Love Mercy

Love Mercy

EARLENE FOWLER

BERKLEY BOOKS, NEW YORK

THE BERKLEY PUBLISHING GROUP
Published by the Penguin Group
Penguin Group (USA) Inc.
375 Hudson Street, New York, New York 10014, USA
Penguin Group (Canada), 90 Eglinton Avenue East, Suite 700, Toronto, Ontario M4P 2Y3, Canada
(a division of Pearson Penguin Canada Inc.)
Penguin Books Ltd., 80 Strand, London WC2R 0RL, England
Penguin Group Ireland, 25 St. Stephen's Green, Dublin 2, Ireland (a division of Penguin Books Ltd.)
Penguin Group (Australia), 250 Camberwell Road, Camberwell, Victoria 3124, Australia
(a division of Pearson Australia Group Pty. Ltd.)
Penguin Books India Pvt. Ltd., 11 Community Centre, Panchsheel Park, New Delhi—110 017, India
Penguin Group (NZ), 67 Apollo Drive, Rosedale, North Shore 0632, New Zealand
(a division of Pearson New Zealand Ltd.)
Penguin Books (South Africa) (Pty.) Ltd., 24 Sturdee Avenue, Rosebank, Johannesburg 2196,
South Africa

Penguin Books Ltd., Registered Offices: 80 Strand, London WC2R 0RL, England

This book is an original publication of The Berkley Publishing Group.

PRINTING HISTORY
Berkley hardcover edition / March 2009

Library of Congress Cataloging-in-Publication Data

Fowler, Earlene.
  Love mercy / Earlene Fowler.
    p. cm.
  ISBN 978-0-425-22597-4
  1. Widows—Fiction. 2. Grandmothers—Fiction. 3. Granddaughters—Fiction. 4. Morro
Bay (Calif.)—Fiction. I. Title.

  PS3556.O828L68 2009
  813'.54—dc22

                                                              2008049051

PRINTED IN THE UNITED STATES OF AMERICA

10   9   8   7   6   5   4   3   2   1

For Jo-Ann Mapson
beloved friend and sister in heart
may you never run out of words or chocolate

and

For Kathy Vieira
dearly loved friend, favorite riding partner
and chosen hermana

Acknowledgments

Love must be sincere. Hate what is evil; cling to what is good. Be devoted to one another in brotherly love. Honor one another above yourselves. Never be lacking in zeal, but keep your spiritual fervor, serving the Lord. Be joyful in hope, patient in affliction, faithful in prayer.

ROMANS 12:9–12

My gratitude to:

Father, Son and Holy Spirit

Ellen Geiger—dynamite agent and wonderful friend—thank you for your support, wisdom and awesome sense of humor!

Kate Seaver—my enthusiastic and talented editor—I appreciate your hard work, your deft touch and your high-spirited encouragement.

Andy Rau—gifted musician, banjo player, songwriter and teacher—thank you for your patience in answering all my crazy questions.

Lela Satterfield—faithful friend, talented musician and writer, sister in Christ—your loving spirit and devotion to Jesus always inspires and amazes me (and thanks for the bridge!).

Tina Davis, Janice Dischner, Jo Ellen Heil, Cathy Higgins, Christine Hill, Karen Meek, Carolyn Miller, Pam Munns, Karen Olson, Laura Ross

Wingfield—some gave information, some prayed, some listened to me whine and some sent chocolate. You are dearly loved and cherished friends. Thank you all.

Always to Allen—all my days—if I had a choice, again I would spend them with you.

Note from the Author

The Central Coast of California holds a special place in my heart, so when I started *Love Mercy*, I decided to set this book in some of the same places I've used in my Benni Harper mystery series. The town of Morro Bay resides in the fictional county of San Celina. The series characters my readers have come to love—Benni Harper, her police chief husband, Gabe, and her gramma, Dove—are minor characters in *Love Mercy*. The difference is that the Benni Harper series is set in the 1990s and *Love Mercy* is set in 2008. And, to those of you who have not read my Benni Harper books, yes, I know that San Celina is improper Spanish. If you want to know the reason why, check my website's FAQ section.

The Love Mercy novels (and I'm hoping there will be more) are not mystery novels, so don't expect a dead body behind every hay bale. But they will deal with another kind of mystery: that of the human heart, especially with how it pertains to family. I'll still write the Benni Harper novels, but I hope you fall as much in love as I have with Love Mercy Johnson, her friends Melina LeBlanc and Magnolia Sanchez, and Love's banjo-playing granddaughter, Rett.

ONE

Rett

The Magic Genie Weight and Fortune machine in the gift shop of Larry's Speedy Time truck stop in Amarillo, Texas, gave Rett her weight but stole her fortune. She smacked the silver machine in frustration. A perfectly good quarter down the drain. Rett needed that fortune. She already knew how much she weighed. One hundred thirteen pounds. In her scuff-toed Justin boots.

"Hon, that contraption ran out of fortunes years ago," said the gum-smacking woman behind the shop's cash register. "It's just a big ole piece of junk, if you ask me."

Rett ducked her head and didn't answer, embarrassed to be caught putting money in something so stupid. She picked up her dirty aqua backpack and black banjo case and headed for the Speedy Skillet café attached to the gift shop. Dwaine said they'd be stuck here for at least six hours.

Loretta Lynn Johnson—who would only answer to Rett despite her mom's insistence that Loretta Lynn was a perfectly nice name—figured a person could have a real full life traveling around the country from truck stop to truck stop. You could do about anything you wanted at a Flying J truck stop or a TravelCenters of America: take a hot shower; get a haircut; buy sugar-free Red Bull, a banana MoonPie or some banjo strings; even learn Spanish from a bilingual Bible.

Rett contemplated becoming a trucker while she chewed her grilled cheese and tomato sandwich. How old did a person have to be to drive long-haul trucks? Her twenty-first birthday was still two and a half years away. Would she have to know how to parallel park? She'd never gotten the hang of that. She wasn't too hot at backing up either. Dimpled trash cans back home in Knoxville, Tennessee, bore witness to that fact.

She nibbled at the gooey sandwich middle and considered her options. She had a for sure ride until Albuquerque with Brother Dwaine Porter Wilburn, a traveling evangelist who held nondenominational church services in the back of a white Peterbilt truck he'd christened the Holy Roller. From there, he was driving north to Denver for the national board meeting of the Jesus Loves Truckers Outreach Ministries. He was vice president this year. Rett was headed for the West Coast.

Brother Dwaine approached her yesterday while she was perusing the candy aisle at a Petro truck stop in Little Rock, Arkansas, trying to decide between a dark chocolate Milky Way and a PayDay candy bar. He said if she needed a safe ride to somewhere, he'd be glad to help her out. He had an accent like Roy, her second stepdad: pure Texas Panhandle.

When he gently repeated his offer, Rett glanced nervously over at the big-haired woman stocking the potato chips shelves. She wore a Petro name tag. The woman smiled and said, "He's okay, girlie. You'll be fine." She reminded Rett of Dolly Parton, so she believed her.

"I reckon I could find you rides with decent people most the ways to where you're going," Dwaine said after he cajoled a little of her story out of her. "Young ladies like yourself shouldn't be out on the road alone. Jesus says to love your fellow man, but I'm here to tell you, there's some bedbug-crazy folks traveling the highways and byways of our fine country."

"Yes, sir," she'd murmured, staring out the window at the toy-sized cars darting around them. She loved the high vantage point of the semi's orange-scented cab. It made her feel like she was in charge of the whole world. On the truck's satellite radio, a gospel group was singing an a cappella version of "Nothing But the Blood of Jesus." The alto was slightly flat.

Normally a statement like his about the dangers of young girls traveling alone would cause her to roll her eyes. But she wasn't stupid. Attitude was fine, but survival was better. Ten years of navigating the fringes of the gospel and bluegrass music business taught her that. It had been her good luck to run into Brother Dwaine. He'd called it God's Providence.

Whatever, she thought. He was kinda preachy, but that was easy enough to tune out. She'd been doing that most of her life. Listening to him definitely beat taking a chance on another van full of college guys, which had been her transportation from Knoxville to Memphis. At the Winn-Dixie two miles from her house, while standing in the ten items or less line, Rett met a Vanderbilt student named Derek. She was buying a bottle of water and some Hershey bars for the road. She'd vaguely thought about taking the bus to California, but she didn't want to waste what little money she had saved. Luckily, the Vanderbilt guy and his buddies were heading in her general direction and offered her a ride. They were okay, didn't hassle her at all and she did pitch in ten bucks for gas. Things were fine until the driver pulled out a Jack Daniel's bottle. She'd ditched them when they'd stopped for snacks at a Wal-Mart outside of Memphis. She wasn't about to become a grease spot in the middle of Interstate 40 because of some drunk frat boy.

She had stood at the side of the road with her thumb out, trying not to think about all the *Dateline NBC* shows she'd seen about serial killers and missing girls. A little later, a girl not much older than Rett picked her up. Her name was Eunice Shumaker, and she drove an older white SUV with a faded pink Mary Kay cosmetics sign plastered on the driver's door. She offered Rett a ride clear to Little Rock, where Eunice's mother was having kidney stone surgery. Eunice dropped her off at the Petro truck stop and handed her some samples of Mary Kay sunscreen.

"Do *not* leave the house without wearing this," she'd warned. "You might have brown hair, but, girl, you got the skin of a redhead."

Brother Dwaine had approached Rett not ten minutes later, a concerned look on his grizzled face.

"More coffee?" The waitress stood in front of Rett holding a stained Bunn coffeepot. She had tired brown eyes and a cool-looking heart-shaped mole on her left cheek. Or maybe it was a tattoo.

"No, thanks," Rett answered, looking down at her plate where a shriveled pickle was the only thing she'd left uneaten.

"Brother Dwaine says this is on his tab," the waitress said in a gravelly, Tanya Tucker voice that Rett immediately envied. "He does that all the time. Cook just baked some peach pie. Want some?"

Rett almost refused, hating to take more of the minister's help, but she thought about the crumpled money tucked down into her dusty red boot. Sixty-eight dollars and forty-three cents, and she still had half the country to travel. She'd started out with a hundred bucks but hadn't paid real close attention to how much she was spending, a trait her mom often pointed out. At the Wal-Mart where she'd ditched the frat boys, she'd bought wool socks, gloves and a red knit hat. It hadn't occurred to her to stick those things in her backpack when she left Knoxville. But it was the first week of December and cold across most of the country. It had seemed likely that she'd be spending most of her trip on the side of the highway with her thumb out.

At the same time she'd foolishly splurged on a Rhonda Vincent CD, the one the bluegrass singer recorded at the Sheldon Concert Hall in Missouri. Rett had the CD at home, but at the last minute decided to leave it since her backpack had been jammed full, and she knew every song lyric and banjo lick by heart. She sighed. If she had an iPod, that would have solved her problem. But Mom was old school, thought they were a waste of money and Rett never had the discipline to save her own money for one. So, unable to resist, Rett tossed the CD in her basket at Wal-Mart. Somehow it made her feel less scared to have it nestled in her backpack against her favorite Nashville Sounds sweatshirt.

"Sure, I'll have some pie," Rett said. She might as well fill up while she could. But, after this, she wouldn't accept any more charity from the minister. If she was careful, her money would last her until she reached Morro Bay. Then, hating that it was her mom's stupidly optimistic words that sprang to her mind first, she'd "reassess her opportunities."

While she waited for the pie, she reached over and rubbed a nail-bitten thumb over a new scar on the black banjo case. Riding in the college student's van had banged it up more than twenty county fair gigs.

"You can leave your banjo in the cab," Dwaine had said when they pulled into the truck stop where he was going to have a pinging sound in the engine checked on. "Won't no one bother it there."

"That's okay," she replied, hugging the case to her chest. "I'll keep it with me."

The preacher would probably be shocked to know the banjo inside the raggedy case was worth twenty-five thousand dollars. And even more shocked to learn it wasn't exactly hers. He'd probably call it stolen. Rett called it getting even.

T W O

Love Mercy

L ove Mercy Johnson stared at the bright computer screen, trying to resist the urge to grind her molars. The uncooperative numbers blurred before her eyes. Balancing the books was her least favorite part of co-owning the Buttercream Café. December was usually a good month, but so far they weren't in the black. She sighed and leaned back in her old office chair, the loud squeak startling her dozing tricolored corgi, Ace. He jumped up from a dead sleep, his full, chesty bark loud enough to rattle the windows of her little bungalow.

She twirled around and laughed. "Calm down, flyboy. It's only my chair. Like the tin man, it just needs a little oil." He shot her a distinctly cranky look and flattened his batlike ears before settling back down on the braided rug in front of her gray river stone fireplace. She stretched her arms out and flexed her long fingers, then turned to the screen, pushing back the discouragement that was starting to build a wall in her chest.

"We can figure this out," she said out loud. "We've been in worse financial straits when Cy and I owned the feed store, right?" Ace didn't lift his head. He was accustomed to Love's conversations with herself.

Unless the Buttercream raised its prices, something that would cause the locals to howl like wounded wolverines, she and Magnolia would have to dip into the money that they'd been saving for a new stove. Dang. Magnolia had mooned over that commercial stove catalog like a teenager would an *American Idol* finalist. Three months ago Love had told her the silver and black Viking stove of her dreams was practically being loaded on the delivery truck. That was before the dishwasher had to be repaired—twice—and the ancient garbage disposal had to be replaced. Plus it seemed people just weren't eating out as often as they used to. Not really a recession, the government kept assuring everyone.

She and her best friend, Magnolia Rosalina Sanchez, bought the restaurant three and a half years ago. It was something they'd fantasized about from the first week they met twenty years ago while working as waitresses in the very same building, back when it was called Freddie's Fish House. A small inheritance from Love's great-aunt Bitsy and Magnolia's ability to squeeze a nickel had helped Love and Magnolia to buy and fix up the café. It had been a struggle from the beginning, but they'd always made a small profit. Until three months ago. Love even used some of the money she'd made when she sold the feed store after Cy died, but she'd had to set back a little to live on. Even though her house was paid off and she lived frugally, that wouldn't last forever. The café had to start making a profit again, or they'd have to sell it.

"What now?" she said, wishing for what seemed the millionth time in the last thirteen months that her calm-spirited husband was here to give his two cents.

"Since when have you ever taken my advice?" he would have asked.

"Not often," she'd have answered, grinning. "But it's always amusing to hear your opinion." The truth was, he wasn't really much better than she was at business. He'd been too much of a soft touch to make a real profit at the feed store, always giving away free dog, cat and bird food to grateful rescue groups and allowing folks credit far longer than he should have. He'd been a sucker for every sad story that trotted up the trail.

How she missed his laid-back personality and that foghorn laugh of his, the laugh that rarely failed to make her join in, even if they'd been quarreling. He'd been totally in favor of her and Magnolia buying the café when it came up for sale. Whenever she worked the counter, he'd come in, pretend he didn't know her and flirt outrageously. He'd leave her a twenty-dollar tip, which she always slipped right into the cash register.

They'd met in Redwater, Kentucky, when he was on leave from Fort Knox. He bid seventy-five dollars for her strawberry-rhubarb pie at the Redwater Baptist Church Vacation Bible School fund-raiser. That was good deal of money in 1967, so it was clear he was announcing to her and the congregation his serious intentions. He was visiting with one of his training buddies, Jim Shore, whose father was head deacon at the church. Both boys were shipped out to Vietnam a few weeks later. After charming her mother, father and twin brother, DJ, Cyrus courted Love the old-fashioned way, through the mail. He wooed her with his square, neat printing, his silly jokes, his kind and thoughtful observations about the Vietnamese people and his mesmerizing descriptions of the Valley oaks, red-tailed hawks and rolling emerald hills of the cattle ranch his family owned on California's Central Coast. They'd married two weeks after he was discharged from the army.

Love glanced at the calendar. Thursdays were Italian day at the Buttercream. This week Magnolia was serving her famous gnocchi and homemade lasagna. Maybe if they cut down on the cheese and imported sausage in the lasagna, they could save a little money. Or they could make the portions a little smaller. Shoot, they could do that with all the menu items. The media was always saying that people ate too much. Would anyone notice?

She shook her head. Even if no one else knew it, Magnolia would, and she'd not stand for it. Her daddy was from Alabama, but her mama was pure Italian. Magnolia had spent every summer of her first eighteen years visiting her mama's sisters on Chicago's Italian West Side. She'd been taught to cook and bake by her aunts Teresa, Marie and Bettina, loving taskmasters who showed her the secret to flaky cannoli and, as Magnolia called it, smack-your-daddy-good spaghetti sauce. Magnolia's recipes were the one reason, Love believed, that *San Celina County Life* readers had voted the Buttercream Café as Best Locally Owned Restaurant for the last two years.

Love turned back to the computer and stared at the unchanging figures. Maybe they could find cheaper hamburger buns that still tasted good. Or quit using the incredible maple syrup from that cute little family in Springfield, New Hampshire. It was unbelievably delicious, but was also a lot more expensive than what they could buy at San Celina's new Costco.

She traced a forefinger over the boat-shaped crystal desk clock next to her computer. It had been a gift to Cy from the guys at the Morro Bay boatyard when he sold his boat shortly after his second round of chemo, when the doctors said things didn't look hopeful. That had been a hard day for everyone.

Cy bought the battered old boat thirty years ago when their son, Tommy, was ten years old. He and Tommy spent countless hours fishing and bird-watching on that boat. They'd sanded, scraped, painted or stained every bit of the old vessel. Cy named it the *Love Mercy*, despite her protests or the fact that she'd ridden on it only a handful of times. She loved the ocean, never grew tired of photographing its endless colors and eclectic variations, but she preferred to remain onshore. She always claimed it was because of her eastern Kentucky genes.

"I'm a backwoods girl," she'd declare when anyone teased her about it. "I prefer solid ground beneath these size-eight feet." The ocean and its mercurial moods were too unpredictable. She remembered that every time she walked by the tiny Anchor Memorial Park on the Embarcadero. The seven-thousand-pound iron anchor set into a concrete square showing the names of the men and women lost at sea reminded her too much of the coal mines in Kentucky that stole so many people from her life.

The boat was the one subject that Cy and Tommy could always discuss when the pangs of adolescence and later, the disagreements between generations had made everything else unapproachable.

After Tommy up and married Karla Rae Murphy and they moved to Nashville a week after the wedding, when Cy missed their son, he would take the boat out and float aimlessly around Morro Rock, watching the peregrine falcons and their chicks through his old binoculars. Love still used those binoculars to watch the ocean from her backyard, placing her fingers in the same spots worn smooth by Cy's calloused fingers. It comforted her to put her hands where she knew his had been.

After Tommy was killed fourteen years ago, working on the boat had been Cy's way of coping with a grief too big for him to talk about, even with her. Love spent hours walking on the beach with only her old Nikon camera for company. The photos she took those first weeks after Tommy's death were packed away in a trunk. Once developed, she'd never looked at the photos, though they were as fresh in her mind as the gash that scarred her heart the moment she received the phone call about Tommy's accident from a friend of Karla Rae's. It always hurt Love that she'd heard the news from someone she didn't even know.

She remembered in detail each photograph she took those weeks of walking. She could still see the loopy wave-diving surf scoters who re- minded her of crazed bodyboarders, the black oystercatchers with their chisel-shaped, blood-colored bills, the frantic western sandpipers who were always running and screaming their high-pitched, teenage-girl screech—a sound that, at the time, she was tempted to mimic—and the peregrine falcons, so majestic and distant, perched high on the sheer edges of Morro Rock, looking down on them all, like they possessed the answers to any number of life's complex questions. But the ones she found the most heartbreaking were the black turnstones: plump, tiny birds with streaks of white in their plumage. They liked rocky areas and, true to their name, spent most of their time turning over stones and seaweed looking for food. Their frantic searching echoed some- thing deep inside her. She spent hours watching them, capturing their struggles to survive on film. Those first few months she and Cy seemed to live on separate planets, each trying to make sense of why their only child was killed by a drunk driver one rainy night in Nashville. The irony of how much that sounded like a country song was something that oc- curred to her during those long, solitary walks.

She pushed her chair away from the computer, rubbing her stinging eyes. A walk. Yes, what she needed was a good long walk with Ace. Stop thinking about all the losses of her life and concentrate on the living. Maybe it would clear out the cobwebs, and she'd figure out how to keep the café going, serve their expected high-quality dishes, not lay off anyone or cut back on portions. She'd take the Nikon and see if something inspired her. Clint would be wanting February's photo and column soon. Then she'd head to the café and talk to Magnolia about how they could cut costs and still keep everyone happy. Wasn't that every middle-aged woman's lament—how do I keep everyone happy? For pity's sake, she thought, who in the heck made us keepers of the world's contentment?

She was in the kitchen pulling Ace's leash off the hook when the phone rang.

"Love, you got to get down to the café right now," Magnolia said.

Love touched her right temple with her fingertips, already feeling a throbbing start. What had broken this time? Where would they get the money to fix it?

"There's this girl here," Magnolia said, her voice as big and lush as the curly black hair that drove her crazy. "She says she needs to talk to you. Darlin', she favors you some around the mouth. I'm thinking she might be one of your granddaughters."

One of her granddaughters? Love's stomach twisted into a knot. Over the phone she could hear the café's normal background sounds, a cacophony of rattling pans and loud laughter. Music twanged from the jukebox, a frenetic, vaguely country-sounding song. Love couldn't make out who was singing, but it didn't matter. As talented as they were, all those narrow-hipped, pretty young girls being pushed by the record companies looked and sounded so much alike. What happened to singers who'd actually lived a little life before they sang about it? Patsy Cline would be appalled. Or have a good belly laugh.

"I offered her one of my cannoli, but she turned me down flat." Magnolia took it real personal when someone turned down her food. "She just ordered coffee. She's sitting there staring at the wall and drinking it."

"Maybe she just ate," Love said, making excuses for the girl before she even knew whether they were related.

"Maybe so." Magnolia's voice sounded doubtful. "Her arms are as skinny as broom handles. A little cannoli would do her a world of good. She said she hitchhiked here."

"Hitchhiked? From where?" The last Love knew, her three grand-daughters and their ditzy mother, Karla Rae, lived in Pensacola, Florida, with Karla's second husband, Pete somebody-or-other, who owned two Ford dealerships. Love hung Ace's leash back up. "Did she tell you her name?"

"Nope," Magnolia said. "Believe me, I tried to squeeze it out of her, but she's a persimmony little thing. All she said is that she has some business with Love Mercy Johnson, then she shut herself up, tight as a tick. What should I tell her? I said I'd call you but that I wasn't about to just hand out your address to any ole person who asked. I told her that, for all I know, she was a serial killer."

Love smiled to herself. "What did she say to that?"

"Not a blessed thing. Just nodded her head and held on to her banjo case like I was going to snatch it from her first chance I got."

Banjo case? Love tried to picture one of her granddaughters fitting her tiny hands around the neck of a banjo. Then again, she hadn't seen them for almost fourteen years. They wouldn't be tiny anymore.

"How old does she look?" Love asked. She had three granddaughters: Patsy Cline, Loretta Lynn and Faith Leann. Their names screamed out their mama's unfulfilled aspirations. Pursuing her singing career was the reason Karla Rae and Tommy had moved to Nashville. Love quickly calculated her granddaughter's ages; Patsy would be nineteen now, Lo-retta would be eighteen and Faith would be fourteen. Faith had been a baby when Tommy was killed. He'd been driving to the Piggly Wiggly to buy diapers for her when a truck broadsided his little Toyota.

Lord, don't let it be Faith, Love automatically sent up a prayer be-fore catching herself. She'd stubbornly been avoiding conversations with God since Cy had died. Still, she didn't take back the prayer, despite a slight feeling of guilt, because the mental image of a fourteen-year-old girl bearing Tommy's sweet, round face hitchhiking on a desolate high-way made her blood freeze in her veins.

"Eighteen? Twenty?" Magnolia guessed.

"It must be Patsy or Loretta," she said, only slightly relieved. "I'll walk on over. Tell her any food she orders is on my tab. Maybe she doesn't have any money and is too embarrassed to say so."

"Okay, but my guess is she has one of those eating disorders so popular with movie stars and whatnot."

"Let's hope she's just broke." Love wouldn't have a clue about how to deal with an eating disorder.

After she hung up, she thought of a question she should have asked Magnolia. Did the girl have red hair? If so, she would probably be Patsy. Loretta had brown hair, like Tommy. At least she did all those years ago. So many years, it felt like someone else's life.

She walked over to the kitchen window that looked out onto her small, grass-covered backyard. Morro Bay and the Pacific Ocean looked like a huge sheet of gray steel. So flat you could fry bacon on it, she could imagine Cy's voice saying in his calm, even baritone that always held a soupçon of laughter.

Soupçon. Now there's a great word. Maybe she could work it into "Love's View," the column she wrote once a month for *San Celina County Life*, a local magazine delivered free to everyone in the county. Well, it wasn't actually a column, she'd tell people, more of a columnette or a column-lite. Though she loved to read and found individual words fascinating, she didn't actually like to write, so what she did was take a photograph of something in San Celina County and then write a short essay about it. The shorter the better. Frankly, she'd be happier if she didn't have to write anything at all, just let the photograph speak for itself. Whenever she tried to explain what she was trying to say with a photo, it seemed to diminish the picture. It was like admitting she'd failed.

January's photo and column were done. She'd taken a picture of an elegantly graceful spider with patterns on her back that reminded Love of a Navajo rug. She—for some reason Love thought of all spiders as female—had built an intricate web at the side of the house, and Love had been observing its progress for days. Her photograph caught it early in the morning, the sun-bright dewdrops on the filaments twinkling like diamonds. In the web, an unfortunate fly awaited its ghastly fate. Her simple caption, "Bless this food we are about to receive," was sure to be misunderstood, causing people to write in to the magazine demanding that she explain what she meant. Some people would be certain that she was somehow being blasphemous or, even worse, *political* (though they wouldn't actually be able to explain why). The boys at the Rowdy Pelican saloon would give her the thumbs-up when she delivered their weekly two dozen Mexican chocolate cupcakes, appreciating her warped sense of humor. It was her shortest "essay" yet. Clint Lawhead, the magazine's owner and publisher, would just laugh, congratulate her for making people think and tease her that it would have saved him a bundle if he'd negotiated paying her by the word rather than the 150 dollars she received for each column.

Soupçon. It meant a very small amount. She imagined a photo of one of the café's white soup bowls holding a teaspoon of bright red tomato soup, maybe a dented Campbell's soup can next to it? No, too Andy Warhol. Besides, she didn't really know what she was trying to say: that soup, which symbolized food, was too expensive? No, not a good thing to put out there when she was contemplating raising the prices at the café. Still, she liked the way the word sounded. And even better, it was a single word. It could be her shortest column ever. But the idea needed work.

She looked down at Ace, who'd followed her to the window, wagging his soupçon of a tail, still hoping for a walk. She bent down and ran her hand along the white, airplane-shaped marking on the black ruff of his neck, the reason Cy had named him Ace. She scratched the top of the dog's nubby butt, making him grin like a wolf.

"If this girl is my granddaughter, she should have given me a soupçon of warning about her visit, don't you think?" Ace cocked his head, his dark, shiny eyes giving her an intelligent look that always made her wonder if he'd one day answer her in a thoughtful Timothy Dalton voice.

When Cy was first diagnosed with lung cancer two years ago, he bought Ace from a breeder in Paso Robles. Always a planner, he told her he didn't want her to be alone after he was gone. Ace, true to the corgi breed, was a handful from the beginning, and he'd accomplished what Cy had desired, forcing Love to go outside for walks and games of

ball even on days when she would have just as soon stayed in her pajamas with the curtains closed, brooding about the unfairness of life, mad
at God, uncontrollable cancer cells, drunk drivers and every happy person in the world. Yes, her husband was wise in bringing this crazy little
dog into her life.

Still and all, you old coyote, she scolded Cy in her head, I wasn't any
less sad when you left me. He isn't *you*.

"Well, flyboy," she said to the dog. "Looks like we'll be having us
some company. If she is who we think she is, anyway."

How long would this girl want to stay? What did she want? Would
she understand why Love hadn't been in contact all these years? The sad
truth was, her granddaughter had only heard her mother's side of the
story. Heaven only knew what the girl thought of her grandma Love.

Karla Rae had never liked Love or Cy much, probably because they
hadn't been very discreet about their displeasure over her and Tommy's
impulsive move to Nashville.

Tommy had met Karla Rae when she was working as a cocktail
waitress at a Los Angeles hotel where he was attending a Farm Bureau
convention. She'd come to California with a band, which broke up
shortly after they arrived when the lead singer landed a solo gig. After
knowing each other only three weeks, Tommy and Karla Rae were en-
gaged. They married a month later under the same scarred oak tree on
the Johnson ranch where Cy and Love had said their second marriage
vows, shortly after his return from Vietnam. Their first legal wedding had
been at the little brown church in Redwater, Kentucky, where they'd met.

In Tennessee, Tommy found work with a local cabinetmaker, and
Karla Rae, with her decent if unremarkable Sunday morning soprano
voice, made the rounds on Music Row and haunted open mike nights in
the city's numerous bars. They had two babies in two years and a third
one four years later. Tommy called Love and Cy, thrilled each time, but
with each child, Karla Rae seemed to sound perpetually more sullen.
She'd not gotten any closer to her dream than singing cover songs in
tourist-filled honky-tonks.

After Tommy's funeral, there had been a small gathering at their
rented house in Nashville. Her father, who lived in Ohio, had sent flowers

but couldn't take off work. Karla Rae's mother had died years before. That made Love a little more sympathetic to her sometimes snippy daughter-in-law. What kind of parent didn't drop everything to come support their child during a time like this? After most of the guests had left, Love went in the kitchen and started washing cups and glasses. As she worked, she wondered about asking Karla Rae if she wanted to come to Morro Bay with the girls and maybe start a new life on the Central Coast. She was picturing the girls playing in the Johnson hay barn where Tommy had played when Karla Rae burst through the swinging kitchen door. She collapsed on one of the red vinyl kitchen chairs.

"Shoot, I'm so tired I could melt into a puddle right here on the floor," she said. "Finally got the girls to bed. Cy's reading them a story."

"You just sit there and relax," Love said, glancing at her. "I'll finish these dishes."

"Good, I'm sick to death of doing dishes." She leaned back in the chair and crossed her arms across her chest. "I'm a bit put out, you know."

"Oh?" Love said, turning back to the sink.

"Tommy only had ten thousand dollars in insurance." She gave an exaggerated sigh. "I don't know how long he expected that to last with three growing girls."

Love froze, shocked that Karla Rae would bring that up on the day of the funeral. She blinked her eyes quickly, trying to focus on the yellow sippy cup she was washing. "I'm sure," she finally said, "that Tommy didn't think he would die so young."

"Well, he should have considered that. It's kinda selfish, if you ask me."

Love slowly turned around, about to snap an irritable reply to her insensitive daughter-in-law, when Cy walked into the room. By his despairing look, Love knew he'd heard Karla Rae's words. Standing behind his daughter-in-law, he shook his head at Love, his green eyes filled with pain. It was his expression that caused Love to press her lips together and say nothing. She would not have done one thing at that moment to make her husband feel any worse than he did. Love turned back to the sink of dirty dishes and took out her frustration on a coffee-stained mug printed with a picture of Bart Simpson.

Love was certain Karla Rae never told the girls that Love had written and called every week after Tommy died, sent checks when she could to help out with expenses. Karla Rae cashed the checks but never sent one word of acknowledgment. When Love called, her granddaughters never seemed to be there; they were at tee ball or a sleepover or an overnight scout function.

About a year after Tommy's death, Love's letters started coming back marked, "Moved, no forwarding address." When Love and Cy tried to call, they got a recording that stated the phone had been disconnected. Love couldn't remember Karla Rae's father's name or the city in Ohio where she vaguely remembered Tommy saying he lived. After three months, they hired a private detective who, with a few phone calls and some Internet searching, discovered that Karla Rae had married a man named Pete Ryan and lived in Pensacola, Florida. Love called the number. Karla Rae's voice didn't sound shocked or embarrassed when she heard who it was.

"Oh, Love!" she exclaimed. "I was going to call you and let you know we'd moved, but you know how it is with kids, just one thing after another. How are you? Did you know that I got married again? He's got a real good job. Such a wonderful father to the girls, buys them every silly little thing they want. I love my new house. The girls all have their own rooms. Isn't that great?"

Love stuttered a moment, amazed at Karla Rae's audacity. "Well, I suppose so."

"We were registered at Pottery Barn, but you can just send us a gift card, if you want."

Though Love couldn't bring herself to send that gift card, she did start writing the girls again, still getting no response. Her letters eventually became birthday and Christmas cards, which also were never acknowledged. It was like having a relationship with imaginary people, all the emotions on one side. To be fair to the girls, Love wasn't even sure they received any of the cards or letters. When she wrote that Cy had cancer, Karla Rae never answered, so Love wasn't surprised when there was no response when she sent a copy of Cy's obituary.

After that, Love was ashamed to admit she just stopped trying. In an odd way, it made her feel better, lighter, like she'd finally accepted the lot in life handed to her by the God she'd trusted since she was a girl, but whose plans for her life now eluded her.

"He does have a plan," Rocky, Magnolia's husband, assured her the one time she flippantly mentioned her disappointment in God at a Labor Day picnic as they watched giggling young kids during a potato sack race.

She'd just nodded and didn't answer, sorry she'd opened her mouth. She dearly loved Rocky both as a friend and as her pastor. She and Cy had first attended his small church, Baytown Christian Fellowship, at Magnolia's request when she and Magnolia first worked together. From the moment they walked into the tiny sky blue church six blocks from their house, they felt at home. They'd instantly connected with Rocky's open personality and no-nonsense take on the Scriptures. And they admired his dedication. Rocky worked full-time as a barber so the small, aging congregation only had to pay him a token salary.

Rocky and Magnolia had been a safe and loving shelter for her those shadowy days after Cy's death. And though she wasn't exactly speaking to God, she still went to church most Sundays. She was waiting, she supposed. For what, she wasn't quite sure.

But, as much as Rocky and Magnolia tried, they couldn't understand. Not really. Their daughters, Jade and Cheyenne, were healthy, happily married and lived here in San Celina County. Except for their elderly parents, Rocky or Magnolia hadn't lost anyone really close to them. When a person lost a child or a spouse, they were definitely dragged, protesting, into membership of a club that no one ever aspired to join.

Love stood up and went to the bathroom to comb her short, strawberry blonde hair, streaked now with white. She couldn't put off meeting this young woman any longer. What would this supposed granddaughter think the first time she saw Love? Would she recognize her? No doubt this girl would consider her as old as Morro Rock, even though the media called fifty-eight the new . . . what? Forty-five?

She stared at her squarish chin and high cheekbones, the face that Cy had always called "majestic."

"What you mean is bony," she'd replied, smiling.

"Angular," he'd countered. "Noble. Katharine Hepburn-ish."

She'd snort at the comparison, but it always secretly thrilled her. She doubted that anyone her granddaughter's age would even know who Katharine Hepburn was. To them, Meryl Streep was a senior citizen. Shoot, these days, Julia Roberts would be considered an older woman.

She bent over the sink, splashing cold water on her face, then straightened up, aligning her spine. Whatever this girl, this granddaughter of hers, needed, she would try to help. Though she had many beloved friends here in San Celina County, including her in-laws, August and Polly, she had no blood family. Fear churned in her chest. Who knew what troubles this girl brought with her? It could end up being the best thing that ever happened to her. Or the worst.

"Only one way to find out, sister," she said to her reflection in the mirror. A determined, slightly thin-lipped woman, one that had made her husband dream of Katharine Hepburn, stared back at her. The woman nodded in agreement and gave her a hopeful smile.

THREE

Mel

Melina Jane LeBlanc, who went by Mel, slipped onto the end stool at the yellow Formica counter of the Buttercream Café. Magnolia placed a stout white coffee mug in front of her and filled it three-quarters full.

"See that little bit of a girl over there?" Magnolia whispered, pushing the lamb-shaped creamer toward Mel. "She might be Love's granddaughter. Love's on her way down here."

Mel studied the thin young woman sitting against the far wall. Training from her eleven years as a Las Vegas police officer kicked in. She narrowed her dark brown eyes, memorizing the girl's statistics: white female, seventeen to twenty-one, five foot three or four, medium brown straight hair, 110 to 115 pounds, roundish face, pale skin, wide-set eyes. Mel was too far away to discern exact color, but they were light—blue or green—their transparent coolness apparent even across the café's dining room.

Mel's suspicious nature, something as organic to her at age thirty-five as her wavy auburn hair, automatically distrusted the girl. Mel knew Love had grandchildren whom she never saw. In the almost three years that they'd been friends, Love had briefly spoken of them twice, her soft Kentucky drawl tinged with regret. No details, just that she and her daughter-in-law were estranged, and because of that, Love didn't have a relationship with her grandchildren. What little Mel knew about the situation, she learned from Cy right before he died.

Mel continued to watch the girl, who didn't look anything like her friend. Love was tall, five nine or ten, with sharp cheekbones that suggested that ubiquitous Cherokee ancestor that everyone and their brother claimed since the sixties when being a Native American became not just acceptable but cool. In Love's case, it could be true, since she told Mel that her family went back generations in eastern Kentucky's Appalachian Mountains. Her great-great-grandmother had written about the Trail of Tears in the big family Bible kept on Love's living room bookshelf.

Love's shaggy, white-streaked hair was reddish gold, not walnut-colored like this girl's. Mel sometimes teased Love by calling her Carrot Top, though her hair color was anything but a garish orange. For as long as Mel could remember, she had never been comfortable around other women. The normal give-and-take laughter and teasing between women remained an unsolvable mystery to her, so it said something about her relationship with Love that she felt comfortable enough to rib her about something as innocuous as hair color.

With this second look, Mel decided the girl, fiddling now for something in her dirt-stained backpack, was likely eighteen or nineteen years old. The girl found what she was looking for, a length of string. She bit it into two pieces and quickly twisted her flyaway hair into slightly crooked braids, finishing them off with the string. She wore tight, grimy blue jeans and a baggy lavender sweatshirt printed with red lettering: Nashville Sounds. It was only because Mel was an avid triple A baseball fan that she knew the Sounds were a farm team for the Milwaukee Brewers.

"Magnolia Rosalina!" called a husky man from a back booth. He wore an ancient, sweat-stained Union Oil cap. "Where's my twice-baked potato omelet?" He tapped his oversized Timex wristwatch.

"Keep your panties on, Lester," Magnolia called back, rolling her bright blue eyes at Mel. A strand of curly black hair, laced with silver, pulled out of her loose bun and fell across her forehead. She brushed it away impatiently and said to Mel, "There are easier ways of making a living, I'm told."

"And harder," Mel answered, looking down and blowing on her coffee more for something to do rather than to cool it down.

Magnolia nodded, acknowledging the difficulty of Mel's former career. She cocked her head over at the girl, who was now staring at one of her grandma's photographs on the wall. "Keep an eye on her while I'm fetching Lester's order."

Mel returned her gaze to the girl. "Count on it." The girl chose that moment to turn her head and stare back at her. She held Mel's eyes without blinking. Then she slowly reached up to scratch her cheek and subtly gave Mel the finger.

Mel felt her bottom lip twitch, wanting to smile. The little brat had nerve; she had to give her that. She apparently didn't appreciate Mel and Magnolia's scrutiny. Though Mel admired chutzpah in any young woman—heaven knows they needed it to survive these days—it also increased her suspicion. This was not some innocent girl wanting to find her grandma so they could exchange family stories and bake sugar cookies. Somewhere this girl had learned to watch out for herself. Mel would have to keep an eye on this one. There was no way she'd let anyone, even a long-lost family member, hurt Love. Mel had promised as much to Cy before he died.

The rusty cowbell clattered when Love opened the Buttercream's front door. A hail of greetings welcomed her from around the room.

"I'm going to kidnap that bell and throw it in the bay," Mel called to Magnolia, who was sliding Lester's omelet in front of him.

"I'll cut off your cannoli supply," she replied amicably.

"You got me there," Mel said, giving one of her rare smiles. She loved Magnolia's cannoli with their tiny bits of cherry, lemon and miniature chocolate chips hiding in the sweet ricotta filling.

Love raised her hand, greeting everyone, then glanced around until she spotted the girl. Her eyes lingered for a moment, then she deliberately walked over to Mel. Mel was glad to see Love appeared to be maintaining a bit of emotional distance.

"Good morning," she said, touching Mel's upper arm briefly. She glanced at the brown and white Stewart's Root Beer clock above the kitchen pass-through. Four orders hung on the stainless turnaround waiting for Shug, Magnolia's second cousin and the Buttercream's primary cook. "Or I guess that's good afternoon, since it's past noon."

"Heard you have family in town," Mel said, stirring her coffee.

Love gave a bemused smile. "Possibly. I see you've been watching her for me."

Magnolia walked back over and gave Love a quick hug, then headed for the swinging kitchen door. "I've got orders waiting in the kitchen. There's a couple of bills over by the register. Don't leave without saying good-bye."

"I won't," Love said. She looked back over at the girl, who stared back without blinking.

"Be careful," Mel said, pushing back her mug.

"I think I can handle her," Love said, turning back to Mel. The sharp tips of her cheekbones flushed pink with some kind of emotion. "Raised her daddy, you know."

"You sure it's your granddaughter?" Mel didn't want to push, but she was worried. "It might be a con."

"It's Loretta Lynn, all right," Love said. "She's the second of my three granddaughters. She looks the same, only older. The only one with brown hair like her daddy's. Other two are . . . well, were the last time I saw them, redheads."

"Want me to stay?" Mel asked, standing up. They were almost the same height, and she looked Love directly in the eyes.

Love's blue eyes softened. "No need. I can handle this. I'm curious, of course. Maybe a little nervous. But she's just a girl." She patted Mel's upper arm. "Don't you have a riding lesson?"

Mel nodded. Four months ago she'd started twice weekly horseback riding lessons. Love needed help working Cy's parents' ranch, and Mel offered, not quite realizing what she was getting into. "I can cancel it. Benni will understand."

Benni Ortiz lived on a ranch neighboring August and Polly Johnson's on the east. She and her husband, Gabe, a retired San Celina police chief, lived there with her dad, her grandmother and Gabe's son, Sam, a San Celina firefighter.

"Don't cancel," Love said. "I can handle one tired, probably scared, eighteen-year-old girl."

Mel stared at her friend's calm, lightly freckled face. Maybe not this one, she wanted to say. "I'll keep my cell phone on in case you need reinforcement."

Love slipped her arm around Mel's shoulders. "Sweetie, don't you worry about me. You just concentrate on staying on your pony. August and Polly are counting on you to ride in the roundup in a few months."

"Dinner tomorrow at the Shrimp?" Mel asked, tucking two one-dollar bills under her empty mug. "We can change the date if you want."

Love and Mel ate dinner together every Friday night at the Happy Shrimp down on Morro Bay's Embarcadero. The ritual had started when Cy was alive, when he first hired Mel and realized she was eating every meal alone. After his death, she and Love continued meeting for dinner without a word and without missing a week.

Mel glanced over at the girl, who was now watching Love suspiciously. The girl's wide mouth turned down in a frown. Did she recognize her grandmother? Mel couldn't tell.

"I'll be there," Love said firmly. "Loretta will either join us or not. She'll have to fit into my life, not the other way around."

Mel picked up her navy corduroy barn jacket and slipped it on. "See you tomorrow then."

She purposely avoided meeting the girl's eyes when she walked out of the café, though she was tempted to shoot her one of the don't-mess-with-me stares that she'd picked up during her years patrolling the streets of North Las Vegas.

But the girl had attitude already, and Mel didn't want to cause any more animosity during this get-reacquainted time between her and Love. There'd be time enough to put the girl in her place if need be.

Outside, the December day had remained cold and foggy despite the fact that it was past noon. She stood on the front step of the café and inhaled deeply, enjoying the damp, salty air. Though many citizens of Morro Bay, especially the new ones, complained when they didn't see the sun for days, this kind of weather energized Mel, made her want to go on a five-mile run, though she hadn't jogged since she'd moved here. She stretched her arms above her head, feeling her stomach pull and tighten. Maybe she should start running again. Or lift some weights. Bucking alfalfa bales and moving saddles around at the feed store had once kept her arms and legs strong, but now she mostly worked the counter. Taking her kayak out on the bay once a week and riding horses could only work her muscles so much.

She walked toward her white Ford Ranger, thinking about Cy and how much he would have loved seeing his granddaughter. They talked about a variety of subjects those last few months of his life when Mel would come sit with him. Love often had to go into San Celina to fetch medical supplies she couldn't buy in Morro Bay. That was when Mel heard the details of Tommy's death and how Cy and Love had a falling-out with Tommy's wife, causing her to keep the girls from them.

"Love tried so hard to mend the rift," Cy had said, his normally ponderous voice weak and old-sounding. "Maybe Karla Rae will feel some compassion when Love calls them about my funeral." He gave Mel a half smile. "Like I always say, some good eventually comes from everything."

Mel swallowed over the painful lump in her throat, not trusting herself to answer. He looked like the pictures she'd seen of concentration camp survivors, all bones and staring fish eyes. The smell of death in the room had been sweet and lingering, like unchanged water in a flower vase.

She climbed into her muddy white truck and started the engine. It coughed a few times, then settled into its normal low growl. The streets were fairly empty on her drive through town toward Highway 1. The turnoff to the Johnson and Ramsey-Ortiz ranches was about halfway between Morro Bay and San Celina. She flipped the heater to high, attempting to warm up the truck cab, but the weather stripping around the windows had deteriorated. A cold draft always whistled down the side of her neck.

She turned off the highway onto Breyer Ranch Road, named for a family who hadn't ranched in San Celina County for fifty years. A late, lingering tule fog hovered three feet off the ground, making it feel like she was driving through that artificial dry-ice smoke many second-rate Vegas magicians used to punch up their magic acts. Tule fog always reminded her of her father, a person she tried to think about as little as possible. A winter-lean squirrel dashed in front of her truck, causing her to brake suddenly, cursing under her breath.

In a few minutes, she passed by the mailbox and long, narrow road that led to August and Polly's ranch. She'd drop by after her lesson with Benni, check on whether they needed any groceries or chores done, her regular Tuesday and Thursday routine. Brad and Evan were covering her afternoon shift at the feed store, like they had since she started helping August and Polly under the pretense of wanting to learn about ranching. The Johnsons paid her minimum wage or sometimes with tomatoes, peppers and squash from Polly's garden. Polly never caught on that Mel was working for them at Love's request.

"Polly and August are typical old-time ranchers," Love told Mel four months ago, when she first asked for Mel's help. "They don't want anyone to know they need assistance." Like many small ranchers, they were land rich but cash poor. "I can get away with checking on them two or three times a week, then they start telling me nicely to mind my own business. If I told them you need the work, they'd feel like they were helping *you* out."

"I'll do it for free," Mel had said.

"I know you would," Love said, squeezing her shoulder. "But they would feel like that's charity. August is getting up there in age and isn't as strong as he used to be. Rocky says he's noticed it too when he's gone out to visit them."

So Mel started going out there Tuesday and Thursday afternoons after her riding lesson with Benni. She'd show August what she'd learned by exercising their two horses, Duke and Daisy. Polly usually had some sort of little chore that she needed done. She'd pay Mel in cash, pressing the soft, old bills into her hand and telling her with a gentle laugh not to spend it all in one place. Mel had saved every penny they paid her, keeping it in a blue Maxwell House coffee can in her cupboard. A stupid hiding place. A burglar with the IQ of a banana slug would find it in twenty seconds. Right now there was 241 dollars. Mel didn't know what to do with the money. It embarrassed her to take money from Polly. She couldn't imagine spending it.

So Mel saw them two days a week, and Love found an excuse to drop by Monday, Wednesday and Friday. Since Polly and August faithfully attended Rocky's church every Sunday, that only left Saturday when someone wasn't checking on them. Love always found some reason to phone on Saturdays. The plan was working, for now.

Mel worked hard at pretending she wanted to learn ranching, though she couldn't imagine anything she'd less want to do. She was a born and raised city girl, a native Las Vegan. Though she loved the quiet, ordinary pattern of Morro Bay town life, ranching and its never-ending chores didn't appeal to her. She liked doing a job and walking away, preferring someone else shoulder the responsibility of the larger issues. That's what she'd liked about patrol work. She did her ten-hour shift, wrote her reports, then, along with the patrol car, turned the whole thing over to the next officer. Unlike a lot of cops, advancing into detective work had never tempted her. She had no desire to delve deeper into victims' lives or to take her work home. Get in, take care of business and get out. That's what had been so perfect about being a street cop. No long-term relationships.

She helped the Johnsons as a favor to Cy and Love, to whom she owed a huge debt for taking her in, though she knew they'd protest that. When she drove into Morro Bay almost three years earlier, she had a desperate agenda that she was sure Cy and Love had eventually guessed, though they never asked her outright about why she came to this town in particular. Their innate kindness and respect for a person's privacy was, she felt sure, what kept them from asking personal questions about her past.

She turned at the long driveway that led to the Ramsey-Ortiz ranch, driving under the wrought-iron archway. In the distance she could see the low, one-story ranch house with the deep front porch. A cheery Christmas flag showing a Nativity scene hung from one of the porch's pillars. When she pulled her truck around the circular driveway and parked in front of the house, Benni's white-haired grandmother, Dove, stepped out on the porch.

"Hey there, missy," she called, as Mel opened her truck door. Her eighty-seven-year-old face was a road map of deep wrinkles, the result of too many unprotected years in the sun. "Before you leave, I have some pumpkin bread for y'all." She made her way slowly down the three porch steps, using her four-pronged cane that was painted with bright red, yellow and green stripes, like a psychedelic barber pole. Her long, waist-length braid flicked like a mare's tail.

"Great," Mel said, coming around the truck to accept the older woman's embrace. Though Mel was not a demonstrative person, she learned the first time they met that there was no use trying to dodge Dove's enthusiastic hugs. They were as much as part of her as her Arkansas roots. "I love pumpkin bread."

"*USA Today* claimed there was a shortage of pumpkins back East this year," Dove said. "Some kind of fungus. Apparently it galloped right past us without stopping, because I have enough pumpkins for ten families."

"Yes, ma'am," Mel said.

"How's things in Morro Bay? You keeping those Rice boys on the straight and narrow?"

"Trying to," Mel said, smiling at Dove, who had bent down to pull some weeds that had dared to stray into her pristine flower beds.

After Cy died thirteen months ago, unable to manage the feed store and help Magnolia with the café, Love sold the feed store to Bill Rice, a millionaire farmer down in Santa Maria. He bought the business for his twentysomething grandsons, Brad and Evan. He renamed it B & E Feed, hoping to instill in them some pride of ownership. Bill asked Mel to stay on, take care of the books and work the counter full-time. He liked how she organized and kept track of the store stock. He decreed that the feed deliveries and heavy lifting be done by Brad and Evan, confessing to Mel that he hoped the physical labor would knock some of the wildness out of the boys, who preferred to spend their time surfing, checking out girls and partying.

Though they were both as flaky as bales of timothy hay, Mel liked the young men, calling them Bert and Ernie or the Muppet Brothers right to their faces, which only made them laugh. They were nice enough guys, especially for growing up so privileged. She understood that Bill had tacitly hired her as an expensive babysitter. She and the boys had an agreement. She'd cover for them when they had hangovers, and they'd pay her double time under the table from their generous trust funds. Because of their little deal, which she suspected their indulgent grandpa was all too aware of, she made enough money to meet her simple needs. And Bill made sure she was covered on his company's health insurance plan. It was a fair exchange.

"Benni's out in the corral," Dove said, sticking the handful of weeds into a plastic grocery sack she pulled from her flowered apron pocket. "Maisie's practicing barrels. She had to change her lessons from Wednesdays to Thursdays because she's taking some kind of special math class or something. She's real good with numbers, Benni says."

"Maisie?"

Dove cocked her head, squinting into the sun. "Maisie Hudson. Guess you two haven't crossed paths. Benni's giving her barrel racing lessons. Her daddy's a deputy sheriff, old friend of the family. He's kind of a smart mouth, but he grows on you. He works cold cases."

"Oh," Mel said, not particularly interested.

Since she'd left the force three years ago, her old life as a cop mostly seemed like a television show she'd watched as a child, familiar in a vague sort of way. Benni's husband, Gabe, a retired police chief who now taught a couple of philosophy and criminal justice classes at Cal Poly, seemed to understand that better than anyone. Whenever they met at a barbecue or when he'd come to buy feed, they'd talk about ranching, the weather, the price of cattle, how the Dodgers were doing. Never about their former law enforcement careers.

"Guess I should get out to the barn," Mel said.

"Don't forget that pumpkin bread before you leave," Dove called after her. "Otherwise I'll have to throw it to the pigs."

"You don't have pigs," Mel called back.

"You are one sharp snickerdoodle," Dove replied, giving a loud cackle.

Out in the corral next to the barn, Benni sat up on the top rail with her dusty boots dangling, watching a copper-haired girl in her late teens canter a gray mare around three blue-striped barrels set in a triangular pattern.

"What's up?" Mel said, joining Benni up on the railing.

"Hey," Benni said, turning to look at her. Her long, red blonde hair was pulled back in a braid almost as long as her grandmother's and dangled through the back of a bright green San Celina Farm Supply cap. "Maisie's almost done. She had to change practice days."

"Yeah, Dove told me."

"Good run," Benni called out to the smiling teenage girl, who held up a hand in reply. "Want me to time you?"

The girl nodded and trotted the horse to one end of the corral. When she got the mare calm and situated, she waved at Benni.

"Okay," Benni called. "Go!" She punched the stopwatch button.

The teenage girl raced around the barrels, hugging her horse's sides with her long, jean-clad legs. It amazed Mel that she stayed in the saddle as the horse flew around the barrels in a cloverleaf pattern. The girl circled the last barrel and raced down the middle of the arena. Benni clicked the stopwatch.

"Twenty-three seconds. Good run!" she called. "You're getting there. Cool off Shoney while Mel and I tack up Redeye." She jumped down off the fence. Mel followed suit.

"So, how's things at the feed store?" Benni asked, her sun-freckled face smiling up at Mel.

Mel smiled back, still a little amazed that she actually looked forward to talking with Benni. The first time they met at one of August and Polly's barbecues, Mel was certain she wouldn't like this woman whose tiny, narrow-hipped body never seemed to stop moving and whose upbeat, talkative personality was the type that would normally set Mel's teeth on edge. But it only took ten minutes for her to discover the kind heart behind Benni's cheery personality and the sharp, often bawdy sense of humor that Mel recognized came from spending so much time around cops and ranchers.

"You know Bert and Ernie," Mel said. "They're a couple of flakes . . . but, as they say, they're my flakes."

"They'll straighten out," Benni said, laughing. "You know Gabe's son, Sam? Gabe and Lydia, Sam's mom, despaired of him at times, but he eventually grew up and became a responsible adult. Though Gabe still teases Sam about where he went wrong since Sam decided to join the fire department."

"I can imagine," Mel said.

They walked into the cool, dim barn where Redeye, the dark red gelding that Mel had been riding for the last few months, stuck his head over his stall door.

"Hey, Red," Mel said, gently rubbing her knuckles over the horse's nose. He blew warm, moist air in reply.

Benni glanced at her watch. "I have to go in and take a roast pan out of the oven for Dove. Her arm's still weak."

"Darn, I meant to ask her how it was feeling," Mel said. Dove had fallen and sprained her shoulder a month ago and was supposed to wear a brace to keep her from using it.

"It's much better," Benni said. "But she ditched the brace despite the doctor's order, and she's not supposed to lift anything heavy. Trying to keep her from doing that is a full-time job. She hates asking for help. I'm trying to just 'accidentally' be there when she needs something lifted or moved."

Mel nodded. "Reminds me of August and Polly."

"Yeah, they're all of a kind. You tack up, and I'll be out shortly."

"No problem."

While she gathered the horse tack, Mel thought about how much time they were all spending trying to help these older people maintain their independence. It felt right to her, like she was part of something bigger and more important than herself.

She opened the stable door, fitted the halter around Redeye's massive head and walked him outside to tie him to the railing. While she brushed his slick, warm coat with long, regular strokes, the scent of horse and hay and the sharp, metallic odor of rich soil floated around her, reminding her of Cy.

"I'm worried," he'd said the last time she saw him, only hours before he died. Love had gone into San Celina for a long-overdue mammogram appointment. Cy insisted she go, though she complained it could wait. Mel suspected that he'd done so because he wanted to talk.

"Why?" She'd been reading to him from *Shane*, one of his favorite novels. She hugged the musty-scented book to her chest, saving their place.

"I didn't think I'd die this young. I'm afraid Love won't have enough to live on. The women in her family are long livers." He managed a shadow of his old grin. "I mean, they live long, not that their livers are—" He started coughing, the fluid in his lungs thick and wet-sounding. It seemed cruel and unfair to Mel that Cy, who had never smoked, would contract lung cancer.

Mel patted him gently on the back until the coughing subsided. She held back her tears with a supreme physical effort, knowing they would distress Cy.

"I'll take care of her," she promised. "Don't worry."

He nodded, unable to speak. His eyes, deep in their sockets, were filled with trust. "She'll fight you," he was finally able to whisper. "You know how independent she is. And you know she's annoyed at me for not trying harder, not going for more chemo." His eyes grew watery. "I'm just so tired . . ."

"No," Mel said. "She's not mad at you. She's . . . we're . . . we just don't want . . ." She choked, then coughed, trying to dislodge the rock that felt like it was cutting off her airway. Don't die, she wanted to cry.

"Chicky, she's gonna have her some tough times. You try to help her, okay? No matter how hard she tries to push you away."

"I will, boss." Chicky was the nickname he'd given her the first day they met. Whenever he called her that, a tiny flower of warmth bloomed inside her chest. "I promise. I . . ." She stuttered, not knowing how to assure him any further that she'd look after Love. "I *promise*." She would have done anything for this man.

It was almost three years ago now, the first week of January, that she drove into Morro Bay, more hopeless than she'd ever felt in her life. She'd quit the force on a Friday morning, spent the day aimlessly driving around Las Vegas, out to Hoover Dam, up and down the streets of Henderson, up to Mt. Charleston, where she drank hot rum toddies and watched skiers in their bright, geometric-print snow jackets and silly knit hats tumble down the powdery runs.

She ended up that night at a stale-smelling casino bar off the Strip. It seemed vaguely familiar to her, and she remembered after her second whiskey that when she was a rookie, she and her partner, an old-timer named Buzz, busted up a fight there between a black guy and a white guy over a bleach-haired cocktail waitress. Around ten p.m. she realized no amount of whiskey would wash away the scene with Sean that kept replaying in her head, a bloody nightmare loop that wouldn't stop—his outstretched hand, face the color of concrete, the sound of the music box knocked over by his fall, the song, "The Entertainer," a cruel joke.

She stumbled out of the casino and found her small white pickup. She started driving, flash-bang images of his empty eyes flitting through her head like a thousand wild bats. Her eyes and head throbbed with a pain that made her pull over in the middle of the desert and puke until electric stars dotted her vision.

When she stopped for coffee in a brightly lit McDonald's outside of Barstow, she remembered Morro Bay. She'd gone there once with her handsome, black-haired father when she was ten years old. It was February, and they stayed for two days and nights in a motel called the Castoff Inn. They ate clam chowder, fried shrimp and stacks of hot, syrupy buttermilk pancakes. He bought her a huge bag of salt water taffy and a red sweatshirt printed with sea lions. They watched seals from a boat ride where, as always, he charmed the other passengers with his winning smile and seemingly impossible card tricks.

In her memories Morro Bay was a magical place, where her father said he'd one day buy them a little house with seashell wind chimes, and they'd live forever next to the ocean. He'd win custody of her, he told her. Her mother didn't really want her, didn't she know that? He put into words what she'd always suspected, that her mother didn't love her but loved the child support. But that didn't matter, because Mel and her dad were going to leave Las Vegas and live in Morro Bay. He would buy her a dog. A big, shaggy one named Ralph or Henry who would follow her everywhere and save her life if she fell into the ocean just like in the movies.

On the third day, they drove back to Las Vegas, and he dropped her off in front of the pink apartment where she lived with her mother, two blocks from downtown. It was late, and Mom was out as usual, probably dating the man who would eventually become her second of five husbands.

"Au revoir, Melina Jane LeBlanc," her father said, flashing his devastating smile. He pulled a shiny silver dollar from behind her ear, bowed and presented it to her with a flourish. Las Vegas's only Cajun magician was how he billed himself. "Be a good *fille* for your old papa." He blew her a kiss and drove away. She never saw Varise Alphonse LeBlanc again.

"Best get over it," her mother said when Mel moped around the phone for weeks, waiting for his call. "He's a magician, little girl. Disappearing is what he does best."

Her vague plan the morning after she quit the force and drove to Morro Bay was to go to the beach near Morro Rock, hopefully deserted that early, and use her .45 one last time. She'd make sure she was close enough to the water that the tide would take her body out to sea, where it would be picked clean by crabs. Even as she mentally planned this on the dark eight-hour drive across Nevada and California toward the ocean, she knew it was a fantasy. Bodies left for any amount of time in a lake or an ocean weren't clean white bones. They were bloated and smelled like rotten fish mixed in a cesspool and were gnawed at and partially consumed by any number of hungry life-forms. But it wouldn't matter, because she would no longer inhabit that body.

It all changed because of a chicken, a Silver Spangled Hamburg, she would later discover. She drove into town when the sun was still a rosy whisper on the horizon. She carefully maneuvered the foggy back streets, trying to find the beach, while her stomach twisted and heaved with the mixture of coffee and alcohol.

Out of the misty gray fog, what looked like a polka-dotted chicken with blue gray legs flew up on her truck's damp hood and performed a clicky-clack, cartoon tap dance. Mel slammed on her brakes. The bird slid off, hit the ground and started running. Another chicken darted in front of the truck. It squawked so loud Mel could hear the agitated sound inside the cab. Another followed, its mouth open in a comical silent chicken scream.

Following them, cursing to beat the band, came a man, six two or three, about two hundred pounds. He was big-chested, had a bushy head of unruly chestnut hair and a full beard. He held up the flat of his hand to Mel, even though she was already stopped, and ran in front of her truck, slapping his wide palm on the right front fender.

"Need some help here!" he called.

Instinctively, she pulled the emergency brake, grabbed her keys and opened the door. It was her duty as a police officer to render assistance, even though she'd officially become a civilian as of noon the day before. She realized in that moment that turning off that part of her wasn't just a matter of saying, "I quit."

Despite the alcohol still in her system, Mel finally caught one of the escaped chickens. She held it under her arm like a football, a flapping, screeching, pecking football.

"What do I do with it?" she yelled to the man who'd managed to capture two and was holding a flapping bird in each of his hands.

"Pen's inside!" He nodded toward the little red tongue-and-groove feed store that she hadn't even noticed was there.

Inside, she managed to drop the hysterical chicken into the pen, whose open gate the man closed and latched. For the next hour she helped the man, who introduced himself as Cy, and his teenage employee, Josh, chase chickens. They were joined by a few locals, retired farmers out for their early morning constitutionals and familiar with the unpredictable ways of poultry. By eight a.m., two hours after Mel's truck had been attacked by the Silver Spangled Hamburg, the frantic fowl were all captured.

The chicken posse was enjoying hot coffee and homemade donuts brought over by one of the neighbors when a bleary-eyed newspaper reporter from the *Morro Bay Post-Gazette* walked up and said someone had called him about a breaking news story on Harbor Street. The story, complete with color photograph, was the next day's front-page news. The caption read, "Harbor Hens Run Amok." The photo showed

Cy, Mel and Josh, each holding a chicken, standing in front of the feed store. Love had been in Kentucky visiting her cousin Tally and never got over the fact that she missed the whole incredible sight.

"Say, Chicky," Cy had said when Mel downed her third chocolate-iced French donut, the best food she'd tasted in months. "You're quite the poultry wrangler. You looking for a job?"

Mel put down the wood-handled brush, remembering that moment like it was yesterday. She scratched Redeye on the spot near his withers that always made his eyes roll with pleasure. She never had a pet growing up, so she wasn't naturally comfortable with animals. In the last few months, as she'd taken the baby steps in learning to ride, Redeye's easygoing personality had wormed its way into her heart. She looked forward to the old horse's nuzzling, amazed that an animal this large and capable of inflicting hurt on a human being could be so gentle. She'd slowly grown to love Redeye, the same way she'd grown to love Morro Bay, August and Polly, the feed store and the Buttercream, Love and Cy.

Yes, that moment with Cy almost three years ago was imprinted on her heart, like an orphaned gosling attaching to the first breathing thing it laid eyes on. That question whose answer would forever change her life. The answer that would *save* her life.

"You looking for a job?" His face had been hopeful.

She remembered taking a few seconds to contemplate what he asked. Then she took a long drag of that strong, hot coffee and replied, to her utter surprise, "Actually, I think I am."

FOUR

Rett

Brother Dwaine's trucker friends took Rett the rest of the way to Morro Bay. Though she would never admit to anyone that she was scared, it was a big relief that she didn't actually have to hitchhike across the country.

Jim, a truck driver from Spokane who had three daughters of his own, dropped her off at a McDonald's in Santa Maria, about an hour or so from Morro Bay. He made a couple of quick cell phone calls and found another of Brother Dwaine's friends who happened to be in Santa Maria visiting someone in the hospital. Rocky Sanchez agreed to drive her to Morro Bay, where he also lived. Though Rett's trust in God's people had gotten a little shaky in the last few years—the small-town county fair and gospel circuit could do that to a person—she had to admit that Brother Dwaine and his friends seemed pretty cool.

Rocky Sanchez told her he was a minister right off, so she gave him points for not trying to fake her out. He could have, because he sure didn't look like any preacher she'd ever met. In the churches where she and her sisters had regularly sung before the the Son Sisters fell apart, thanks to her freakazoid older sister, Patsy, the ministers tended to wear baggy gray or navy blue suits with lapel pins of little gold crosses or American flags. Rocky had a shaved head, a tattoo on his right forearm of a bleeding red heart surrounding a greenish black crown of thorns, and a gooselike laugh that reminded Rett of Brother Dwaine's truck horn. It made her smile, something her mom always complained she didn't do enough.

On the drive to Morro Bay in an old Chevy pickup sun-faded to a pale pink, he talked nonstop, which she kind of liked, because it meant she only had to nod her head. She found out he was born and raised in Phoenix, Arizona, where he once sold drugs and served time in prison for various drug-related crimes. In prison, he found Jesus after seeing him in a dream and used the time inside to get his bachelor's degree in pastoral care. He also worked in the prison barbershop. Two weeks after he got out, he met his wife, Magnolia Rosalina Fabrizio, at a casino in Las Vegas.

"I was passing out tracts at the old Aladdin," he said. "Magnolia was the freebie headliner in the bar that night. Man, she could sing the hair off a dead man's chest." His laugh filled the truck's warm cab. He swatted at the wooden cross hanging from the rearview mirror. "I fell for her like a lodge pine to a chain saw. Asked her out that night. We ate pancakes and sausage at Denny's on the Strip. Been together ever since." He smiled to himself, keeping his eyes on the road. "Thirty-one incredible years. We have two girls. Jade is twenty-nine, and Cheyenne is thirty." Rocky looked over at Rett; his dark brown skin seemed to glow when he spoke of his wife. "She doesn't sing in bars anymore, except on the third Wednesday of the month at the Rowdy Pelican saloon."

"Why there?" Rett asked.

"For four hours, from six to ten p.m., they agree not to serve liquor. Then she sings all the songs that made me want to marry her the first moment I heard her. She won't sing anymore while people are drinking, and her fans love her enough to honor her beliefs. That's her picture there." He gestured at a photo paper clipped to Rett's sunshade. It showed a woman with curly, dark hair and a gleaming smile holding a red pan-cake spatula across her heart. Somehow the photograph made her look like she had a halo, which Rett thought looked kind of cool.

"Her best friend took that photo," he said. "Really caught her personality."

"Oh," Rett said.

True to his profession, he did try to find out if she was in any kind of physical or spiritual trouble. But at least he wasn't sneaky. He just flat-out asked if she needed any advice, then left her alone when she made it clear she was fine and didn't want to discuss why she was coming to Morro Bay.

"Say," he said, glancing at her banjo case. "Do you know 'On the Rock Where Moses Stood?'"

"Sure." His request impressed her. The old guy really knew his bluegrass gospel. Normally when people saw a banjo, they always asked her to play "Dueling Banjos," like that was the be all and end all of banjo music. "Can't play it alone," she always lied. People were so lame sometimes.

She pulled out Dale's . . . *her* . . . banjo and started tuning it by ear.

"Beautiful instrument," Rocky said, glancing over.

"It's a 1933 prewar Gibson Granada," she said, pretending it was actually hers. "Who knows how many people have played it? It has all its original parts. And the rim has never been cut."

"I don't know what all that means, but I do know old fiddles often play the sweetest," Rocky said, smiling.

She played the old gospel song, giving it a bluesy sound by throwing in some sharps and flats. After that, she played song after song, losing herself in the notes like she always did when she was scared. She did every fancy slide, hammer-down and pull-off that she knew, just because this old banjo, with all its history, felt so solid and wise. It seemed like only a few minutes went by when he pulled off the exit marked Morro Bay.

"Where to now?" he asked, as he slowed down on the off-ramp curve.

"The Buttercream Café?" It was a place her grandma mentioned in the letter Rett found at the bottom of her mom's closet last month when she was looking for spare change. She carefully put the banjo back into the lined case.

"What a coincidence! My wife and her best friend own the Butter-cream." A few minutes later, he pulled up in front of a white stucco build-ing set between a bead shop and a store that sold office supplies. A sign in the shape of an old-fashioned butter churn swung in the morning breeze. Yellow gingham curtains framed the large front window. "Good luck," Rocky said. "You'll be in my prayers tonight."

"Thanks."

"I guess I should say God bless you," he said, when she stepped out of the truck. "But that has always sounded kind of strange to me. He'll bless you whether I request it or not." He smiled and handed her a church bulletin. A round coffee stain haloed the name: Baytown Chris-tian Fellowship. "Drop by if you have a chance. We're a pretty nice group, if not a little long in the tooth, but we do have a few people around your age."

She took the bulletin, planning on ditching it later. "Thanks for the ride, Mr. Sanchez."

"Call me Rocky."

Once inside the café, Rett obeyed the sign and seated herself, choos-ing a table next to the back wall. While she pretended to scan the menu, she peeked at Rocky's wife, Magnolia, who looked just like her photo-graph. She was a good-sized woman, not fat, but definitely substantial. Unlike Rett's mom, who always freaked when she got bigger than a size six, this woman looked like she couldn't give a flying flip about what size jeans she wore. She seemed to be in a dozen places at once, firing off orders, talking to the people sitting at the counter, filling people's cof-fee cups and greeting new customers by name when they came through the door.

Rett glanced around at the café. On the tables were every kind of weird coffee creamer you could imagine, many of them different types of animals, one an ear of corn. Whoever owned this place—Mrs. Rocky and her best friend—must have bought most of the crazy creamers off eBay. On the wall next to her table, the farm and animal theme was car-ried out in framed photographs of butter churns, cows and creamers. The photos at first looked normal, until you really studied them. Then you saw that the photographer had a kind of weird sense of humor; the

butter churns had odd things hanging off them like frilly wedding gar-
ters and spiked dog collars. The creamers, in the shapes of scowling pigs
and wild-eyed collie dogs, were posed next to empty whiskey bottles
and one-armed Barbie dolls with cornrowed hair wearing tattered wedding dresses and cowboy hats. One photo showed a bunch of plastic
cows crowded into a bright red pie pan sitting in the middle of a red-
checked table. Rett thought about it for a moment, then smiled. *Cow
pie.* They were funny in a lame kind of way.

Today all the framed photos were decorated with red and green gar-
lands for Christmas. A manger scene carved from some kind of light
brown wood held a special spot in the big, round communal table in
the middle of the café filled with laughing men and women who looked
and talked as if they were eating in their own dining room. They all
looked really old, like in their sixties.

Mrs. Rocky walked up, pulling a pencil from her thick, curly black
hair, fashioned in a loose bun. Her plastic name tag said Magnolia.

"What can I get you, sugar?" Magnolia poised her pencil over a half-
used order pad.

Alabama, Rett thought. Down near Mobile. Definitely not Mont-
gomery or the hilly northern part. Rett had a kind of knack for accents,
especially Southern ones. Probably because she'd spent so much of her
childhood traveling around the South singing at church reunions and
revival meetings.

Rett thought quickly, remembering that she needed to be careful with
her money in case her grandma was a total whack job and Rett needed
to get out of town fast. "Uh, water. And a donut." She felt her face turn
warm. That sounded stupid, like what a kid would order. "No, make it
coffee. Just coffee."

Magnolia stared at her a moment, her blue eyes thoughtful. "You
just getting into town?"

Rett stared back at her and nodded.

"Where in the South you from?"

Rett hesitated a moment. Her first instinct was to lie, though one
didn't automatically present itself. Then again, she had nothing to hide.
She was here to find her grandma. Maybe this woman could help.

Morro Bay wasn't a big town. It was likely her grandma ate here. The letter she found in her mom's closet had no envelope, so no return address. And Rett couldn't find any free information on the Internet about Love Mercy Johnson except a Morro Bay post office box. She didn't have the money to pay for more information. Luckily, her grandma mentioned the name of this café in the letter.

"Tennessee," Rett said.

Magnolia's full bottom lip tightened slightly. "Long ways for a young girl to be traveling all by herself."

Rett felt the flush start on her neck and work its way slowly up to her cheeks. "I'm eighteen. That's a legal adult."

"So they say," Magnolia said, lifting one eyebrow.

"It is." Rett heard the stubborn, childlike whine in her voice and cringed. It would have been better if she'd kept her mouth shut. Leave it to her to be in a place only two minutes and already be arguing with some adult.

"So, Miss Legal Adult. How'd you get to Morro Bay from Tennessee?" Magnolia asked.

Rett felt her own lower lip stiffen. "Hitchhiked." Take that, you nosy old bat.

Magnolia shook her head, obviously disapproving. "You come to Morro Bay for any particular reason?"

Mind your own darn business, Rett wanted to say. The woman's nosiness was probably the Alabama part of her personality. According to Rocky, his wife was half Southern (that's the Magnolia part, he'd said), half Italian and all business.

"She keeps me and most of the town on the straight and narrow path," he said, obviously proud of his strong-willed wife.

Though Rett knew how to fend off a curious Southerner—heaven knows she'd done it often enough—she was less inclined to deliberately antagonize an Italian lady. She'd known one once when they moved to Pensacola with Mom's second husband, Pete. The woman's name was Mrs. Coscarelli. She lived next door to them and made these awesome lacy cookies that tasted like Good and Plenty candy. The neighborhood kids learned fast that you didn't want to make her mad. Once, the boy across the street, Johnny Dillard, picked her pink roses and threw them all over the street just because he was a jerk who was all over messing up things for no reason. Mrs. Coscarelli went totally postal and turned from a nice, cookie-baking old lady to a freaking maniac. She chased him down the street with a rolling pin dusty with flour, which was funny when you thought about it, kind of like those back-in-the-day cartoons: *Heckle and Jeckle* or *Tom and Jerry*.

Rett shifted in her seat, wishing this woman would go find someone else to interrogate. "I'm looking for Love Mercy Johnson. I have some business with her." That was all she was going to say.

"That right?" Magnolia said. "Well, I happen to know Love Johnson pretty good. I'll give her a ring and let her know you're here waitin' on her. What did you say your name was?"

"Didn't."

That shut Rocky's wife right up and, Rett was guessing, put her on Magnolia's bad girl list for all eternity. Oh, well, she doubted she'd be in this town for very long. Probably her grandma would let her stay a night or two, then wish her good luck and a nice life. Fine, she'd head down to L.A. The music scene there was supposed to be pretty good.

Magnolia picked up the menu and said with a sharp voice, "You sure you don't want the lunch special? Or a cannoli to go with your coffee?"

"I'm sure."

Magnolia's face softened. "No charge, sugar."

Rett frowned. She didn't take charity. "I have money. I'm just not hungry."

Magnolia shrugged. "Suit yourself." A few minutes later, she brought Rett a cup of coffee and a little collie dog–shaped pitcher of cream.

Rett stared out the café window and inhaled deeply, trying to ignore the combination of emptiness and anxiety in her stomach. She'd skipped breakfast this morning, her stomach upset by the stress of meeting her grandma. Maybe she should have taken Magnolia's offer of free food. But she was obviously offering Rett the food out of pity, and Rett hated pity. She didn't want to be beholden to anyone.

Beholden. She liked the way the word sounded. It rolled off your tongue like Karo syrup and butter. And it rhymed with *golden*, which was a good songwriting word. She dug through her backpack and found her songwriting notebook, one of those steno kind with the metal spirals across the top.

She wrote down the words *beholden/golden*. A tune was already starting to tickle her brain. That was what it was like, she once told a newspaper reporter in a little town in Arkansas when she and her sisters were being interviewed by the local newspaper. They were singing at a country fair near Mt. Ida, not on the big permanent stage, but the temporary one near the pig races. Sometimes there'd only be five or six people in the audience, usually eating lunch. Her sister Patsy called it singing to the corn dogs. The Son Sisters sing your favorite bluegrass and gospel hits. Free mustard and relish all around.

It killed something inside Rett when they took the stage just to watch people finish their deep-fried Snickers, then stand up and walk away. After their show, they sold—or tried to sell—the only CD they'd recorded. Ten bucks a piece or three for twenty-five dollars. Like anyone would ever want three. One of Mom's boyfriends paid to have it made when he was so gaga in love with her. That was Mom's biggest talent for sure, getting men to fall in love with her and do whatever she wanted. For a while, anyway.

"It's sort of like an itch," she'd answered the reporter's question about how she wrote a song. She'd been fifteen at the time and had already written twenty-seven and a half songs, though none of them were recorded on their CD. Mom had only let them cover other people's songs on the CD, so it would, in Mom's words, "Have an actual chance of selling." Her words had cut Rett's heart like a knife.

"I just have to kind of scratch at it," Rett told the reporter. "And the words start coming. Sometimes with the music, sometimes not. Sometimes the music comes first, sometimes last. Then I put them together, like a puzzle."

She still remembered the gagging sound that Patsy made deep in her throat. Rett knew what it meant, that she'd said something totally dumb.

The reporter, who was already all over Patsy like about a zillion guys before him, exchanged a look with her pretty older sister, while he feebly attempted to keep a straight face. Rett could see the laugher in his eyes, how all he was interested in was looking cool to her sister with his phony sophistication, so Rett clammed right up. She let Patsy take over the interview, even though her sister couldn't write a song to save her life. Though Patsy was only a year older than Rett, she'd figured out early how to say the right thing to both media types and adults, give them the sound bites they wanted to hear. She was definitely the prettiest of the Johnson girls, so photographers always wanted to put her in the forefront of the photo. That part Rett didn't mind. She tried to hide behind her banjo or guitar whenever she could. And their younger sister, Faith, was mostly in a world of her own, dreaming about dogs and horses and exotic birds. Faith was the type who always went along to get along. She hated any kind of conflict.

Rett inhaled the sweet, toasty scents of the café. The chalkboard next to the cash register read in fancy letters, Italian Day! Man, was she hungry. She glanced over at the table next to her. That plate of lasagna looked killer.

She wished her grandma Johnson would hurry up. She contemplated going outside to wait but quickly squelched that. It was way too cold. She wished she had packed something warmer than this sweatshirt, but she thought California was all sunshine, all the time. That's sure how they made it look on television.

The pastor's wife was talking to a dark-haired woman who sat at the long counter. The woman kept giving Rett suspicious glances that she didn't try to hide, even after Rett gave her the finger, something she kinda regretted. Still, the lady ought to mind her own business and quit staring at her like she was going to steal the sugar or something.

The woman was obviously younger than Magnolia, who looked like she was in her fifties. This other woman looked like she was thirty-something. She wore the cool kind of jeans, cut low and tight. Like Magnolia, she also looked like someone you wouldn't want to mess with, but in a way that Rett couldn't put her finger on. Magnolia was like a really tough grandma. This lady she was whispering to sort of reminded Rett of the female studio musicians she'd met a few times. Those women had bones made of steel. They were used to working with men and seemed like they'd just as soon punch you as speak to you. Still, they'd always been real nice to Rett and her sisters. Rett admired them, wished she could be like that: hard but nice. She always felt one sharp word away from crybaby tears when something went totally wrong in her life.

Like all the weird things about her personality, she blamed that on her mom, Karla Rae Murphy Johnson Ryan Wilson, the queen of excess emo. Mama Diva was what Rett and her sisters called their mom behind her back. Maybe this break from her mom and coming out West to see where her dad was raised might bring out his side in her. Not that she knew what that might be. She barely remembered her father, because her mom hardly ever spoke about him. Tommy Cyrus Johnson was a low, laughing voice and a spicy, elusive scent that Rett had been searching for all her life. A couple of times she'd even tried writing a song about him, but she always got stuck after the first few lines.

Rett was digging through her backpack for her last stick of sour orange gum when Magnolia walked up to her table and plopped a big plate of lasagna in front of her.

"Eat," she said. "No argument. Your grandmama's paid for it already."

"Yes, ma'am," Rett said automatically, grateful for the food and even more grateful that someone made a decision for her.

She was halfway finished with the pasta when the door to the café opened, and a tall, kind of bony woman with reddish hair walked in. When Rett heard a couple of men call out her name—Love—she knew it was her grandma. The woman glanced over at Rett, her pale eyes lingering for a split second. Before Rett could react, her grandma turned to speak to the woman that Rett had flipped off.

Great, she thought. They're probably best friends or something. Her grandma would hate her before they even met. Rett immediately started thinking about where she could go from here. Her money wouldn't get her far. She hated thinking about it, but she might have to pawn the banjo. Though the thought of pawning the gorgeous instrument kinda killed her, it also made her smile. Dale would bust a vein. Would serve him right. Maybe she'd send him a postcard with a little cartoon showing the banjo in a jail cell. Just like all those cute little cartoons he drew on Hampton Inn stationery and sent her when he was on the road. All the time he was probably sending Patsy the same cartoons along with love notes reliving what they'd done.

Just thinking about Dale and Patsy made her eyes burn. She bit the inside of her cheek, making herself concentrate on the physical pain, so she wouldn't think about the ache in her chest. She'd sung he-done-me-wrong songs since she was barely five years old, but this was the first time she understood what those women were talking about.

She pushed the lasagna away, her appetite gone. Forget about Dale, she lectured herself. You've got to figure a way to make some money and get out of here. She was certain she'd used up whatever good girl, spiritual savings she'd acquired with the Mister upstairs, so she doubted whether someone like Brother Dwaine would show up and drive her to L.A. Maybe she could get a job bartending, though she didn't have any idea how to make any kind of drink except a sloe gin fizz. She tried to remember the ratio between sloe gin and fizzy water. Was lemon juice involved somehow? Maybe she could Google it. She'd need to find a fake ID too.

"Hello, Loretta."

Rett looked up, surprised to see her grandma standing next to her. She was struck dumb for a moment. She looked right into her eyes, then back down at the table. "I go by Rett now."

She looked back up to see her grandma's reaction. For some reason, she knew this moment would be one she'd remember her whole life. She tasted the sweet-tangy marinara sauce in the back of her throat. The contents of her stomach crashed and broke like an ocean wave. It suddenly struck her that this was her father's mother. She'd given birth and raised the man that was Rett's dad. What would this woman think of her? What if her grandma didn't want to have anything to do with her?

"Rett Johnson." Her grandma cocked her head and rolled the name off her tongue as if she were tasting it. Her voice was pitched low, like a blues singer. "I like that." A soft Kentucky twang still echoed in the shadows of her vowels. Her thin, pale lips turned up into a smile. "Well, Rett, welcome home."

FIVE

Mel

Mel had finished her riding lesson and was currying the sweat and dirt off Redeye's back when Maisie came up behind her.

"Benni says you were a cop," Maisie remarked, leaning against the metal hitching rail where the horse was tied.

Mel kept grooming and didn't answer.

"In Las Vegas," Maisie persisted.

According to Benni, Maisie's father had called and said he'd be late, so she had hung around during Mel's lesson supposedly helping Gabe build a new chicken coop. Throughout her lesson, Mel had heard the young woman's clear voice talking a mile a minute to Gabe.

"*Were* being the operative word," Mel said, glancing over at the curious young woman. Strands of Maisie's hair had worked their way loose from her braid, causing tiny curls to form around her heart-shaped face. She appeared to be the same age as Love's granddaughter, but the two girls seemed as far apart in looks and attitude as Mel was from the actress Reese Witherspoon.

"My daddy's a cop," Maisie replied. "He says, 'Once a cop, always a cop.'"

Benni walked around the corner in time to hear Maisie's statement. "Amen to that. Though I have to admit, since Gabe retired, he's becoming a little less suspicious of every person who looks crosswise at him."

Mel didn't answer, just kept currying the horse's broad back.

"Do you still carry a gun?" Maisie asked Mel.

Mel glanced over at Benni and arched one eyebrow. For a cop's kid, this one was awfully snoopy.

"Hey, Maisie," Benni said. "Would you go inside and help Dove pack up the pumpkin bread for Mel and the others? You know my gramma. She'll probably be trying to do it herself, and she's not supposed to use that arm."

"In other words, quit asking questions and get lost." Maisie gave Mel a wide grin and wiped her hands down her tight Wranglers. "Sorry if I'm a pain. Daddy says I should have come equipped with a snap on my mouth." She gave a high giggle.

Maisie had an infectiously cheerful way about her, an innocence that Mel envied. She exuded the easy confidence that a person seemed to acquire only if they'd been cherished early in their life. Mel wanted to dislike the girl for it, but instead, she found herself smiling back.

"No harm, no foul," Mel said, tossing the currycomb into the metal bucket. She pulled a hoof pick from her back pocket.

"Thanks! See you later." Maisie ran toward the back door of the ranch house, giving a little skip every third step or so.

"She's a good kid," Benni said. "She reminds me of myself at that age."

"Well, lucky you." Mel felt a twinge inside. She hadn't meant the words to sound quite so sarcastic.

Benni cocked her head, not appearing to be insulted. "Yes, I was. But I can't take any credit for it. I didn't pick my family, I was born into it. Lucky sperm club, as Gabe would say." She smiled. "I always correct him. Lucky sperm *and* egg club. I didn't deserve my good fortune any more than someone deserves a bad family. I just thank God for it."

Mel gently tugged at Redeye's back fetlock until he lifted his leg. She pulled his foot between her knees and dug at the mud and debris caught in the frog of his hoof. It always made her uncomfortable when someone talked about God in such a familiar way, like he was a person they just called on their cell phone, one of their five favorite people, as one phone company advertised. She didn't know how to respond. The whole concept of a being who created this screwed-up world seemed beyond rational belief, though she'd have to admit, if pressed, that she didn't have any better explanation for how or why humans existed or what made them do things, good and bad.

"Are you going to the lighted boat parade on Saturday?" Benni asked.

"Yep. Bert and Ernie and four of their buddies are attempting some kind of kayak formation." She let Redeye's leg down carefully and moved to the next one.

"I've seen single kayaks in the parade," Benni said. "They always cover themselves with Christmas lights. But I don't think there's ever been a whole fleet of them. Is that what you'd call it, a fleet of kayaks? A bevy? A cartel?"

Mel didn't look up from Red's hoof. "In this case, I'd probably call it a foolishness of kayaks."

Benni's clear laugh rang out. "Mel, you are a hoot. Are you going to paddle with them?"

"With how cold it is out there on the water? No way. I'm the official photographer and designated cheerleader."

"Smart lady." Benni checked her watch. "I'd better go inside and make sure Dove isn't doing something she's not supposed to be doing. Same time next week?"

Mel nodded. "I'll practice with opening and closing gates before then. I'm going over to August and Polly's after this."

"You're doing great, but riding a horse is like riding a bicycle. You need to do it enough that it becomes second nature. That's the best way to avoid a wreck."

Ten minutes later, Mel had finished with the horse's last hoof and was combing out his tangled mane when a man came strolling around the corner of the barn. She swore softly to herself. Grooming Redeye was her favorite part of her lessons with Benni, and she really preferred doing it alone. There was a certain rhythm to the brushing, combing, picking his hooves, checking his body for sore spots. Making another creature feel comfortable and calm seemed a worthwhile task and set-tled something inside her in an uncomplicated, peaceful way.

So it annoyed her when the man, whistling an off-key tune, walked right up to her. He was average height, five eleven or so, middle to late forties, short brownish silver hair parted on the side, dark eyes. He had a self-assured, slightly aggressive walk that instantly gave him away. Cop or career military. Maisie's dad, she guessed.

"Hey, how's it going?" he asked. He wore a faded plaid flannel shirt, jeans and round-toed brown boots. His black ball cap read Tulane University.

"Fine."

"Is Maisie back here?"

"Nope." She continued to run the steel comb through Redeye's mane. His accent had a drawl to it. Texas, she guessed.

"Know where she went?" He squinted his coffee brown eyes against the warm afternoon sun and rested his hands on his hips. Though she hated that she noticed, he was attractive, good-looking in that Eddie Bauer–L.L. Bean male-model way. All he needed was a rake in his hand, a yellow Lab at his feet and a bar code across his feet.

"Last I heard she was headed toward the house."

"No one's in the house."

Mel shrugged. "That's all I know."

She waited for him to go away, but he didn't. She could feel the tension start in the pit of her stomach, reminding her of the feeling when she was a patrol officer, that millisecond she knew that the person she'd pulled over was going to be a pain in the ass.

"You must be Mel," he said, his voice friendly, deliberately ignoring her not-interested signals.

"Yep." She started vigorously working at a knotted place in Red-eye's mane. When she tugged too hard, the horse tossed his head in an-noyance. "Sorry, boy," she murmured.

"You're taking lessons from Benni too," the man said. "Maisie talks about you all the time. Says you're the bomb. That's good, I think. But you're young. I guess you'd know that. Actually, Maisie just talks all the time, so don't take it personal. She used to be shy as a kid, then something happened when she hit puberty, and it's been magpie city ever since. Sometimes I put on my Bose headphones and tell her I'm listening to music when all I'm doing is listening to the quiet. I'm her dad, by the way." While he talked, he'd moved over to the other side of the horse.

Mel peered at him over Redeye's back, unsmiling. "Like daughter, like father."

Without missing a beat, he threw back his head and laughed. "Touché, Ms. Melina Jane LeBlanc. I've been known to bend someone's ear once in a great while."

His use of her full name caused her neck to stiffen. She didn't like it when someone knew more about her than she did about them. Then again, he was a cop and an obviously protective father, so it made sense that he'd do some checking on a person who was around his daughter, even peripherally. She reluctantly gave him credit for that. A parent couldn't be too cautious these days, what with pedophiles on practically every street corner. Still, his familiarity grated on her nerves.

She gave him a cool look. "That all you need, Maisie's dad?"

He grinned at her, a cocky smile that she was certain always worked for him with the badge bunnies who flocked around the diners and bars where law enforcement officers hung out. "Sorry, name's Hud. Short for Ford Hudson. Don't laugh. My late, not-so-great father was crazy as a drunk barn rat. Story goes if I had been a girl, my name was going to be Cadillac."

Mel didn't smile back. He gave the spiel so easily that she knew it was his go-to line for picking up women. It probably worked more times than not.

"Daddy!" Maisie's voice rang out when she walked around the corner of the barn and saw them. She was carrying a mewing calico kitten. Benni followed behind her. "Dove's house cat had kittens . . ."

"No," he said, automatically. Then added, "Ask your mama."

"I will," Maisie said, cuddling the kitten against her chest. "And she'll say no. But I thought I'd try."

"Boo is too old to be getting used to a kitten," Hud said. He looked back at Mel. "He's her corgi. Half uncle or cousin twice removed or something to Love Johnson's dog, Ace."

"Oh," Mel said, untying Redeye's lead. She looked over at Benni. "Pasture or barn?"

"Barn," Benni said. "Give him an extra measure of grain. He worked hard today, and we've been having some cold nights."

After Mel settled the horse in his stall, she walked back out into the backyard, relieved to see that everyone was gone. Up on the front porch of the ranch house, she hesitated before walking in. Though Dove had admonished her many times to feel free to come on in whenever she needed to use the bathroom, get a drink or something to eat, Mel didn't feel right about entering someone's home without knocking. She couldn't imagine someone doing that in her little house. She compromised by making it a habit of opening the screen door and calling out, "Anyone here?"

"In the kitchen." Benni's voice was a muffled reply.

Inside the warm red and yellow farm kitchen, Mel found Benni standing next to the large stainless steel stove stirring a pot that sent a wonderful nutmeg-infused scent throughout the room.

"There's your pumpkin bread." She nodded at the four green gift bags tied with red and white curly ribbon.

"Thanks," Mel said and closed her eyes for a second, inhaling deeply. The smell reminded her of her tenth Christmas, the last one her mom and dad were still together. They'd driven to Idyllwild, California, a small town in the San Jacinto Mountains above Palm Springs, at the invitation of her dad's mother. Her grandmother Suzette worked as a baker for Wes & Laura's Chowdown Inn, a local café and bakery. They stayed with Grand-mère Suzette for four days. Every day except for Christmas, Mel rose at two a.m. and went with her grandmother to work. She helped make scones, donuts, oatmeal cookies and Grand-mère Suzette's famous pie plate cinnamon rolls. But it was her grandmother's nutmeg donuts that people drove up the mountain to buy, ordering dozens of them to take home, especially during the holidays.

"You a good little baker, you," Grand-mère Suzette told her. Her faint Cajun French accent fascinated Mel. "And my perfect *latite fille*." She smiled at Mel. "That is how you say granddaughter in Cajun."

Her praise and Mel's feeling of accomplishment when they slipped the large metal pans of baked goods into the glass cases was something that Mel forced herself to remember when she felt like her life was worthless.

"*Je t'aime*, Melina," Grand-mère Suzette had said, kissing both Mel's cheeks when they left, the day after Christmas. Her father had a two-week gig at a casino in Reno that started at eleven p.m. that night. "You be a good girl, you. A happy girl. Come bake with me again, no?" She pressed a tissue-wrapped package in Mel's hands. It was the red and white checked apron that her grandmother had tied around Mel's neck when they sprinkled cinnamon and rolled out cookie dough.

"Let's go, Varise," Mel's mother, Genetta, had said to her father, impatient to leave the small town. She'd been complaining about being bored since they arrived.

"Au revoir, Mama," her father said. "I'll call."

Grand-mère Suzette glanced over at Mel, her eyes sad. Mel was beginning to realize that her father promised many things but carried out few of them. "Take care of Melina, Varise and Genetta. Don't forget her."

"Oh, for heaven's sake, Suzette," Mel's mother said, rolling her eyes. "She's our daughter. How could we forget her?"

"Good-bye, good-bye!" Mel hung out the window of their new 1981 Cadillac, the car that would be repossessed two months later. "Don't forget me, Grand-mère!"

"*Dieu te beni*, sweet Melina," her grandmother called back. "God bless you."

Eight months later, her mother told her bluntly that Grand-mère Suzette had died of a heart attack. They'd found her one morning lying next to the bakery's refrigerator, a pound of wrapped butter in her hand.

"Good memories?" Benni said, bringing Mel back to the present.

Mel opened her eyes, embarrassed to be caught in such a vulnerable moment. But this was Benni, someone she almost considered a friend.

"Nutmeg reminds me of my grandmother Suzette," Mel said. "She was a baker. Her specialty was nutmeg donuts."

"Sounds delicious," Benni said. "I'm stirring this for Dove. She's making peach cobbler. No one makes it like she does. I think grammas have something special they add to food that just makes it taste better. Magic gramma seasoning."

"You may be right. Who are all these for again?" She nodded at the gift bags lined up on the tile counter.

"One's for you, one's for Love, one's for August and Polly. You said you're going there next, right?"

Mel nodded.

"The last one is for Rocky and Magnolia. Can you drop it by the church office when you get back to Morro Bay? He loves Dove's pumpkin bread. Don't tell Shug, but he says he likes Dove's better."

"Want to bet he tells Shug the same thing about his pumpkin bread?" Mel said, gathering up the bags by their white handles.

Benni laughed. "You're probably right. Guess when you're a minister you learn the fine art of food complimenting early, or you find yourself another gig. Our church found out the surest way to divide a congregation is to have a pie contest. The one time we tried it, our two judges, Jo Ellen and Goldie, practically had to go into the witness protection program."

"Tell Dove thanks for the pumpkin bread. See you Saturday."

"No doubt. Stay safe."

"You too."

On the ten-minute drive to August and Polly's ranch, though Mel mentally fought it, Sean came to mind. She'd been proud of the fact that sometimes she went for days without thinking about him. After three years, Cy's wise words to her were finally beginning to come true.

"Whatever horrible thing you went through," he'd said once when she told him only that she left the force because someone she respected let her down, "it will soften with age. I'm not saying it'll ever stop hurting. God knows that whenever I think about Tommy dying all alone on that street in Nashville, my heart hurts like it happened yesterday. But, to be honest, there are weeks that go by when I don't think about it. I don't mean that I don't think about Tommy. I think about him every day, but I remember the good things. I don't know when that will happen for you, but if you had any good times with this person, then someday those times will maybe equal whatever bad happened between you."

Good times. Yes, she and Sean had those. But they seemed vague and fuzzy in her memory, still overshadowed by the sight of his glassy marble eyes, not seeing her, not seeing anything. In her dreams his blood-splattered hand reached out to her, fingers splayed and stained red brown, wanting her help, wanting her to join the nightmare his life had become. Those first few minutes when she discovered his body was time she'd give away everything she owned to wipe from her memory.

Stop it, she commanded herself. There's no point in thinking about it. It's over. She slowed down when she spotted the avocado grove. The tractor-shaped mailbox, orange *Morro Bay Post-Gazette* newspaper holder and a hand-painted sign stating Eggs for Sale announced the entrance to the quarter-mile driveway to the Johnson ranch. The avocados were August's latest attempt to keep the ranch solvent. He'd said he broke even on the deal, though she and Love suspected he lost money, even with all their volunteer help. The truth was that August and Polly couldn't make a living off the ranch any longer, and they didn't want to admit it. Mel thought they should just sell the place, take the million dollars or more it had to be worth and enjoy the end of their life.

"August is eighty-four years old," Mel complained to Love a few weeks ago. "Polly's eighty and with no one to . . ." She instantly closed her mouth, realizing a split second too late how cruel her comment would sound to Love. What was she thinking? Open mouth, insert size-nine foot, chew vigorously.

"Oh, man, I'm so sorry," she said, dropping her head to stare at her plate. "That was truly one of the stupidest things I almost said."

Love patted Mel's hand. "It's okay. I understand your frustration. And I agree with you. Now that Cy is gone, they don't have anyone to save the ranch for, but I think the real problem is they just don't know what to do with themselves. August and Polly have ranched their whole lives. I can't picture them sitting in a house in town playing Scrabble at the senior center."

Mel nodded. "Still, what happens when one of them dies? Neither of them can stay out there alone."

Love's face darkened with worry. "I know, I know. I'm being absolutely foolish by not facing reality. But, to be honest, I don't have any idea about how to talk to them about changing their lives. I'm sure they'll fight me on it."

They had left it at that, unresolved, and went on to discuss Love's column two months ago about banana pudding, which she was still hearing about. The photo showed two bowls, one clear red, one clear blue. The blue bowl had banana pudding with whipped cream topping, the red bowl brown-tipped meringue. Her caption read, "What difference does it really make?" Both bowls were surrounded by packages of bologna. The photo had apparently started a huge controversy about what she "meant" when she assigned meringue to the red bowl.

"Another letter to the editor in yesterday's *Post-Gazette* said I was implying that people who vote red are lightweights and people who vote blue have substance." Love shook her head. "Clint's loving it, of course. And, get this, someone said I was making a statement about racism with the brown tips on my meringue! You know why I chose the red bowl for the meringue? It was closer! And meringue *browns* when you bake it! And no one even *mentioned* the bologna part of the photo, which is what my real statement was. People are nuts."

"You're preaching to the choir," Mel had said, smiling.

She was right about August and Polly, Mel thought, as she drove up the narrow gravel driveway. There was no way the couple would voluntarily move away from the house they'd lived in their whole married life, sixty years come February. August had been born and raised in that house, only leaving once to serve in WWII.

"I missed this old place every minute I was fighting those Germans in Italy," he'd told Mel one time when they were picking corn in Polly's garden. "It and Polly were the reason I made it home. No one was going to keep me from them."

Polly was sweeping the two-story farmhouse's deep front porch when Mel pulled up. Her short gray hair was tied up in a red bandanna, knotted in the back, like an outlaw motorcycle rider. She wore a flowered cotton dress and a full apron like the kind Mel had seen on housewives in 1930s movies.

"Hey, Miss Polly," Mel called, climbing down from her truck. She grabbed one of the green bags of pumpkin bread. "With that do-rag on your head, all you need is some black leather chaps, and you'd be the queen of the bikers on some old guy's thirty-thousand-dollar hog."

Polly stopped sweeping and came down the three wooden porch steps and gave her tinkly music box laugh. "I have no idea what you just said. The only hogs I know are the kind you raise for ham. And there's not a one of them I'd ride, not even for thirty thousand dollars." Then she paused a moment, thinking. "Well, maybe for thirty thousand dollars. The barn needs a new roof."

Mel handed her the green bag. "Pumpkin bread from Dove."

"Oh, good," Polly said, opening the bag to look. "She makes the best in the county. Don't tell Shug."

"Got it." Mel mimed zipping her lips. "So, what's on the chore list today besides exercising Duke and Daisy?"

"You'd best check with August," she said. "He's out back in the barn. Only thing I need done today is getting the Christmas decorations from the attic."

"I can help you with that."

"We'll see," she said, setting the broom against the porch railing. "August might have a long list for you."

"I'll just head out there then. Anything you want me to tell him?"

"Supper is at five. Chicken pot pie and . . ." She held up the green bag. "Pumpkin bread! You'll stay, won't you?"

"Wouldn't miss it," Mel said.

She walked down the path beside the house to the weathered brown barn set about fifty yards from the house. As she got closer, August's border collie, Ring, bounded out from the barn, barking his greeting.

"Hey, Ring-a-ding-ding," she said. He instantly rolled over and offered his black-and-white-spotted stomach. She was giving him an enthusiastic scratching when August limped out of the tack room.

"Hey, gimpy," she called, standing up. Ring jumped up and ran toward August, who was using a handmade wooden walking stick. Though he didn't have a beard and was a few inches shorter, he looked like what she imagined Cy would have looked like had he lived to his eighties.

And, after seeing Cy's granddaughter this morning, she recognized the same wide eyes and high forehead passed down through the generations. It suddenly occurred to her that she'd forgotten to ask Love whether she should mention that August and Polly's great-granddaughter was in town. She decided that, just like when she was a cop, when in doubt, keep your mouth shut.

"Hey, yourself, Miss Smarty Pants," he replied, good-naturedly. He'd stumbled while attempting to fix a broken gate a week ago, twisting his ankle and banging his head. A dark brown scab decorated his forehead along with a purplish bruise on his cheek. "What're you doing here?"

She paused for a moment, uncertain about what to say. This had been happening the last few months, and it vaguely worried her. She'd been coming to the ranch twice a week for months now. A few times in the last month or so when she came, August acted truly surprised to see her. Once she teased him about it, but without warning, he snapped at her, obviously embarrassed, so she'd backed off. Now she just pretended every visit was spur-of-the-moment.

"Thought the horses might need exercising," she said. "Just had my lesson at Benni's, so I'm all loose and ready to ride."

He nodded. "They can always use some riding. How's things in the city?"

She smiled. Even after living in Morro Bay for almost three years, it amused Mel how differently people here viewed life. The first time Cy told Mel he was going to the city, the first week she worked at the feed store, she assumed he meant San Francisco or Los Angeles. It had floored her when she realized he'd meant San Celina, the county seat, a town of about forty thousand people.

So, a few weeks after that, when August asked her how things were going in the "city," she'd smugly replied, "Don't know. I haven't been to San Celina for a while."

"No, I mean Morro Bay," he'd said, his face completely serious.

"How's that ankle healing?" she asked, glancing down at his dirt-encrusted Redwing work boot.

"Put some of Polly's arthritis ointment on it at night and wrap it during the day. I'll live."

Though she didn't imagine the ointment would do much except heat up his skin and smell funky, it probably wouldn't hurt it. It was the bump on his head that worried her and Love, but August had brushed away their suggestion he see a doctor. "Polly said supper was at five p.m. Chicken pot pie and Dove's pumpkin bread."

His sun-browned face broke into a deep-creviced smile. "I love her pumpkin bread. I do believe it's even better than . . ."

"I know, I know, Shug's. And I won't tell him."

His eyes turned hazy. "Shug? What kind of name is that? You hire someone new at the feed store?"

Mel paused a moment, trying not let the worry she felt show on her face. "Shug's the cook at the Buttercream, August. Magnolia's cousin. He's worked there since they bought it."

August stared at her a moment, then turned his head and called Ring. "Here, you old hound. You want to chase this here stick?" He picked up a small piece of firewood and chucked it toward the corral. Ring bounded after it, grabbed the stick and ran off.

"Worthless mutt," August said, chuckling.

"So, horses first, then what?" Mel asked, sticking her hands in the back pockets of her jeans. It was cold today, and she'd forgotten to bring gloves.

"Got some fence down up on the pasture near Tripod Hill," he said. "It's kinda steep getting up there and . . ."

"Got it," Mel said. "I'll ride Duke up there and kill two birds with one stone. Anything else?"

"That'll take you a good little while," he said. "Daisy's a bit lame today, so it might be better if she rests." He leaned against his knobby stick. "I tell you, Mel, seems like everything and everyone around this place is going to pot." He shook his head. "And I don't mean that stuff the hippies smoke."

Mel smiled. "Hippies? I think you're about thirty years behind. No, make that forty years."

He peered at her through sharp, sky blue eyes. "You said it, girlie. And times were better back then too."

"I wouldn't know. I was still five years away from being born."

"Trust me, times were better." He looked past her, his cheeks drawing inward.

She didn't argue with him, but wanted to say, not better, August. You were just younger and so was Polly. Your son was still alive, and the world was full of hope.

"I'll get to that fence," she said, glancing at her watch. One thirty. "Probably take me until suppertime."

"Fence?" His face looked genuinely confused.

Her chest felt like it held a brick. "Over by Tripod Hill. It needs fixing."

"Does? Then you'd best take a flashlight with you. And Ring. I'd go with you myself if I wasn't so stoved up."

"That's okay. I think Polly might need your help inside. She said something about getting the Christmas decorations down from the attic."

"Guess we should go looking for a tree." He poked the dry ground with his walking stick. "Darn Christmas. Seems like we just had one."

"We did," Mel said, smiling. "About a year ago."

His grin was as mischievous as a young boy's. "So, why do we need to do it again?"

"Who knows? But I'll cut down a pine tree on my way back from fixing that fence. I think I saw one a good one a few weeks ago."

"Fence?" he asked. "What fence?"

SIX

Love Mercy

Love and Rett's ten-minute walk from the Buttercream to Love's house was mostly silent and definitely awkward.

"Are you sure I can't carry something?" Love asked Rett again. She'd offered when they stepped out of the café, but her granddaughter refused any help, even though the banjo case and backpack looked heavy.

"I'm sure." Rett shifted the awkward case to her other hand, switching places with her backpack.

Love was curious about her granddaughter's trip, about who'd given her rides, but when she gently quizzed her, Rett was evasive in that frustrating way that adolescents perfected from the minute their hormones starting churning. That shouldn't have surprised her. Though Tommy had been an uncomplicated child to raise, even he had his moments when a veil dropped over his eyes and he refused to relate to anyone except his friends.

After they'd used up the sparse conversation about her trip, Love fell back on that always dependable subject, weather. She told Rett that it might be a damper cold than she was used to in Tennessee, but that Love had many sweatshirts and jackets she could use.

"Thanks," Rett replied, stopping again to reposition her grip.

When Love opened the door to her house, Ace, after sniffing Rett's outstretched hand, instantly attached himself to her, shadowing her like a pesky younger brother.

"Would you look at that?" Love said. "You know, he's usually a bit standoffish with strangers. I think he knows you're family."

A small smile softened Rett's serious face. Love immediately wished she had her camera so she could photograph the moment. She stared down at the fawning dog. It *was* odd how Ace warmed up to her right away. Could he smell Love and Cy's DNA on Rett?

Love gave her a quick tour of her three-bedroom house, telling her that it was one of Morro Bay's oldest beach cottages, built at the turn of the twentieth century. "Back in 1968 when your granddad replaced some boards in the built-in bookcase next to the fireplace, he found some old letters. One was addressed to someone named Liberty from a man named Jim and was obviously a love letter. When I showed it to one of our older members of the county historical society—she was ninety-six back then—she said, 'I didn't know she was dating Jim!' Apparently, Liberty had been one of her best friends back in the thirties, and Jim was married to someone else at the time." The words tumbled out of Love's mouth like rocks down a hillside.

Rett's expression was polite but slightly bored.

"Well, never mind that," Love said, embarrassed that she'd sounded like a historical home tour guide. "Here's the guest room. Make yourself at home. I use the bathroom off the master bedroom, so the hall bathroom is all yours."

Rett glanced up at her, and then back down at the glossy oak floor. "Thanks." Ace sat down on the trout-shaped rug next to the maple bed.

"Ace, give her some space," Love scolded the dog in a good-natured tone.

"He can stay," Rett said, bending down to run her hand down his long back. "I like him."

"Okay, then." Love waited, not sure what to do.

Rett nodded, closing the door softly.

Love stood in the hallway, trying to sort out the questions running through her mind. How long did Rett plan to stay? Did Karla Rae know she was here? Was her granddaughter in some kind of trouble? She walked over to the living room window that looked out at the backyard and, farther out, the bay and the Pacific Ocean. Her house was old and small, so not much that happened inside the rooms was private. She could hear Rett's settling-in noises, the toilet flushing, the opening and closing of closet doors. After the last thirteen months alone, hearing human sounds other than her own in this house was odd, both comforting and unsettling.

"Oh, Cy," she whispered, watching the whitecaps dance on the gray blue water. "I wish you were here to see your granddaughter. She's beautiful."

For a moment, a lit match of anger flared behind her eyes. "You could have been here." In the next instance, remorse extinguished the flame. She hadn't had these feelings in months. Something about seeing Loretta—Rett, she corrected herself—brought back all the pain of losing Cy, of the one argument she'd had with him about the cancer. That's how she'd referred to it: The Cancer. Not *his* cancer. She never wanted him to take it as his own, like if they didn't give it a pronoun, it couldn't become real. It couldn't overcome him. Couldn't steal him from her.

Except it did. And the disease caused her to do things, feel things that she'd regret the rest of her life. She couldn't forget the day he confessed to her that he was tired of fighting, that he wanted to stop treatment, he wanted to just go home. At first, she thought he meant their house in Morro Bay. But his next sentence made it all too clear.

They were in the hallway of the medical center in San Celina. The doctor had said they could try again, another round of chemo and radiation, but the chances of remission were slim and, in his weakened state, the side effects would be even rougher this time.

"Love," he said. "It's time. I want to see Tommy."

"No," she'd lashed out, exhausted by months of inadequate sleep, worry over his pain and struggles with hospitals, doctors, pharmacies and insurance companies. All the nights on the Internet, reading through websites, Listservs, chat room archives, looking for some hope in this vast inner space of souls.

"Please," he'd said. That was all. Just *please*.

Like a spoiled five-year-old she'd pressed her hands over her ears. She knew what he was asking. "No, no, no," she said and walked away from him. She couldn't . . . wouldn't give him what he wanted. Permission to leave her. How could she bring herself to give him that? How could he ask that of her? If he left, she would have no one. She ran out of the building, leaving him there.

He found her three blocks away sitting on a curb in front of a taco stand popular with Cal Poly students. He sat down beside her and, without a word, took her hand and kissed her palm, his lips chapped and dry. It was his customary way of asking for her forgiveness.

"Okay," she whispered, staring into the gutter, unable to meet his eyes.

She called hospice the next day, and the focus of their life moved from helping him live to helping him die. To this day, she regretted that she never apologized to him for making that moment harder than it had to be. She never said she was sorry for behaving so selfishly. But, the truth was, she never stopped being angry. God forgive her, but she couldn't help wondering if he'd just hung in there, something would have happened, he would have conquered the cancer. He would *be* here to see his granddaughter.

She shook her head, trying to dislodge her troubling thoughts and concentrate on the joy of seeing Rett again.

It was disconcerting to see this almost grown woman in the place of the four-year-old burned into her memories. So many years lost. Love closed her eyes and tried to recall the particular things she remembered about Rett. The last time she saw her, she was playing with stuffed animals; Love vaguely remembered a pink and black skunk named Lily. Rett carried it with her everywhere, even throwing a little tantrum when Karla Rae wouldn't let her take it to Tommy's funeral. Or was that Patsy? The two girls, so close in age, blended in Love's memories, despite the fact that physically they'd been very different. Patsy was tall and redheaded, like Love. Rett was shorter, thin, but solid-boned, like Polly.

Polly and August. Heavenly stars, it just occurred to her that she needed to call them. They'd want to know right away that their great-granddaughter was in town. Polly had mourned the lack of relationship almost as much as Love had, though August had been more pragmatic.

"You marry a person, you marry everything that ever happened to them," August had stated bluntly after hearing what happened at Tommy's funeral. They'd wanted to come, but Polly had been recovering from a hysterectomy. "Tommy didn't look close enough at what kind of history he was taking on."

There were a thousand things Love longed to ask Rett about so she could fill in the gaps of the last fourteen years. But how and when should she do that?

First things first. She turned away from the window and picked up the telephone. Polly and August would never forgive her if she didn't tell them about Rett right away. Gossip flew around this town faster than a sea otter. She should have called the minute Magnolia told her about Rett.

She'd dialed the first three numbers, when the guest room door flew open. She set the phone back down.

"All settled in?" she asked, walking toward Rett.

Rett stood in the bedroom's doorway, her cheeks flushed a dark pink; a stricken expression covered her face. Behind her, the contents of her backpack were strewn across the Ocean Waves quilt, a Christmas present from Polly ten years ago.

Love's mother instincts kicked in. "Are you all right?"

Rett's eyes blinked rapidly. "I . . . I . . . it's . . ." The stutter caused her to clamp her lips tightly. She took a deep breath and spoke slowly. "I guess I didn't realize what time of the month . . . Is there a drugstore . . . ?"

"Oh." Love let out a sigh of relief. The girl had started her period. That crisis was one Love could handle. "The drugstore is over by the highway. I can drive there in five minutes. Any certain brand?"

Rett shook her head, her face still red. "Any is fine. Tampons, that is."

"I'm sorry I don't have any here. It's been years since I've had to worry about that."

Rett let out a small huff of air. "Lucky."

Love shrugged. "There's good and bad with both, like most things. Make yourself at home. There's food and drinks in the kitchen. I've got cable, more channels than I'll watch in a lifetime. I don't know how to find most of them, but I'm sure you can figure it out. How about steak for dinner? I have a couple in the freezer." She brought a hand up to her cheek. "If you're vegetarian, I can always make macaroni and cheese. Or if you don't eat dairy . . ." Why was fixing someone dinner so hard anymore?

Rett held up her hand. "I'm not a vegan. Steak is fine."

"Then, I'll be off. Like I said, make yourself at home."

Rett hesitated, then said, "Okay."

At Goody's Drug Supermart, Love wandered up and down the women's personal care aisle, not certain what brand to buy. The tinny sound of Christmas Muzak—"Santa Claus Is Coming to Town"—played over the store's PA system. At fifty-eight, it had been years since she'd bought these products. She paused in front of a display of brightly colored boxes, the brand a familiar name. Someone had placed a small, neatly written flag under the flowery boxes. Great Stocking Stuffer!

Who in the world would consider a box of tampons a stocking stuffer? Was that a joke? She chose a box that had a young-looking design, hoping it would be the right one. She already had every kind of pain medication at home if Rett had cramps. What else did one need at that time of month? A hot water bottle? No, that was old-fashioned, something her mother used to do back in Kentucky, before pharmaceuticals rescued them all. Still, when she walked down another aisle, she saw a display of hot water bottles and bought one on a whim. It came with a pink flannel cover decorated with little red hearts. She added a navy blue sweatshirt, size small, with a discreet Morro Bay, California, embroidered on the chest in light blue thread. Maybe Rett had a thing about borrowing clothes. Maybe she'd think anything that Love had would be too old ladyish, even though she bought most of her clothes from Columbia and L.L. Bean. Weren't their styles ageless?

Standing in the checkout line, she gazed down at her purchases.

They would be the first gifts she'd given to her granddaughter in four-teen years: a box of tampons, a hot water bottle and a sweatshirt. What did they signify? She was always looking at how things connected, what they looked like on the surface as compared to what they really meant. A photo and column about gifts and what they symbolized started form-ing in her head. She loved the idea of using the offbeat sign describing the tampons as a great stocking stuffer. But she could never use these particular details. Imagine the embarrassment of a teenage girl's grand-mother writing about tampons. Love would write a column about pres-ents, but it could not include the things that actually inspired the essay.

It struck her with a pang how meager these gifts were. Would Rett stay long enough to celebrate Christmas? Maybe Love could do better if she stayed through the holidays. Christmas was only a few weeks away, but surely she would discover some hint as to what her grand-daughter would like. Something to do with her banjo? The thought of shopping for someone she was related to by blood, her *granddaughter*, filled her with an inexplicable joy and an equal feeling of panic.

On the drive back, she turned on the radio. The local oldies station was playing "Moon River," one of Cy's favorite songs, one of the songs that Magnolia performed at his funeral. Love hummed the melody, and when the song came to the words "my huckleberry friend," her eyes didn't tear up like they would have yesterday. Instead, she sang them softly out loud, her heart more hopeful than it had been in a long time.

SEVEN

Rett

I have to talk fast," Rett said to Lissa, her best friend and the only person in Knoxville who knew where she was. "I only have seventeen minutes left on my cell phone."

Lissa had given Rett the cell phone as a good-bye gift. It was one of those kind you can buy at Wal-Mart where you can add minutes, if you had the money. Rett had started out with sixty minutes.

"What's the deal with California?" Lissa asked.

"It's foggy. The Pacific Ocean is really cool."

"What about your grandmother?"

Rett paused, choosing her words carefully. "She's okay. Kinda nervous. She totally knows everyone in town. It's like some kind of back-in-the-day TV show. She seems okay, but you never can tell."

"For sure." Her friend's voice was knowing. "Sometimes the ones who act the nicest are the ones you have to watch out for." Lissa's mother and father had been married seven times between them. She was experienced getting to know new people. Right now, she lived with her dad. "So, do you think you'll stay?"

"I don't know, but at least I have a place to stay for tonight. I may go to L.A. in a few days."

"Sweet," Lissa said. "Maybe I'll hit my dad up for some bucks and fly out to see you."

Rett glanced nervously at the clock next to the bed. "My time is running out. Has my mom called again?"

"Like only fifty times. It's so funny. She's even called my dad to tell him to tell me to tell her where you are. Like I'd even listen to what *he* says."

"Thanks. I just don't want to talk to her right now. *Don't* give her this phone number. Or Dale either. Promise."

"Okay, okay, I hear you."

Rett sat down on the bed, leaned over and ran her hand down Ace's silky head. "She has an awesome dog. His name is Ace. He's a corgi."

"If you get stuck and need money, just call me. I can squeeze some out of my dad if I have to. He's dating a girl only five years older than me and feels all guilty. Ha, I'm like, who cares? Buy me a Wii and I'll feel better."

"What's her name?"

"Ashley Clarabelle. Can you believe it? I call her Ghastly Clarasmell. She was a runner-up for Miss Apple Fritter or Miss Catfish Queen or something stupid. She weighs, like, thirty pounds. My dad's a freak."

"I'll try and call you tomorrow."

"Okay, kiss a surfer dude for me."

"You wish. I'm out." Rett punched the End button.

She wandered into the glassed-in sunroom, taking the time alone in her grandma's house to try to figure her out. It reminded Rett of one of those reality shows she kind of liked, something like *Trading Spouses*. At the beginning of the show, both mothers go through each other's houses before the new family comes home. The snarky things the women said about each other always cracked Rett up. But more often than not, the first impressions the women had of each other were so right.

The tiny sunroom that faced the bay held a desk with a computer and an office chair on one end, an overstuffed chair in a leafy pattern, a small end table and a lamp on the other. A pile of books was neatly stacked on the end table. She picked up the top book. It showed a bunch of photographs by somebody named Dorothea Lange. They were pretty awesome, even though they were black-and-white and were mostly of tired-looking poor people in overalls and old-timey flowered dresses. Next to the books was a framed photo that someone had taken of Ace and a sailboat. He was in the backyard staring out to sea, and the photographer had framed the sailboat using the corgi's triangular ears. It was a cool effect, like the camera was sitting on the dog's back.

She peered through the window, past the bay to the Pacific Ocean. It was overwhelming, not like any lake she'd ever seen. It reminded her of the Grand Canyon, which she'd seen once when she was nine on a pathetic attempt at a family vacation with her mom and first stepdad, Pete, who she always secretly called the Hulk, because he totally loved the color green. Her little sister, Faith, had spent most of the trip being carsick. Patsy, a smooth talker even at ten, had convinced their mom to let her stay at a friend's house, so she didn't have to go. No one ever said no to Patsy when she really wanted something. Even Dale. Well, Rett couldn't help thinking, things finally came back to bite her in the butt. She wanted to gloat about Patsy's pregnancy, but instead, it made her feel sick to her stomach.

Forget her, she told herself, glancing over the surface of her grandma's desk. She sat down in the high-backed office chair and spun around, trying to imagine what her grandma would use a computer for. What did old people look at on the Internet? It was a fairly new Sony with a large flat screen. Though Rett was tempted, she didn't turn it on. She studied the neat desktop. There was a crystal clock shaped like a boat, a couple of smooth speckled rocks about the size of eggs being used as paperweights, a lumpy brown and blue, definitely handmade ceramic mug that held pens and pencils, a mouse pad that showed a picture of Ace wearing a red and green velvet Christmas collar and a navy blue mug half filled with—she took a sniff—cold tea.

Had her grandma been working on the computer when she got the call about Rett from Rocky's wife at the café? It appeared that she rushed out without even rinsing out her mug of tea. That kind of made

Rett feel flattered. Maybe her grandma *was* glad to see her. Then again, her grandma had *never* come out to see them in Florida or Knoxville. What was the deal with that?

She twirled around in the chair again, then stopped it with her foot. The movement didn't make her feel so good. She'd had a vague sort of throbbing in her head for the last day or so, one of those headaches that seemed to hide behind your eyes, waiting to squeeze your brain when you least expected it. She suspected she was getting sick but kept mentally pushing the symptoms back, using every bit of her stubborn will to stop whatever bug was crawling through her body. She couldn't get sick. There was no time for that.

She carefully stood up and walked back into the living room, which was so quiet that she could hear seagulls calling to each other outside. Ace clicked softly next to her. She bent down and stroked his head. She liked her grandma's house. The rooms were plain and simple, not a lot of clutter, like Mom's fussy decorating, which was heavy on crocheted doilies, silk ivy and handmade wreaths. Distressed French country, her mom called it. Shabby chic. Rett called it gaggy vanilla froufrou.

Her grandma's furniture looked like something Rett might buy. The living room sofa and chair were a dark blue denim with pillows that were red and white checks. One of the pillows was a needlepoint of a boat. She peered closer at the name on the boat: *Love Mercy*. That was kind of hokey, but her grandma was old, so that was understandable. There was a quilt draped over the sofa in some kind of triangle pattern in dozens of shades of blue. An old green trunk served as a coffee table. Rett wondered what was inside it. A shallow wooden bowl that looked a zillion years old sat on the trunk and held a half dozen magazines: *Oxford American, Gun and Garden, U.S. News & World Report, Aperture, National Geographic, San Celina County Life*. The lumpy wood end tables looked old and sort of handmade. The lamps were a plain kind of beaten copper. The oak entertainment center held a television, a CD player and a bunch of CDs. Obviously she'd never heard of iTunes.

Despite the pounding behind her eyes, Rett stooped down to flip through some of the CD titles. A person's taste in music told more about them than just about anything. At first glance, her grandma's tastes seemed pretty predictable: George Strait, Alan Jackson, Tony Bennett, Harry Connick Jr., Norah Jones. But there were a few surprises: Gillian Welch, Elizabeth Cook, Kelly Willis, Ralph Stanley and the group Uncle Earl, who Rett thought was awesome. Her grandma obviously thought more outside the norm when it came to music, which gave Rett a ray of hope that she might like what Rett wrote. She pulled out Gillian Welch's CD *Revival*. Her song "Orphan Girl" just blew Rett away. It felt like Rett's life story. Whenever she heard it, the beautiful words and melody filled her with both joy and despair. Would she ever write anything so totally perfect?

She stood up, gripping the edge of the entertainment center. Her stomach roiled, and she felt like throwing up the lasagna she'd eaten earlier. The room began to spin and turn crazy. Beads of sweat popped on her upper lip, and her forehead felt like somebody had sprayed it with a water pistol full of boiling water. Then suddenly she was cold. She bent over, shivering, holding herself. Her head felt like it was going to explode.

Was this what it felt like to be pregnant? Is this what Patsy was feeling when she hugged the toilet a week ago, the sounds of her retching reaching through the wall of their house and taunting Rett, confirming what an idiot she was?

Rett wasn't pregnant; she knew that for sure. No, she'd not given in to Dale when he wanted *that*. She'd been stupid enough in other ways, but not *that*. Obviously, Patsy hadn't been quite so careful.

Or, a little voice in Rett's head mocked, maybe you just were not as irresistible as your sister. It was a fact that when Rett said no, Dale immediately backed off, laughing that crazy, sexy laugh of his, holding up his hands and calling her jailbait. Though technically she wasn't the last few months they were . . . what would you call it? Not hooked up, but kind of being with each other. Except he was really with Patsy, as Patsy's early morning sickness proved. Their mom figured it out about two seconds after Patsy's first retch, and the screaming matches between the two went primal as Mom tried to find out who ruined—as she put it—*the star of the family*, the *one* daughter she thought would make it in the music world.

Thanks a lot, Rett thought, sitting in her bedroom, her back against her closed door. She left two days later, and as far as she knew, Patsy still hadn't revealed who the father was.

A wave of nausea hit Rett again, causing her to sit down hard on the carpeted floor. She used every bit of willpower she had to keep from barfing. Ace came up to her, whining softly, nosing her shoulder.

"It's okay, boy," she whispered, even though it wasn't. She curled up in a ball, her head pounding like twenty snare drums. The dog's warm tongue licked her ear.

She curled tighter, trying to make herself as small as possible, waiting for the blackness to overtake her. At this moment, if she'd been connected to a lie dectector and asked if she cared about living, she could have honestly said no. If she could have spat the words out, she would have said, Bring on that dark curtain, Mister God, and let me die in peace.

EIGHT

Mel

It was past seven p.m. when Mel finished eating supper with August
and Polly. Afterward, she helped August fit the Christmas tree she'd
brought back into the battered green and red metal stand.

"We'll wait and decorate it with Love," Polly said, going through the
boxes of ornaments that August brought down from the attic.

"Good idea," Mel said. Maybe that great-granddaughter of theirs
would be around to help. Mel hoped the girl didn't hurt these two
gentle, good-hearted people. Likely, her hopes would be dashed. She'd
learned early that more often than not, the kids with great families, loving families, were too spoiled and self-centered to appreciate their good
fortune. Still, she hoped that wouldn't be the case with Love's granddaughter.

"Thank you for your hard work, sweetie," Polly said, pressing some
folded bills into Mel's hand. "You're such a big help to me and August."

"Thanks," Mel said, pocketing the money quickly. "Will I see you at
the lighted boat parade this Saturday?"

"Haven't missed it in forty-seven years," August said, turning the
tree so the fuller side faced the living room.

"We're watching it from inside this year," Polly said. "We reserved a table at the Happy Shrimp for the Old-Timers' Club. It's right next to the window. Best seats in the house, they said."

"Which you deserve," Mel said. "I'll be braving the elements outside."

"You're welcome to join us," August said. "Always room for one more."

"Thanks, but I promised the Muppet Brothers I'd take pictures of their kayak brigade. I'm staking out a place near the start, over by the Taffy Shak."

"Oh, I do love their Georgia peach taffy," Polly said. "The peppermint's good too."

Mel smiled at her. "Maybe Santa will bring you some." Good; she'd been having a hard time deciding what to buy Polly for Christmas.

"Let me walk out with you," August said. They took it slow, and Mel resisted the urge to help him down the porch steps, knowing he'd brush her off with an irritated grunt.

"What's up?" she asked him when they reached her truck.

"Wondered if you could come by this weekend," he said, his wiry, salt-and-pepper eyebrows pulled together in a frown.

"No problem. I have to work both Saturday and Sunday, but just in the mornings. The waves are supposed to be good, and the boys want to go surfing. What do you need me to do?"

"Saw something over at Big Barn that I want you to check out."

Her cop antenna instantly went up. Big Barn was an old, half-collapsed barn about a mile from the ranch house. It was a place that Cy showed her on their first jeep ride around the ranch. She'd worked for him at the feed store for about three months.

"I used to play here when I was a boy," Cy had told her when they stepped into the cool, quiet building. The part that hadn't collapsed from the elements creaked and sagged, ready to fall with the next rainstorm or minor earthquake. She walked to the back of it, feeling slightly nervous in the dappled sunlight, flinching with every creak of the overhead beams.

"Look here," he called to her, his voice sounding hollow and farther away than it actually was. He stood next to a huge middle beam that she doubted she could encircle even with her long arms.

She turned on her small SureFire flashlight with one thumb, causing the intense white light to illuminate the post and Cy. The flashlight was one of the few physical things she'd saved from her law enforcement days. She walked over to the beam where he pointed to the carving in the wood: *CJ was here—1961.*

"Practically ruined the blade on my new Swiss Army knife doing that," he'd told her. "I used to come up here and sulk when I was a teenager and my parents were being . . . well, parents." He'd laughed, shaking his head.

"Do you need me to check on the barn today?" she asked August, wishing he'd mentioned this a few hours ago when she first arrived. But that was August for you. He ruminated things to death and then dealt with them on his own timetable. Then it occurred to her, maybe he'd forgotten it, like her coming here every Tuesday and Thursday or who Shug was.

"Nah," August said. "It can wait. Been waiting a couple weeks now."

Mel wished in that moment that August was actually related to her, that they had a relationship that was a little less polite and careful. If he'd been her grandfather, she would have nagged him to tell her what he found, threaten to tell Polly or Love, use the familiarity of a blood relationship to make him reveal what was bothering him.

But she was essentially just an employee. A friend too, she'd venture to admit, but not close enough to push him . . . much. "I have time to hear about it now."

"You're on your way home. It'll wait."

"You're the boss," she said tartly.

A flash of hurt came over his face, and she realized a second too late that the words had sounded sharper than she intended. She touched his flannel-clad forearm with two fingers. "Sorry, August. I'm a little tired."

"What're you talking about, girlie?" he answered, winking at her. "You go have yourself a mug of whiskey at the Pelican. Take a long sip for me."

"A mug would put even me under the table," she said, smiling. "But I may add a little rum to my hot cocoa tonight."

"Sounds good. May do that myself."

She waved at him as she backed out, his solitary figure outlined by the porch light. A brief sense of doom fell over her when she pulled out onto the highway leading back to town. She'd had this feeling only one other time in her life: the day she walked out of the apartment after her last shouting match with Sean. The neighbors had threatened to call the cops, even though they knew Mel and Sean were police officers. Mel left before that could happen, saving them both the embarrassment.

Like so many times before, she'd driven around town, up and down dark streets, ignoring the insect vibration of her cell phone, finally turning it off without checking her voice mail. Her life was so narrow then, so friendless. There were only two phone calls that would have come over her cell: to go in to work or Sean trying to explain again why he felt he had the right to that money. Neither had been something she felt like dealing with at that moment.

Bribery. Graft. Kickback. Payola. Hush money. Like a sick board game, she tried to think of more synonyms for what Sean did, but her mind went blank. Before she discovered the hidden money, she'd defended him to her old partner, Buzz. He'd come to her the month before and told her he'd heard over the grapevine that Sean was on the take.

"That's bull," she'd said. "I practically live with the guy. Don't you think I'd see something suspicious? We were looking at flat-screen televisions the other day, and he said that he'd have to wait until his tax return came in. If he was on the take, believe me, we'd have had that sucker up and running in time for the next game."

Buzz just shrugged, probably realizing that you couldn't talk sense into someone who was crazy in love. And she had been from the first moment Sean turned his Irish green eyes on her. She'd been flat-out, no-turning-back, crazy-as-a-loon in love with him. She'd even considered introducing him to her mother, something she'd never done with any of the men she'd hooked up with. It had to have been love if she was willing to subject herself to her mother's smug look when she saw that Mel had thrown her own life aside for a man just like her mother had so many times. That old saying about the acorn not falling far from the tree was a cliché for a reason.

Finding the plastic-wrapped stack of hundred-dollar bills in the bottom of a ten-pound bag of stale flour had changed everything. What a lame place to hide the money, a television-cop-show kind of place. She was certain he'd hidden it there because he thought it was the one place that Mel would never look. In the two years they were together, she'd never once shown an inclination toward baking. Her idea of a home-cooked meal was sticking a hunk of roast beef and some potatoes in a Crock-Pot. And that was a rare occasion. Mostly they ate out, because they rarely worked the same shift. She'd pulled the bag of flour out in a frenzy of cleaning when Sean was at work because she'd discovered some mouse droppings under the kitchen sink. She'd almost thrown it into the large trash bag with the other open food. But her fingers felt something odd, so she unfolded the bag, dumping the contents into the kitchen sink.

She stared at the plastic-wrapped bundle of money for a long time, not wanting to believe it was there. Resisting the urge to count it, she left it in the sink for Sean to find when he came home from his shift three hours later. By that time she'd packed all the belongings she'd left at his place, filling three plastic shopping bags, and drove back to her own apartment two miles away, where she had sat staring at a blank television screen, waiting for his call.

"Let it go," she said out loud, her words sounding hollow inside the truck's cab. She drove slowly down Ocean Avenue, past the Buttercream, which looked cheery and bright in the already encroaching fog. She contemplated stopping by for a cup of coffee, perhaps find out from Magnolia, if she was still there, if she'd heard any news about what was going on with Love and her granddaughter. But it was almost eight p.m., their normal closing time. Besides, these days any caffeine after three or four p.m. made it impossible for her to get to sleep before midnight. Not a problem usually, but she had to open the feed store at six a.m. tomorrow. She'd find out about the granddaughter tomorrow.

Mel's small rented house looked forlorn in the swirling, cat's feet fog. Maybe she should get one of those automatic timers for her living room lamp, so she'd at least have the illusion of coming home to something other than a cold, empty house. Maybe she should get a dog. Or a bird. No, a light timer would be easier to use and easier to leave.

She quickly unlocked the door, flipping the light switch next to the door. The floor lamp turned her compact living room a warm amber. The simple brown plaid sofa and matching chair, the old-fashioned maple end tables, the small stack of books from the library, a basket of magazines, her favorite leather slippers, the brown and orange flame stitch afghan Polly crocheted for her last year looked suddenly very precious to her, and she was surprised to feel a burning behind her eyes. She shook her head, fighting the emotion, glad that no one could see her childish reaction.

She put Dove's pumpkin bread in the refrigerator and filled her teakettle with water. A cup of peppermint tea, a habit she'd picked up from Polly, would help take the chill off her bones. Maybe she'd add a dollop of Maker's Mark bourbon, a semi-healthy evening toddy.

It was only after she'd changed into warm sweatpants and a faded red Cy's Feed and Seed T-shirt and went into the living room with her drink that she noticed the flashing light on her phone, set in the far corner because it was the only place that had an outlet. The phone was one she'd bought cheap at Costco and hadn't bothered to read its description. It didn't have an audio message indicator . . . or if it did, she couldn't figure out how to turn it on. And, of course, she'd lost the instruction book that came with it. Half the time, the person who left her a message had to call her again, hoping to catch her at home, because she forgot to check for the tiny flashing red light.

She hit the Message button.

"You have one new message," the phone woman's bland voice informed her.

"Ma's dead," the voice said. Its Boston accent sent a steel wire of painful memory down Mel's spine. "We gotta talk."

NINE

Love Mercy

On the drive back home from the drugstore, Love decided that she'd drop off the things she bought Rett, then go to the grocery store. Those steaks had been in her freezer for a month. She wanted everything fresh for her granddaughter's first dinner in Morro Bay. She'd buy some Romaine lettuce for a Caesar salad and some sourdough bread. A couple of baking potatoes. Corn on the cob. Everyone loved corn on the cob. She could make garlic bread, if Rett liked garlic. She wished she'd had time to bake some cupcakes. Butterscotch spice, maybe. With cream cheese frosting. But, she could defrost that cake she had in the freezer.

She pulled into the driveway and climbed out of her Honda, laughing at herself. For heaven's sake, she was as nervous as a girl on her first date. Rett would either like her or not. She'd either understand when Love explained her side of what happened or not. Whatever conversation took place about it, Love would not, if she could help it, say anything negative about Karla Rae. Criticizing someone's mother had just never seemed right to her. She'd be as truthful as she could, but not accept *all* the blame. More than anything she wanted Rett to know that she'd always thought about her, always loved her and that she was happy they'd have a chance to start a new relationship. Things would work out.

She opened the door leading from the garage into the kitchen. Ace's mournful howl was the first sound she heard. Love froze. Ace was not a howler, not even at the rare fire truck or police siren. The only other time she'd heard that sound was when she let him in the bedroom to see Cy right after he died. She ran into the living room, calling Rett's name.

Rett lay curled up on the floor in a fetal position, thin arms hugging her chest, shaking like she'd been cold for a hundred years. Ace stopped howling the minute he saw Love and started barking.

"Oh, Sweet Pea!" Love cried, the name she'd called her as a child. She dropped down to kneel next to Rett. "What happened?"

"I'm sick," Rett whispered, her teeth chattering so dramatically Love was afraid she'd chip one.

She leaned over and placed her lips on Rett's forehead, testing for a fever in the same way she had with Tommy when he was a boy. Her skin was burning up.

"We need to get you in bed," she said, helping her sit up. "It's probably just the flu."

Please, God, Love automatically thought. Let it only be the flu. She actually had no idea what was wrong, because she knew virtually nothing about this girl.

"I have to go to the bathroom," Rett said. "Please."

"Can you make it by yourself?"

Rett nodded. "But . . ." Her face was a pale green.

"I've got them in the kitchen," Love said.

She helped Rett into the bathroom, hesitating while she clung to the porcelain sink.

"I'll be okay," Rett whispered.

Love reluctantly stepped out of the bathroom and rushed into the kitchen, grabbed the drugstore bag. Back in the bathroom, she thrust it at Rett, who sat on the toilet's closed lid.

"Thanks," Rett said, taking the bag. Her face, tight and determined, reminded Love so much of Cy and his last days when he sometimes refused pain medication because it drugged him too much, and he couldn't talk to his many visitors.

Love closed the door but lingered right outside, ready to rush in and help the minute she heard any sounds of distress. The minutes dragged, then she heard the toilet flush and the water run. Finally, she couldn't help herself. "Are you okay? Is there anything I can do?"

The door opened slowly, and Rett, gripping the doorjamb, looked up at her. "I think I need to lie down."

Rett's words slurred slightly, her Southern accent more prominent in her weakened state. Cy used to say that Love was the same way, that her mountain drawl would show itself more when she was tired or sick.

"Let me help you," she said, putting her arm around Rett's thin shoulders. She felt a sharp pang inside. It was the first time she'd held Rett since she was four years old. The depth of feeling caught Love by surprise, reminding her of that first time she cradled Tommy, moments after he was born, that overwhelming feeling that she'd do anything, *anything*, to protect him.

Rett didn't protest when Love helped her out of her jeans and T-shirt and into a pair of Love's own cotton pajamas, the legs miles too long for her. Heat, like a raging furnace, radiated from Rett's body.

Rett closed her eyes when Love settled the sheet over her body.

"Are you allergic to any medications?" Love asked.

Rett shook her head no.

"Maybe I can give you some Tylenol for the fever." Love brushed a strand of hair from across Rett's pale, smooth forehead.

She went to the kitchen cupboard where she kept her medicine and stood in front of the open cabinet door, contemplating what she should do. Should she give Rett anything when she didn't have any idea what was wrong? What if . . . oh, Lord, what if she was pregnant? Was Tylenol okay if you were having a baby? She couldn't remember. It had been almost forty years since she'd been pregnant, and so much had changed. She didn't keep up on it simply because it was information she'd never had any use for. No, wait, Rett couldn't be pregnant. Her period was the reason Love went to the drugstore. Unless she was lying.

Heavenly stars, she thought. This was going to be more complicated than she anticipated.

Then she remembered something. Her boss, Clint, the owner of *San Celina County Life* magazine, had a son who was a family physician in the Bay Area. And, as luck would have it, he was visiting his father this week. Clint had complained a few days ago about this annual father-son bonding week that Clint said they suffered through because he'd promised his late wife before she died. Mostly, Clint said, he and his son watched sports on television and argued about politics.

She closed the cabinet door and picked up the phone. Clint answered on the second ring.

"Good afternoon, Clint," she said.

"Hey, Love," he said.

"I have a problem—"

"No, you can't have an extra day for your column. I need it yesterday. You know Bob the printer gets his panties all in a bunch if I ask him to work even a modicum of overtime. And he charges me an arm, a leg and a couple of fingers even without overtime. I ought to sell this rag. What was I thinking? It's nothing but a money pit."

"No, Clint, I—"

"I'm serious. Owning a magazine might have been my dream at one time, but it's turning into Dante's nightmare. Is that a correct literary reference? Probably not, but nevertheless, it's exactly what it feels like. I should have stayed at my old job. Putting rapists and wife beaters in jail was much less stressful."

Four years ago, after thirty years on the bench as one of the toughest, most feared criminal judges in San Bernardino County, he'd retired to the Central Coast. After six months of fishing, he was ready to retire from retirement, so he bought the struggling regional magazine.

"I—" Love started again.

"Okay," he interrupted. "For you, I'll do it. Only because I'm a sucker for smart, good-looking broads with silver red hair who bake killer chocolate rum cupcakes. Have the cupcakes in my office by nine a.m. tomorrow. With a mug of joe."

"Judge, I need your help."

His voice grew serious in a flash. She only called him Judge when she was upset. "What's wrong?"

"Isn't your son visiting you this week?"

"He's probably reclining on my leather sofa gobbling down my favorite Wasabi-flavored potato chips and watching a police-chase video as we speak. Why?"

"My granddaughter is sick, and I'd like him to look at her. I'm sure it's just the flu, but I . . . I don't know that much about her health."

There were ten seconds of silence. "Your granddaughter? I didn't know you and Cy had a granddaughter."

"Actually, we have three. Long story. I'll tell you all about it someday, but right now I need your son."

"Nine-one-one?"

"No, I think it's just the flu, but I'd feel better—"

"He can be there in ten minutes. Would you like me to come by?"

"Not tonight. I want you to meet Rett, but I'm sure she'd prefer feeling a little better before I inflict my friends on her."

"Inflict? Knife to the heart, Love. I'll have you know young women have always adored me. The young law clerks often compared me to Paul Newman." He paused, and Love knew the punch line was coming. "Or maybe it was Alfred E. Neuman."

"You, my dear friend, are a little of both," she said, relieved. "Thank you. I will make you those cupcakes."

"Wait until after my son leaves. He's a human garbage disposal. I honestly have no idea how he stays so thin."

"I can make a double batch. What is his name again?"

"Garth."

"That's right, like the country singer."

"Actually, Beth named him after the illustrator, but no one realizes that now."

"Of course. Garth Williams. The Little House books. Thanks again. My column and photo will be on your desk in a few days. I promise."

"I knew that. What is it about?"

She paused a moment before answering. "Gifts." Actually, the one she had finished was about hearts, since it was for the February issue. But Rett's arrival, the moments at the drugstore, made her want to explore the idea of gifts.

"Appropriate for Valentine's Day. As always, I'll look forward to giving it a vicious critique."

She laughed with him, both of them knowing that he wouldn't change a thing. When he bought the magazine and was considering changing the format and content, he'd seen her photographs with their humorous captions in the Buttercream and thought they were just what he was looking for. He proposed she write a monthly column illustrated by her sometimes mystifying and always controversial photographs.

"Only if I have complete creative control," she'd told him.

"Sold," he said. "My only request is that they be controversial. I love it when people get all hot and bothered."

She cemented her place in his heart with her first column about the magazine's new publisher. The photograph showed the scales of justice sporting a grinning Ken doll head on one scale and a fresh fish head on the other. The caption read, "What kind of name is Clint Lawhead?"

To his delight, people talked about what it "meant" for weeks. The reason he and Love clicked was because they both understood, it didn't really *mean* anything.

"Judge Lawhead, you're the tower of pizza," she said.

"Or at least a bowl of ravioli. Let me know how she's doing."

After they hung up, she checked on Rett again. Ace lay next to the bed, his head down on his paws, his liquid brown eyes worried. Rett's eyes were closed, her breathing slow and even.

"She'll be all right," Love said, bending over to stroke the dog's head. "She'll be playing ball with you in no time. I promise."

"For sure," Rett murmured.

Love bent closer. "Rett, I've called a friend who is a doctor to come and look at you. I didn't want to give you any medication until he checked you over."

"Okay," she whispered. "But, really, I'm fine."

"Your mother—" Love started.

Rett's eyes flew open. "*No.* Do not call her."

She didn't want to upset her granddaughter so early in their relationship, but it bothered her that Karla Rae might be wondering where
Rett was, worrying if she was safe. Rett had never been a mother. She
didn't know that heart-in-the-throat feeling of panic a parent felt when
they didn't know if their child was safe. No matter what kind of relationship Rett had with her mother, Karla Rae had a right to know that
her daughter was all right.

"Rett, she'll be worried."

"Doubt that." Rett closed her eyes again.

She stared at Rett's vulnerable face; its smooth, flushed skin; the fine,
strong line of her chin. Love wished she could capture this moment on
film. In Rett's wide, high cheekbones, Love could see her mother; in her
long, dusky eyelashes, Love's brother, DJ, lived again. When she was a
girl, Love used to complain that DJ got the eyelashes she should have
received.

"Don't call my mom," Rett said again, her voice weak but determined.

Love didn't answer. The girl had inherited Cy's stubbornness too. It
wouldn't do any good to argue with her right now, but like it or not,
Love would find out where Karla Rae lived and let her know Rett was
safe. She dreaded speaking to her daughter-in-law, but it was the right
thing to do.

Less than fifteen minutes later, there was a knock on the front door
causing Ace to dash out of the bedroom, barking.

"Hush," she told the dog, grabbing his collar.

Love opened the door to find a fortyish man wearing a San Francisco Giants T-shirt and baggy tan chinos. He clutched an old-fashioned
leather doctor's bag, something that surprised her. The only photos she'd
seen of Garth were in Clint's office. He had been in his UCLA football
uniform and much younger. She was struck by the physical resemblance
to his sixty-two-year-old father. Both had silver-streaked chestnut hair
and tall, long-limbed bodies.

"I'm Garth Lawhead. Where's the patient?"

Ace growled and pulled against Love's hand. "It's okay," she told the
dog. "Friend."

Garth held out his hand for Ace to sniff, then once the dog was satisfied, scratched Ace's white chest.

She let go of Ace's collar. "I'm Love Johnson. Nice to finally meet you. Thank you so much for humoring a worried grandmother."

He grinned. "It's a grandma's prerogative and duty to worry. Glad to help out. Dad promised me some awesome cupcakes for my effort."

"Oh, you share your dad's sweet tooth," she said, ushering him into the house.

"When it comes to sweets, we try not to share at all," he said, laughing. "The cupcakes are *mine*."

"I'll make a double batch. Rett's in the bedroom at the end of the hall."

He followed her into the bedroom, his manner turning completely professional when he walked over the threshold.

"Hello, Ms. . . . ." He turned to Love, his face questioning.

"Rett Johnson," Love said.

He turned back to Rett, whose eyes were open and suspicious. "Hello, Ms. Johnson. I'm Dr. Lawhead, a friend of your grandma's. She says you're feeling a little under the weather."

"I'm okay," Rett said, struggling to sit up, her face flushing with embarrassment.

"I'm sure you are," Garth said. "But let's just set her mind at ease. I'll do a quick examination. I promise I have a real license and everything. Are you eighteen?"

She closed her eyes. "Eighteen and a half."

He glanced over at Love, and she nodded, verifying her age. "So, this'll just take a minute." He smiled at Love and waited.

"Oh, yes," she said, taking his hint. "I'll go into the living room."

Less than ten minutes later, Garth came out of the bedroom, zipping up his doctor's bag.

"Well, Grandma Love, you called it right. My professional guess is it's just a little flu. Considering all the truck stops she's been in the last few days, she was exposed to about a billion germs. She's young and healthy, so my diagnosis is she'll be over the worst of it in a few days. Tylenol, lots of liquids, dry toast and maybe some chicken soup when she's up to it. Last, but very important, I prescribe an occasional hug from Grandma. That should do the trick."

"Truck stops?" she couldn't help repeating.

He put a finger to his lips. "That was supposed to be between Rett and me. She had quite the little adventure getting to the West Coast from Knoxville. I'm sure she'll eventually tell you about it." He shrugged. "Problems between her mother and her. Not so unusual. I barely spoke to Dad from age eighteen to twenty-one. And seeing as I was quite the jerk during those years, he might have been okay with that."

"Did she say anything else?"

He shook his head no. "But I'm sure she'll open up sooner or later."

Love wasn't as sure, but she thanked him anyway while walking him to the door. "Tell your dad I'll have the cupcakes at his office to-morrow afternoon."

"Good. I'm leaving day after tomorrow. I'll bring them back to the wife and daughters. If what Dad says about the cupcakes is true, I might be off the hook for Christmas presents."

She smiled, shaking her head. "They aren't that good, but I think your wife will like them if she likes chocolate. How old are your girls?"

"Eight and ten."

"Then you have a ways to go before they start hitchhiking across the country to escape you."

"From your lips to God's ears," he said, looking up to the ceiling. "Right now, they still think I'm relatively cool."

"Enjoy it while you can."

After Garth left, Love made up a tray of ice water, toast, a glass of ginger ale and two Tylenol. She carried it carefully into the bedroom where Rett lay on her side, her back to the door.

"Rett, are you awake?"

Rett turned over slowly to look at her. "Yes, ma'am."

"The doctor said Tylenol would make you feel better. I wasn't sure if you were hungry, but I made you some toast."

"Just the Tylenol," Rett said, sitting up.

"I'll leave the tray here." She set it down on the maple desk across from the bed. "I'll put the water on the nightstand next to you. Why don't you try to rest, let the Tylenol go to work?"

"Okay." Rett swallowed the pills with a sip of water and lay back against the down pillows, her face relaxing.

Just as Love closed the bedroom door, she heard a faint. "Thanks."

"You're welcome," she answered softly.

She went into the kitchen, fed Ace, then made herself some cocoa and toast with peanut butter. She carried them into the sunroom and sat down in her easy chair, staring out at the darkness. She knew she should try to find Karla Rae's phone number and call her, let her know that Rett was here. The thought of talking to her daughter-in-law filled her with dread. Though it *was* cruel, she decided to collect her bearings before she spoke to Karla Rae.

So, her next photograph would have to have something to do with gifts. But what? It was such a loaded subject. Gifts represented so many things to people. People spent their whole lives trying to give the perfect gift or longing to be given the perfect gift. What was it about gifts that held such power? Something that should be easy and fun was fraught with a vast array of frightening, confusing and complex emotions. No doubt how people felt about gifts—giving and receiving—could likely be traced back to their earliest years, to those first gifts they both gave and received.

The question was, of course, how would she say all that in a photograph? That was always the dilemma. Something would come to her. She sipped her cocoa, wishing she could just sit here forever and never make that phone call. Ace settled at her feet and gave a wide yawn.

"Well, flyboy," she said, leaning over and massaging his neck, "we have to let Rett's mama know that she is safe, even if my granddaughter hates me forever. I'm just going to take it on faith that by doing the right thing, it will eventually come back to reward me."

She stood up and turned on her computer. This was definitely one time that the efficiency and downright convenience of the Internet would come in handy. She Googled Karla Rae's maiden name and came up with fifteen people, none of whom lived in Florida or Tennessee. She found an old address book and looked for Karla Rae's name. Next to it she'd, thank goodness, written her second husband's last name, Ryan. She Googled that. It gave an even a longer list: forty-two names. She could pay forty bucks to find out more, but she was afraid she'd just pay good money to get the address she already had. Then she dialed information in Pensacola, Florida, and quietly asked for Karla Rae or Pete Ryan. There was no listing. Did they move? She knew from Magnolia that Rett hitchhiked from Tennessee. Wait, Garth had said Knoxville. She called Knoxville information and asked for Karla or Pete Ryan. No listing. They probably had a private number if they had a landline at all. So many people were getting rid of theirs these days.

Then it hit her. Rett's cell phone. Surely she had her mother's number listed in her phone's address book. Love quietly opened the guest room door. Rett was sound asleep. Within minutes she had Karla Rae's phone number and was back in the living room, proud of her sleuthing.

She stared at the ten digits for a long five minutes before she screwed up the courage to dial them. On the third ring, a woman answered.

"Karla Rae?" Love asked.

"No, this is her friend, Ann. May I tell her who's calling?"

She swallowed and said, "This is her mother-in-law, Love Johnson. In California."

"Is Rett there?" Ann said, her voice excited.

"Yes, she is. She's—" But before Love could finish her sentence, she heard the phone drop.

Ann's voice yelled, "Karla! It's your mother-in-law." Then Ann came back on the line and asked, "Which one, ma'am?"

For pity's sake, Love thought, how many has she had? "I was the first." She heard her own voice turn to steel. "I am Rett's *real* grandmother."

"No, not Roy's mom," Ann called to a voice in the background. "Not Pete's either. Honey, it's your first husband's mama."

Love gritted her back teeth at the woman's words.

Seconds later, a husky, familiar voice came on the line.

"What have you done with my daughter?" Karla Rae demanded.

TEN

Mel

W e're the original Irish cliché," Sean O'Reilly told Mel on their first
date, a pastrami sandwich at the New York–New York Hotel &
Casino. He was the last-born of a large Irish Catholic family that went
back a hundred years in Boston. "My blessed mother spends all her time
saying rosaries for her wayward sons and daughters, though most of us
are pretty much on the up-and-up."

He'd held up his fingers and counted off his siblings. "In birth order,
Patrick is a police sergeant, Kathleen is a housewife and married to a
police captain, Michael sells insurance, Moira is a singing nun, Brian is
a fireman, Kelly Marie is a teacher, Timothy is an accountant, Mary
Margaret is a parole officer—something every Irish family needs—and
then there's me, the black sheep of the family."

"You have a sister who is a singing nun?" Mel asked, thinking that
perhaps Sean wouldn't find her parents so odd after all.

He gave his wonderful, deep laugh, a sound that filled her with a
crazy desire that she'd never known existed until she met him. "Well,
she's a nun and she does occasionally sing. She gets annoyed when I call

her that, but I told her that I had to do something to punch up her image. Being a plain old nun is just too boring."

She'd stared at him, fascinated by a life she couldn't even imagine. A household filled with people who looked like you, who shared your life from the time you were born, people who would understand when one of your parents did something weird or exasperating. She'd seen it before with people she'd worked with, kids she'd known in school; they could just look at their siblings and with a flicker of an eye, communicate everything that needed to be said. She'd always longed for that kind of bond.

"You became a cop, just like your dad and Patrick," she said. "Why are you the black sheep?"

The irony of her question haunted her to this day. Was he taking bribes even when she asked that innocent question?

He laughed. "I left Boston and moved to Sin City."

The memories tumbled back as she dialed the number Sean's brother left on her answering machine.

"O'Reilly," he answered in a voice that was an older, more gravelly version of Sean's.

"Hello, Patrick," she said, forcing her voice to be calm. "This is Melina LeBlanc."

"It's about time you called."

"I'm sorry to hear about your mother," she answered, ignoring his tone. How had he found her? She answered herself in a flash. He was a cop. Of course he could find her.

"Yeah, yeah, well, she's up in heaven or wherever probably still saying her rosaries for us sinners down here. We have to talk."

"Was it her heart?" Sean had told her his mother had heart problems. Mel felt a perverse need to force Patrick to tell her the details. It wasn't so much that she cared. She'd only met Sean's mother once, at his funeral. She shook the sobbing woman's hand and gave her condolences without his mother even realizing that Mel was not only her son's lover but also part of his downfall. Patrick bustled his mother away, shooting Mel a hard look. Only Patrick knew about Mel and, apparently, had not told anyone else in his family. No doubt one of Sean's so-called friends on the force had informed Patrick about her. When Internal Affairs came to her and asked if she had ever seen anything unusual with Sean, she didn't lie and told them about the money she'd found in the pantry. And that was that. With one statement, she ended her career as a cop. No one would ever really trust her again. Though she was cleared of being involved with his kickbacks, IA would always look at her with suspicion, and her fellow officers would always see her as someone they couldn't trust.

"What do you care how she died?" Patrick snapped.

The details of Mrs. O'Reilly's death didn't actually matter to Mel, but she was avoiding what she knew Patrick wanted to discuss. She'd dodged it for almost three years, hoping the words he'd said at Sean's funeral were just the ranting of a grieving brother. "I was just being polite."

"It was a heart attack. She was always saying that we'd give her one, and I guess we finally did."

"I'm sorry."

"She didn't suffer," he said bluntly. "One pain and she was gone. Truth was, she was never the same after Sean died."

Neither was I, she thought.

"She's gone now, so like I promised at Sean's funeral, I'm going to pursue this now. Where's the rest of the money?"

She took a deep breath before answering. "Like I told you then, I don't know."

An angry puff of breath echoed through the phone. Mel could almost smell the whiskey scent of it, recalling Patrick's same question when he pulled her aside at Patrick's funeral in Las Vegas. "Look, I don't want to have to come out there, but I'm telling you, I'm not about to let this go. My baby brother died for that money, and it belongs to his family."

Mel let herself grow cold and indifferent inside, channeling the persona she'd developed as a street cop. "Your baby brother killed himself because he was on the take, was going to get caught and sent to prison. That's dirty money, Patrick. I would think that you wouldn't want anything to do with it."

"Money is money," Patrick said. "It's all dirty. But it's still ours."

"And I still don't know where it is. Or even if it exists."

"My brother wouldn't risk his career for ten grand. I know that he had to have more."

"Because he was likely on the take for years?"

Patrick let out a stream of curse words. "My brother had a problem. He was sick."

"He was a drunk and a drug addict," she said, hating herself even as she said the words. And because of him, she thought, I'll have to wonder for the next ten years whether I contracted HIV.

"Where's the money?"

"I—don't—know."

"This isn't over." He slammed the phone down, cutting off their connection. She stood with the phone to her ear for thirty seconds, listening to the dial tone.

She set the receiver carefully back in place, trying to will away the trembling in her hand. She'd known this day was coming.

She sat down hard on the sofa, staring at the floor. It still bothered her that Sean had somehow hidden his drug addiction from her. Or more likely, she just hadn't wanted to see it. He'd always been a cheerful, upbeat guy, the life of any party they attended. And there were a lot of parties, something that she still sometimes missed, that camaraderie, that being a part of a brotherhood, knowing—or at least believing—that these people would have your back if need be.

"I love being the center of attention," he said when they first dated. "Psychologists say that's because I'm the baby of the family. Hope it doesn't bother you."

"Not at all," she'd said, and it was true. She was happy to be the quiet one, the girl who nursed a single drink all night long, then drove Sean home, often passed out in the seat next to her. It was easy to be with him, to absorb his vitality, to be part of his "posse," as he liked to call it. Everyone loved Sean. He was generous, always buying drinks for people or lending them twenty or fifty bucks. She'd occasionally wondered how he could afford it. Now she knew.

She had no idea what Patrick would do. She wouldn't put it past him to come out here and confront her directly. The thought of her old life encroaching on this fragile, new existence she'd built made her feel desperate. She knew—hoped—that her new friends here would believe her, that they'd not assume the worst, but she didn't want to put their loyalty to the test. Though Love and Magnolia and Rocky and the Johnsons and the rest of the people she'd come to call friends knew she'd been a cop in Las Vegas, that was the extent of it. Thankfully, no one ever asked her why she left the force.

She'd told only one person the whole story: Cy. It all spilled out the day before he died when he was lying in bed, groggy from pain medication and, she hoped, uncomprehending. He'd finally conceded to Love's pleading to allow an increase in his pain meds. She couldn't bear to see him suffer. He agreed, he'd told Mel, only for Love. So she wouldn't fret.

Telling him about her past at that moment was, Mel felt, a horrible thing to do, something she was ashamed of to this day. But she couldn't let Cy die without him knowing about her. He'd saved her life. He deserved to know the truth about her. Had he heard anything she said that day?

Mel waited until he dozed off and Magnolia had convinced Love to go for a walk. As Mel held his dry hand, the words tumbled over themselves like stones in a fast river. It took twenty minutes, and by the end, she could barely breathe.

"Thank you, Cy," she whispered. "Thank you for my life."

Then—and to this day she didn't know if it was real or just her longing—she thought she felt a small squeeze from his hand. He never opened his eyes, never spoke another word to anyone. He died the next day.

She glanced around her small house, a two-bedroom, one-bath beach cottage she'd grown to love. She rented it from an older woman who lived in Cambria, a woman whose husband made his fortune with computer stocks. The owner, Mrs. Melville, was a friend of Love and Cy's and had rented Mel this house as a favor to them. Slowly, over the last three years, Mel had made it her home; she even had an herb garden in the kitchen window, though she never cooked and did nothing except use the mint leaves in her iced tea. Her small collection of ceramic chickens, bought mostly by Cy and Love, sat on a bookshelf she'd found in a secondhand store and refinished herself, following instructions in a book she'd borrowed from Morro Bay's tiny library. On the walls were photos Love had taken of the ocean, of Cy's boat, of Morro Rock, of the feed store. Above her sofa she hung an acrylic painting of the Buttercream Café done by a local artist, Stewart Allison. Everything she owned was secondhand or bought for her by Love, who would tell her, when Mel tried to refuse her gifts, that she was doing Love a favor accepting the towels, sheets, red plaid kitchen curtains and cheery matching drinking glasses that she found at Target or Wal-Mart or the outlet mall in Pismo Beach.

"I have no one to buy for but you and Magnolia," Love always told her. "Polly just wants gift certificates so she can pick things out herself."

And now she might lose it all. Before she'd let Patrick ruin her life here, she'd leave. Go somewhere else and start over. It would be easy enough; she knew how to invent a new identity, though she doubted she'd have to go that far. But she'd leave no trace, so that Patrick couldn't hurt any of the people in Morro Bay who'd been so kind to her. When he asked them where she was, they wouldn't have to lie, because she'd make sure they didn't know.

The phone call from Patrick had agitated her enough that she knew she wouldn't be able to settle down. She wondered how Love was faring with her new granddaughter. She pictured them sitting at the pine kitchen table, like Mel had with Love and Cy so many times, sharing a meal and laughing. Was that what was happening? Mel suspected it wasn't quite that simple. That young girl looked like she brought with her a boatload of trouble. That would be another reason Mel would leave if Patrick followed through on his threat to come out here. Love would have her hands full with her granddaughter. She didn't need to worry about Mel.

She glanced over at the sunburst clock hanging next to the potbellied stove sitting in the corner of the living room. It was nine fifteen p.m. Too late for a piece of pie at the Buttercream. But she was restless, wanting to be on the move yet not knowing where to go. She grabbed her keys and left her house, driving her truck out of Morro Bay toward San Celina. She wanted a drink but didn't want to go where anyone knew her. She had a lot to think about. If she was going to leave, she'd better start thinking about what she'd take, because it would happen fast, the minute that Patrick showed up on her doorstep.

In downtown San Celina, Mel parked in one of the new parking structures and walked down to Lopez Street, the town's main drag. The old-fashioned streetlamps were decorated for Christmas with artificial pine boughs, giant red bows and gold trumpets. There were twinkling lights in the trees, giving the entire downtown a festive, Disney-like aura. They were cleaning up from the town's famous Thursday night farmers' market. The bars at the south end of the street were just starting to liven up, rowdy groups of Cal Poly students pouring out on the streets, loud, laughing and obnoxious. At least they seemed obnoxious to Mel, who not only had never lived that carefree college life but had spent a lot of her early years as a patrol officer hauling these overly privileged, drunk, puke-covered kids into the police station.

She walked down to the end of the street with her hands in the pockets of her flannel-lined barn jacket, trying to decide if she wanted to push through the crowds and find a quiet corner. She finally gave up and walked back up the street toward Blind Harry's Bookstore, where she'd make do with a chai latte, even though what she craved was a double Irish coffee, a drink she'd grown to love when she was with Sean.

The bookstore was crowded with Christmas shoppers, and she realized that Blind Harry's was having a special "open until midnight" sale. That worked for her. She hadn't bought a Christmas gift for Love yet, and though she wasn't sure if she'd even be around in a few weeks, she'd try to find something that she could leave with Polly to give to Love on Christmas Day.

It didn't take her long to find what she hoped was the perfect gift. It was a book of photographs by the late Isaac Lyons, a famous photographer Love took a class from once and who had been married to Benni Ortiz's grandmother, Dove. She picked it up and ran her fingers over the faux leather front cover.

"It just came in today," said a pretty Hispanic woman who looked to be in her midforties. Her name tag read Elvia. "He was a local for many years. Married to the grandmother of a friend of mine before he passed away last year." She straightened a stack of Christmas cards. "We miss him terribly."

Mel nodded. "Benni and Dove. They have the ranch next to the Johnsons. I work for Polly and August occasionally." She handed her the book. "I'll take it. It's actually a gift for Love Johnson."

"Oh, my goodness, I've known Love forever. She's a wonderful customer." The woman smiled at Mel. "She'll love it. I'd be happy to wrap it for you. No extra charge."

"Sold," Mel said. "Thank you."

Happy that she'd found something Love would like, Mel carried her package to the basement coffeehouse to buy her latte, maybe read the newspapers always lying around on the round wooden tables. It was better she didn't stay home and brood. There would be enough time for that later on tonight, when she wouldn't be able to sleep. She ordered a decaf, hoping that her virtuous choice would stave off the insomnia gremlins.

She was perusing one of the bookshelves filled with used books that lined all the walls of the coffeehouse, waiting for her order to be called, when a vaguely familiar male voice said her name.

"Melina LeBlanc. As I live and breathe."

She turned to look at the man, studying his animated face, trying to remember where she'd met him. He wore a navy blue cowboy shirt, jeans and a pair of dark, shiny cowboy boots made with the skin of some unfortunate lizard.

He smiled and held out his hand. "I'm absolutely crushed that you don't remember me. Ford Hudson. Hud. Maisie's dad."

"Oh, yeah, hi." The annoying sheriff's deputy. She shook his hand firmly, one cop to another.

"Doing some holiday shopping?" He tilted his head, glancing at the red and silver Blind Harry's bag. "Or a book for yourself?"

"A gift," she said, glancing around, trying to figure out a way to extricate herself from this encounter. She'd driven to San Celina specifically because she didn't want to talk to anyone.

"You have an appointment?" he asked, his dark eyes laughing at her.

She hesitated, not a natural liar but wanting to use the excuse to leave.

"I won't bite. At least not until we've known each other a little longer."

She frowned and looked him directly in the eyes. "I don't find your flirting particularly amusing."

"Flirting, *moi*?" He pretended to be shocked. "My daughter would inform you that I am way too elderly to flirt. According to her, people should stop dating or havin' any fun at all after the age of thirty-five."

She just stared at him, not wanting this conversation to continue. She had too much on her mind tonight to word wrestle with some middle-aged wannabe cowboy.

"I'm from Texas," he said, completely out of the blue.

"Too bad," she replied.

"You got something against Texans?"

She inhaled, holding it in for a few seconds before letting out a long breath. "Look, Mr. Hudson—"

"Hud. Mr. Hudson was—"

"I know, I know, your father. Look, I just want to be alone tonight, okay? I'm sure you're a nice guy and that there are women who go for guys like you. So why don't you go run your little spiel on them? I'm sure they'd appreciate it a lot more than me."

"I'm very rich." He said it matter-of-factly, with a friendly smile like he'd just said, I own a basset hound or I like fried chicken.

She felt her mouth drop open slightly. "That's the most obnoxious pickup line I've ever heard."

"It got your attention, didn't it? Don't you want to know how I got rich? I swear, it's not graft."

It felt like someone punched her in the stomach. His words had to be a coincidence, but they still seemed to crumble around her like a brick house in an earthquake.

"I gotta go," she said, her voice jagged in her ears. She ran up the steps, vaguely hearing her order being called. When she reached the street, she stood for a moment inhaling the cold night air, her chest heaving, trying to catch her breath. It felt like she was under water, like she was going to suffocate.

"Here," Hud said, suddenly beside her. He pulled her into the alley next to Blind Harry's. He took her Blind Harry's bag and handed her a brown paper sack. "Put it over your—"

"I know," she gasped and put the sack over her mouth, breathing slowly in and out, mentally telling herself to calm down, don't panic, there's no way this man could know about her and Sean. Was there? In a few minutes, she was breathing normally again, and she lowered the sack. She hadn't had an attack like that for years. She used to hyperventilate when she was a kid, so much that she carried a paper lunch bag around in her backpack like the way a person susceptible to anaphylactic shock carries an EpiPen.

"Better?" Hud said, his voice gentle.

She looked up at him, knowing she should be grateful for his help, but all she wanted to do was crumple the bag in a hard ball and throw it in his face. Yes, he helped her by realizing she was hyperventilating and bringing her the thing she needed, but he also *caused* the attack to begin with. And by the look on his face, he was going to ask her why she reacted like she did.

"Look," he said. "I'm not going to ask you what's wrong, but it's obvious to me that something traumatic is going on in your life." He took his wallet from his back pocket, pulled out a white business card and wrote on the back of it. "Here's my home phone number, my cell and my work number. If you need any help—"

"I don't." She started folding the paper bag in neat squares, making it smaller and smaller until she couldn't fold it anymore. "I'm fine. I just . . . have these attacks once in a while."

He held out her Blind Harry's bag and the business card. "I've gone through some rough times in my life. If you need someone to talk to . . ."

She grabbed the bag that held Love's gift. "I don't even know you."

"We both know Benni Harper. And we're her friends. That makes us friends once removed."

Man, this guy was persistent. "Thanks, but I'm fine."

He stuck his card in her jacket's pocket. "Just in case."

She turned abruptly away from him, walking up Lopez Street, her back teeth aching from tension. With guys like him, the only thing you could do was walk away. Usually their egos kept them from chasing after you. When a few minutes later she was still alone, she sighed in relief. The last thing she needed was a guy, especially one who was a cop. As she walked down the crowded street, the sound of Christmas music in the air, she couldn't help wondering where she would be at this time next year. She'd always suspected that her life in Morro Bay had been too good to last. When Cy died and she and Love continued their Friday night dinners, she'd been relieved. Though she knew that it was pity that Cy and Love had felt for her initially, she hoped that it had turned into a true caring, maybe even something close to a family.

But now Love had her real family here. A girl that might or might not appreciate how lucky she was to have Love as her grandmother. At any rate, this girl and possibly her sisters and her mother would fill up Love's life, and though Mel was glad for Love, really happy for her, she was sad for herself. Maybe the call from Patrick had been a sign that it was time for Mel to move on.

A sharp wind came up when she was a block away from the parking structure. She looped the handled Blind Harry's bag over the crook of her elbow and stuck her cold hands deep into her pockets. Her right fingers touched the folded paper bag that had given her back her breath only moments before; her left hand pulled out the card from the deputy who talked as smooth as melted chocolate, someone who reminded her way too much of a man she'd once loved. Right before she started up the stairs to the second level where her truck was parked, she threw the folded paper bag in an overflowing garbage can. Then, with only the slightest hesitation, she tossed the business card after it.

ELEVEN

Rett

R ett could hear her grandma talking on the phone, her voice a low murmur. She wanted to get up and hear who she was talking to since she had a sneaking feeling that the conversation was about her. But when she sat up, her head thrummed like a bass fiddle, so she carefully lowered herself back down. Why did she have to get sick now? For a moment, she almost wished that she was back home, that the voice in the background was her mother's. Mom wasn't so bad when you were sick. It was the only time she seemed to be nice. It was a miracle that she, Patsy and Faith hadn't all become total hypochondriacs.

She rolled over on her back and stared at the ceiling. The moonlight through the thin white window shades gave shape to the furniture in the room, simple pieces that looked like they'd been around a while. Her grandma didn't look rich, just normal. How did she make a living? There was so much Rett didn't know about her dad's family. Thinking about that made her angry with her mom all over again.

Love's voice became a little louder, causing Rett to struggle up and swing her legs over to the side of the bed, ignoring her throbbing head. It sounded like her grandma Love was arguing. A deep dread in Rett's stomach told her that, despite her protests, her grandma had contacted Mom.

She stood up, gripping the side of the bed as the room spun around while she inched her way over to the partially closed door. Love's words became clearer.

"I assure you, Karla Rae, I had no idea she was coming out here. For heaven's sake, I didn't . . . don't even know where y'all live. If not for Rett's cell phone, I still wouldn't know how to get in touch with you, which means I couldn't have been in touch with her." There was a pause, then her grandma said, "She's eighteen, Karla. I can't *make* her do anything."

All right, Grandma, Rett thought. She could imagine her mom's deep voice spewing accusations. Accusations that were totally bogus. Though Rett had thought about calling her grandma first and seeing if she even cared about seeing her, that wasn't how Rett did things. Jump right in was her philosophy. Don't think too much about stuff you want to do, because you'd probably chicken out. It was how she made friends— maybe not the smartest way, considering what happened with Dale— and it was how she wrote songs. She remembered Pete, her first stepdad, saying to her when she was nine or ten, "Rett, you are much too happy flying by the seat of your pants. Someday you're going to be right sorry you don't put a little more thought into what you do."

She didn't think about the last part of his comment because she'd zeroed in on that first image. She pictured herself on a flying carpet hurtling over the earth looking down on everyone as she dipped and flew her way to someplace more exciting than her life as the second Son Sister. That feeling had come back to her when she rode in the cab of Brother Dwaine's big rig. Not that she thought she was better than other people. She just wanted to go her own way and do what she wanted without being bugged. What was wrong with that? She wasn't hurting anyone, so why couldn't they just leave her alone?

She edged closer to the door as Love's voice grew softer.

"Karla Rae—excuse me—Karla—I'm sorry you were so worried. That was why I tried to find you. I understand. No, I can't put her on the phone. She's got the flu, and she's asleep."

There was a long pause, probably because her mom was nagging her grandma's ear off. Rett felt a quick stab of regret for putting Love through this. But it was kinda her own fault. Rett *told* her not to call Karla.

"I'll ask her to call you the minute she gets up," Love said, her voice way more calm than Rett's would have been, she was sure. Another short pause. "I can't guarantee anything, Karla. As I said before, she's a legal adult."

All right, Grandma, Rett silently cheered, suddenly feeling a lot better about her spontaneous trip here. Maybe everything would turn out okay. There was still Dale's banjo she had to think about. It was only a matter of time before he forced Lissa into telling him where Rett was. She didn't expect her girlfriend to hold out forever, and Rett sure knew how persuasive Dale could be. What would he do when he found out she took his precious banjo? Would he come out here and try to get it back? The thought of pawning it still rolled around in her head, but since it was technically stolen, she didn't want to do something that might land her in jail. Though, she thought, that would give her some interesting material for songs and a bio that was way cooler than being one-third of a second-rate girl bluegrass-gospel group. Well, she'd figure out what to do if Dale actually showed up.

Love hung up the phone. Rett hobbled back to bed and climbed in. She didn't want her grandma to think she was some kind of weirdo snoop. Rett suspected that her grandma would check on her right now and probably lots of times during the night. She seemed like that kind of person. Rett sighed, feeling like she could sleep for a week. She snuggled down into the soft comforter with the intention of closing her eyes and pretending to be asleep when her grandma checked, but before she even heard her grandma open the bedroom door, she wasn't pretending.

TWELVE

Love Mercy

Love collapsed in Cy's old leather chair. This wasn't the end of it between her and Karla Rae by any stretch of the imagination. *Karla,* Love reminded herself. Her daughter-in-law had informed her she no longer went by Karla Rae.

Well, at least Love couldn't be accused of trying to hide Rett from her. It would be up to Rett now to stay in contact with her mother. Her former daughter-in-law's accusations that Love was somehow involved with Rett running away from home still rang in Love's ears. Fourteen years hadn't done much to soften Karla.

Love stood up and walked into the guest room to check on Rett. The poor girl was sound asleep, her hair spread in a wild disarray on the white pillow. Love gently touched her forehead with her fingertips. It was damp and cool. The Tylenol had broken the fever. She studied her granddaughter's peaceful face, feeling a combination of joy and sorrow. Seeing Rett made the loss of Cy and Tommy so much more tangible. She managed to go for days at a time not mourning her life, thinking about how her whole family had been snatched from her. When she saw families down on the Embarcadero, visiting from L.A. or the Valley, eating ice cream, laughing at family jokes, she just barely managed to squelch the resentment she felt, the anger that she harbored against God.

Love had grown up attending the little Baptist church in Redwater, Kentucky, where she and Cy met. Her faith back then was as simple as the church's unpainted pine walls. It was a faith taught to her by her mother, Nora, who had the sort of honest and trusting faith in God and Jesus that never questioned, as far as Love knew, why bad things happened, not even when the coal mine took first her son through a mine collapse, then her husband through black lung. Bad things just happened, seemed to be her mother's unspoken credo, and a person was supposed to endure and trust that better times were coming. It wasn't proper to ask God why, not respectful to demand an explanation. Job and his travails was a popular sermon topic in Redwater.

Something deep inside Love always rebelled against that. It was that attitude that made her want to leave Redwater, find someplace where there was more hope. Though at the time, she'd said to her heartbroken mother that it was a wife's duty to follow her husband, Love knew that though she loved Cy with all her heart, even if he hadn't come along, she would have eventually fled Kentucky. It was pure luck on her part to fall in love with a man who wasn't a local boy, but she'd decided to leave Kentucky the day the Redwater mine manager walked up to their screen door with the news that her eighteen-year-old twin brother, DJ, had been killed. In that moment, Kentucky lost her forever.

She had to shake her head at her naive young self now. She'd thought by fleeing the hollers and coal mines of her childhood, she could outrun sadness, outmaneuver tragedy. How wrong she'd been. Everyone she had given her heart to lay in graveyards here or in Redwater. And despite what her mother taught her, Love questioned God. When he didn't answer, she'd just stopped talking. She did go to church one or two Sundays a month, not wanting to disappoint Rocky or Magnolia. She listened to Rocky's sermons, enjoyed Magnolia's beautiful solos, and she silently moved her lips to the familiar old gospel songs. She did it all with a heart that she was sure if it could be photographed inside her chest would look exactly like a dried corncob, one scraped bare of any sweet kernels, as barren as an old seashell.

On the Sundays she skipped church, a practice her good friends, bless their hearts, never questioned, she took photos of churches. It had grown into almost a compulsion. She liked taking the photos on Sunday afternoons or evenings, right after they'd emptied of worshippers. There seemed an almost-palpable something in the air then, something that seemed to tinge the photographs, a mistiness that gave them a haunted look. Though she had a digital camera that she was slowly learning to work with, for these outings she preferred her old Nikon SLR with real film. She actually liked not knowing what her photographs looked like until they were developed. One of her favorites was of a tiny wood-frame church in Cayucos. She took the photo at sunset, certain that no one was on the premises. When she had the photos developed the next week, there was, to her surprise, a blurred arm showing from the left side of the church; it almost appeared to be waving. It seemed a ghostly message of something, though she never could figure out what it was trying to say.

For the second time she studied the lines and planes of her granddaughter's face. Love felt like she could see the whole history of Appalachia on Rett's smooth cheeks. She wondered if she could convince Rett to pose for a portrait before she left. Love planned it in her head, shooting it up at the ranch next to the lightning oak. It would be dusk— blue time—and she'd take it at an angle, half of Rett's face in shadows, hinting at the murky kudzu-filled hollers of her ancestors.

Like a water moccasin, a ripple of fear shimmied through Love. She wanted to love this girl, but there were no guarantees. Could she survive losing someone she loved again? She remembered what Mama told her the day of DJ's funeral only three weeks after they'd celebrated their eighteenth birthday, when the smell of all those lilies and roses made her want to gag. The world looked like she was watching it through a waterfall.

"How can you stand it?" she asked her mother who had spent the day comforting other people.

"No choice, child," Mama had told her. Her mother's wrinkled face had been as luminous as an old painting. "If you love, you grieve."

Love closed the bedroom door halfway so that she could hear Rett if she needed something during the night. Ace followed Love from the living room into the kitchen, where she sat at the kitchen table. What to do now? Wait was the answer that came to mind. Something she was experienced at.

The clock on the stove read eight thirty. Still early enough to call Polly and August. They needed to hear about Rett from her.

"You almost missed us," Polly said.

"Were you two going out to paint the town red?" She chuckled, knowing exactly what Polly meant.

"No, going upstairs to read the insides of our eyelids."

"I have some news that might make you feel like painting the town red. We've got company in town."

"Do say?"

"Your second great-granddaughter, Loretta Lynn, dropped in for a visit. She likes to be called Rett."

"Well, I'll be. August will be thrilled. How old is the girl now?"

"Eighteen, believe it or not."

"Did you know . . . no, forget I asked that. Of course you didn't know she was coming."

"She just showed up at the Buttercream, and Magnolia called me. It's been a rather exciting few hours. About two minutes after she stepped over the threshold of my place, she got sick."

"Poor little thing. With what?"

"Looks like the flu. Clint's son, the doctor, is visiting him, so I traded chocolate cupcakes for a house call. I'll bring her by as soon as she starts feeling better."

"Does Karla Rae know she's here?"

"She does now. I found her number in Rett's cell phone. Oh, and she prefers to be called just Karla now."

"What did just Karla say?"

"She accused me of being behind Rett's running away. I think there's something else going on in the family besides a tiff between daughter and mother. Hopefully, I'll be able to convince Rett to tell me what it is."

"Well, I'm just going to have to knit Rett a scarf for Christmas. I'll go to town tomorrow and buy some new yarn. You bring her around just as soon as you can. Mel brought us our Christmas tree today, and we were waiting on you to decorate it. Now, it'll be even better with Rett here."

"Yes," Love said, thinking, Let's hope so.

"Sweet dreams, Love."

The next person she called was Magnolia. She knew her friend was dying to know what happened this evening.

"She has the flu," Love said. "At least, that's what Garth thinks."

"The judge's son is still here? I thought he was supposed to leave yesterday." Magnolia always knew everything from soup to nuts that went on in Morro Bay.

"Thank goodness he didn't. I was afraid to give her anything, since I know nothing about her medical background. She had a fever."

"How's she doing now?"

"She's asleep. The Tylenol broke her fever."

"So, what's her story?"

"I don't really know yet. I managed to get ahold of Karla." She picked at a rough spot on the pine dining table.

"You did the right thing, calling her."

"Rett didn't want me to call."

"Well, she'll just have to deal with it. You couldn't let her mama worry, no matter how crazy Karla Rae is. So, what's next?"

"Just Karla. She's dropped the Rae. Anyway, I have no idea. Rett and I didn't really get a chance to discuss her plans before she got sick."

"August and Polly know she's here?"

"I just called. Polly took it in stride, like she does everything. She'll be up at dawn baking and planning a special meal. I'll make a wild guess that we'll be eating lunch there tomorrow."

"It's going to work out fine. There's a reason she showed up on your doorstep."

Love promised to call Magnolia as soon as she learned anything new. What would she do without her good friend? Without Magnolia and her down-to-earth practicality, Love was sure she'd have long ago dug a hole and just crawled right in. Especially after Cy died. Her heart had felt so torn and ragged, so used up, but no matter how cranky or short she was, Magnolia took it in stride, barged right past her bad mood with her deep laugh and cranberry coffee cake.

"I'll knock on your door until you can't stand the noise and answer," she'd said. She meant it literally and emotionally. "It is nigh on impossible to ignore an Italian Southern girl."

They'd become friends because she'd walked right up to Love on the first day she'd come to work at the diner and said, "Girl, I like the way you look. I think we could be best friends."

Love was taken aback for a moment. Like her Appalachian ancestors, she had a tendency to be suspicious of most folks, certain that they were up to no good, as so many smiling, fork-tongued people had been throughout the history of Appalachia. But Magnolia was as open and sweet as the flower she was named for. Mama used to tell Love and DJ, you can only trust two things in life: the Good Lord and family. Love added friends to that list. You can trust good, true friends like Magnolia and Rocky.

An old cliché popped into her head: don't wish for something, you might just get it. She'd always wanted—no, *yearned* for—family, and now here it was in the form of a complicated runaway teenager who may or may not stay.

Still, there was an undeniable lightness in her heart when she checked Rett one last time before going to bed herself. She left both bedroom doors open, worried that her long-unused mother radar had gone dormant.

In bed, she settled the quilt over her legs and turned out the light, knowing she should get on her knees and thank God that one of her granddaughters had finally come home. But, though she wasn't the most faithful of followers, the one thing she'd always been in her often bumpy relationship with God was honest. She always figured she might as well be. If God was truly God and could read her thoughts, see what she was doing when no one else could, what was the point of pretending he couldn't? She hoped that it counted for something.

We'll see, Lord, she thought. We'll just see.

THIRTEEN

Rett

Rett's cell phone woke her out of a deep sleep. The room was tinted a pale yellow, and the clock on the bedside table read nine thirty. Man, she must have slept twelve hours.

"Don't be mad," Lissa blurted out.

Before Rett could answer, there was a soft knock on the partially closed bedroom door.

"Rett, are you up?" Love called in a low voice.

"Yes, ma'am."

"How do you feel? Would you like some breakfast?"

"I'm okay. I'll be right there. Give me five minutes."

"No hurry. I'll be in the kitchen."

Rett waited until she heard her grandma's footsteps fade away, then she hissed, "You told Dale where I was?"

"Oh, Rett, I swear it just slipped out." Lissa's voice turned whiny in that way that always drove Rett clear up a brick wall. She could hear her best friend take a drag off her cigarette.

"I can't believe you ratted me out," Rett said.

"I didn't say *exactly* where you were. I just told him enough to get him off my front porch. And I didn't give him your number."

Rett wasn't actually surprised. She'd known the minute she took the banjo from behind the seat of Dale's truck that it was only a matter of time before he realized it was her. It wasn't like she'd stolen his beloved Vietnam-era Zippo cigarette lighter that he bought at the Arkansas State Fair last year. This was way bigger.

"Quick, tell me what he said. I think my minutes are just about to run out." She'd have to find a Wal-Mart and use some of her precious money to pay for thirty more minutes. She just couldn't be without a cell phone.

"I only told him you went to see your grandma on the West Coast."

"Did he ask about the banjo?"

"Yes, he wanted to know if you took it, except before I could lie and say you didn't, he said he knew you had it. He's real pissed, Rett."

"All you told him is I went to the West Coast?"

"That's all, I swear. I don't even remember the name of the town where your grandma lives. I think he believed me, 'cause he just stomped off cussing, sayin' he'd better f-ing get it back before the tour started."

Rett smiled to herself. She knew he was freaking out, because he'd gotten a once-in-a-lifetime gig. The Flat Top Onions, a hot new alt country-bluegrass band that was the talk of the circuit—they'd been nominated for a Grammy last year—needed a temporary banjo picker. Their regular banjo guy had gone back to Mississippi to help care for his brother, who was dying of some brain disease. It was Dale's first full-time paying gig with a successful band. Like most new musicians, to make ends meet, he'd always worked other jobs, teaching banjo or guitar, working retail or busing tables. This was a shot at the big time. And she knew he needed his beloved Gibson prewar banjo. He loved that banjo more than his own mama.

"Well, I just hope he doesn't talk to my mom. She knows where I am, and I wouldn't put it past her to tell him."

"How'd she find out?"

"My grandma called her."

"That sucks."

"Whatever. I'll deal with her later." Much later, she hoped. She knew that between fighting with Patsy about her pregnancy and arguing with Rett's second stepdad, Roy, something that had been happening a lot lately, she doubted her mom would have the time to come out here. She'd probably just call and try to fight over the phone. Rett would just not take her calls. Simple as pie.

"I'll call you when I can buy more minutes," she told Lissa. "Just don't say another word. Promise."

"I swear on my stepmom's Day-of-the-Dead Rocketbuster boots that I am so totally going to steal someday."

Rett didn't believe for a minute that Lissa would be able to keep where Rett was a secret from Dale, but she figured she had a few days lead time if she could just depend on her mom not to tell Dale anything. But Dale had the ability to charm any woman, even old ones like Mom.

Rett pondered for a moment how she could keep that from happening and realized she couldn't. She'd have to ask her mom not to tell Dale where she was, and Mom would want to know why he wanted to know and why Rett didn't want him to know. She'd squeeze out of Rett that she and Dale had had a "thing." Mom could be like one of those persistent animals Rett had seen on one of the shows on *Animal Planet* that took hold of something and didn't let it go until it totally died. Was it a badger? That's how Karla would be about finding out who Patsy's baby daddy was.

So, like writing a killer song or landing a sweet gig, it was a matter of timing. And, like those two things, there wasn't a whole lot a person could do to change what was bound to happen. Rett was pragmatic about that. It was a word she'd just learned and really liked because she felt it described her perfectly. She pragmatically flew by the seat of her pants.

What she really hoped was that she was left out of the whole dang thing when the crap hit the fan about Patsy and her little brat.

Even as she thought the word, a little voice inside her remarked, *That little brat that will be your first niece or nephew.* She had to admit, that kind of seemed cool. Aunt Rett. She'd be the awesome aunt, the successful musician who blew into town and bought really sweet presents, then left again before anyone knew what hit them. Patsy and Dale would be old and boring and totally envy her cool new life.

She swung her legs out of bed and tentatively stood up. Her head felt a million times better this morning. Whatever it was she had last night seemed mostly gone. She actually felt kinda hungry. She opened the bedroom door and found Ace lying on the oak floor. If she hadn't been paying attention, she would have tripped over him.

"Hey, boy, how're you doing?" She stooped down to stroke his long, wolflike head. He grinned at her and stood up, wagging his butt. "Let's go see what Grandma Love has cooking in the kitchen."

FOURTEEN

Love Mercy

Love stood at the kitchen sink filling the coffee carafe with water and singing to herself. ". . . a little lamb who's lost in the woods . . ."

"I know that song," Rett said, startling her.

"Oh," she said, turning around, sloshing water on the floor.

"I kinda remember my dad singing it to us," Rett said, hugging herself. Standing in the doorway, she didn't look much older than twelve in Love's blue-striped pajamas. Her toes peeked out from the folds of flannel puddled on the kitchen floor. "I never knew its name."

" 'Someone to Watch Over Me.' Before your daddy sang it to you, your grandpa Cy sang it to your daddy."

"Cy for Cyrus."

Love nodded. "That's right."

"He died last year."

Her bluntness surprised Love. "Yes, a year ago November. From lung cancer." She hesitated, then said, "He never smoked." She didn't know why she felt compelled to state that.

"Sorry." Rett ducked her head and studied the fabric covering her feet.

"You would have liked him. He was . . . he laughed a lot." Love paused. "He would have loved you."

Rett looked up, her eyes unreadable.

"Anything you particularly want for breakfast?" Love asked.

Rett pushed up the sleeves of her pajamas. "Whatever. I'm not picky."

Well, Love thought, turning back to the sink, she's not the most verbal person. She certainly didn't take after Cy or Tommy that way. Both of them could have talked the ears off an elephant. She smiled to herself while scooping coffee into the basket. No, Rett wasn't like Cy or Tommy that way; she was like Love. She'd been told more than once after she finally became friends with someone that she wasn't the most forthcoming person right off.

"It's amazing you and Mel have managed to become friends," Magnolia said once. "I never see y'all just *talk*."

Love laughed at her verbose friend. "We talk enough."

She started the coffee, then turned back to her granddaughter. Rett sat down at the yellow dining table, picking up the tennis ball Ace dropped at her feet.

"Ace," Love said, "let the girl eat her breakfast first. There are banana muffins in the freezer. That okay?"

Rett nodded and tossed the ball across the kitchen floor, Ace bounding happily after it. She played with Ace while the coffee brewed and Love unwrapped the muffins, putting them in the microwave to defrost and heat. In a few minutes, they were buttering muffins and sipping their coffees like an old married couple.

Love felt her heart thrum in her chest. She felt an overwhelming urge to touch Rett, hug her, feel the texture of her hair, her skin, to try to absorb and recapture those lost years. Seeing Rett brought back a sharp memory of bathing her when she was four years old, scrubbing her tender baby back, her fine brown hair bubbling with shampoo. It was the night before Tommy's funeral. Love was toweling Rett dry, and she remembered her granddaughter shivering with delight from the cold air hitting her wet skin, letting out a happy squeal and running in place. Where was that innocent little four-year-old? Was she buried behind the down-turned eyes of this reserved young woman?

"So," Love finally said. "Tell me about yourself. It's been a long time."

Rett looked up from her half-eaten muffin. "Why?"

Her response took Love by surprise. "What?"

"Why has it been a long time? How come you never came to visit us? How come you never called? Or, like, even sent a postcard?" Her tone was accusing, making Love's hackles rise.

Love slowly set down her coffee mug. This conversation was happening sooner than she anticipated. She couldn't help noticing a bit of Karla's pushiness in Rett's blunt questions. Her daughter-in-law had always been so sure of herself, so sure she was in the right, no matter what anyone else thought or felt. Why did it surprise Love that Rett was as bold as her mother? She was, after all, as much a Murphy as she was a Johnson.

"It's complicated," Love said, choosing her words carefully. "I'm not sure—"

"That I'll get it? Believe me, I *totally* get how screwed-up families can be."

Love wasn't certain how to continue this conversation. Except for the occasional teenager or twentysomething she spoke to at church or served at the café, she didn't know anyone from this age group. All she knew about this Generation Y or Millennials or whatever they were currently being called by the media was what she read in magazines or saw on television. A lot was made about how they'd never lived in a world without computers, had grown up being told they could do or be anything, that they were more open-minded, less concerned about convention and more self-centered than the baby boomers. A lot of articles lamented that the world was doomed with this generation, that they, and therefore the world, were slip-sliding down a perdition-bound road.

It amused Love to read blanket statements like that. The doomsday predictors didn't scare her. Anyone who read the least little bit of history knew that every generation said similar things about the next generation. Her parents said that about the baby boomers, and she imagined the people who were adults during the Depression said it about the WWII generation.

"These crazy kids," she could imagine her grandmother saying about her parents and their friends. "Now that the war is over they want to spend all their time having babies and buying every sort of newfangled appliance and car that rolls down the pike."

She smiled. As wise old King Solomon once declared, there's really nothing new under the sun. Comparing the generations would make a good column, though she wasn't sure what kind of photo would best illustrate it.

"What's so funny?" Rett asked, frowning.

"I'm sorry. It had nothing to do with you. Sometimes my mind goes off on these tangents, and I completely forget where I am. Used to drive your grandpa Cy crazy."

Rett's frown softened. "Yeah, I do that sometimes. Like when I'm thinking about a song that I'm writing."

Love cocked her head. "You write songs?"

Rett's face flushed pink. "None have actually been, like, bought or anything. I . . . I mess around."

"I take photos," Love said, feeling like she should share something about herself, trying to relieve Rett's embarrassment. "I have a monthly column for a local magazine. I take a picture, then sort of comment on it. The magazine's publisher is the father of the doctor who examined you last night." She put two fingers to her cheek, laughing softly. "That sounds really small town, doesn't it?"

Rett's eyes lit up. "You're published in a magazine? Cool."

Love lifted one shoulder, trying not to look overly pleased at her granddaughter's approval. She would have liked to continue this conversational detour, but they had unfinished business that was best taken care of now. "About what happened with our family. Let's just get that out of the way. I'll answer your questions flat out, okay?"

Rett nodded, her face serious.

"When Tommy . . . your daddy . . . passed away, your mother and I were both very hurt and very sad and, I guess, looking back now, we both felt cheated. She lost her husband, and I lost my only child." Love stopped, taking a deep breath. Just saying it out loud was still hard. And she wanted to tread carefully, not make Karla sound horrible. "Instead of being able to comfort each other, I think we both wanted to be mad at someone, so we chose each other. Grief makes people do strange things sometimes. But I did try to make up with her once I got back to California. I sent cards and letters and we even came to visit you once, but—"

"The Disney World trip," Rett said softly.

That surprised Love. "How do you know about that? You were just a tiny girl." The remembered humiliation of that visit still caused Love's blood pressure to rise.

Rett started picking the half-eaten muffin on her plate into little pieces, not meeting Love's eyes. "When I was eight, I heard Mom talk about it to a friend. Mom said you could visit, then we went to Disney World before you got there. That was totally mean of her." She looked up at Love. "Why does she hate you so much?"

Love bit the inside of her cheek. Rett's candid words hurt more than she probably realized. "I guess it boils down to the fact that we both loved Tommy and thought we knew what was best for him, and they weren't the same thing."

"What she did to you was so wrong," Rett said.

Though she wanted to jump up and hug her granddaughter, Love held back. "We have both said and thought hurtful things, Rett. I know your daddy loved your mama and you girls to the last day of his life."

Rett stared at her hands, clasped together, fingers entwined as if in prayer. She didn't reply for a long time, causing Love to wonder if she'd made a mistake in being so honest. When Rett lifted her head, her pupils were large black spots.

"It wasn't you. It was Mom. She's always been so, I don't know, pissed off at life. She never got over not making it as a country singer, and she is sure that one of us girls will do it for her." Rett gave a bitter laugh. "That's not exactly true. She wants Patsy to be the big old Nashville star. And that's screwed up royally now. Don't worry about Mom being upset about me being here. That not what's really bugging her. What's freaking her out is that her shining star has gotten pregnant. The only reason she wants me to come back is that she thinks I can talk Patsy into telling her who the daddy is. I'm sick of being the person who always has to tell everyone what everyone else is doing. Let them punch it out. I'm so over the whole stupid thing with Dale."

Love stared at Rett, floored by this unexpected cascade of information. "Patsy's pregnant? Who's Dale?"

Rett's face seemed to collapse, and she turned her head, staring out the kitchen window at the navy-colored ocean. In that instant, Love pieced together the whole story. Rett was in love with this Dale, who got her sister pregnant, and she was running away from the situation.

Heavenly stars, she thought. It sounds just like a soap opera episode. Or a country western song. She gently asked, "Dale is the father of Patsy's baby?"

Rett nodded silently.

"And you and Dale had a relationship too?"

Rett nodded again.

Love took a deep breath. "Does your mother know the whole story?"

Rett shook her head, her eyes glistening. "I told you, Mom doesn't even know Dale is the father. At least, she didn't know when I left three days ago."

"And you and this Dale?"

"Mom doesn't know about that either. Neither does Patsy. At least I don't think she does. No one knew except me and Dale." Her expression was both defiant and apologetic. "I didn't know about him and Patsy. I'd never be that skanky."

"I believe you." Love wanted to strangle this Dale creature with her bare hands. She reached over and touched her granddaughter's hand. It was as cold as a winter tide pool. She was almost afraid to ask the next question. "How old is Dale?"

Rett raised her chin. "Not that old. I'm eighteen."

"But how old is *he*?"

"I've known him, like, forever. Since I was thirteen. He played Dobro and banjo in our backup band when we cut our CD a few years ago."

Love just looked at her and waited.

Rett's chin went a little higher. "Twenty-six, okay? So he's a little older. So what."

Love felt her neck grow hot with anger at this man who'd taken advantage of her granddaughters. But that wasn't something she could do anything about. Not at the moment. She cleared her throat. "We've been very adult and been perfectly honest with each other. I can't think of a better way to start our new relationship, can you?"

Rett started playing with her already mangled muffin and squirmed just enough to make Love suspicious.

"What else, Rett?" she asked. "If we're going to have a good relationship, we need to be honest with each other. Don't you think there have been enough secrets and misunderstandings in this family?"

Rett nodded, her face miserable. "I kind of . . . well . . . I sort of . . . borrowed something from someone?"

Now Love was really confused.

"I guess, sort of without asking."

Love could feel the vein in her right temple start to throb. "In other words, you've stolen something." She panicked, thinking, What do I do if she's robbed a liquor store, and the police are after her? For a split second, she contemplated the places on the Johnson ranch where she could hide her granddaughter.

"What did you take?" Love's voice jumped an octave.

"My banjo," Rett said. "I mean, his banjo. It's Dale's banjo. It was his grandfather's. I took it out of the back of his truck. Dale's, I mean. Not his grandfather. His grandfather died ten years ago." She sat up straight and looked Love in the eye. "I don't care. Dale deserved it. He's a creep."

"I won't argue with the fact that he is a creep, but that doesn't make it right for you to take something that belongs to him."

Rett narrowed her eyes. "What he did was way worse. He lied to me. I'm not giving it back."

Love was not quite certain how far she should pursue this. After all, as she'd pointed out to Karla last night, Rett was a grown woman. If she wanted to steal her cheating ex-boyfriend's banjo, why should Love care? How much could a banjo be worth, anyway? Granted, if it was his grandfather's, it would have some sentimental value. Love was certain that once Rett cooled down, she'd let Love send it back to this cockroach of a man.

"So, just to keep things aboveboard, how much would you say this instrument is worth?" Love was thinking, Four, five hundred dollars, tops.

Rett wouldn't meet her eyes. "Kind of a lot."

"Meaning?"

"Twenty-five . . . umm . . ."

Love felt her stomach drop. "Twenty-five hundred dollars?"

There was a long pause. "Uh . . . thousand."

"Twenty-five thousand dollars? That banjo is worth *twenty-five thousand* dollars?"

Rett's expression was sheepish and a little fearful.

Love had always believed there were dramatic moments in every Protestant believer's life when they fervently wished they were Catholic just so they could cross themselves, when that comforting holy gesture seemed the only conceivable response to a situation. This was, without a doubt, one of those moments for her.

FIFTEEN

Mel

Before she went to sleep, Mel loaded her .38 pistol and placed it on the bed next to her, something she hadn't done since she left Las Vegas. She managed to get a few hours' sleep, though she tossed and turned most of the night, dreaming of plastic-wrapped money and Patrick's leering face.

When the alarm clock went off at five a.m., she turned on her bedside light and was surprised to see terra-cotta-colored spots dotting her pale blue pillowcase. Her bottom lip throbbed, and she touched the soft, swollen flesh with a tentative finger. Sometime during the night she'd bitten her lip. Ice cubes wrapped in a dish towel and pressed to her lip made it presentable. It took two large mugs of coffee before she felt able to get dressed. Though normally she didn't mind covering for Brad and Evan's surfing, this morning she cursed their flakiness and swore she'd find a job where she wasn't at the beck and call of two horny guys with boy-band looks and excessive trust funds.

By the time she opened the feed store at six a.m., she was a little less cranky. They'd promised to be here by nine a.m. Coffee would sustain her until then. Once they took over, she'd go to the Buttercream for some of Shug's sourdough-banana pancakes.

From the first day that Cy hired her, she'd felt at home in this small wooden structure with the huge back lot. Though at first foreign, now the malty smell of hay, toasty cracked corn, sweet new leather and grassiness of rabbit pellets was like a heady perfume to her, a sensory memory road to long, easy days when Cy patiently taught her the ins and outs of running a feed store.

"Though most folks round here don't want to face it, ranching isn't going to be the top moneymaker in this county forever," he'd said while they counted bags of dog and cat chow. "But there'll be enough die-hard ranchers, rancher wannabes, weekend farmers and pet owners to make an okay living for a feed store if we stay up with the times. This county will always have its dogs and cats and goats and rabbits and horses. Whatever critters people want to own or raise, we'll be here to take care of their needs." He grinned at her. "Besides, the barbershop can't be the only place where men go to gossip."

She glanced over the to-do list she made yesterday. The shipments of Nature's Variety and Paul Newman dog food were coming in today. At first, the new owner, Bill, was reluctant to carry any of the fancy organic dog foods, afraid their higher prices would scare customers off. But she convinced him that the new breed of pet owners moving into the once primarily rural San Celina County were not people who would balk at buying the best for their pets. Her next idea that she was going to run by Bill was stocking the ever-growing-in-popularity raw food diet touted by magazines like *Whole Dog Journal* and *Bark*. Then she'd broach the lucrative suggestion of pet toys and beds. Bill was old school, but he trusted Mel enough to give these new products a try. Last month the store actually made money, which made Bill happy. He'd really only expected it to be a place for his grandsons to appear to be working.

Mel had been there only a half hour when her first customer of the day, Rocky Sanchez, walked through the door. She was cleaning an old saddle that Mrs. Tenorio, a widow lady from Cayucos, wanted to sell. It had been her husband, Oscar's, she told Mel when she brought it in yesterday in the back of her ancient Ford pickup. He used it for fifty-seven years, starting when he worked for the Hearst Ranch back in the fifties. He died last year of a heart attack. Mrs. Tenorio didn't want to sell it, but the taxes were due on her little house, and she didn't have the money to pay them. She was hoping someone would buy the saddle since, she said, they hadn't kept horses for years and had no children to leave it to. It was filthy and stiff from nonuse, and Mel couldn't imagine anyone wanting to buy it, but she spontaneously offered to clean it in hopes that some kind person would see its homely beauty and feel drawn to it.

"Beautiful carving," Rocky said, reaching over to touch the fender that Mel had been meticulously cleaning with saddle soap.

"Yeah, I was surprised. It's an old working saddle that looked kinda tacky when Mrs. Tenorio brought it in. Wasn't sure anyone would buy it, but now I'm thinking it might have a chance."

Rocky's broad, smooth face looked thoughtful. "I preached Oscar's funeral. Great old guy. Lived to be ninety-six and was still riding the last year of his life. Gracie's had it a little tough financially since he's been gone. Both their children died before they turned eighteen." He shook his shiny bald head at the tragedy.

"That's rough," Mel said, setting down her chamois cloth and grabbing a paper towel to wipe off her slick hands. The smell of the saddle soap always reminded her of August, who first taught her how to clean leather. "What can I get you, Padre Sanchez?"

"Rabbit feed," he said. "I'm doing visitations today, and I'm going to see Lenora up in Cayucos, and she needs some food for her floppy ears. Maybe I'll drop by Gracie's house as long as I'm up there. How much she asking for the saddle?"

Mel went over to the aisle where they stocked the rabbit food. "Three- or five-pound bag?"

"Make it five. That'll last her awhile."

Mel tucked it under her arm and walked back to the counter. "That'll be six fifty."

He pulled a worn leather wallet from the back pocket of his dark blue Levi's. "About Gracie's saddle . . ."

"Oh, forgot to say. I sold it." She made the decision on the spur of the moment. She knew what Rocky was going to do: buy the saddle himself so Mrs. Tenorio could pay her tax bill. He was always doing things like that, which is why, she'd heard Magnolia complain in an indulgent voice, they had an almost-full storage unit they rented over by the golf course. She kept threatening him that they'd have a big old garage sale someday. Not, he told her seriously, until the people whose possessions he'd bought had died.

He looked at her from under thick, bushy eyebrows, not fooled a bit. "Do tell? And who bought the old thing?"

She just smiled at him. "Now, you know I can't tell you that." Gracie Tenorio had wanted three hundred dollars for it. Mel had about almost two fifty saved in the blue Maxwell House coffee can. She'd find the rest somewhere.

"You're a good girl," Rocky said, patting her shoulder. "God will reward you for your kind heart."

She avoided his eyes. "You going to the lighted boat parade tomorrow night?"

He nodded. "Magnolia and I are wimping out this year. We've reserved a table inside the Happy Shrimp."

"So did August and Polly. I think you all are smart. I'll be out in the cold freezing my tail off taking photos of Bert and Ernie and their kayak brigade."

"Wear your long underwear, and pray for no wind."

"That's your department."

"He doesn't listen any better to me than he would you; that's a fact."

She looked him directly in the eyes. "I'm not so sure about that."

Rocky gave her a big smile, white, white teeth against dark brown skin. "Well, I am, and I am an educated man. I've got a piece of pretty parchment paper that declares it to be so."

"Tell Mrs. T. that I've got her money here. I can mail her a check or pay her cash."

"I'll tell her."

After Rocky left, business picked up, and there was a steady stream of customers for the rest of the morning. Mel was glad, because it gave her little time to think about Patrick. She knew that he wouldn't just go away. He was absolutely convinced that she had the rest of Sean's money. Somehow she would have to persuade him that she didn't even believe it existed.

The boys finally showed up about noon, three hours late, their sun-streaked hair still damp and wild from surfing. She was hungry, her nerves jangly from apprehension and too much coffee. She was in no mood for their jokes.

"Hey, Mama Mel," said Brad, the older by ten months. "Business been good?" He flashed a perfect smile, thanks to thousands of dollars of orthodontia and an image-conscious society mother. They both could have posed for *Surfer* magazine or an Abercrombie & Fitch ad.

"You said you'd be here by nine," she snapped.

"Man, the waves were awesome," Evan said, picking up her freshly poured fifth cup of coffee and taking a swig. "You gotta go with the flow." He was shorter than his brother by two inches and had a slightly broader nose. Other than that, they could have been sun-kissed twins.

"That sounds like bad Beach Boys dialogue," she said. "And that's my coffee."

"Ah, don't be mad," Brad said. "This enough?" He pulled out a damp wallet and took out three fifty-dollar bills.

She growled, grabbed the soggy money and stuffed it in her front pocket. Her official wage was ten bucks an hour, so this was a lot for six hours' work. The boys knew she could be bought, and though she had once had vague misgivings about taking their money, that false pride vanished long ago. She always needed money, and they had it to spare. The fact that they were born into so much wealth wasn't her business or her problem. This money would more than make up the bulk of what she needed to buy Mrs. Tenorio's saddle.

She gave them a quick rundown on what had been delivered today, who was coming in to pick up feed and other things they'd ordered.

"John Preston's picking up that fencing for his Labrador puppies," she told Evan who had settled down on the stool behind the counter, making eyes at a young woman who was perusing the new horse blankets Mel had ordered from a family of Spanish weavers in northern New Mexico. They were going like hotcakes despite the fact that they were five times as expensive as normal horse blankets. The young, afflu-ent horse girls going to Cal Poly loved the bright, Native American–style patterns and were using them to decorate their dorm rooms. Bill would be pleased at the profit margin.

"Yeah, okay," Evan said, not looking at her. The girl, a willowy red-head with a French braid, giggled to her girlfriend and made eyes back.

Mel sighed, then reached over and knocked on his head like she was testing a cantaloupe. "Earth to Ernie. Just don't close before he gets here. He'll be here by four."

"Okay, okay," he said, turning to grin at her. "John Preston. Puppy fencing. Four o'clock."

"You've got the camera all charged up for tomorrow night?" Brad asked.

"Don't worry, it has plenty of time to charge."

"So, got a wild Friday night planned?" Brad laughed.

"The wildest," she said, her voice sardonic. They knew that the row-diest thing she ever did was go to dinner with Love. Sometimes, after Love went home, Mel went for a beer and some pool at the Rowdy Pelican. But usually she just walked home. "Don't forget to balance the cash register."

"Okay," Evan said.

"No, I meant Brad," she said.

"Got it," Brad said. "What's with the grody saddle?"

"It's mine," she said. "I'm going to put it in the back. When I finish cleaning it, I think I'll take it out to the Johnsons', see if it fits one of their horses." In reality, she was going to stick it in the corner of her liv-ing room. She kind of liked the idea of Oscar Tenorio's benevolent cow-boy spirit watching over the place while she wasn't there.

"Whatever." Brad lifted one shoulder.

Deciding to fix herself a sandwich at home rather than go to the Buttercream, she walked the five blocks to her house. The streets were starting to get busy. Tourists were already straggling in for the lighted boat parade tomorrow night. Though many locals complained about out-of-towners coming in and taking over Morro Bay, Mel had a more practical view. She'd grown up in Las Vegas, a town that depended on tourists to survive. She knew that without tourists from L.A. or San Francisco or the Central Valley, the town of Morro Bay would eventually dry up and blow away. Though it had originally started as a fishing village, commercial fishing hadn't truly supported the city for many years. And with ranching rapidly becoming a thing in the county's bucolic historical past, tourism and the state university in San Celina twelve miles away were becoming more important in keeping Morro Bay's little businesses alive. Yes, the tourists could be a pain in the butt sometimes, but the town needed them. When locals complained at the Buttercream, Mel rarely joined in. She was tempted to say, You haven't seen truly world-class jackass behavior until you've worked the eleven p.m. to seven a.m. Las Vegas Boulevard beat. Every bad behavior known to man and woman was quintupled in Las Vegas.

She unlocked the front door of her house and immediately checked the answering machine. There was one flashing light. Her left temple started throbbing. Patrick again? She was tempted to just grab her personal papers, a few clothes and her favorite books and take off. But she couldn't do that. A part of her was stubborn enough to think, it's *my* life here. I'm not going to be intimidated by anyone. She'd figure out some way to convince Patrick that he was barking up a tree that was completely empty. Mel punched the Listen button with more force than needed. She was relieved to hear Love's voice.

"Hi, it's Love. I guess you've already gone to the feed store. I won't bother you there, but give me a call when you hear this. I'll fill you in on the latest about my granddaughter. Bye, now." The call came in at seven thirty a.m.

Mel played the tape another time, trying to discern from her friend's voice whether things were going well or not. But Love rarely showed in her manner or her voice what she was really feeling. She was one of the most even-tempered and calm people that Mel had ever known. Such a contrast to Genetta LeBlanc, Mel's mother, who still lived in Las Vegas with her fifth husband. At least, Mel thought it was her mother's fifth. She didn't really try to keep track anymore. She hadn't gone into details with Genetta about what really happened with Sean. Though it had been in the newspapers for weeks, her mother wasn't the type to pay attention to the news. Drinking, dancing and playing blackjack were about all that interested her mother. She'd been that way for as long as Mel could remember. Genetta had been beautiful at one time, was a showgirl at the old Stardust hotel, where she'd met Mel's dad. Now, at fifty-nine, she looked ten years older, though she tried to hide her age with glitzy clothes and thick pancake makeup. Just another aging show-girl drinking watered-down whiskey sours and dreaming of the big jackpot. Had Patrick called Genetta to find out where Mel was living? Once Mel settled down in Morro Bay, she'd told her mother not to tell anyone where she was, though she also knew that if Patrick called Genetta when she was drinking, she'd probably reel off Mel's whereabouts without a second thought.

It was more likely that Patrick just used his police connections to find Mel or paid some computer geek to find her online, despite the fact she'd tried to stay under the radar by not opening up any bank accounts or credit cards, and not giving her old job a forwarding address. Still, she did have a social security number and did pay her income taxes. That put her on the grid. Maybe the next place she went, she should just work for cash under the table.

She picked up the phone and dialed Love. Listening to someone else's problems would help her forget her own. While the phone rang, she tried to ignore the heavy feeling that crowded her chest, like a balloon filling with helium. Would Patrick call again? Or worse, show up on her doorstep?

"Hello?" Love's voice was strong, upbeat.

"It's Mel. How're things going with the kid?"

"We're managing." Love gave a quick laugh. "She's got the flu. Oh, dear, I didn't mean to laugh. It's not funny, just ironic."

"She going to be okay?"

"Yes, she's much better this morning. I asked Clint's son to look at her last night. He's a doctor."

"He made a house call? Man, you do have pull in this town."

Love laughed again, more relaxed this time. "I think Clint just wants to make sure I get my column in on time. Do you mind if Rett joins us for dinner tonight? If she's up to it, of course."

Mel took a deep breath. "Sure. Actually, I thought you might want to have dinner with her alone."

"Plenty of time for that. I like *our* dinners. I don't want to miss one."

"Me either." Mel almost said thanks but kept silent. Did Love understand what a profound thing she just said? Mel would have totally understood if Love had said she needed time to visit with her granddaughter, that her friendship with Mel would have to take a backseat. But she essentially told Mel, you're just as important to me as family. It made Mel's chest tight with gratitude.

"Okay, see you at the Shrimp," Love said. "Bye, now."

When Mel hung up the phone, stubbornness started to take hold inside her chest. Like her father's Cajun ancestors, she had a deep-seated sense of survival. No one was going to take her new life away from her. She'd dig her heels into this loamy soil and fight to keep it. It's what Cy would tell her to do. It's what Grand-mère Suzette would expect from her.

"Bring it on, Patrick O'Reilly," she said out loud to the empty room. "If you come here and mess with what I have, I'll make you wish you hadn't."

SIXTEEN

Rett

O h, my dear little Loretta," Polly cried, when Rett climbed out of
Love's truck. The old woman's wrinkled cheeks were a shiny rose
color. "I'm your great-grandma Polly, and I never thought I was going
to see you again this side of heaven!" She came down the front steps of
the brown and white two-story clapboard ranch house.

Rett walked tentatively across the mottled grass toward the woman
who was dressed in a full print skirt, a high-necked white blouse and
new-looking red sneakers. On the fifteen-minute drive to the ranch,
Love told her a little about the Johnsons, Rett's great-grandma and great-
grandpa, how the ranch had been in the family for almost a hundred
years, how August once worked at some famous guy's ranch, Hertz or
something, who built a castle for his girlfriend. The castle was somewhere around here. She told Rett how Polly had made a hundred quilts
by hand to give away to foster kids. It was like some weird dream or a
Lifetime cable movie.

Rett let the woman hug her and ramble on while Love unloaded the
bags of milk, butter and cheese they'd bought at the grocery store. The
woman—her great-grandma—smelled like cinnamon and flowers. Rett

circled the woman's narrow shoulders with her own arms, feeling like a complete idiot. What was she supposed to say?

"Uh, it's good to see you too." Now that sounded totally lame and bogus. Why hadn't she thought up something cool to say? Some creative artist she was.

"Come in, come in," Polly said. "Do you like chicken salad? I baked a peach pie this morning. Peaches from our own trees from last summer. Used my last frozen bag. They weren't as good this year as last, but still pretty tasty." She glanced over at Love. "Do you need any help, sweetie?"

Love smiled at them both. "You two just go on in. I can manage."

Polly looped her arm through Rett's and practically pulled her up the steps. When they got to the top step, an old man came out of the front door. He wore a pair of faded overalls and a plaid shirt. He stooped a little at the shoulders, reminding Rett of the gnarly old apple tree that grew in the backyard of their house in Knoxville.

"Now, who is this?" the old man said, not moving toward Rett.

"This is Loretta," Polly said. "Your great-granddaughter from Tennessee. "Loretta, this is your great-grandpa August."

August stared at her a moment, then he smiled. "Oh, Polly, you kidder. You think I don't know my own baby sister, Agnes?" He came over and hugged Rett. "You're looking good, Aggie. How's things in Kansas City? That husband of yours keeping you busy?"

Rett turned her head to look at Love, who had just come up the steps in time to hear the old man's comment. What was she supposed to do now? Did this crazy old guy really think she was his sister in Kansas City?

"August, quit your teasing," Polly said, her smile stretching across her face. "Let's go have lunch." She moved past Rett and opened the wooden screen door, letting it slam behind her with a thunk.

"How about giving your favorite daughter-in-law a hug, August," Love said, rescuing Rett, trying to communicate something with her eyes, though Rett couldn't figure out what.

"You wait your turn," he said, giving a deep, rumbling laugh. "I haven't seen Aggie in years."

"This is Rett," Love said evenly, holding out a bag of groceries.

He automatically reached for it, letting go of Rett. Rett moved quickly away, not sure what was going on here.

"Rett?" he said.

"Yes, this is your great-granddaughter, Loretta Johnson. But she likes to be called Rett."

He smiled over at her, touched a free finger to his green sun-faded Farm Supply cap. "As in Butler?"

Rett was on familiar ground now. Old people always said that. "Yeah, except there's no *h* in my name. And I'm a girl."

"Well, so you are," he said. "Hope you like peach pie, Rett who is a girl." He opened the screen door and went inside without waiting for her answer.

"What's going on?" she whispered to Love.

Love touched her bottom lip with her fingers. "Aggie was his little sister who died sixty years ago. He gets a little confused sometimes."

A little? Rett thought. Get a clue, Grandma. He thinks I'm a dead woman.

"Let's just go in and enjoy lunch," Love said with a sigh.

"Whatever," Rett said under her breath, following her into the house. What was she supposed to do if he called her Aggie again, pretend that she was this dead woman?

Rett could tell everyone was on edge, trying to be friendly. She wished she could just tell them to chill, that she wasn't going to bite. Then again, it was kind of cool, in a mean-girl sort of way, to be the one people were trying to impress. Usually it was she who was all nervous and shaking in her boots.

They ate in the dining room seated at a round oak dining table with claw feet. There was enough food to feed twenty people.

"We'll eat like fancy folks this time," Polly said, "because it's your first visit. After this, it's lunch at the kitchen table like any other member of the family."

Love winked at Rett. "I had to marry their son before I was allowed to eat in the kitchen."

"That's when you became family," Polly said, completely serious. "Rett was family the moment she was born."

Rett looked at Love, expecting her to be mad. It seemed like kind of a snarky remark. But Love just smiled.

After lunch, her great-grandpa suggested taking Rett on a tour of the ranch.

"We can all go," Love agreed.

"I'll stay here," Polly said when Rett helped her carry the dirty dishes into the big yellow and blue goose-themed kitchen. "I've seen every inch of this ranch a million times. When you get back, we'll have peach pie with ice cream."

When they went to the barn, Love argued with August about who was going to drive the jeep. The rust-eaten vehicle was from the fifties and it no longer had windows and the windshield had a long crack down the passenger side. Rett would have loved to have driven it, but she wasn't in the running.

"I need the practice on the stick shift, Pop," Love said, climbing into the driver's seat.

He grumbled but took the front passenger seat, anyway. "Women these days. You all want to run the world."

"Yes, sir, we do," Love said, starting the engine. "You know it all began during the war when they let us start wearing pants." She turned and gestured at Rett to hop in the backseat. "Why don't you tell Rett what you did in the war? She hasn't heard your stories a hundred times like the rest of us."

"You're the youngest," Love said when they came to the first gate. "That means you're in charge of the gates."

"I'm what?" Rett said.

"You jump out and open and close the gates behind us," August said, chuckling. "Youngest cowboy always gets that job."

She didn't mind it too much except that each gate seemed to have a different kind of lock or homemade hooking system so each one took her forever. Couldn't these people, like, buy one kind in bulk at Costco?

They drove around the ranch on narrow dirt roads Love told her

were built by August; her grandfather, Cy; and her father, Tommy. After
pointing out different wildflowers and trees, so many that there was no
way Rett would remember them all, August told stories about his time
as a signalman on a ship—the U.S.S. *Teal*—outside the Aleutian Islands
during the war.

"I couldn't wait to get back to California," he said, turning back to
give Rett a wide, yellow-toothed smile. "No siree, Bob. We knew what
war was. And it was cold up there! Makes a man appreciate the Central
Coast. But sometimes I miss it. Wonderful men I worked alongside. You
kids now don't know squat about fighting a *real* war. Our war was a real
war."

"You mean Vietnam?" Rett asked, not exactly certain where the
Aleutian Islands were. The shocked look on his face made her realize
her mistake. "Oh, I get it. World War II. Like my—" She almost said
boyfriend's. "My banjo. It's a prewar Gibson."

August's wrinkled lips turned up in a smile. "You play banjo?"

She nodded, feeling on more comfortable ground now. "Also the
guitar, some mandolin and a little fiddle. But mostly I like the banjo."

"Do say," August said. "Maybe you'll play for us sometime."

"Sure," Rett said, embarrassed now that she'd bragged about an instrument that wasn't technically hers. The thought of giving it back
made her stomach hurt. That was stupid. Was she in love with Dale or
his banjo? His dark eyes suddenly painted themselves inside her head,
and she shivered, remembering the feel of his full bottom lip. She
blinked quickly, trying to outrun the tears. Would she ever be able to
think about him without feeling like she'd been slapped in the face?
What was it going to be like to see a reminder of him every time she saw
her niece or nephew? What if he and Patsy got married? She pressed a
fist on her stomach, feeling like she was going to throw up.

Love didn't join the conversation, though Rett thought she saw her
grandma's back stiffen when Rett called it her banjo. Fine, so her
grandma thought she was a total thief. Who cared? Except that deep
inside, Rett knew she really did. She wanted her grandma to . . . she
wasn't sure what . . . be proud of her? Why did she care about what
someone who didn't even know her thought?

After the hour-long tour, when they were back in sight of the ranch house, Love brought the jeep to a stop under a huge oak tree in the middle of a smooth pasture.

"This was where your grandpa and I got married," Love said. "So did Polly and August."

Rett jumped out of the jeep to look closer at the huge oak tree. Its trunk was scratchy to her touch and about a million shades of gray and brown. A black lightning-shaped mark scarred the trunk. "Did Mom and Dad . . . ?"

Love shook her head. "Your mom preferred getting married at the Episcopalian church in San Celina. It *is* a beautiful old stone church."

"We call it the lightning tree," August said. "That mark's been there since I was twelve. Remember the storm that brought it. Flooding like I've never seen before or since. We lost fifty head of Angus. Ever so often one of the newspapers does a story on it, sends out a person to take a picture."

"Cool," Rett said, running her fingers over it.

After pie and ice cream, Rett and Love started back to Morro Bay with the promise they'd come on Sunday to help decorate the Christmas tree. Rett was thankful that her grandma didn't want to talk on the drive back. She was exhausted from trying to make conversation with old people. It was three thirty when they returned to Morro Bay.

"At five thirty I have a weekly dinner with a good friend of mine," Love said, while they put away the leftover food pressed on them by Polly. "You're welcome to come. It's at my favorite restaurant down on the Embarcadero. Best fried shrimp on the coast." She opened the freezer door and started putting plastic bags of peaches and strawberries in the almost-empty space. "Do you like fish?"

Rett thought for a moment. She loved fried shrimp, but the idea of spending time with more old people seemed like more than she could handle.

"It'll only be about an hour," Love said. "I think you'll like Mel."

Rett looked at her grandma in surprise. Her friend was a man? Was he, like, her grandma's boyfriend or something? Now she was curious. "Okay."

Her grandma pointed to the Embarcadero from her back porch. It was a long street that ran along the bay. "At one time," Love said, "this town's whole identity was wrapped around the fishermen and their boats. But the biggest thing for sale now is our quaintness. That and salt water taffy." She gave a wide yawn. "I think I'll take a quick nap. Feel free to watch television or whatever. Oh, there's some photo albums next to the sofa. Lots of photos of your dad. Some of you girls."

After her grandma's bedroom door closed, Rett was tempted to call Lissa and see if she'd heard from Dale again. But she resisted. She only had nine minutes left on her phone, and she needed to save them. Instead, she sat in the living room and looked through the photo albums.

Even when her dad was in high school he didn't look much different than he did at twenty-three, the age he was when he was killed. Her mom didn't have many early pictures of Dad, so this was really weird for Rett, seeing him grow up in these photos. Since her grandma Love wasn't in most of them, she assumed that she'd taken them. She'd noticed the old Nikon sitting next to Love's chair on the sunporch. It wasn't a digital, so her grandma must take pictures the old way. That would be hard, she thought, 'cause you really didn't know what you were getting; you kind of had to do it by faith. Digital was so much better.

There were a few pictures of her and her sisters, though they ended after Rett was four, obviously when her grandma and her mom stopped talking. She studied her grandma's wedding photos, Love and Cy posed under the lightning tree. There was another photo of Mom and Dad underneath the same tree, a photo that Rett had never seen before. Dad's grin was as big as a pie plate, and Mom squinted into the sun, sort of half smiling. He wore a plaid shirt and jeans, and Mom wore a short denim skirt, a yellow tank top and about a dozen thin bangle bracelets. Rett remembered playing with those bracelets when she was a little girl. For some reason, the photo made Rett sad.

Two hours later, after feeding Ace, they started for the restaurant. Though they could see the Embarcadero from the cottage's back porch, they had to walk around the corner and down two blocks to reach it. It was colder than Rett expected, and she was glad that Love suggested she bring the blue hoodie that her grandma bought at the drugstore.

"It's crowded like this on Fridays," Love said, as they walked along the street that was filled with T-shirt shops, gift boutiques and fish restaurants. "During the summer or holidays, people from the Valley come here to escape the heat or just have a weekend away. The locals like to complain about them. But I've got many friends who live in the Valley. They remind me of my cousins back in Kentucky. Good-hearted, hard-working people without a lot of pretense."

"Valley?" Rett asked. "What valley?"

Love laughed and opened the shiny red doors of the Happy Shrimp restaurant. It stood between a tiny bookstore called Books by the Bay and a salt water taffy store called Louann's Taffy. "The Central Valley. Haven't you ever looked at a map of California? The Central Valley is one of the biggest sections of farmland in the United States."

"Oh," Rett said, feeling halfway dumb and halfway that she didn't care. She didn't want to ask any more because already she was beginning to catch on that her grandma liked to tell stuff to people, kind of like a teacher. It was okay, except that Rett sometimes had a hard time paying attention, especially when it was something she wasn't that interested in.

There was a line when they walked in, but Love moved past the people and gazed around the crowded restaurant. Three of the restaurant's walls were windows and, since it was dark, Rett could just barely make out Morro Rock, lit tonight by a cartoony crescent moon. There were pictures of shrimp everywhere: realistic, cartoons and some bold paintings showing shrimp wearing different types of hats. Love waved at someone and turned to Rett, "Mel's already got a table for us."

Rett followed her to a table in the corner where a dark-haired thirty-ish woman was standing up, one hand held high. Oh, crap, Rett thought. Mel was a woman. And not just any woman. She was the woman Rett flipped off yesterday in the Buttercream.

"Hey, Love," the woman said, giving Rett a cursory glance.

"Hey, yourself," Love replied. She turned to Rett. "This is my friend,

Melina LeBlanc. She likes to be called Mel. Mel, this is my granddaughter, Loretta Johnson. She likes to be called Rett."

"Hi, Rett." Mel's face held no expression.

"Hi," Rett said, feeling her face turn hot. What in the heck should she do now? Had this woman told her grandma that Rett flipped her off?

Before she had to think of something to say, the waitress came and reeled off the specials, all of them fish of some kind. Rett didn't hear a word and just ordered the shrimp and chips and a Coke.

"How was your day with Polly and August?" Mel asked, looking first at Love, then Rett. Rett's churning stomach calmed a little. Maybe this woman wouldn't tell her grandma that Rett gave her the finger. For some reason, she didn't want Love to hear about that. It was bad enough she thought Rett was a thief.

"They were thrilled, of course," Love said. "August and I took Rett for a tour of the ranch."

"What did you think?" Mel asked Rett.

Rett shrugged. "It's okay, I guess. It was pretty."

"Don't let your enthusiasm drown out the crowd," Mel said.

Rett glared at her. "I said it was pretty." What else did this woman expect her to say?

"So," Love interrupted. "What interesting people did you see today, Mel?" She looked sideways at Rett. "Mel runs B & E Feed over by the fire department. Your grandpa Cy and I used to own it. Mel worked for your grandpa."

Whoopee, Rett thought. She picked up a package of oyster crackers and started crushing them with her fingers.

Mel started telling Love something about a saddle and a cowboy named Oscar. Rett tuned them out and for the rest of the meal stared out the window at the sailboats bobbing on the moonlit purple and blue bay. The musical murmur of voices, the mysterious smell of the ocean, the briny taste of salt on her lips, the damp chill that seemed to reach into her bones, the foghorn in the distance, all those sensations made her feel like she was in a dream. Her life in Tennessee, Dale, Patsy, her mom, Lissa, her messy bedroom seemed like a life she'd lived years ago. And the thing was, she didn't miss it. Not any of it. Not even Lissa. She was ready to start a new life. She didn't care if she ever saw any of them again. Even Dale. Especially Dale.

"Anything else I can get you ladies?" the waitress asked, laying the check down on the table.

"Would you like dessert, Rett?" her grandma asked.

Rett looked down at her plastic basket, surprised to see that she'd finished everything. She didn't even remember eating. "No, thanks."

"I guess we should head on home," Love said. "Rett should probably get to bed early since she was not feeling well yesterday."

"I wasn't that sick," Rett said, irritated that Love was kind of trying to tell her what to do.

"Listen to your grandma," Mel said. "She's had a bit more experience than you at those sorts of things."

Rett had to hold back the urge to flip Mel off again. She acted like she was queen of the universe or something. Rett gave her a phony smile. "Who died and left you prison guard of the world?"

"Rett!" Her grandma gave a quick, nervous laugh.

Mel's bottom lip tightened, and Rett could tell she was holding back a reply. Though she'd never admit it, this lady kinda scared Rett. She looked like she'd go all Columbine on you.

"Let's call it a night," Love said evenly, standing up. "We'll see you at the lighted boat parade tomorrow night, Mel." She fumbled with her purse, searching for her wallet.

"Don't worry about it," Mel said, waving at her. "Dinner's on me."

"Thanks, sweetie," she said. They exchanged a look, which kind of pissed Rett off. At the same time it kind of made her sad. It was like they could talk without actually saying words. Rett had always wanted a friend like that. She'd thought she'd had it with Dale. The synonym for Rett Johnson should be *stupid girl*.

She followed her grandma out without saying another word to Mel. Just as they left the restaurant, she turned back to look at the woman, thinking she would be watching Rett and Love, probably still wearing that know-it-all expression. But Mel was staring at the black hole that was Morro Rock. Her face held a look that even Rett could tell from where she stood was one of deep despair.

The next morning while Rett was eating her second English muffin, the phone rang. Love answered the extension hanging on the wall next to the microwave.

"Yes, this is Love Johnson. Well, yes she is. May I tell her who's calling?" Love listened a few more seconds. "Just a minute. I'll see if she's available." She put her hand over the phone's mouthpiece. "It's Dale," she mouthed.

Rett froze, not certain what to do. Either Lissa had told him where she was, or Rett's mother had. It didn't matter, because the fact was, he found her. She chewed on her lower lip, wondering how much of a head start she had.

Love cocked her head, waiting.

"May as well get it over with," Rett said, tossing her half-eaten muffin on her plate. She could tell by the look on her grandma's face that she was happy Rett chose that route. She took the phone and said, "What?" She watched her grandma go into the living room, closing the kitchen door behind her, giving Rett her privacy. Thank you, Grandma, she thought.

"I'll tell you what," Dale said. "I want my friggin' banjo back."

Even though his words were angry, the sound of his throaty voice, a baritone pitched at just the perfect place, made her heart beat faster. She hated how it caused a longing that made her go all soft inside. How could she still feel like this about someone so creepy? She had to be the most pathetic girl alive.

"Yeah, well, I think I'd like my heart back, you stupid jerk." The minute she said the words, she wished she had said something else. Her line sounded so needy and lame and, worst of all, unoriginal.

"Rett," he said, his voice growing softer. "Look, I'm sorry—"

"Save it for the soaps," she interrupted. "Save it for my *pregnant* sister."

"Look," he said. "It's not what you think—"

"Not what I think!" she said, hearing her voice go all shrill, like her mother's did when she was mad. "You were screwing my sister at the same time you were telling me you loved me! What exactly does that sound like to you? Not something that would win any prizes from Dr. Phil, that's for sure."

"I just meant—"

"I don't care what you meant. Go tell it to my sister. Maybe she gives a crap, because I sure don't."

His voice grew cold over the phone. "Look, I've got a lot on my plate right now, Rett. All I want is my banjo back. You know how much it means to me, and I need it for this new gig. It's my big chance. We can discuss this whole mess some other time."

"Or like maybe, never." Take that, you donkey.

"I'm in San Celina. I know where your grandma lives. I can be there in a half hour."

Shocked, she slammed the phone down and ran through the living room past her openmouthed grandma. Ace followed her, barking, excited by the game. She pulled off her pajamas, threw on jeans, a sweatshirt and her boots. Almost tripping over the still-yapping dog, she grabbed the black banjo case.

"Oh, man, sorry, Ace." She bent down and patted his head. "Gotta go." She ran past her grandma. "Dale's on his way. Stall him for me."

"Wait!" she heard her grandma call after her. But Rett was young and fast and was down the street, leaving Love standing in the front doorway. Rett felt like the rottenest person on the planet leaving her grandma to talk to Dale, but she just couldn't see him right now. Not yet. And she wasn't ready to surrender the banjo.

Five minutes of running with the heavy banjo case was all she could manage. She slowed down to a walk, wondering what she should do now. She didn't know anyone in this town. Once again, she'd been totally stupid and jumped before she thought. She knew eventually she'd have to go back to her grandma's house where, no doubt, Dale would be waiting. Still, she could hold out as long as she could and decided to keep walking.

"Okay, Mister God," she murmured. "I'm asking for some kind of

sign here. I know that thieves aren't exactly your favorite kind of people, but you know I didn't steal Dale's banjo for no reason. He deserves
to be worried for a while. Look what he did."

She knew, even as she said the words, that really, they wouldn't convince God any more than they convinced her. Stealing was stealing.
Look at how people justify stealing music over the Internet, saying its,
like, public domain or whatever. They wouldn't be so casual about it if
they'd spent months writing a song, trying to get it right, and then if
they were lucky enough to get someone to publish it, people downloaded it for free. No, she knew that asking God to help her right now
was being the phoniest of phonies. Still, she thought, *still.*

She kept walking, turning back every once in a while to look at
Morro Rock, a beacon that told her that she couldn't really get lost in
this town, the rock that watched over the town like a sentry guard. Like
how all the songs she'd sung growing up in the church called Jesus the
rock. She kind of got it now. From so much of this town a person could
see Morro Rock. But even if you couldn't see it, it was still there. Like,
well, like God. It's not like she never thought about what she sang about
as a kid, but now it was beginning to kind of get deeper; she could see
where the songwriters were coming from when they compared things.
It made her want to go see Morro Rock up close, see exactly what it
was made of, what it felt like, how it smelled.

But first she had to figure out a way to get out of this mess. For a
moment, she regretted everything: stealing Dale's banjo, running away
from home, even being so pissed at her older sister. How much simpler
life would have been if she'd just pretended like she didn't care when
she found out Patsy was pregnant by Dale. She could have just been
cool about it, kept her face expressionless, like that lady Mel did.
Though Rett didn't like her very much, she did admire her ability to stay
cool. How did a person learn that? Rett sure wished someone could
teach her.

She stopped, out of breath, and looked around. She'd stayed away
from the main downtown street and was walking along a side street.
She wasn't stupid; she knew that if Love or Dale wanted to, they could
find her in two minutes if they were driving. She didn't have a watch,

but she figured it had to be at least a half hour, so it was likely he was at her grandma's house right now. What would Love do? Would she stall him or help him find Rett? She didn't have a clue. Her grandma seemed like the kind of person who did the right thing. But would her right thing be to protect Rett or help a guy recover his stolen property?

To her left was the post office, busy this Saturday morning. People were carrying in packages decorated with Christmas stickers. For a moment, Rett wondered what they were doing in Knoxville. Mom always had the coolest Christmas trees. Rett had to give her that. Their Christmas trees were always famous wherever they lived. They were a different theme every year. Last year it was soldiers and flags, honoring those serving in Iraq. The local paper even took a picture of it and put it on the front page. Mom smiled for days afterward. Christmas was always a good time in their house, though Rett doubted it would be this year.

She walked past the post office, trying to ignore the sad feeling. Next to the post office was the fire department. The yellow fire truck had a fake green Christmas bough with a fancy gold bow attached to its grill. Next to the fire department was B & E Feed. She stopped and stared at the red wooden building. A chalkboard next to the open door said, "Don't forget your feathered friends this holiday season! Wild bird-seed—half price—today only."

This was the feed store her grandpa once owned. She'd seen a picture of it in one of Love's albums when it was called Cy's Feed and Seed. It was where Love had told Rett that her dad had worked. It occurred to Rett in that moment that these were the streets her dad, that man she remembered holding her, his laugh a deep rumble against her tiny ear, lived and played and learned to do, well, everything a person had to learn to be a grown-up. Her *father*. Her chest felt like someone had pumped air into it, and with one prick she'd explode like a balloon. He grew up here. His father owned this feed store. Whenever she'd heard the word *family*, it was her mother and sisters who instantly came to mind. Maybe, if pressed, her grandfather Murphy, though he was mostly someone who was good for a check on her birthday and at Christmas. In that moment her concept of family changed. My people—she'd heard that remark hundreds of times in the little churches they sang at throughout

Tennessee, Georgia, Arkansas and Alabama. Old people were always talking about "their people" and "your people." The words had never meant much to her. Until now. She kind of got it now.

She switched the banjo case to the other hand and walked into the feed store. It was warm inside and smelled nutty, like cooked oatmeal. Before she could glance around, Mel walked out of a back room behind the counter, holding a sheaf of papers. Her head was down when she asked, "May I help you?"

She glanced up before Rett could answer.

"Oh!" Mel said. Her face didn't look mad or sad, just surprised.

Rett hesitated a moment, thinking, well, Mister God, maybe this is your answer? Was it just an accident she picked this street to walk down? Or was it just some big cosmic joke? Whatever it was, right now, this woman Mel was her only hope.

"Actually," Rett said. "I kind of do need your help." She paused, then reluctantly added, "Please?"

SEVENTEEN

Love Mercy

"I'm here to see Rett." The man's low, melodious voice sounded like water gliding over smooth river stones.

Love peered at him through the screen door. Though she had never been the kind of woman who looked at every man she met as a potential source of romance, she also wasn't blind to the charms of the opposite sex. There was no doubt that this young man with the thick auburn hair who stood at the bottom of her porch steps was a fine-looking specimen. Yes, this man with the smoldering dark eyes and long, thick sideburns straight out of the seventies definitely exuded pheromones or whatever it was that drew good women to bad men like ants to sugar water.

She narrowed her eyes, not a bit fooled by nature's peacock display. This man had also broken the hearts of not one, but two of her granddaughters and she was ready to let this *child molester* have the full brunt of her anger.

Dale came up to the second porch step, causing Ace to throw his bullet-shaped body against the screen door. The man backed down, startled by Ace's deep bark. When he looked closer and saw Ace's size, he gave a relaxed chortle.

"All bark—" he started.

"Plenty of bite," Love snapped. "Stay where you are, young man."

"Ma'am," he said, his sexy voice taking on a little steel. "I don't mean to bother you, but, like I said, I'm here to see Rett, not you."

"I don't know where she is." She tried not to imagine this experienced male's voice whispering silky promises to both Rett and Patsy.

"She's got my banjo, and I want it back."

She pushed Ace gently aside with her foot and stepped out on the front porch, cradling Cy's shotgun in her arms.

"Whoa, now," the man said, holding up his hands and backing down the steps. "No need for that." He nervously touched the side of his shiny dark hair, combed in an Elvis-like rockabilly pompadour that reminded Love of the backwoods Kentucky boys at Redwater High who drove two-tone Chevys and ran 'shine for their daddies.

"I don't know where she is," Love said. "And I don't have your banjo. Now get yourself gone right now."

He hesitated, not certain if she was serious.

"I'm from Redwater, Kentucky, son," she said, exaggerating her drawl. "We don't cotton to older men taking advantage of young girls."

His eyes darted from side to side like a panicked bull.

She couldn't help feeling a tiny bit sorry for him. She had been the mother of a young man. She knew that they were often brash, unthinking and way too ruled by hormones. Look at how her Tommy had just up and left his whole life behind because he'd fallen in love and lust.

Still and all, her son married the girl. He took responsibility for his actions. This man had wantonly used two young girls, *her granddaughters*. She wasn't about to let some vague motherly feelings let him off the hook.

"Rett is not here, and neither is your . . . the banjo," she repeated.

"You got it right the first time. It's my banjo."

"I told you she's not here."

"She's in town. I just talked to her. I won't leave without my banjo."

They glared at each other in a stalemate. She knew that legally he was completely in the right. But all she could think of was that she had to protect Rett, help her resolve this situation, though she didn't have a clue how. When in doubt, stall for time had always been Love's philosophy. Then hightail it to someone who knew more than you did about the subject in question.

Using her sweetest cajoling tone, Love said, "Look, Dale. Rett is real hurt and angry, and from what I understand, has a mighty good right to be. I know that takin' your instrument wasn't the wisest thing she could've done, but try to see her point of view." She drew out the try, using a long *a*—traah. She paused. Should she bring up Patsy's pregnancy? No, best keep things as calm as possible, at least until she found Rett and talked her into giving this boy back his instrument. The situation with Patsy could be dealt with later.

"I'll go to the police," he said, his cheeks flushing pink.

She readjusted the shotgun in her arms, causing him to flinch. But he held his ground. She was tempted to smack his shoulder and tell him to grow up. Instead, she inhaled deeply and said, "There is no need to go to the police. Let me find her. I'm sure I can talk her into givin' you the banjo, and everyone can walk away . . ." She almost said happy, but that certainly wasn't an emotion that was likely going to result from any of this. "Satisfied. Just give me a little time."

His chest filled with air, reminding her of one of those lizards who tried to make themselves look bigger to intimidate an enemy.

"Okay," he finally said. "I'll give you three hours before I go to the cops. I'm staying at the Holiday Inn Express in San Celina."

"I may need a little more time," she said. "Come back at six p.m. That gives me . . ." She looked at her watch. It was eleven twenty-five. "A little more than six hours. After all the trouble you've caused, you can surely give me six hours to straighten things out."

He narrowed his eyes, trying to look dangerous. "No way. I—"

She matched his look with one of her own. "Exactly how old was Rett and Patsy when you started . . ." She didn't know what they called it these days—hooking up? Doing the horizontal hula? She shook her head. "I don't know what the laws in Tennessee are, but here in California, the legal system takes a dim view of adults who take sexual advantage of minors."

His smooth face changed from anger to panic in a millisecond. "Patsy was eighteen! I swear . . ."

She almost laughed at how easy he was to fool. Then she quickly sobered. It was a situation where one of her granddaughters was pregnant and the other was brokenhearted and guilty of grand theft . . . banjo. Nothing funny about either of those things. Well, the grand theft banjo part might be someday.

He pulled his cell phone out of his pocket and checked the time. "I'll be back at six p.m. My banjo better be here, or else." Before she could say another word, he turned around and headed down the walkway to the rental car parked on the street. The car spewed a puff of white smoke when he drove away.

It was now eleven forty. She had a little more than six hours to figure out how to save her crazy-in-love granddaughter's hide. She looked up and down the street, wondering where Rett could have gone. She sighed and went inside to fetch her car keys. Morro Bay wasn't that big, and she knew this town as well as she did her own front teeth. Rett couldn't have made it far on foot, and she barely knew anyone in town. Someone had to have seen her in the last half hour. Why hadn't Love thought to write down her cell phone number? Then again, Rett probably wouldn't have answered.

After driving around for ten minutes, she pulled over and decided to call for reinforcements. Then she would need some legal advice. Her first call was to Magnolia.

"Oh, Lord, I wish I had a picture of that. You totin' a shotgun to the door." Magnolia's laugh echoed through the phone. "We could hang it in the café next to the cash register. Scare the deadbeats into paying their tabs."

"Well, it wasn't loaded," Love said. "But he didn't know that."

"I'll find that girl within the hour or I'll give up my claim to bein' a true cracker. Well, half cracker."

"Thank you, Magnolia," Love said. "You're a peach, not a cracker. I'm heading over to Clint's office to see what he can advise me about the legal mess Rett might be in for taking this young man's property."

Magnolia's deep chuckle rang through the phone lines. "Well, butter my lips and call me a square of corn bread, you're finding out the joys of havin' a family pretty darn quick."

For a split second, Love was annoyed at her friend. "You don't have to sound so happy about my problems."

Magnolia's voice was instantly contrite. "Oh, Love, I'm sorry. I'm not laughing at you, I'm laughing with you. You've been to the moon and back with me and my girls. Remember when Cheyenne dyed her hair that horrible shade of purple? For heaven's sake, her head looked like a grape snow cone. I was about ready to hold her down, shave it all off and lock her in the basement—if I had one. You made me laugh, told me if that was the worst thing she ever did, I was lucky. It was just hair, you said. Then when Jade went and started dating her college professor? That nut job with the two ex-wives and scraggly goatee? He looked like Satan come to life. You said to keep my mouth shut and act like it didn't bother me one bit, that Jade was a smart girl, and she'd find out on her own he was a loser. And she did. All I'm sayin' is, you'll figure this out and everything will be okay . . . eventually. That's just part of bein' a family, havin' crazy times like this. I promise, when all the wash has gone through the cycle and is dried and put away, you'll be glad you went through this. It's a *bonding* experience. Hold on a minute."

Her voice moved away from the phone, and Love heard her take money, ring it up in the cash register and wish the person a grand day. "I'm back. I'm sorry if I was bein' flippant. All I'm sayin' is that this is just what family does. They drive you nuts, and then you forgive them. Trust me, you'll eventually pay Rett back by drivin' her nuts. You've kind of forgotten that's what family's about."

Love's annoyance flew out the window. "I know you're right. I guess I was just hoping that Rett and I could have a few nice times before we dove into an emotional quagmire like this."

"This emotional quagmire is why she showed up on your doorstep," Magnolia said. "It's really a blessing when you think about it. Maybe she would have never come lookin' for you if she'd been totally happy with her life."

Love contemplated her words. "It's weird to be thankful for something like what has happened with Rett and Patsy, but you're right; if it hadn't happened, there's no telling if I'd ever have seen the girls again."

"So, just deal with this and wait for the good times that are surely coming. Now, go on and talk to Clint. It's always good to know your legal options. I'll get to working on finding our little sneak thief, bless her crooked little heart."

"I'll have my cell phone on. Ring me the minute you find her."

"You got it, baby doll."

Clint Lawhead's office was down on the Embarcadero over a long-time Morro Bay gift shop, the Missing Shell. The owner of the shell shop, Belle Lebovitz, was seventy-five years old. She moved to California from Brooklyn in 1957, the same year the Dodgers came to Los Angeles. She'd married the man who started the gift shop that specialized in all types of seashells and seashell bric-a-brac. He died in a boating accident seven months after their wedding. She never remarried and never went back East.

"I'm a Dodgers fan," she'd tell people who asked why she never returned to Brooklyn despite the fact that all her family lived there. "When they go back, so will I." When Clint rented the upstairs offices from her when he started the magazine, she became his unofficial receptionist.

Love poked her head inside the store. Belle was perched on her rickety wooden stool behind the cash register, keeping one eye on her black-and-white television and the other on the three preteen girls picking through some buckets of neon-colored sand dollars.

"Hey, Belle," Love said. "The judge in?"

Belle slid off her stool and shrank four inches. She was barely four ten, though she claimed five feet. Her head of white hair was tinted a soft conch shell pink. "Where else does he have to go? How's things with the new grandmonster?" Her black eyes sparkled. "She give back that stolen banjo yet?"

Love wasn't a bit surprised that Belle knew the story. That was one of the things about being part of a small town you learned to live with. Since she'd always lived in one, here and in Kentucky, she couldn't even imagine having privacy. "I'm working on it. I need to ask Clint about the legal ramifications."

Belle laughed, a sharp goose honk. "That's the real reason I never went back to Brooklyn. Family's best taken once a year, like a flu shot. A quick poke, a little fever and you're set until next year."

Love smiled and didn't answer. Belle had the exact opposite view of family than Magnolia. Magnolia would have her whole family live on a big old compound, all within shouting distance, something her two girls complained about frequently. Love suspected her own comfort zone resided somewhere in between these two extremes.

"Tell Clint he's late with the rent," Belle said. "Tell him I'm thinking about talking to my lawyer." She goose honked again.

"You bet," she said, smiling. It was a joke that Belle said every time Love came to see Clint. "Let me know if you see my granddaughter."

"I'm on the case," she said, turning her eyes back on her three young customers. "Hey, girlies, if you ain't going to buy, quit fondling the shells."

Love walked around to the side of the building and up the wooden steps. She could have gone up to his office without checking with Belle, but the older woman loved being asked. That too was one of the things about living in a small town. Everyone put up with everyone else's eccentricities. It made a person slow down, whether they wanted to or not. There's an idea for a column, she thought. The things that slow us down in life—good and bad. She could take a photo of something to do with a stop sign. Stop signs were great to photograph, the more beat up, the better.

She walked into the small foyer that held a metal secretary desk. It was tidy as a doctor's exam room. Clint actually had five part-time employees, but none of them worked on Saturday.

"Clint?" she called out. His office door was closed, but through the pebbled glass door she could see the lights were on.

"Come on in," he called out.

He came around the wide oak executive desk when she opened the door. As always, his smile was genuine, and she started to feel herself relax. He was the kind of person who, the minute he walked in the room, made things feel calmer, like someone sprinkled the air with magical peace dust. She wondered if it was his years as a judge that gave him that sort of psychic power.

"It's good to see you, Love," he said, gesturing to a padded visitor's chair. "How's Rett feeling?"

"Fine," she said, taking a seat. "Physically, anyway. It might have just been a bit of travel fatigue. She seemed to get over it quick enough."

He took the other visitor's chair, scooting it around so they faced each other. His silver-streaked hair needed a trim, something that he said he never seemed to find time to do now that he was retired. His face, tanned and lined, had the look of someone who enjoyed the sun and didn't use sunscreen as much as he should. It made his light gray eyes look almost spooky, like the eerie, all-seeing eyes of an Australian shepherd. Love could imagine what power that gaze had on anyone standing before his bench. Final judgment eyes, Magnolia called them.

"Ah, the resilience of youth," Clint said, his eyes slitting with humor. "My own little whirlwind of mayhem went back home this morning. My potato chips are safe for the time being."

Love smiled. "Admit it. You miss him like crazy. He's a sweet boy, Clint."

"No thanks to me," he said lightly, grinning at her. "His mother was a saint."

Then it suddenly hit her. Garth's payment for his home visit. "Oh, Clint, I'm so sorry. I forgot to make Garth his cupcakes."

"No problem," he said. "He and I both knew you were a little distracted. We'll take a rain check. Trust me, he'll be back. Now, what can I do for you?"

"It is about Rett. She's . . ." She felt her neck start to get warm. For some reason, this was starting to be embarrassing. The thought of spilling her family's messy background in front of this man she admired and liked made her feel like running out the door. "This is a little embarrassing . . ."

Clint leaned over and took her hand, placing his on top of it the same way Rocky did when he wanted to comfort one of his flock. "Love, this is your old pal, Clint. Nothing you tell me can shock me or make me think any less of you."

"I'm not so sure about that. But I need some advice quick. My granddaughter has . . ." She almost said *borrowed*. "Oh, for Pete's sake, she stole a young man's banjo. A man who she had a relationship with, and they had a quarrel . . ." Oh, well, in for a penny. "They broke up because he was also having a relationship with my oldest granddaughter, Patsy, who is now pregnant. Patsy, that is, not Rett. Rett took this boy's—man's—banjo and hitchhiked here from Knoxville. He followed her and wants it back. He's threatening to go to the police. She took off before he came to my house, and I managed to convince him to wait until six this evening before doing that. Right now, I don't know exactly where she is. Magnolia's tracking her down. I'm afraid my granddaughter will go to jail, and I don't know what to do."

True to his judge training, Clint waited a long, thoughtful moment before answering. "Dale is this boy's name?"

She nodded.

"How old is he?"

"Twenty-six."

"How old is your granddaughter?"

She put both hands on her jittery thighs. "I know where this is going. Yes, she was underage when he was seeing her. I've tried that card already. That's why he's waiting until six before going to the cops while I try to find her. She's eighteen now, so I'm not sure what the law is on that, but that doesn't change that she stole his banjo."

He nodded. "Yes, you're right. How much is this banjo worth?"

She looked down at her hands clenching her thighs. "Twenty-five thousand."

Clint let out a low whistle and leaned forward, resting his elbows on his wrinkled khakis.

"It's not good, is it?"

Clint pressed his lips together, his brow furrowed. "No, it's not. That makes it grand theft. Crossing a state line makes it even worse. The sooner we can find her and convince her to give him back his banjo, the better."

"And if she doesn't, and he goes to the police?"

He stood up, running his hands down the sides of his slacks. "Let's not worry about that yet. Let's find her and see if we can talk her into being sensible. I'm guessing this young man would just as soon not have the police involved. He's not exactly squeaky clean."

"Okay," she said, feeling both helpless and relieved. If there was trouble, Clint Lawhead was someone you wanted to have on your side. Rett had no idea how lucky she was that Love had so many friends here in Morro Bay willing to help them.

"I'll get back in the car and start looking for her," she said.

"Good idea. Let me know as soon as you find her. I'll do some checking on my own. What's this guy's last name?"

She felt like groaning again. "I don't know. I didn't even think to ask."

"Where's he staying?"

"Holiday Inn Express in San Celina."

"I'll make some calls. I should be able to find out his name, and then I'll see what I can find out about him."

"Thanks, Clint. I owe you—"

"February's column and some cupcakes," he finished, laughing.

"Really, thanks . . ."

He placed a finger over his lips. "Shhh. Not a bother. Go find your fugitive granddaughter."

She was driving down Main Street on her way to the highway, thinking that maybe Rett was trying to hitchhike out of town, when her cell phone rang. She pulled over and answered it on the fourth ring, right before it went to voice mail.

"Hello, Magnolia? Did you find Rett?"

"It's Mel. Don't you look at your screen before you answer?"

She slumped back in the seat. "I usually do, but I wasn't paying attention. I'm a bit frazzled right now. Rett's run off—"

"She's fine. She's on her way back to your house. Evan's dropping her off."

"How did you . . . What did she . . . Oh, I don't even know what to ask."

"She came in here looking to hide from her pond scum of an ex-boyfriend. She told me the whole story, by the way."

She rested her forehead on the steering wheel. "I was going to tell you everything, but it's been a little crazy since she arrived."

"I have the banjo. It's locked in a closet at the feed store. What are you planning on doing?"

"I talked to Clint, and things are a little more complicated than I thought. Apparently the instrument is worth quite a bit of money."

"If I'd been her, I would have tossed it in the bay."

"Please, don't even say those words out loud! She could go to jail, Mel. We have to get that banjo back to Dale and convince him to leave, to forget this ever happened."

Mel was quiet for a moment. Love could hear her soft breathing over the phone line. "Hard to do with a baby on the way."

"Yes, it is. But first things first. We need to make sure that Rett is out of trouble, then we can worry about the baby."

"Your first great-grandchild."

Love lifted her head and looked through the windshield. She could see the old Bay Theater, just recently renovated by its new owner. A quiet, solitary few hours watching a movie sure sounded good right now. "You know, that didn't even occur to me until you said it. Makes me feel . . ."

"Old?" Mel laughed.

She paused a moment, then said, "Yes, but more sad. Cy would have been so excited."

Mel was quiet for a moment. "Yeah."

"Oh, Mel, I miss him so much."

"Me too."

She straightened her spine. There was no time to fall into a funk. "Okay, thanks for helping. I'll let you know when we need the banjo. Guess I'll see you at the lighted boat parade tonight."

"You bet."

When she arrived home, there was no sign of Rett. But as she was opening the side door that led to the kitchen, she heard Ace's excited barking. She looked out the kitchen window and saw Rett tossing a ball to him on the small patch of backyard grass. She set her purse down and walked out on the deck.

"Hey," Rett said, looking up at her.

"Hey," Love replied. She watched them play for a while, wanting to put off as much as Rett did the discussion they needed to have. A few minutes passed. "Rett, you know we have to talk."

Rett picked up the tennis ball and bounced it up and down in her hand. Ace sat her feet, his dark eyes boring a hole into the bright yellow ball. She tossed it, laughing as he scampered across the yard. Then she turned to Love, her smile falling away when she saw Love's sober expression. "Yeah, I know."

Love went back inside the house. A few seconds later, Rett followed, Ace at her heels.

"Let's sit down at the kitchen table," Love said. "I'll make some tea."

Rett shrugged and pulled out a kitchen chair, flopping down in it, attitude sticking out of her like prickles on a desert pear.

Love started talking as she filled the kettle with water, figuring it would be easier if they weren't just staring across the table at each other. "Dale came by. He's quite angry."

"He can join the party," she said bitterly.

She nodded, acknowledging that Rett had a reason to be mad. "As hurt as you are—"

"I'm not hurt; I'm pissed," she interrupted.

"Okay," Love said, turning on the stove and setting the kettle on the burner. "Duly noted. And with good reason. Nevertheless, you being angry at something he did . . ." She paused and added, "Something really, really cruel, doesn't make it right for you to steal his property." She grabbed two mugs from the tree and put a tea bag in each one.

"Doesn't the Bible say an eye for an eye? That's what I'm doing. He hurt me, so I'm gonna hurt him. I ought to just chop up that banjo in little pieces and see how he likes *that*."

Love was thankful that the banjo was safely in Mel's hands. "First, that saying is taken out of context almost all the time. Jesus actually says in Matthew that—"

Rett glared at her. "Yeah, yeah, that we're not supposed to actually try to get back at someone who wronged us, but that we're supposed to turn the other cheek."

Love raised her eyebrows, surprised.

"I spent, like, my whole life in Baptist churches. Some of it rubbed off."

"Then I don't need to remind you that we're supposed to love our enemies, forgive what they do to us."

Her pale blue eyes turned sly. "Like you have my mom?"

Love turned away, her heart beating double time. Her first thought was, You little brat. Then she had to admit . . . Rett was right. She'd never really forgiven Karla and, to be truthful, she wasn't sure she wanted to even now. She kept her back to Rett, wishing for a split second that her granddaughter had never showed up at her door. It was hard enough missing Cy, trying to learn how to make a life without him. He'd been gone only a little more than a year. It still felt like one of her arms was missing. And it was hard enough trying to figure out what she should do with August and his obvious descent into dementia, how she could help him and Polly stay at the ranch. Not to mention her friends and the life she had here, the daily problems of just being part of a community. Her eyes itched with the desire to cry. She swallowed hard, tasting bitter salt. She didn't need a smart-mouthed teenager on top of all that. She just didn't.

"Where is Dale now?" Rett said.

Love turned around and frowned at her. Rett was sharp enough to know when to let something go. The issue of Karla and Love would no doubt come up again someday . . . if Rett stuck around.

"He's at the Holiday Inn Express in San Celina," Love said. "I convinced him to wait until six p.m. before he called the police. I think you need to talk to him." She set the sugar bowl in the middle of the table.

Rett contemplated the information. "You know what? I will." She went to the wall phone, dialed a number from heart. She waited, obviously getting his voice mail. Where was he that he couldn't answer his cell phone?

"Dale Bailey, this is your old pal, Rett Johnson. Y'all better leave me and my grandma the heck alone, or I'll throw your precious banjo in the ocean and see how well it can surf. And you know I'll do it too. You call the police, and I swear I'll tell them you and I were doing it when I was fourteen. No, make that twelve, you lyin', cheatin' water mocca-sin." She set the phone down in the cradle and smiled at Love. "He didn't pick up, but I left a message."

Love tried not to show the dismay that permeated her body like a su-per virus. "Well, that's not likely to be much help," she eventually man-aged to get out. She definitely needed to talk to Clint again. And maybe Rocky. Both legal and spiritual intervention was, no doubt, going to be required.

"He'll back off for a little while," Rett said. "I'm going to take a shower. Aren't we going somewhere tonight?" She looked much too happy for someone who would possibly be going to jail by nightfall.

"The lighted boat parade," Love said, trying to erase the mental pic-ture of Rett's thin body in a baggy orange jumpsuit. Her granddaughter's constant bouncing between confidence and despair was beginning to wear on Love. Sometimes Rett seemed like a ten-year-old and sometimes she seemed like she was forty. "We watch it from the Embarcadero."

"Cool," she said, smiling. "What time do we leave?"

EIGHTEEN

Mel

H ey, Mel, get a shot of this!"
    Brad or Evan—she couldn't tell because of the garish Santa
Claus mask—held a Christmas-light-covered kayak paddle over his head.
The tiny bulbs twinkled like Disney fireflies.

She centered on the grinning Santa through the Canon's screen and
snapped a couple of shots, then gave him a wave. Surrounding him were
five other kayaks, all the paddlers wearing masks. There were two San-
tas, two elves, a Scrooge and a shark with glow-in-the-dark teeth and a
Christmas wreath around its rubbery neck.

She walked along the crowded Embarcadero looking for a good spot
on the dock to take photographs. The boys had loaned her their new
Canon digital with a zoom lens. They'd worked the afternoon shift, giving her time to sit in the back office, read the instruction book and figure out the camera's bells and whistles. It was a relief to have something
complicated and foreign to concentrate on. It certainly beat worrying
about when Patrick would pop up like some papier-mâché monster on
a third-class carnival ride. Unwanted surprises made her think of Love
and her on-the-lam granddaughter.

Shock was not an accurate enough word to describe what she felt this morning at the feed store when she found Rett standing in front of her, her pale, round face tear-streaked, her expression, half-scared, half-mad.

"What's wrong?" Mel demanded, thinking the girl and Love had gotten into a fight.

Rett's haltingly told story made Mel soften her harsh tone. Her heart went out to the girl. She certainly knew what it felt like to go all stupid over a guy.

Except, a little voice inside smugly commented, she's a kid and you're thirty-five *you-should-know-better* years old.

After hearing the girl's story, Mel agreed to hide the banjo until Rett could talk to this guy. But Mel didn't promise not to tell Love what was going on. So, when Evan showed up, she asked him to drive Rett home, and she called Love. She didn't like getting involved with this—mediating family problems had been her least favorite part of being a cop—but Love was her friend. When Evan returned to the feed store, Mel went home, telling him she'd see them tonight. She didn't tell him about the banjo. The less people who knew, the better.

She walked along the Embarcadero, her eyes involuntarily scanning the crowd, searching for Patrick's ruddy face—an older version of Sean's lean good looks. It annoyed her that Patrick had the advantage, that he could show up any moment without warning, and she'd be forced to deal with him on the spot. How could she convince him that she didn't have any of Sean's stolen money? How could she keep him from ruining this new life she'd carefully constructed? She knew she should have told Love about her past a long time ago, but there never seemed to be a right moment. She was fairly certain Love would have understood, would have believed that Mel was innocent. At least she hoped so.

She turned up one of the short T-piers that led to the edge of the bay. People stood three deep next to the metal railing, waiting for the boat parade to start. The air was crisp and cold, and the crowd murmur was congenial as people sipped mugs of hot chocolate, coffee and apple cider. Kids ran in circles, frantic and chirpy as seagulls, high on salt water taffy, the laughing crowd and the coming Christmas holiday. In the distance, she heard a boat horn sound—three short blasts—the signal for the parade to begin. Anticipating the boats, the crowd's collective sound rose, their laughter took on a sharp vibrato. A man with wide shoulders pushed in front of her without excusing himself. She shook her head but just turned around, looking for a less crowded spot when she ran right into August Johnson's broad chest.

"Hey, missy," he said. He wore his standard faded denim overalls and a red plaid flannel shirt.

"Hey, August," she replied, letting the camera drop to her chest, held in place by a thick strap. "I thought you and Polly reserved a table at the Shrimp."

His gray eyebrows furrowed. "Now what would we be doing with shrimp at a roundup? You know Mr. Hearst only serves tri-tip. Polly's back at the house making her pumpkin cobbler. She'll be coming by right about suppertime."

Mel stared at him a moment, at a loss for words. She searched his red-rimmed eyes for a twinkle, indicating that he was joking. They were friendly, normal-looking. This was August Johnson, Cy's father, the man who taught her how to drive a tractor, how to mend a barbed wire fence and tell the difference between a wild mushroom you could eat and one that would kill you.

"August, we're at the lighted boat parade." She talked slowly, choosing her words carefully. "In Morro Bay. The Christmas boat parade."

His heavy brows remained together. "We're going to the parade in Morro Bay, me and Polly. I'll pick her up in the truck right after I find those calves." He peered over Mel's shoulder, and she turned around, half expecting to see a herd of bawling calves waiting to be tagged and vaccinated. Instead, she saw a family of five dressed alike in green Christmas sweaters decorated with Rudolph and his red nose.

She lightly touched his forearm. "Let's find Polly. We have to help her carry that cobbler."

His eyes darted from side to side. He looked down, then back up and gave Mel a tentative smile. "Apples make good cobbler, but I believe I like pumpkin better."

"Me too," Mel said, gently leading him down the street toward the Happy Shrimp. "Let's find Polly. I bet she's waiting supper on us."

He nodded, going along with Mel with the trusting innocence of a child. That frightened her more than anything when she thought about all the psychos waiting to prey upon the weak and the helpless.

A block away from the restaurant they saw Benni Harper and Ford Hudson walking toward them.

"Hi, August," Benni called out. She wore a bright emerald cowboy shirt and a black felt cowboy hat with tiny green and red bells circling the narrow hatband. "You've got people looking for you, mister." She gave August a quick hug. Her animated face belied her worried eyes.

"We're going to pick up Polly," August said, smiling at her. "She's bringing her pumpkin cobbler to the roundup. Got calves waiting."

"I love Polly's cobbler," Benni said, looping her arm through his. "Let's go find her." Catching Mel's eye, she raised one eyebrow a fraction of an inch.

August narrowed his eyes, peering over at Hud. "I don't recognize you, young man. You must be new. You can show us what you can do by tagging those calves. But be careful, the chute's been a bit cranky lately."

"Yes, sir," Hud said evenly, touching a finger to the rim of his gray felt cowboy hat. He wore dark jeans and a fleece-lined Levi's jacket. "I'll be real careful."

"We might be able to keep you on if you can do the work. But Mr. Hearst don't hold with slackers. Keep that in mind." He shook his head. "That's a mighty fancy hat to be wearing to work on calves. I'd put it on a post if I was you."

"Good idea, sir," Hud said, his face completely serious.

At that moment, Gabe, Benni's husband, walked up. "August, your beautiful bride is looking for you." He and Benni exchanged troubled looks.

"We're going to find her now," Benni said, tucking August's arm next to hers. They watched as Benni led August toward the Happy Shrimp.

"Thanks," Mel said when they were out of earshot. "I think he just got a little confused." She cleared her throat.

"Polly noticed he'd been in the restroom a little too long," Gabe said. "Hud and I went to check on him. When he wasn't there, we were hoping he hadn't gotten far."

"I ran into him a few minutes before you showed up," Mel said. "He thought he was going to a roundup at the Hearst Ranch."

"He worked there in his younger years," Gabe said. "Has he been evaluated by a doctor?" Gabe tugged absentmindedly at the corner of his thick, silver-laced black mustache. Though he wore faded Levi's and a dark red sweater, he still exuded a police chief's authority.

"Not that I know of," Mel said, resisting the urge to say "sir." "We have noticed some memory lapses for the last few months, but nothing like this. It started a little while after Cy died." She ducked her head, the last two words causing her eyes to burn. She didn't want either of these men to notice.

"Has he had any falls?" Gabe asked.

"He fell a few weeks ago, banged up his leg and scraped his head. He was alone in the barn when it happened, so we don't know how bad the fall was. He wouldn't go see a doctor. You know August."

"He's like my father-in-law, Ben," Gabe said, smiling. "Those old ranchers would sooner stitch up their own legs than let, as Ben would say, a money-hungry sawbones near him. Drives Benni crazy."

"Love and I are doing the best we can, but . . ." Mel shrugged, not knowing what else to say. "Polly's going along with him. I think she doesn't want to face that he might have . . ." She couldn't finish the sentence. As superstitious as it was, it felt like just saying the word *Alzheimer's* would make it a reality.

"There are people who can help," Gabe said gently. "Call his doctor and tell him or her what's going on. Sometimes it's best to let an outside person intervene. There are drugs now that can slow the disease down."

Mel nodded. "I'll talk to Love about it. Thanks."

He reached over and patted her shoulder. "Take care, Mel. And don't worry about August and Polly tonight. Benni and I will make sure they get home safely."

"I appreciate that. Love has her hands full with her granddaughter right now."

Gabe smiled. "So I've heard. Tell her from me that she has my deepest sympathy."

"Sure will." She turned and started walking away. In seconds, Hud was beside her, matching her long strides, his hands stuck deep into the pockets of his jacket.

"Nice to see you too," he said, bumping her shoulder with his.

"See you later. I've got things to do."

"I could help. I could hold your . . . uh, purse. Hey, why don't you have a purse? All women carry purses."

She glanced over at him and frowned. "Stupid remark."

He grinned. "Cut me some slack, Ms. LeBlanc. I'm trying to work with what I have here."

"Leave me alone."

"When we're having so much fun?"

She stopped, turned and started walking the opposite way.

"Hey," he said, double-stepping to catch up with her. "Good evasive maneuver. Learn that in Sin City cop school?"

She stopped again and looked him in the eye. "Look, Mr. Hudson. I'm not going to play games. We both know I'm not some badge bunny who finds your adolescent patter amusing. I don't care to spar with you. I don't care to date you. I don't care if we ever speak again. You need to leave me alone. I've got enough problems in my life. Are we clear on this?"

He studied her a moment, then lifted his hands in surrender, his brown eyes opaque and unblinking. "My mistake. I apologize. I won't bother you again." He walked away and, for a moment, she felt like the biggest jerk in the world. He had been really nice to August.

"Hey, detective," she called. "Thanks. I mean, with August."

He lifted a hand and kept walking.

Okay, she thought. Well, okay. She again felt like a jerk, and sort of hurt. Then again, he asked for it. Man, she didn't *need* this right now. Forget him.

She went back to the parade and snapped another twenty or so shots of Brad, Evan and the rest of the kayakers. After some shots of other decorated boats, she decided to call it a night. The crowed made her nervous; it was hard to tell if she was being watched. Besides, the incident with August had unnerved her. Next to Cy, he'd been the other male constant in her life for the last three years, as close to a grandfather as she'd ever known. It pained her to see him lose touch with reality even for a few minutes.

The walk back to her house through the almost-vacant streets helped calm her nerves. She passed the Buttercream, where she could see Shug through the window standing next to the Bunn coffeepot. He wore an Arkansas Razorbacks T-shirt and was chatting with Maria, one of the dinner waitresses. Only two old guys were in the café, sitting at the counter nursing cups of coffee. After the parade, people would start drifting in, wanting a bowl of Shug's homemade green chile–corn chowder or some of Magnolia's hot apple cider pie, with homemade cinnamon ice cream. All the shops on Main Street were open, waiting for customers to meander uptown from the Embarcadero, Christmas money burning a hole in their pockets. She paused briefly in front of Baytown Stained Glass to look at the stained glass hanging showing a detailed Christmas tree complete with angel tree topper. She'd thought about buying it, even though she was not much for decorating for the holidays. The colors of the glass, the incredible details of the toys under the tree and the ornaments fascinated her. She kept expecting someone else to buy it, for it to be gone when she walked by every day on her way to breakfast at the Buttercream. But it remained in the window. Waiting for her? No, it would just be one more thing she'd have to leave behind.

She turned the corner to her street, sticking her hands deep into her coat pockets. She was always forgetting gloves. Why didn't she just buy extra ones and keep them in her jacket pockets?

Most of the houses on her street were owned by retirees with plenty of spare time, so the yards and windows of most of them were elaborately decorated for Christmas with all manner of lights, blow-up Santa Clauses and waving snowmen. She'd been teased by her neighbors on both sides saying she needed to get on over to Target and buy herself some lights, join the neighborhood. They almost had her convinced. She inhaled deeply, tasting salt. The air was sharp with the scent of eucalyptus and pine, reminding her of the ointment her father used to smear under her nose when she had a cold as a child, telling her it would make her breathe better. She realized now that it was just illusion, that it only seemed like she could breathe better. It didn't do one thing to unplug her swollen nostrils.

She didn't notice anything was wrong with her house until she walked close enough to her front porch to set off her automatic porch light. An involuntary gasp burst from her lips. Painted across the pale blue expanse of her one-car garage in crooked black letters: THIEF.

NINETEEN

Love Mercy

Love didn't enjoy a minute of the parade because she was too busy looking over her shoulder for Dale to show up toting a scowling police officer. After Rett's little "solution" to her problem, Love felt the overwhelming urge to call Clint again. She held back, not wanting to appear completely incompetent. Not to mention she was a little embarrassed by her volatile granddaughter. She'd figure something out.

Rett and Love agreed on a spot down by the aquarium. It seemed to Love there were more people at the parade than last year. All the restaurants overflowed with those who decided to watch the lighted boats in a more comfortable, less chilly environment. She'd seen the parade from behind a glass restaurant window herself a few times, but she preferred the brisk experience of watching the parade outside. Though the boats strung with twinkling lights, homemade painted Santa Claus figures and glow-in-the-dark Nativity scenes would have likely made people in Newport Beach or Huntington Harbour in Southern California laugh, she loved their small-town parade where the boats were owned and piloted by people who ate breakfast at the Buttercream, who Magnolia bought fish from or who had at one time or another shared one of Morro Bay's popsicle-colored sunsets with Love.

For someone who'd possibly guaranteed herself a stay in the San Celina County Jail, Rett seemed remarkably calm and happy. Was it a facade? One of the things that especially tugged at Love's heart was the fact that this girl and her sisters were strangers to Love. If she'd grown up close by . . . or at least visited once a year, Love would have babysat Rett, Patsy and Faith, brushed their hair, argued with them about bedtimes, watched Disney movies with them. Then maybe she'd be better able to discern Rett's motivation right now. Could she possibly be that uncaring or that foolish? Love snuck a glance at the girl's face while she laughed at a bunch of guys in kayaks—Brad, Evan and friends, Love assumed—and wondered if she felt any anxiety at all. Was it all just bravado? When Love was her age, if she had been in the same situation, she was certain she would have been huddled in the corner of her bedroom, waiting for the police to break down the door. Rett looked like she could just hop onto a kayak with the boys down there and paddle off to China.

After the parade, they pointedly avoided the topic of Dale when they walked back home clutching paper cups of hot chocolate dotted with tiny marshmallows. Rett chattered about the floats while Love worried about the San Celina police car she was certain would be idling in front of her house.

"I think the fishing boat with the twinkly lights set to the twelve days of Christmas was the prettiest," Rett said. "But I loved the kayak guys. I've never been in a kayak. I'd like to try one. I wonder if anyone's ever written a song about a kayak? That would be hilarious. But maybe kinda dumb. This parade was pretty cool. What else does this town do at Christmas?"

"That's about it," Love said. "You missed the lighting of the Christmas tree in the park. That was the first week of December. Some churches and civic groups will likely do some caroling. And there are a few Christmas programs and cantatas. But the lighted boat parade is pretty much the highlight of our city festivities."

"Well, it was pretty sweet." She smiled, looking, for the first time since she arrived, carefree and excited, like one of the college students at Cal Poly.

They turned the corner, and Love was relieved to see that the only car parked in front was her own dew-damp Honda Accord. Maybe Rett's threats to Dale had caused him to temporarily back off. Love knew that it was only a reprieve. He'd be back. By her blasé attitude, Rett obviously hadn't realized that yet. Or didn't care.

Rett was in her bedroom talking to Ace when her cell phone rang. It was inside her backpack, tossed casually on the floor next to the front door.

"Rett, your phone!" Love called, not certain she could hear it.

She flew out of the bedroom with Ace at her heels. "Thanks!" She punched it without checking the screen, her face animated until she heard the caller. Instantly, her smiling lips turned down at the corners.

"Oh, hi, Patsy," she said, her voice cool. She was silent for a minute before saying, "And why should I?" She listened a little longer, her lips straightening. Ace picked up an orange tennis ball, then dropped it at her feet. After a few seconds, he picked it up and dropped it again.

"Ace, not now," Love whispered.

He gave her a baleful look, looked back to Rett and picked up the ball again. She held out her hand and took the ball. She threw it across the room with a force that could have broken glass. Instead, it put a reddish orange mark on Love's ecru living room wall. Ace scampered after it with a happy, triumphant grin.

Love almost reprimanded her, then decided it would be better to just remain an observer. When Ace brought the ball back to Rett, she ignored him.

"That's too bad," she finally said to her sister. "I'm surprised Roy stayed as long as he did in our nutso family. Anyway, I can't come back now. I have . . . a situation here I need to take care of." She listened a little longer. "I have no idea. Why don't you call him? Bye." She punched a button, stared at the tiny screen, then tossed it back in her backpack. "I'm almost out of minutes," she said, not looking at me. "Is there a Wal-Mart anywhere close?"

"Paso Robles," Love said. "What was that about?" She was sorry

Rett hung up before she could say hello to Patsy. She would have liked to have heard her voice, asked her if there was anything Love could do for her. The poor girl had to be scared to death.

Rett shrugged, picked up the ball and raised up her arm.

Love felt a flash of anger. "Don't. I just had the living room painted."

"Sorry," she said and threw it gently underhand across the floor. Ace bounded after it, happy and oblivious in his doggie world.

"Is Patsy okay?" Love asked.

"I guess."

"Rett, it sounded like something is going on. Who's Roy?"

"Mama's third husband. He's leaving her. No surprise there. I knew he wouldn't stick around."

Her cynicism shocked Love a little, even though she knew that many kids her age experienced broken homes. She couldn't help wondering what would have happened had Tommy not died so young. Would he and Karla have made it, or would their marriage have become a statistic? Though Love knew her son had been profoundly in love with Karla, she suspected by some of the hints he'd dropped during his phone calls home that their marriage was already starting to fray at the edges.

"Why not?" Love asked, trying to keep the conversation going.

"They didn't really, like, love each other," she said, flipping back a strand of hair.

Love almost said, and how would you know, then decided that it would be better to remain impartial. "That's too bad," she said instead.

Rett shrugged again, apparently not concerned about any other woman's disappointment in love. "Whatever. She'll find someone else eventually. Mom's real good at that. She's pretty, like Patsy. That makes it easier."

I'm not going anywhere near that subject, Love thought. "How is Patsy feeling? Physically, I mean."

"Don't know. Don't care."

This time Love was irritated. "Rett, she's your sister, and she's pregnant. I know it's awkward, but—"

Rett put her hands on her narrow hips. "Awkward! Well, I guess so. But the way I figure it: you play, you pay. She got herself pregnant. She can just deal with the crappy stuff that comes with it. Oh, don't look so judgmental. You have no idea how it feels to have your sister totally stab you in the back."

Love fought the urge to snap at her. Instead, she let her voice grow cool. "You're right, I don't know how it feels. My only sibling died in a coal-mining accident two weeks after he turned eighteen. I wish he were here so we could quarrel."

Love's words startled Rett silent. Her eyes widened, the pupils large and black. "I'm sorry. I didn't know you had a brother."

Love turned away, tears coating the back of her eyes. How could the thought of DJ still make her this emotional? It had been almost forty years since Mama received the visit from the mine manager, standing on their front porch, his fancy hat in his hands. Two of the mine's security men in pressed khaki uniforms stood on each side of him like stone-faced bookends. Did he really think her five foot two, one-hundred-pound mother would get violent?

Mama knew what was wrong the minute she opened the door. They had heard the siren telling everyone within hearing distance that there'd been an accident at the mine. Daddy was already bedridden by then, his lungs as pitted and black-stained as their windowsills.

When the mine manager said, "Mrs. Johnson, I'm sorry . . ." Mama cried, "No," and turned away, running down the hallway of their shotgun house. Mr. Wyatt gave Love the news, warning her that the reporters would soon be contacting them and they should just reply "no comment" when they asked the family about anything. A small part of the mine had collapsed, and though they'd dug quickly, they hadn't been fast enough. Both men, DJ and his best friend, Nate, were dead.

"We did our best." The manager's basset hound eyes pretended sadness. His only son worked in the air-conditioned office, safe from collapsed mine tunnels.

"Did you?" Love wanted to ask, but didn't. Oh, how she regretted that now. She wished she would have taken his expensive hat and stomped it flat. She wished she would have spat in his face.

"He would have been your great-uncle," she told Rett. "His given name was Do Justly. We called him DJ."

"DJ," she whispered to herself. "Uncle DJ." Then she looked up. "Do Justly. That's a verse from Micah. Do justly and love mercy. Micah 6:8."

Love nodded. "We were twins."

She took a deep breath. "I'm sorry your brother died, but that still doesn't change what Patsy did."

"And Dale. He was an equal part of this."

Her blue eyes flashed. "I know that. I'm mad at both of them."

"But did Patsy know you and he—" But before Love could go further, the kitchen phone rang. It was Mel.

"Hey," she said. "You busy?"

She almost said yes, that she'd call her back, but there was something in Mel's voice that told Love to stay on the line. "I can talk."

"I'll take Ace for a walk," Rett said, her expression relieved.

"Everything okay with her and the cradle-robber?" Mel asked.

Love grimaced to herself, trying not to think about this Dale eying her granddaughters when they were thirteen and fourteen when he would have been twenty-one. What kind of twenty-one-year-old man looked at little girls that way? "So far the cops haven't shown up at our door. Rett's got herself some backbone, I have to give her that." She told Mel how Rett threatened Dale.

Mel laughed. "Good for her."

"Please, do not tell her that. I don't want to encourage her for—"

"Sticking up for herself?"

"I just want to keep her out of jail. Don't forget, her sister, Patsy, is my granddaughter too. I'm hoping to have a relationship with all three girls. I know Rett is hurt, but Patsy is hurting too and has a bigger problem."

Mel was silent for a moment. When she spoke, her tone was subdued. "I'm sorry, Love. I don't mean to make light of this. I know it must be hard."

She sighed and switched the phone to her other ear. "No need to apologize. It's not exactly the relationship I'd always imagined having with my grandchildren."

"Nothing ever is what we imagine, is it?" Mel's voice sounded so sad and, not for the first time, Love wondered about her family. In their three years of friendship, she'd rarely spoken of her parents. If she'd ever said anything to Cy, she'd obviously sworn him to secrecy, and as close as Cy and Love were, he would have honored his promise.

"Sweetie, are you all right?" Love asked. Though she knew Mel's mother lived in Las Vegas, she didn't know anything about her father, if he was alive or just gone. The holidays had to be hard for her. She'd shared three Christmases with Cy, Love, Polly and August. As far as Love knew, she'd never gone home to Las Vegas.

"I'm fine," Mel said, her voice revealing nothing. "Look, I have to tell you about what happened tonight at the boat parade."

During the story about August getting lost, Love felt herself falling further into a funk. She was going to have to face the fact that he and Polly could not live alone at the ranch much longer. The problem was, of course, how best to convince them a change needed to be made.

"I'm sorry," Mel said when she finished. "I mean, sorry this has happened."

"Yes, it's a horrible thing, but we aren't the first people to have to face this. I'll go by tomorrow and try to talk to them about it."

"I'll do whatever I can to help."

"I know you will. Thanks for letting me know."

Love hung up the phone just as Rett was clumping up the back steps. Throughout her conversation with Mel, Love sensed that there was something else besides what happened with August. But as was normal for Mel, she kept whatever was bothering her close to her chest. Love chalked it up to holiday depression. Heaven knows, she certainly felt a little blue about this Christmas despite the joy of seeing her granddaughter. It would be her second one without Cy. The second of how many? She didn't even want to think about it.

After unhooking Ace's leash, Rett excused herself to go to bed. Love made her a snack and knocked on her door.

"It's open," Rett called.

She sat cross-legged on the bed, flipping through a steno notepad filled with words and what looked like musical doodlings. She didn't try to hide it when Love set the tray of cold milk and a slice of five-layer caramel cake on her nightstand.

"Thanks," Rett said. "That looks awesome."

"Let it thaw a little. Should be ready to eat in about fifteen minutes," Love said. "I usually have a cake in the freezer. Cakes are kind of my specialty. I try to bake them once a week for the café." She looked down at her notebook. "Are those your songs?"

Rett nodded.

"How long have you been writing them?"

"Since I was eight," she said, ducking her head. "Those first ones were dumb, of course. I was just learning."

"Well, you know that no one was born knowing how to do something well. Everyone starts as a beginner, just at different times in their lives." Love sat down on the edge of the bed. "You're luckier than most people."

She raised her head to look at Love, her eyes transparent in that way a person was before life handed them their own personal plate of sorrow. "Why?"

"You know what you want to do. Sounds like you've always known. Some people search their whole life for the one thing that makes them happy."

"This is all I want to do . . . write songs." She bit her lip. "Do you think that it's something that's really possible? I mean to do for a living?"

Love didn't answer right away, guessing that her words would be something Rett would always remember. "Other people have done it. Why wouldn't it be possible for you?"

Rett seemed to consider Love's words, then she smiled. The answer seemed to satisfy her. "Thanks for taking me to the boat parade. It was pretty cool."

"It was my pleasure," Love said. "Guess I'll see you in the morning."

"Sure," Rett said, looking back down at her notebook.

When Love closed the bedroom door and walked back to the kitchen, she couldn't help wondering. Would there ever be a time when Rett and she had the same comfortable relationship she'd seen with Magnolia and her kids or Benni and her grandmother Dove? Please, Love thought. Oh, please, yes.

The rattling of pans, the smell of smoky bacon and a sharp bark woke Love the next morning. Though she had no idea why, it was the best night's sleep she'd had since Cy had died. She hadn't jerked awake once during the night in a pool of damp desperation, his presence hovering at the edge of her dreams, so close she sometimes felt like she could touch the warmth of him. She went into the kitchen still wearing her lavender flannel pajamas printed with flying pink pigs, a birthday gift from Magnolia.

Rett stood at the stove flipping pancakes and frying bacon. Ace tap-danced around her feet, smiling his hopeful corgi smile.

"What's going on?" Love asked.

"Crazy pj's, Grandma," she said. "I was going to send Ace in to wake you up. Breakfast is almost ready. I made coffee, if you want it. Or I can make you tea." She gestured with her spatula over at the Mr. Coffee.

"Coffee's fine." She poured herself a cup and sat down at the table. It felt strange having another woman standing in front of her stove.

"I warmed up the syrup," she said, setting the platter of pancakes and bacon on the table. "Oh, and I fed Ace."

"How did you know how much . . . ?"

"I've watched you. I figured it out."

"Oh," Love said, sitting there with her hands in her lap. It stunned her a bit, seeing Rett switch back and forth between an almost-mature woman to a stubborn, willful adolescent. It had been a long time since Love was that age. Had she been like that too? How she longed at that moment for Mama to be alive so she could call her and ask that simple question. She stood up and went over to the phone. "I want to give Polly a call and make sure they're okay. Then I'll be ready for breakfast."

Polly answered on the fourth ring. "Mel came by about six a.m. this morning," she said. "It was a real nice surprise. Had breakfast with us, and she and August are out gathering eggs."

Thank you, Mel, Love thought, leaning against the wall. "Great, just wanted to see how you were doing and let you know we'll be seeing you at church." She'd not gone for two weeks, so this seemed as good a Sunday to attend as any. Rocky would love seeing her and Rett there.

"We probably won't be there this morning," Polly said. "August is a little stoved up from being out and about last night."

"Then we'll see you later. What time do you want to decorate the tree?"

"Come any time. We got plenty in the refrigerator to make up a meal."

"Okay, we'll probably see you right after church."

Love sat back down at the table and took the cloth napkin Rett had neatly folded and placed on top of her plate. "This looks delicious. I didn't know you could cook."

Rett shrugged and sat down, unfolding her own napkin. "Mom was always busy booking us gigs or dealing with business stuff." She gave a rueful smile. "Or trying to find new husbands. In Florida, our neighbor taught me some stuff. I used to cook for Faith and me. It was something to do."

While they ate, Love told her about what happened to August. She listened intently, not commenting until Love was finished.

"So, he's got Alzheimer's?" Rett said.

"We don't actually know yet. He needs to be tested. I looked some stuff up on the Internet, and there are apparently many types of dementia. It could be any one of them."

"But the problem is the same, no matter what kind he has?"

Love nodded. "About their living situation? Yes, it is."

"That sucks."

Though she'd never really liked that word, she had to admit it perfectly described the situation. "Yes, Rett, it definitely does."

"So, how can I help?" she asked, cutting a pie wedge of pancake and putting it into her mouth.

Love inhaled deeply before answering. They were getting along so well, but her question demanded the truth. "Getting this situation with Dale straightened out would help the most."

She scowled. "I'm working on it."

"Telling him you'll accuse him of child molestation is not working on it. It's putting gasoline on an already huge fire."

"He deserves to be the freaked-out one for a change."

"I might agree with that, but you need to look at the larger picture. What would help the most is for you to give him back his banjo and let bygones be bygones."

"That's a stupid saying. What's a bygone anyway?"

"Rett, don't change the subject."

"Whatever."

Love bit the end off a strip of crisp bacon. "You asked how you could help, and I told you. What you really want is to dictate how you can help."

She shrugged and didn't answer, but the word *whatever* lingered unspoken in the air between them. Love wondered briefly if there was a way to vote a word out of the English language. Parents of adolescents everywhere would surely write their name on a petition to rid the world of that irritating word.

"Okay," Love said. "Let's just put all our cards on the table right now. Are you planning on staying for very long?"

She cut another piece of pancake and studied it for a moment before putting it in her mouth. "Don't know."

"That's not a good enough answer. As you saw last night, I need to start making plans, and if you're going to stay, you'll need to be part of those plans."

"I might go down to L.A. Or maybe to Nashville."

Love's heart dropped, but she was determined not to let her disappointment show. "You're a grown woman, so you certainly have the right to go where you want. I just need to know so I can make plans."

"I might, umm . . ." Her sentence dropped off into a garbled mutter.

"Excuse me," Love said, leaning forward. "I didn't hear what you said."

She looked up, her round eyes unblinking. "I said I might have to get a job before I move on. I'm kinda broke."

Was it horrible, Love thought, to be thrilled at her granddaughter's financial dilemma? She would have to stay for however long it took her to earn the money to leave.

"That makes perfect sense," Love said calmly. "You getting a job, I mean. Exactly how much money do you have, if you don't mind me asking?"

Her eyes shifted to the side. "Some."

Okay, she wasn't going to give Love that. "All right, how about I loan you fifty dollars to tide you over while you look for a job? You're welcome to stay here, free room and board, as long as you help out around the house."

She considered Love's words. "Like doing what?"

Love stood up and took her empty breakfast plate to the sink. "You know, help with the dishes, keep your room clean, walk Ace. I have a gardener come once a month to do the yard, and really, there's not much maintenance to this house. You seem to be pretty neat . . ."

She sat up straight. "I am."

"And so am I. So living together shouldn't be very hard. The only thing I do request is that through the holidays you participate in things, like going out today to your great-grandparents' and helping them decorate their tree."

"Oh, that's fun stuff," she said, picking up her plate. "I don't mind."

"Then I'd say the first thing on your agenda is taking care of this problem with Dale—" Before Love could finish, the phone rang. Was she ever going to finish a conversation with Rett about this Dale?

"A happy Sunday morning to you, Love," Clint said. "I call with glad tidings and good news."

"Great," Love said, watching her granddaughter rinse off the plates and open the dishwasher door. "I could use some good news."

"I contacted Mr. Dale Bailey and, as they say in the legal biz, we cut a deal."

"Oh?"

"Yes, we had a nice conversation with me doing most of the talking about things like how you should treat women, how the law might be interpreted in certain circumstances, and a few other things that randy young men should consider before jumping into relationships with girls under the age of consent. Offered to pay his hotel bill and meals for the next three days. That gives you time to talk your granddaughter into handing over the stolen goods."

Love swore if Clint had been standing in front of her, she would have given him a bear hug. "That really is good news. I think we're only inches away from that." Rett walked out of the room, and Love lowered her voice. "I know where the banjo is, so if worse comes to worst, I'll give it to him and face my granddaughter's wrath."

"But at least she won't be a jailbird."

"Yes and that's my biggest goal right now. Having some kind of relationship with her might have to take a backseat to that." She gave a big sigh. "Clint, I owe you forever for this. Thank you."

"No problem. Got to watch out for my employees. What're her plans after she gives back the banjo?"

"She'll be here a little while because she just informed me she's broke and needs to find a job."

"I could have her work in the office here. Skye could use someone to help catch up on our filing."

Love contemplated that a moment, then said, "No, I think it would be better if she found one herself. It would be too easy for me to smooth that path for her, and I don't think that's necessarily the best start to our relationship."

"Wise woman. Just let me know if I can do anything else to help."

"You've done so much already. Again, thank you."

"My pleasure. Talk to you soon."

She stared at the phone for a moment, listening to the dial tone. What Clint did truly was above and beyond the call of duty for a boss and a friend. It caused her to remember something that Cy had told her during the months before he died.

"That boss of yours," he'd said. "You listen to him. He's a nice fella. I like him a lot. He's one to consider, Lovebug, when you start looking again."

Her chest grew tight, remembering the silly nickname he gave her early in their relationship. "Don't you dare talk like that, Cyrus Johnson," she'd said. "You act like you're trying to set me up."

He'd given her his familiar lopsided grin. It seemed to reach from ear to ear, covering his face, which seemed wider and rounder with the loss of his thick, bushy hair. "I'll put the judge on the list of possibilities." He winked at her and mimed writing on his palm.

"Eat your banana pudding, you crazy man," Love had replied, laughing through her tears, wondering how in the world she would ever live without him. "Or I swear I'll throw it to the pigs."

TWENTY

Rett

W ould you like to come to church with me?" Love asked Rett. Her voice was neutral, but Rett could tell by her eyes that she wanted her to say yes.

"Okay," Rett said, surprising them both.

"We're pretty casual at Baytown Christian," Love said. "You can dress any way you like." She hesitated a moment, then added, "Well, I mean . . ."

"No worries, Grandma," Rett said. "I won't wear anything that'll make the front-row ladies call the prayer chain."

An expression of surprise swept over her grandma's face, then she smiled and winked at Rett, acknowledging the truth to what she said. Rett really liked her grandma's smile. She probably thinks she hides what she feels, Rett thought, but she had a face like an open book. Then Rett chided herself and tried to think of something that wasn't a cliché. Like Morro Rock. Her face was as open as Morro Rock, like something you couldn't avoid seeing.

The minute they walked into the small brown and white wooden church—Baytown Christian Fellowship—Rett liked it. There were about seventy-five or eighty people there, most of them old, like her grandma, some even older, like in their seventies or eighties. They were a combination of white people and Hispanics, something that sort of surprised her, though she didn't know why. This was California, after all. There was only one black person, a really old lady wearing a lavender hat with netting and fake flowers. She was playing the wheezy old organ.

The simple lines of the building and the smooth wooden pews reminded her of the little churches throughout the South where the Son Sisters sang when they first started. That was before Mom went all crazy and thought they had the potential to become famous and make tons of money. Those churches never paid them outright but instead took up a "love offering." It was always exciting to watch Mom count it afterward, trying to guess the amount. It was never much and certainly never enough for Mom, but it helped with gas and sometimes a motel. Churches always volunteered housing, staying in someone's den-turned-guest-room or the bedroom left vacant by a child off to college or the military, but Mama preferred a motel, where she said they could let their hair down, which meant she could smoke a cigarette.

Rett and her sisters liked the motels because they usually had pools and Coke machines, though they'd stayed in some pretty weird ones. The funniest was the one in Alabama that looked like little cabins. Faith spilled Coke on the bedsheet, and when they pulled it off to wash, they discovered there was graffiti written with purple felt-tip pen on the mattress: Wanda loves Bobby. They laughed so hard their stomachs ached.

The food was always wonderful at those church gatherings: homemade angel food cakes, maple-cured ham and butter beans, oniony hush puppies, fried chicken and sour cream biscuits the size of compact discs. During the time between Mom's second and third husbands, they struggled for money, but they had fun. Back then, Mom sometimes harmonized along with them on songs, though never in public.

"You babies will be the stars," she'd tell them. "My time has passed."

Rett followed her grandma to the third pew on the right and slid in next to her. She liked churches with permanent pews. They felt real, not like you were sitting at a school assembly like so many modern churches felt like now. She pulled out one of the hymnals and was humming the song on page one, "How Great Thou Art," when a familiar voice called out her name.

"Rett!" Rocky said.

Her head came up, her bottom lip dropping open in surprise. "Uh, hi."

"How wonderful to see you and your *abuela* on this fine winter morning." He bent over and gave Love a hug, holding out his free hand to Rett.

"Yeah, it's cool," she said, shaking his hand. "I mean, to see you again."

She was surprised, though maybe she shouldn't have been. He'd given her an old church program, and she remembered sticking it in her backpack without a glance. If she had looked at the name of the church, she would have recognized it. But the church sign outside said the pastor's name was Roberto Sanchez, and he'd introduced himself as Rocky. It was kinda spooky when you thought about it, the coincidence of this being her grandma Love's church. There ain't no kind of coincidences on God's earth, Brother Dwaine would have told her. It's Divine Providence. Maybe he was right.

"Hope you're able to visit us here in Morro Bay a little while," he said, then moved on to greet some old ladies behind them. She hoped that since he didn't make a big deal about meeting her before, he wouldn't make some kind of announcement from the pulpit about her visiting her grandma.

He didn't, so she settled into the pew, thinking she'd just let her mind drift away while waiting for the service to end. But she didn't. First, the special music was pretty awesome with two old guys on a guitar and a fiddle, the old black lady rocking out on the organ and a cute guy in his twenties with spiky black hair who was the real musician. He played a beat-up old Gibson guitar and performed a few unexpected licks that made her lean closer to watch his fingers. He was good, far better than the other musicians, but he was cool about it. He gave them their time, respected their ability and never stopped smiling even when the old fiddler dude fumbled the song's timing and the young guy had to really think fast to recapture his own time and place in the song. They played a combination of old-time hymns and a couple of praise songs that weren't all boring and singsong.

She was glad that Rocky was of the "if you can't say it in a half hour, it probably isn't worth saying" group of ministers. It was a group she thought was way too small. She'd endured her fair share of preachers who made their point the first twenty minutes of their sermon and then spent the next hour and a half repeating it over and over with slightly different words, like "Dueling Banjos" set on perpetual repeat.

"God often doesn't answer our prayers, at least right off," Rocky stated, once he took the pulpit. "And that really annoys me sometimes."

Rett found herself fascinated by his gravelly Johnny Cash voice, one that sounded like a real person who'd been through tough times. He probably sounded like rocks in a washing machine when he sang.

"Here's some reasons why I think he might do that. We'll be studying this subject in depth through January, but I'll just lay out the facts for you right now, so you can ponder them. Remember, my e-mail is always open to discuss anything I talk about. Or come on down to the barbershop. My coffeepot is always on. Don't be afraid to give me your input. We're all learning together here."

He looked down at his open Bible, where Rett could see the wire rim of a steno notebook. Rocky took notes for his sermons on the same kind of notebook she used to write down song lyrics and melodies.

"Here's what I came up with. One: We don't always understand all the circumstances about a situation, so what we're asking for might mess up something else in God's long-term eternal plan for the world. Two: We don't understand God's higher spiritual purposes, so what we ask for is what will make us feel better. Three: We forget that others have free will and that our Lord won't force someone to do something he or she doesn't want to do. Four: We don't understand that life on earth is not perfect, that Satan does have limited power here and can sometimes mess with our plans (and under four a—just so you don't lose hope— remember it isn't going to be that way forever). Five: We all go through hard times, and unanswered prayers would definitely qualify, but it makes us seek out God. That, ideally, should result in us having a closer relationship with him. And that is the ultimate goal of *all* prayer . . . a closer relationship with our Creator."

As he went on to delve a little deeper into the first reason, Rett found her thoughts homing in on number three. Though she'd never admit it out loud to one single person on this earth, she'd continued to pray that the minute Dale saw her, he would realize that she was the one he truly loved. And, deeper inside, she sort of hoped this baby would just disappear. She'd never thought the word *miscarriage*, not wanting to go that far. And she certainly didn't pray for it, though if she was being honest, wasn't hoping for a baby to disappear kind of the same thing? She didn't want to wrap her mind around that, because that would make her the most horrible, evil person alive. This baby, this physical combination of Dale and Patsy's DNA, didn't actually seem real to her yet. Despite everything, all Rett could think about was the feel of Dale's calloused fingertips on her cheeks, the sweet way her stomach felt when he kissed her.

Before she realized it, Rocky's sermon was over, and the congregation was standing. Where had her brain gone to? Sometimes it freaked her out how she could lose time like that, be in this solitary world of her thoughts and look up and find that minutes and hours had passed, leaving only the echo of what had happened around her while she was gone, like the reverberating sound of a train seconds after it was out of sight.

She sang the last song by heart—"Blessed Assurance." She was surprised that Rocky closed with such a traditional hymn. His final prayer surprised her even more, because he prayed first in Spanish, then in English.

"*El Señor, nosotros les damos gracias para sus bendiciones, le paticionamos para nuestras necesidades, anoramos su guía y nosotros le honoramos su majestad. Usted, nuestro redentor, nuestra piedra, nuestro padre eterno, nuestra esperanza y nuestra salvacion. Nos ofrecemos a usted esta semana y oramos que usted nos ayude a servir a sus personas y usted. En el nombre del santeo hijo, amen.*

"Oh, Lord, we thank you for your blessings, we petition you for our needs, we yearn for your guidance and honor you for your majesty. You are our redeemer, our rock, our everlasting father, our hope and our salvation. We offer ourselves to you this week and pray that you help us to serve your people and you. In your son, Jesus's holy name, amen."

The Spanish sounded cool. *El Señor?* She knew from the few Spanish classes she was forced to take in high school that *el* meant "the" and *señor* was "mister." The Mister? That was so like Mister God that it freaked her out. She thought she was the only person who called him that.

After the service, as they stood in line to shake Rocky's hand, Love introduced her to so many people that Rett's smiling face started to hurt. She tried to be nice, not wanting to ruin this moment for her grandma, but after the tenth, "Why, you don't look at all like Love," she was ready to haul butt for home.

When they finally made it to the front of the line, she saw that Magnolia, the lady who owned the Buttercream, stood at Rocky's side. She'd forgotten that she was Rocky's wife. Why hadn't she been in the service? Maybe she had been sitting in back. Magnolia hugged Love enthusiastically.

"I got roped into nursery duty today," Magnolia said. "We had three babies and five toddlers. Thank the good Lord I took my Flintstone vitamins this morning."

"We missed your voice," Love said, glancing over at Rett. "Magnolia was a professional singer for years. Her voice would knock your boots off."

Rett nodded, not knowing how to answer.

"Oh, that was a million and a half years ago," Magnolia said, giving Rett a quick up-and-down look. "Rett doesn't want to hear about my days as a lounge singer."

You got that one right, Rett thought, giving Magnolia a small smile.

"We're heading out to the ranch after church to help August and Polly decorate their tree," Love said.

"We're heading out there ourselves after lunch. We're meeting Father Mark at Liddie's in San Celina. A bunch of churches are coordinating Christmas dinner at the homeless shelter this year, trying to maximize our contributions."

"Put me down for a two-hour shift," Love said. "More if you need slots filled."

When they started to discuss the details of the holiday meal, Rett wandered away and sat on the small brick fence that surrounded the church sign. She could see Morro Rock from her perch. It glistened in the bright noon sunlight, looking like someone had sprayed it with carbonated water. She wondered what the rock looked like close up. Was it made of that shiny black rock—what was it called—obsidian? She'd seen an obsidian penholder once on the desk of a church pastor in Louisiana. He'd said it came from lava.

"It's cool you came to our church," a guy's voice said, interrupting Rett's contemplation of Morro Rock. "Was it okay for you?"

She looked up into the smiling face of the guy in the band who played the awesome guitar licks. He looked younger up close than he did from the front of the church, maybe nineteen or twenty at the most. He was tanned the color of almonds and had hazel eyes with gold in the center.

"I'm Zane," he said, holding out his hand. "Zane Gray."

"Oh, man, I'm so sorry," she said, standing up and laughing as she shook his hand.

"Yeah," he said, laughing with her. "My dad's favorite book was *Riders of the Purple Sage.* Obviously."

"It could have been worse. He could have named you Pearl."

He moved in front of her to shade her face from the sun. "Wow, you know your obscure Zane Grey facts."

She twisted a strand of her hair. "Who would name their son Pearl?"

He laughed again. "So, who are you, anyway?"

"Rett Johnson. I'm Love Johnson's granddaughter."

He nodded. "She's awesome. Her cakes are wicked good." A grin, one that caused his greenish eyes to turn to slits, stretched across his face. "She was my Sunday school teacher when I was fourteen. She always made each of us our favorite cake for our birthday. Mine was banana with caramel frosting. Nice to meet you, Rett. Is that, like, in Butler?"

Even though she'd heard *that* a million times, he was nice, so she decided to make him feel better about his name by telling him her real name. "I like to be called Rett, but my full name is Loretta Lynn Johnson."

He threw back his head and laughed. Rett stared at his tanned throat, intrigued. She wondered if he sang and what his voice sounded like.

"Sorry back at you," he said. "What was your parents' deal?"

"Mom was a wannabe country singer," she said.

"Dad sold insurance, but he wanted to be a writer," Zane said, nodding. "He died when I was six. My mom and my great-aunt Zoey are veterinarians over in Paso. That's what we call Paso Robles here."

"Got it. That's kinda cool, I mean, your mom and great-aunt both being vets."

He stuck his hands into the pockets of his baggy jeans. "I suppose, except it stops with me. I want to be a musician, which, according to my mom, is breaking her heart."

"Ready to go, Rett?" Love called over to her.

"Hey, see you around," he said.

"Sure," she replied.

Love and Rett swung by the house to pick up Ace, who was waiting eagerly by the kitchen door.

"Ace loves his excursions to the ranch," Love said, helping him into the backseat of her car, where she hooked him into a special padded dog car seat built high enough for him to see out the window. "He's like a weekend gentleman rancher. He pretends he knows what to do with a herd of cattle."

"Wow, he's not spoiled or anything," Rett said, turning around in the passenger seat to scratch him under his white chin. He licked her nose, causing her to giggle.

"Oh, no, not a bit," Love said.

On the drive to the ranch, Love fretted out loud about Polly and August living there alone. "Polly's in denial, I think," she said, as they turned into the long driveway. "I guess I can understand. Sometimes it's hard to see what's right in front of our face, especially if it's something we don't *want* to see."

Polly sat on the porch waiting for them, a red mixing bowl in her lap. The minute Ace hit the ground, he darted around the house.

"Where's he going?" Rett asked.

"To find Ring. They're old buddies," Love said.

"You like snap peas?" Polly asked Rett when she walked up to the porch.

Rett hesitated a moment, then said, "Not really, ma'am."

Polly smiled at her. "No matter. We have lots of other things for dinner. I'm assuming you do like roast chicken and mashed potatoes?"

Rett nodded and smiled back. "But I really like desserts."

"Got plenty of those." Polly stood up and opened the screen door. "Help me set the table. Love, August is in the barn with Mel. Tell 'em that dinner will be served in ten minutes."

"Thanks, Mom," Love said, winking at Rett, though Rett wasn't sure why.

Rett liked helping Polly set the table with the flowery, mismatched dishes and worn silverware. Since Polly missed church that morning, she asked Rett to tell her about Rocky's sermon. Once she starting talking, Rett realized that she'd absorbed more than she realized. She gave her great-grandma the highlights, while they moved platters and bowls of food to the table: pepper-scented roast chicken, buttermilk mashed potatoes, snap peas, corn, baking powder biscuits and three kinds of pickles in a crystal condiment dish.

"He talked about unanswered prayers and how sometimes what we pray for isn't what God wants for us," Rett said, "or for other people, so that's why he doesn't answer." She stuck a small sour pickle in her mouth. It made Rett's lips purse, and Polly laughed. "Well, Rocky says he does answer, but it's not always what we want to hear. And some stuff about how people have free will, so even if we pray for changes in their life, they, like, have to allow the changes to happen."

"How well I know that," Polly said, setting a bowl of black olives next to the pickles. She wiped her hands down her blue and white checked apron.

"So, then, why bother praying?" Rett heard herself ask, then wished she'd kept quiet. The last thing she felt like doing right now was getting into some kind of theological argument.

Polly put both hands on her hips, and Rett thought, Oh, no, here it comes. But her great-grandma surprised her.

"Well, I don't really know, Rett," she said. "I always figured that

God told us to pray, and if I don't always see what good it does, that doesn't change the fact that he told us to do it. It's like being the rancher as compared to the ranch hand. When you're the rancher, you see the whole picture of what you know the ranch needs to prosper. So you tell the hands, you work on this fence, you clear out this bunch of brush, you doctor the cattle. The hands don't know everything that's going on, and if they just up and said, I think I'd rather clean tack today or rebuild the corral, they're messing with the overall plan that you have for the ranch."

Rett set out forks and knives, contemplating what Polly said. "What if the rancher sees things wrong? What if he—"

"Or she," Polly said, chuckling.

Rett smiled. "Okay, or she, totally has things all screwed up and is doing things wrong. What do you do then?"

Polly wiped her hands on her apron and said, "If that's the case, maybe you shouldn't be working for a rancher you don't trust."

At that moment, Love, August and Mel came into the house, stomping their feet and laughing. Ace darted into the kitchen, immediately lay down in front of the refrigerator and barked. Ring bounded in seconds later and joined Ace.

"They want cheese," Polly explained, opening the door and reaching into a drawer. "It's our ritual." She broke off two small pieces of cheddar cheese and fed one to each dog.

In a flurry of talk and removing jackets, everyone eventually found places around the table. After a quick prayer of thanks, they started eating, with Ace and Ring moving from one person to another, noses upturned in hope.

"We'll decorate the tree after lunch," Polly said. "I have all the ornaments out." She turned to Rett. "You'll be with us for Christmas, won't you?"

Everyone turned to stare at her, waiting for her answer. "Uh, I don't know yet. I . . . maybe I'll go back to . . ."

She stopped, not wanting to lie, but not wanting to let Polly think that she was for sure going to stay here. She had absolutely no intention of going back to Tennessee. She just couldn't look Patsy in the face right now. But staying here felt weird. To be honest, she just wished that she could skip Christmas this year. It was too full of emotional minefields. She stared down into her pile of mashed potatoes, watching the pat of butter melt into a murky yellow pond.

"Well, you know, I think I'm going to have to call the police," August said, biting off a large chunk of biscuit. "Pretty darn soon."

Everyone turned their faces from Rett to August. She exhaled in relief.

He looked over at Mel, then at Love, his face serious; his blue eyes seemed as clear and still as a mountain lake.

"What?" Love said, voicing what they were all thinking.

For one crazy moment, Rett thought he meant he'd have to call the police on her for stealing Dale's banjo. Had Mel told him she was hiding it at the feed store?

"I can't figure it out," August said, shaking his head.

"Figure out what?" Mel asked, carefully placing her fork across her plate.

"Aliens," he said. "They're writing all over the walls of Big Barn."

TWENTY-ONE

Mel

Everyone was shocked silent. Mel was the first one to speak. "August, are you pulling our legs?" She reached over and gently punched his shoulder. Please, she thought, make it be a joke.

His deeply creviced face remained unsmiling. "Now, why would I be doing that? They're writing all over the walls of Big Barn, and I'm telling you, I'm sick and tired of it."

"Who wants pie?" Polly said, standing up. She picked up her half-full plate and started for the kitchen. "I've got peach and pecan. Vanilla ice cream or whipped cream. There's more chicken too." She bustled through the swinging kitchen door, Ace and Ring trailing behind her.

Mel focused on August's face, hoping he'd suddenly grin and laugh. August had fooled them before.

"What does it say, August?" Mel asked in her calmest voice, the voice she used when dealing with people wearing tinfoil crowns who claimed there were talking dragons in their vegetable bins.

"That's what I'm trying to tell you." He took an aggressive bite from his chicken leg. "I don't know what it says. That's why we need to call the police. They have people who know these kinds of things, secret codes and whatnot."

Mel glanced over at Love, whose face looked like a cameo. Not a muscle moved, her lips set in a frozen smile.

"I'm good with codes," Mel said, keeping her voice casual. "How about after we have dessert, I ride up there and take a look."

"I'll saddle up the horses—" he started.

"I'll ride with her, Pops," Love said. "I think Polly and Rett could use help hanging the lights." She glanced over at Rett and raised one eyebrow a fraction of an inch.

"We do," Rett said without hesitation. "I don't really like ladders, so you have to do the high stuff."

Quick on the draw, Mel thought. Her opinion of the girl went up a notch.

August smiled at Rett and raised his shaggy eyebrows. "Afraid of heights, are you? Did you know your daddy was too?"

"No, I didn't," Rett said, smiling back at him.

August launched into a long story about Tommy getting stuck in an oak tree when he was ten, how it took August and Cy two hours to talk him down. Mel watched, amazed, as August completely forgot about the alien writing on Big Barn and told one story after another about Tommy's escapades as a boy.

Rocky and Magnolia arrived a few minutes later, while Polly and Love were serving pie and ice cream. Love whispered something to Magnolia, and they went to the kitchen with the excuse that they were fetching more napkins. Mel figured she was probably cluing Magnolia in on the story about the alien writing.

After dessert, Rocky walked with Mel and Love out to the barn, telling the others he just wanted to say hello to the horses, that he'd be back to help them decorate the tree in a few minutes.

"That's just like a preacher," August grumbled good-naturedly. "Leave the hard work of untangling the lights to us common folk."

"August, be nice," Polly said, patting her husband on his arm. Magnolia was pulling out boxes of ornaments, telling Rett about the time she helped Tommy make a set of clay bells to give to Love for Christmas.

Out in the corral, Mel caught both horses while she listened to Love tell Rocky what August said at lunch.

"I don't understand how it could be happening so fast," Love said, a catch in her voice. "He seemed fine a few weeks ago."

"Dementia patients often change quickly," Rocky said. "We really need to get him in for a medical workup. Have you talked to Polly about it?"

Love shook her head no, grabbing Daisy's lead rope from Mel. "I think she's just trying to ignore it, hoping it'll go away. I sure understand that."

Rocky sighed. "Do you want me to talk to them?"

Love led the horse over to the hitching post next to the tack room. "I'd appreciate that so much. Do you think we can wait until after Christmas? I mean, with Rett here and all. I don't know how long she'll stay and, well, I'd just like things to be . . . normal. It will likely cause a huge fight. You know how August feels about doctors and change."

"I do," Rocky said. "We'll have to be vigilant on watching him until we can convince him to see the doctor."

"I can't ask you and Magnolia to do any more," Love said, currying and brushing Duke's dusty back before throwing on a saddle pad. "Especially this time of year and with your own family . . ."

"Don't worry about it. I'll put out the word in the church and see what we can come up with. I think I could talk Zane into coming out here for a few weeks. He told me his mom and great-aunt were closing the clinic for a week and going on a cruise over the holidays. He's not going because he has a couple of gigs in San Celina over the Christmas holidays. He could stay out here nights. I could cook up a story about him being thrown out of his apartment or something. You know that Polly would let him stay with them if she thought he was homeless."

Mel walked up leading Duke. "Isn't it double bad when a preacher lies?" she asked.

Rocky grinned at her. "I think the Lord might forgive this particular bending of the truth."

"It sounds workable," Love said, throwing the saddle over Daisy's back. "We'll pay Zane, of course. Right now, Mel and I just need to think up something to tell August about Big Barn."

"Check it out first," Rocky suggested. "It might all be in his imagination. There's also a good chance he's already forgotten about it."

Love turned her back on Rocky to buckle the cinch and pull it tight. He couldn't see her face, but Mel, tacking up Duke, could. Bright tears glistened in her friend's eyes. Mel felt sick, wishing she could do something to help Love.

"I hate this," Love said. "To quote my granddaughter, it really sucks."

Rocky walked over and patted her shoulder. "I know it does. Be careful on your ride."

For the first ten minutes, Mel and Love didn't speak. They kept the horses at a walk up the narrow cattle path toward Big Barn, about a mile ride from the house. The air was clear and sweet-smelling, the sky a crisp metallic blue. Mel started to relax, and her thoughts of August and Patrick and everything that was going on seemed to melt away with each step Duke took. She knew that this was only a short respite, that these things would need to be faced, but right now, all she wanted to do was inhale this honey air, watch the red-tailed hawks circle overhead and feel the sun on her face. But even the perfect moment she was experiencing right now couldn't replace the memory of her vandalized garage door. It had only taken her fifteen minutes to paint over it, but the word was burned into her brain like a brand on a calf.

She glanced over at Love. "You okay?"

Love gave a half smile. "As okay as I can be under the circumstances. I knew this was going to be another hard Christmas, but if you'd told me three months ago what we'd be facing, I might have locked myself in my house and not come out until January."

"How're things going with Rett?" Mel clicked softly under her breath when Duke slowed down and attempted to sample some grass. "Let's go, boy. We got miles to go before we sleep."

"Robert Frost," Love said, smiling.

Mel's eyebrows went up. "What?"

"Who you just quoted. Robert Frost. The poet."

Mel gave a wry smile. "I didn't really know that. I think I heard it on a TV commercial. For a car."

Love laughed. "Things are going pretty well. But, until she settles this thing with Dale, I'm not sure she can move on."

Mel picked a burr from Duke's coarse black mane. "It's certainly complicated." Mel thought that, maybe, not having siblings wasn't so bad.

"To say the least. Patsy's pregnancy is something we haven't really discussed in great detail yet. But returning this boy's banjo and making sure Rett doesn't end up in jail are first on our agenda right now." Love shifted in her saddle, the creaking leather a comforting sound to Mel. It occurred to her that it was a sound she'd only become familiar with in the last few years.

From a small rise, they could look down on Big Barn. Next to the tumbledown structure was a wooden, half-rotted corral. In an earlier era, the barn had been used to store extra hay and shelter young heifers. In faded pictures that August once showed Mel, there had been a rustic cabin on the other side of the corral. August told her about nights he'd camped out there with his father when they worked the cattle until long past dark. The only thing left of the cabin was its cracked foundation and a soot-stained stone chimney that looked to Mel like the saddest thing she'd ever seen.

"Let's tie up the horses here," Mel said, hopping off Duke. "We should walk in." It occurred to Mel that August might be seeing some kind of illegal activity. Many of the remote sections of ranches in the county had been used by people setting up portable meth labs and marijuana farmers cultivating their crops. They caused no shortage of headaches for ranchers as well as law enforcement, since cleanup was always on the rancher's dime. An old barn on the ranch of an elderly couple who didn't ride around their land much anymore would be the perfect spot for drug activity.

"Stay here," Mel said, pulling her little .38 pistol from her jacket pocket.

"I didn't know you were packing heat," Love said. "And I will not stay behind. I'm coming with you."

"Packing heat?" Mel said, giving a low laugh. "What is this, *Dragnet*? Just keep behind me then."

"Yes, ma'am. We might need this." Love held up a small flashlight.

"Good idea," Mel said. The sun was still out, dusk an hour or so away, but it would likely be hard to see inside the barn.

When they reached a tree near the barn, she took the flashlight from Love. "Stay behind this tree for a minute. Let me check things out first. Really, it's safer this way. I'm trained for this."

"Okay," Love said, moving behind the oak's thick trunk. "But be careful."

"Count on it." Mel crept up to the barn, staying low. When she reached the building, she carefully moved around its perimeter, her gun held low to her side. She peered through gaps in the boards, unable to see much in the murky interior. But there was no sound coming from the barn, and no light likely meant that no one was inside.

After she walked completely around the building, she came back to Love, who stood next to the tree, her cell phone ready.

"Well?" Love asked.

"Doesn't look like anyone's in there," Mel said. "Still, we'd better be careful going inside. Pull the door open and keep to the side."

When Love pulled the rickety barn door open, Mel stood on the other side and shone the flashlight into the barn's dim interior. It was empty except for a few old pieces of farm equipment. Unseen birds rustled in the rafters. A startled mouse scampered across a moldy hay bale.

"Clear," she called to Love.

Love was at her side in seconds. "You know, this might not be the smartest thing we've ever done. I tried my cell, and the signal came and went. What if someone was actually in here doing something illegal?"

"Too late now." Mel forced her voice to be nonchalant, though she knew Love was right. They probably should have called the sheriff. But she also knew that something this ambiguous would get low priority. She flashed the light around the walls. Pale December sunshine leaked through the wide boards, zebra-striping the dirt floor. When the flashlight's beam hit the north wall, she let out a small, surprised oath.

"Oh, my stars," Love said, gazing up at the wall. It was covered with a long row of markings in blue, green, red and florescent pink. "It does look like some kind of code." She cocked her head, studying the colorful marks. "I think . . ." She reached up, touched one of the bars and brought her fingers to her nose. "Yep, smells greasy. It's paint sticks."

"What?" Mel shone the light directly on the markings. They were about six feet off the ground.

"You know, those sticks we use to mark heifers."

Mel stared at the colored figures.

```
. _ _ . . . . . . . _ . . . _ _ . _ _ . _ _ . _ _ . _ _ _ _ . . . _ . . _ _ _ . . . _ . _ _
. . . . . . _ . _ _ . . . _ _ _ . . . . _ _ _ . . . . _ _ _ . . _ _ _ . . _ _ _
. . . _ _ _ . . . _ _ _ . . . _ _ _ . . .
```

After a moment, she slapped the side of her leg and laughed. "That crafty old codger. It's Morse code!" She only knew that because her dad had tried to teach it to her when she was a little girl. Occasionally he used it to communicate with his assistant during his magic shows. She slipped her pistol into her jacket pocket. "August really did pull one over on us. I bet he's laughing his socks off right now."

"Maybe," Love said, pressing her lips together. She pulled a tiny digital camera out of her Levi's jacket. "I'll take some photos, and we'll see what he has to say."

"Good idea." Mel's voice was casual, but inwardly she was cursing herself again. Why hadn't she thought of bringing a camera? What if it hadn't been a joke, and the writing was something important? She was losing her edge, her ability to be prepared for situations. It made her slightly afraid, knowing that Patrick was out there, likely more devious and prepared than she was.

When they arrived back at the ranch house and walked into the warm cinnamon-scented living room, Magnolia was playing "O Tannenbaum" on the old upright piano, and everyone was attempting to sing it in German. The laughter at their silly attempts to pronounce the German words sounded better to Mel's ears than any famous singer she'd ever heard in Vegas.

"Hello, ladies," Rocky said, handing Love a box of old, glittery ornaments. "Grab a cup of cider and join the festivities." He turned to Magnolia and grinned. "Maybe "Feliz Navidad" will be easier for this group."

Love and Mel waited for August to say something about their ride to Big Barn. But August didn't even seem to notice they'd been gone. Finally, Mel couldn't stand it any longer. She got another cup of cider and sat down next to August on the sofa.

"Things are okay at Big Barn," she said. She elbowed him gently, grinning. "You really got us this time, August."

August tilted his head. "Do say? When'd you go up there?"

Mel inhaled slowly, feeling her grin fade. "About half an hour ago. Love and I went to check out the writing on the wall."

August scratched his whiskered chin. "That barn's needed painting for years, but it won't really pay to do it. Old place is falling down. We really should doze it." Mel studied his expression. Not a speck of guile. He had no memory of telling them about the writing.

Mel looked over at Love, not knowing what to do.

Love shook her head: *Let it go.*

So Mel did, simply because it seemed something too big to face right at this moment. For the next hour, it felt like she'd fallen down Alice's dark rabbit hole into another world, a world where normal people lived, where Christmas trees were decorated together, not alone because your parents either had gigs or were out drinking, and people sang Christmas carols as if there were some truth to them. Though she had a hard time believing that a little baby who would be the world's savior was actually born in a manger over two thousand years ago, when Magnolia sang "O Holy Night," Mel's chest grew tight, and she wished there was someplace to put this feeling that seemed too ponderous and swollen to live inside her.

It was past five p.m. and dark when they finished decorating the tree and everyone started searching for jackets and scarves, ready to head home. Mel felt a stab of panic in her gut, not wanting to face her little house with its freshly painted garage door. Had Patrick come back and repainted the accusing words? She couldn't imagine him trying it in daylight. He'd surely notice that her neighbors were retired folks. He'd know that people like that would call the police without hesitation. Patrick had a rare opportunity last night during the parade. He was smart enough to know that. But who knew what else he might do?

On the drive home she came to the uneasy conclusion that she'd have to have it out with Patrick. How else could she convince him that she truly didn't have any of Sean's graft money? She wished that she had someone to talk it over with, someone who could assess the situation with a practical, unemotional eye. She swallowed hard and turned down her street. She wanted to talk to Cy. A tiny sob burst from her throat, surprising her.

"Damn it, Cy." She felt her chest start to heave. "Why'd you have to go and die on me? Why?" She heard the word reverberate through the truck's cab. "We needed you. *I* needed you." She glanced up at the cab's ceiling, then back to the road. "Some God you are. You stole the only person . . ." She stopped, feeling ridiculous. Who did she think was listening? And what she was about to voice wasn't actually true. The only person who loved her. She knew that Love cared about her, as did Magnolia and Rocky, August and Polly and even the Muppet Brothers. The truth was, if she was sitting in some cosmic witness chair, she'd have to admit to whomever was questioning her, for the first time in her life, she belonged. She was a part of a community.

She pulled into her short driveway and cut the engine. Next door, the Biermanns, a German couple who once owned a popular bakery in the San Fernando Valley, were having a party. Their blue and gray saltbox house was lit up like a Macy's department store window, and people overflowed the little house into their small sailboat-themed front yard.

"Hey, Mel," Fritz Biermann called. "Come on over and have some Christmas cheer." He held up a punch cup of red liquid.

"Thanks, Fritz," she said. "But I think I've had enough holiday cheer tonight. Rain check?"

"You bet," he said. "We'll be eating leftover spinach dip for two weeks."

She knew that the party next door would not likely be late. The Biermanns and all their friends were always in bed by ten p.m. It was one of the peaceful things she liked about this neighborhood. Patrick wouldn't try anything with all of those people as witnesses. She checked her answering machine. No messages. Same with her cell. She turned her cell off . . . then back on. If he was going to call or text, it would be wiser if she didn't ignore it.

She changed out of her jeans and sweatshirt into a pair of sweats and another brick red Cy's Feed and Seed T-shirt. When Bill bought the feed store and changed the name, he offered Love the stock of T-shirts printed with the old name. Love asked Mel if she wanted them. Mel took them gratefully, all thirty-two. Somehow, wearing one always made her feel closer to Cy.

Though she knew there was a party going on next door, every time she heard an unfamiliar noise, she started, like a puppy on its first night away from its mother. When the last person said good-bye around nine thirty, she actually felt calmer. It became quiet, like normal, so any noise out of the ordinary would be obvious. She sat in her recliner with her .38 on the end table next to her. She wished she had a good watchdog, one as alert as Ace. It would allow her to sleep in peace. She didn't realize she'd dozed off until her doorbell rang, jolting her awake. She jumped up and grabbed the gun. The digital clock on top of her television read ten after ten.

When she looked out the security peephole in the door, the porch was empty. Was Patrick playing some kind of crazy cat and mouse game with her? She felt sweat dampen the small of her back. Had she dreamed the doorbell ringing? Now that she thought about it, it hadn't sounded like her doorbell here—a high, old-fashioned ding-dong—but a cheery tring-tring, like the doorbell of her grand-mère's house in Idyllwild. It must have been a dream.

She went into the kitchen to pour herself a drink. She searched every cabinet and drawer looking for something stronger than vanilla extract. Cursing under her breath, she remembered now that she'd finished her last bottle of whiskey a couple of weekends ago when she had a head cold and had made herself a couple of hot toddies.

She pulled on jeans and boots with the intention of walking the four blocks to Larry's Liquors and buying a fifth of Jack Daniel's. She dug through the box shoved under her bed until she found her old holster. She strapped it on and pulled on her barn jacket.

When she stepped outside, she hesitated. Maybe she should drive. She'd be less vulnerable inside her truck. A flash of anger warmed her chest. How dare Patrick O'Reilly make her afraid to walk the streets of her own town. Still, she wasn't stupid. Walking made her too easy a target. Before she got to Larry's, she passed the Rowdy Pelican. She suddenly craved company, not people she knew well, just people to sit next to and drink, make comments about the latest football game and how stupid politicians were.

She took one of the five empty stools at the Pelican's knife-scarred wooden bar. The bartender tonight was new, a woman with bleached pink blonde hair pulled back into a high fifties-style ponytail. A red ruby protruded from the side of her nose, and her unnaturally long fake eyelashes reminded Mel of low-end Vegas hookers, the ones who lingered around the convention center. She always felt sorry for those women; most had kids at home, turned tricks because they were desperate for drugs or needed food for their babies. She understood desperation, didn't look down on them the way Sean and his buddies did. She'd always suspected that had she not accidentally stumbled into a job fair years ago and started chatting with a Las Vegas Metro Police officer, she might have ended up in the same place as those hookers.

The woman served Mel a whiskey and water with a polite nod, then went back to her conversation with a young man in a Frank's Sea Charters sweatshirt. Mel was glad there was no one in the bar she knew.

Her solitude lasted about five minutes.

"Excuse me, is that stool taken?" a man's husky voice asked.

Without turning to look, she said, "Nope." She took a sip of her whiskey. If he started talking, she'd politely shut him down by moving to a booth. It was a slow night, and half the bar's eight booths were empty.

"Thanks," he said. "Nice seeing you again."

His comment caused her to swing her head to look. She cursed to herself. She hadn't recognized Ford Hudson's voice. And he wasn't wearing his ubiquitous Stetson but a navy watch cap.

"Don't get too close," he said, pulling off his knit cap. "Getting a cold. Thought a hot toddy might help me sleep."

She didn't answer. Why did this guy turn up everywhere she went? If it wasn't being absolutely paranoid—a condition she might be only two shakes away from—she'd swear he was following her. Where in the heck did he live?

"I live in Morro Bay," he said, freaking her out. "I've actually lived all over the county since I moved here fourteen or fifteen years ago, but about six months ago I finally settled down and bought myself a place here in Morro Bay. I like how it doesn't seem to change, even when the rest of the county is becoming like a mini Orange County. Or maybe Santa Barbara's a better comparison."

She looked away and stared at the counter in front of her drink.

He called to the ponytailed bartender, ordering a double Irish decaf coffee. "I'd ask you if you come here often, but I know you don't, because I do, and I've never seen you here before."

"I come here some," Mel said.

"Guess we haven't crossed paths."

"Guess not."

She sipped her drink, letting the conversation falter, hoping he'd take the hint and move on.

When she finished her drink, he gestured at the bartender again. "Another of whatever this lovely lady is drinking." In seconds, another glass of whiskey was in front of Mel.

"What if I don't want this?" she asked in a tight voice, even though she did.

"Then the bartender can dump it in the fake fern," he said. "But I'm guessing you do. I hate Christmas. No, wait, let me rephrase that. I don't actually hate Christmas. I hate the hullabaloo surrounding it. Just puts a big ole crack in my heart. What about you?"

She hesitated before picking up the drink he'd bought her. If she drank it, there was the implication that she would owe him conversation or, at the very least, politeness.

"It's just a drink," he said softly, again reading her thoughts. "No obligation. I swear."

She didn't look at him but took a sip. Silently they watched the television over the bar. It was showing flickered replays of the National Finals Rodeo a few weeks ago in Las Vegas. There was a collective groan from the bar patrons when a young man was dragged by a black and white spotted bull across the dusty ground like a dog's ragged play toy. One of the crazy-brave rodeo clowns distracted the enraged bull, and the young man limped toward an open gate.

"Double ouch," Hud said to her. "Those dudes are insane. There's got to be better ways to make a living."

"Not to those boys," she commented, remembering the young men she'd warned and sometimes arrested during that crazy two weeks during National Finals. "But they are the craziest bunch I've ever seen, bar none."

Hud shook his head. "Yeah, and a good plenty of them are from Texas."

She glanced over at him, almost smiling. "A good plenty?"

He grinned. "Sorry, I swear as I get older my grandpa Iry's words seem to come out of my mouth more often than not." He looked down into his coffee. "Lost him last year. My mama the year before that. Miss them like crazy."

"Sorry," she said stiffly, shifting on her stool.

He sipped his drink and didn't look at her. "Thanks. My mama'd been sick a long time, didn't really know me. Iry . . . well, he was the one person who always seemed to understand me. I guess I miss him for selfish reasons."

"Maybe," she said, thinking of Cy. It never occurred to her that missing him would be selfish. But she understood what this guy was trying to articulate.

He looked up at the television screen where another young man in red chaps with green and purple sparkly fringe was trying to stay on a bull. "When did cowboys get so fashion conscious?"

She'd almost finished her second drink and was starting to feel a bit more friendly toward people, even this annoying sheriff's detective. "Glitz sells. I think it changed when National Finals moved from Oklahoma to Vegas."

He shook his head in mock sorrow. "A sad day in cowboydom."

For some reason, that made her laugh. "Did you say cowboy dung?"

He grinned at her. "You've got yourself a real nice laugh, Miss Melina LeBlanc."

She felt her stomach warm at his words. Or maybe it was just the whiskey. "Mel."

"Then you have to call me Hud."

She gestured at the bartender for another drink. "So, Hud," she said, feeling magnanimous. "Are you all ready for Santa to come to your house? Is he going to bring Maisie a pony?" She chuckled, feeling confident and amusing. Drinking always did that for her, made her feel stronger and more in control. Deep inside she knew it was an illusion. She knew that Patrick's hate and Sean's death and losing Cy and August going nutty on them and all the rest of the horrible world lay outside this bar, outside this glass. But right now, she felt good and strong and happy. Well, maybe not happy, but at least not sad. She gulped the whiskey down in one swallow. "Is *not sad* the opposite of *happy*?" she wondered out loud.

Hud contemplated her question, then said, "I think it's more cattycorner. But it's not a bad place to be. Maybe it's better than happy. More like being satisfied. And *that* is much easier to maintain than out-and-out happiness."

She laughed again. The bartender came over with the bottle of Jack Daniel's, and Mel nodded at her to fill her shot glass.

"Double it," she said, knowing this was foolish. She shouldn't be drinking this much when she needed to stay alert. But something inside her felt like it was crumbling away, and these drinks seemed to patch it all back together. Or at least make her not care if she crumbled. She finished the drink with two swallows, feeling Hud's eyes watching her.

Then a tiny, sensible part of her that the alcohol hadn't reached kicked in. She needed to get home, eat something, get sober. By not staying in control, she was leaving herself wide-open and giving Patrick the advantage.

"I have to go," she said, abruptly standing up. The bar wavered in front of her eyes, and she suddenly felt like puking.

"Whoa," Hud said, standing up and grabbing her shoulder. "When was the last time you ate?"

She stared at him, his features soft and blurry.

"I have to go," she repeated, digging through her pockets and finding a twenty and four ones. She dropped them on the bar. Was that enough? Oh, well, they knew her here. She could come back and settle up later. "Bye, now, Mr. Hud."

She took a step and stumbled over her feet. He was quick and caught her.

"Ma'am, are you all right?" the blonde bartender called. "Should I call you a cab?"

"I'll help her get home," Hud said.

Mel jerked her arm out of his grasp. "I'm fine."

The bartender walked over, an empty glass in her hand. "This dude bothering you, hon? Want me to call someone?"

Mel stared at her for a moment, trying to piece the words together. "Oh, him? No, he's okay. He's a cop. Show her your badge, Hudson."

Hud pulled out his wallet and showed the bartender his sheriff's badge. She studied it a moment. "I'm new to this area. How do I know that's not fake?"

A large man with a bushy mustache walked over. "What's goin' on, Wanda?"

"You know this guy?" She nodded her head at Hud. "Says he's a cop."

The guy nodded. "Yeah, that's Hud. He lives here in Morro Bay. Comes in here all the time. He really is a cop. He's good people."

"Okay," Wanda said, her face still doubtful. "Just didn't want to let her go off with some weirdo psycho nut job."

Mel heard someone giggle. It took a few seconds to realize it was her. Oh, man, she was drunk. "Thanks," she heard herself say. "I do kind of draw the line at weirdo nut job psychos."

The woman gave her a sympathetic look. "You want some coffee before you leave?"

Mel considered her offer. "No, but thank you very much for your hospi . . . hospi . . . hospi . . ." Mel couldn't get the rest of the word out. "Help."

"No worries. It's my job."

Once they were outside, Mel looked up and down the street, trying to decide which way to start walking. Had she walked? No, wait, she drove here. That much she remembered. Where was her truck? Maybe she shouldn't have made that last drink a double.

"Did you drive here?" Hud asked.

She thought for a moment, then shook her head no, then yes. She didn't want to admit she'd forgotten where she parked.

"Your truck's over there." He pointed across the street. "Let me drive you home. I walked here."

"How'd . . . ?"

"Saw it at Benni's ranch." She handed him her keys and carefully climbed into the passenger seat. Though a part of her wanted to protest his blatant taking over, insist she could make it home on her own, she also felt relieved that someone was taking control. The man back in the bar said this Hud was good people. Whatever that meant. Hud could be a serial killer for all she knew. She settled back into the seat. Right now, she couldn't care less.

When they pulled up in front of her house, she began to grow anxious. She pressed her elbow to her side, feeling for her gun in her jacket pocket.

"It's still there," Hud said, amicably. "Though I probably should have taken it from you."

"Try."

"Wouldn't think of it." He cut the truck's engine. The houses on both sides of hers were dark.

"I'll walk you in," he said, opening his door.

"No, thanks," she said, climbing out of the truck and walking slowly toward her front door. She stubbed her toe on the small front step of her porch. She cursed and lifted her other foot high to avoid repeating her move. Her foot came down hard, causing her to bite her tongue. She cursed again and started patting her coat pockets for her house keys.

"I have them right—" Hud's voice was right behind her.

"Leave . . . me . . . alone." Without turning around, she swatted at him like she was being attacked by horseflies.

Hud reached around and unlocked the front door. "Would you like me to make some coffee?"

"No."

He stood in the open doorway, her car and house keys in his hand. In the dim illumination of the entryway's night-light, in her half-drunken state, he sort of reminded her of Sean. A strangled noise came from the back of her throat.

"Hey," he said. "Someone left you a note." He bent down to pick up the half-folded page lying facedown on the hardwood floor. It had obviously been thrust through the mail slot. He unfolded it and started reading.

"Do you mind?" she said, grabbing the sheet of paper.

"What does that mean?" he asked. "I want the money. Are you in trouble, Mel? Do you owe someone money? Is there anything I can do to help?"

His face looked so kind, the expression so much like one Cy would have had. It wasn't fair that he died. Cy would have helped her. Cy would have known what to do. He would have . . .

"Mel . . ." Hud started, reaching out to her.

She pushed his hand away and stumbled into the living room, clutching the paper. "You can't help me. No one can."

"Sit," he said, gesturing to her chair. "Let me fix you something to eat."

Too tired and sad to protest, she sat down hard in her plaid easy chair. In a few moments, she blacked out, only to be wakened by Hud what seemed like hours later.

"What time is it?" She jumped up when he touched her forearm.

"Time to eat something," he said. He handed her a plate with a peanut butter and jelly sandwich. "Your cupboards are pretty bare, Ms. LeBlanc."

"I eat out." She looked down at the plate, her eyes trying to focus on the sandwich.

"Eat a few bites," he said, sitting down on the sofa opposite her. "Won't really sober you up, but at least your stomach won't be screaming in protest."

She took a bite, then set the plate aside. "Thanks, but I'm fine. You can go now."

"Who do you owe money to?"

She looked away. "I don't owe anyone money."

"The note."

"That's my business."

"Mel, whatever it is, I assure you I've been there before. You look like you—"

"Shut up," she said, clutching her stomach, willing herself not to puke all over his boots. "You don't have any right to tell me what I look like, what I need or what you *think* I need."

He sat down on the sofa and crossed his arms over his chest. "I want to help."

She sat forward in her chair, her stomach careening in protest. "Leave."

"No."

She stared at him in disbelief. Was he serious? Did he really think that if he sat here long enough she'd pour out her whole life story to him? She'd never be that drunk. Never.

"Mel," Hud said. "I knew Cy a long time. He was a true friend to a good many people, including me. He'd want you to tell me what's wrong."

She stood up and pointed a shaky finger at him. "Don't you dare tell me what Cy would want. You don't know. No one does. He's dead. So no one could say what he wants. Not you. Not me. No one. He's dead. He's *dead*."

Then, to her utter humiliation, she burst into tears.

TWENTY-TWO

Mel

I'm sorry," Hud said. He appeared to be floating underwater.

"Go away," she said, resisting the urge to wipe the tears from her cheeks with the back of her hand. Acknowledging them seemed weak.

"I can help," he said, not moving from the sofa.

"Why?" she burst out. "Why would you want to help someone you don't even know?" She sat back down hard, jarring her back teeth. "People don't do things for no reason. Why would you want to help me?"

"I know what it's like to be desperate."

She gave a cynical laugh, not believing him. "My dad's a magician. He could make you disappear. But he's better at making himself disappear." She pressed her lips together, horrified at her words. What possessed her to say that?

"Trust me, my father has your father beat in being the biggest jackass in the country," Hud said. "Not that it's a contest or anything. And it sounds like your dad is still alive, so he would have the edge. My dear daddy passed on to that great golf course down below many years ago."

"I don't owe anyone money," she said, sorry she'd brought up fathers.

"It's just some guy who thinks . . ." She stopped, not wanting to reveal more. "I can handle him. It's just a misunderstanding."

He sat forward on the sofa. In the amber light of her single living room lamp, she caught a glimpse of what he must have looked like as a younger man, before time and sun had textured his face. He was still a handsome man.

"Look," he said. "Sometimes a person who barely knows you can see a situation more clearly. Like telling your problems to someone on a plane, someone you'll never see again. They don't actually help you solve anything, they're just a sounding board."

"But you're not an anonymous person on a plane."

"True, but you and I are not actually friends. My opinion would be purely objective. I'm assuming it has something to do with your life back in Las Vegas. Something or someone that has come up from there." He waited a moment. "You know, we're both Cajuns, so we're kind of like family."

She stared at him. "How do you know I'm Cajun? I could be Canadian. I could be from France."

"I just know. We can't hide from each other. My mama's side is Cajun, by the way. My daddy's side is moral misfits."

She closed her eyes, remembering her grand-mère Suzette. "Say something in Cajun."

"I want to help. We're *pareil comme deux gouttes d'eau.*"

The silky, familiar sound of the Cajun French made her think of her grandmother. And her father. Where was Varise LeBlanc? Would she ever see him again? Did she want to?

She opened her eyes. "What did you say?"

"We're alike as two peas in a pod." He smiled at her. "My grandpapa Iry used to call me T-Hud." His eyes turned down when his smile faded. "Man, I miss him."

Maybe it was the liquor still coursing through her veins like liquid truth serum or maybe it was Cy's spirit telling her to trust this guy. Or maybe she just didn't care about what he thought. Maybe if he saw who she really was, maybe he'd figure she was too much trouble and leave.

Without looking at him once, she haltingly started to talk, telling him about Sean, about finding the money, about the investigation, what her fellow officers believed about her. She didn't mention her father. Or her mother. Or the reason she came to Morro Bay. She told him about Patrick and his accusations. All of the information came out disjointed and out of order, mimicking her life.

"Cy gave me a job," she said, winding down, wishing now she'd kept her mouth shut. "He never knew any of this." Not until the end, anyway. But she wouldn't tell Hud that. "Love doesn't know. I don't want her to know."

"She wouldn't feel any different about you. She's not a judgmental person. And she's your friend."

She looked at him grimly. "If you tell her, I'll—" She almost said kill you. But she knew that was just a phony threat. "I'll leave Morro Bay."

"I won't tell her. I can talk to this Patrick. Man-to-man."

She glared at him.

"Sorry," he said, holding up his hands. "That was a stupid, sexist remark. I meant I . . . shoot howdy, I don't know what I mean."

For a moment she was silent, then she gave a small laugh. "That's the most honest thing you've said in three hours."

"Tell me how I can help."

She sighed. "You can't. This is between me and Patrick. I can handle it. I don't need some man rushing in on a white stallion."

"Chestnut."

"What?" He was making no sense.

"My horse, Brandy. She's a chestnut quarter horse. And she's a mare."

She stood up, one hand still on the chair arm. "Look, I appreciate you listening to my tale of woe. But I'll deal with Patrick. Thanks for the ride home."

He stood up. "Okay, I can take a hint." He pulled a card out of his back pocket and laid it on the coffee table. "In case you misplaced my other one. Home phone and cell phone is on the back. Call any time."

"Thanks." She would toss this one out too, after he left. "Have a merry Christmas."

He walked toward the front door, turning to face her before he opened it. "You too, Melina. Don't be afraid."

"I'm *not*," she said, suddenly angry.

"Call me if you need me." He left, closing the door softly behind him.

"Never gonna happen, buddy," she said to the wooden door. She went over and locked it, turning the dead bolt with more force than necessary.

TWENTY-THREE

Love Mercy

It was a little past noon, and Love had already put in a four-hour shift at the café. One of their new waitresses, a Cal Poly girl, had just up and quit without so much as a how-do-you-do. Oh, well, one less salary to pay, she thought, trying to look on the bright side.

"What is wrong with kids these days?" Magnolia grumbled while they refilled creamers. "Hey, how do you like that new creamer over on table six? Got it on eBay." It was the head of a collie dog.

"We'll have to watch that one," Love said. "It's so cute, it might just up and walk its way out of here." They'd had trouble before with their creamers being stolen. Now *that* made Love wonder what was wrong with people more than fickle college kids who quit without warning. Honestly, people who would break a commandment for a gewgaw. Crazy.

Love had brought home some clam chowder and sourdough rolls, and she and Rett had just sat down to eat lunch when the always dependable corgi doorbell told them that someone was parking in front of the house.

"It better not be another pound of fudge," she said to Rett. "I know people want to celebrate this time of year by reaching out to their neighbors, but I've already got four pounds of the stuff."

"I'll take it," Rett said, smiling. "I love fudge."

When Love opened the front door, her heart started pounding. It was Dale. Sensing her agitation, Ace started growling until she stooped down and rested her hand on the back of his neck.

"It's okay, Ace." She stood back up. "What are you doing here? I thought you and the judge had a deal." Love kept her voice low, hoping Rett wouldn't come out of the kitchen to see who it was.

Today he wore a pair of tight black jeans, a black T-shirt with Hank Williams's face printed in silver, and those heavy black Redwing work boots that were once worn only by men for whom work meant dirt-encrusted nails and banged-up thumbs.

His face held a forced Elvis sneer. "Tell that friend of yours, that judge dude, that I thought about it and changed my mind. I don't have time to hang around this lame-ass town. The band is leaving two days after Christmas, and I have to go with them. I want my banjo."

"Well, now," she said, trying to buy some time. "Let's not—"

"Tell Rett I need . . ." The sneer faded, too difficult to maintain for longer than a minute. He swallowed hard, reminding her of a child. "I want to talk to her. To explain."

She peered at him through the screen door. Though Love wanted to spare Rett the pain, there was no way she could keep her from eventually talking to this man. And Love had always believed you might as well get bad stuff over with right off, just take it on the chin and move on. So she grabbed Ace's collar and opened the screen door. "She's in the kitchen eating lunch. You may as well join us." She stroked the dog's head. "Ace, this boy's a . . . friend." She almost choked on the word. "No bite."

Ace gave Dale a suspicious look, then ran to the kitchen. Rett's head was bent over petting him when Dale walked into the room. Love stood back, wondering if she should leave these two alone yet not trusting this young man enough to do that.

"Rett, baby," he said, his voice husky in a way that told Love more than she wanted to know about their relationship.

Her head popped up, and a small animal sound escaped from the back of her throat. The stricken look on her face made Love wonder if she'd made the right decision. Then, like a lamp clicking off, Rett's expression turned hard.

"I have nothing to say to you." She turned back to her soup and took a sip, calm as a nun.

"Baby, we need to talk."

She jumped out of her chair. "Don't you call me that. Don't you ever call me that, you big, stupid jerk. Get out of here. I said I don't want to talk to you." She ran out of the kitchen into her bedroom, Ace at her heels. The door slammed behind them.

Dale turned to Love, his cocky expression replaced by one of boyish panic. "Do something! Make her . . ." He stood there with his unfinished sentence, his long arms dangling at his side.

"I can't make her do anything," she said calmly. "I can *ask* her if she'll talk to you."

"Please, ma'am," he said, sounding like a ten-year-old.

She inhaled deeply and said, "Go outside and sit in the backyard."

"Thanks," he said, relieved.

She pointed to the kitchen's back door. "You can reach the yard through there. Stay out there until I come get you."

"Yes, ma'am."

Dollars to donuts he's his mama's favorite, she thought. Probably an only son or the youngest—his mama's sweet baby. He was way too willing to let someone else step in and take care of his problems.

She rapped softly on Rett's door. "Can I come in?"

"Okay," she said.

Love opened the door and found Rett sitting on the floor next to her bed, her arms encircling Ace's squat body. He looked as if he were laughing to himself, which Love thought he must often do while he observed the nutty humans trying to maneuver their way-too-complicated relationships.

"Are you all right?" Love asked, sitting down on the overstuffed chair.

"I guess," she said, burying her face in Ace's fluffy neck. "Is he still here?"

"Yes. He's out on the patio cooling his heels."

"What's that mean, anyway?"

"It means to wait for something. It originally meant to cool your feet when they became hot from too much walking. It has been in use since the sixteen hundreds when people were forced to rest after a long walk. I'm assuming they meant the peasants. Kings and queens probably had horses and carriages."

Rett gave a small smile. "How do you know those things?"

"Google," Love said, smiling back. "And I read a lot."

Rett gave Ace a last hug, then stood up and went over to the window, her back to Love. "I wish I didn't have to talk to him. I wish he'd just go away."

"You don't have to talk to him. But you do need to give him back his banjo. It's stealing, Rett. No matter what he did, it's still stealing."

She didn't turn around. "I know that. But . . ."

"Rett . . ."

She spun around and threw up her hands. "Okay, okay. I just wanted to mess with his head for a while. I didn't ever plan on keeping it." Her eyes started blinking, teenage emotional Morse code.

Love wanted so badly to go across the room and put her arms around her. But they weren't at that point yet. She didn't think she could have stood the pain of Rett pushing her away.

"You know," Love said, leaning her elbow on the padded chair arm. "If you really want to start a new life, it might be better if you talked this out with him now. Yell, scream, whatever makes you feel better." She gave a half smile. "You might want to stop at actual physical violence. But sometimes it's better to just move on. You'll have to eventually make your peace with him. Like it or not, he's the father of your future niece or nephew."

Rett sat down on the bed and looked down at her hands, studying her long fingers. It occurred to Love that she hadn't yet heard her granddaughter play or sing. Was she any good? How much did banjos cost? Not a fancy one like Dale's, but a good one. Magnolia would know. Maybe Love could buy Rett one for Christmas.

"But it's not fair," she said.

Love felt like laughing and crying at the same time. "Sweet Pea, life isn't fair. It just . . . is. But things even out. You'll be happy again. I promise."

Rett looked over at Love, her eyes red-rimmed. This time Love couldn't help herself. She went over, sat next to her granddaughter and put her arms around her. Rett laid her head on Love's shoulder. Love could smell the flowery scent of her hair. Her heart throbbed with sadness, wishing she could take her granddaughter's pain into her own body.

Rett pulled away. Sniffing loudly, she went over to the dresser, grabbed a wad of tissue and blew her nose. "I'm going to tell him exactly what I think of him. Then I'll give him his stupid banjo."

"Wise plan," Love said, standing up. "Can I say something to you as a sort of writer to another writer?"

Rett looked at her warily, then nodded.

"This hurts, I know. But suffering is often what spurs on our most creative moments. Think about the song 'Crazy.' I imagine Willie Nelson had to be rejected by someone he really cared about before he could write that song. And I don't think Patsy Cline could have sung it quite the way she did without going through some real heartache of her own."

Rett's eyes held Love's, then she nodded and squared her shoulders before walking out to the backyard. Love resisted spying on them and went into the kitchen to wash the lunch dishes. A little while later, they came through the back door.

"We're going for a drive," Rett said.

Love almost protested, not wanting to let Rett go anywhere with this irresponsible young man. But Rett was eighteen, and Love couldn't stop her.

"No worries, Grandma," Rett said, grabbing her backpack. "I'll be fine. We won't be long."

Love looked over at Dale, standing in the doorway looking sheepish. She pointed a finger at him. "I have your number, young man. And so does my friend, the judge. So help me God, if you harm a—"

"I won't, Mrs. Johnson. I swear, ma'am. I know you have friends who can—"

"Yes, I do," she said, trying to sound fierce. "And they would. At the drop of a hat." She hoped her vague warning sounded threatening rather than like dialogue from a *Sopranos* episode.

Without a backward glance, Rett walked away with him. Ace and Love stood on the front porch and watched them drive away.

She hadn't been back inside the house three minutes when she heard the sound of tinkling music. Rett's cell phone lay on the kitchen counter being recharged. Now Love was really nervous. How would Rett call for help if she needed it? Love picked it up and hit the green Answer button.

"Rett? Is that you?" a young woman asked.

"I'm sorry, Rett isn't here right now. Can I take a message?" She should have let it go to voice mail.

"Grandma Love?"

Her heart leapt like a dancing trout. "Patsy?"

"Grandma? Is that you?" Her voice sounded like Rett's, but didn't. It was higher, softer, a soprano rather than the alto Love suspected Rett was.

"It is. It's so good to hear your voice. How are you?" Thank goodness Rett used some of the money Love gave her yesterday to buy more minutes.

There was a moment of silence. "I've been . . . better."

"I know, honey. This must be so hard for you."

A strangled sob came over the phone. "Mom's really mad and I don't know where Dale is and I'm so scared." In the background, Love could hear music playing and the murmur of people talking.

"Are you at home?"

"No, I'm at Starbucks with my girlfriend, Liz. Mom is about to drive me insane with wanting to talk every minute about what we should do. I just couldn't take it anymore."

Love didn't envy what Karla was going through. One heartbroken daughter on the lam with stolen goods, one daughter pregnant, with the same man responsible for both problems. Did Karla know about Dale yet? "What can I do to help you?"

She sighed. "Nothing, I guess. I mean, it's Rett I need to talk to. If you could tell her to call me the minute she gets back, I'd sure appreciate it. Tell her . . ." There was a pause. "Tell her I know about Dale and her. Tell her we have to talk."

"Okay," Love said, hating that she had the information that would set Patsy's mind at ease, at least temporarily. Knowing where Dale was and keeping it from her seemed unkind. But was it Love's place to tell her?

She made a sudden decision that she hoped she wouldn't regret later. "Patsy, this might not be my place to tell you . . ." She paused. "Dale is here. Rett took his banjo when she left, and he came after it. They are out talking now. I thought you should know." Rett and Patsy would both probably hate her, but at least everything was out in the open now.

Patsy sighed again. "I figured as much when he wouldn't answer his cell. I mean, he did once, when I texted him. He said don't worry, that he had something to take care of, that he'd text me soon. That was two days ago, and I've called and texted him, like, thirty times."

Love didn't know what to say to Patsy. This was a horrible situation, one that would, undoubtedly, taint her and Rett's relationship forever. She made a vow to go see Rocky. They all definitely needed a wise and impartial view on all this. "Patsy, I wish I had some advice for you, but I'll be honest, I don't know what to tell you. Do you love this Dale? Is there any chance for a . . ." She wanted to say marriage, but these days that wasn't always the first thing people did when the woman became pregnant. But, shoot, that's what Love meant. "Any chance you and this boy will get married?"

"I love him," she said. "I think . . . I thought he loved me. He said he did." Another sob choked her. "But he probably said that to Rett too."

"Sounds like it," Love said.

"I don't know what to do."

Love sure didn't know what to tell her, so she decided to just keep asking questions. "How's your mother doing?"

"She's crazy," Patsy said. "I've totally disappointed her. She's told me that at least a hundred times in the last two days. She's all bent out of shape about her and Roy too. Can you believe he went on a business trip to Orlando and called her from the hotel, said when he got back he was going to move into an apartment he'd rented. It's one of those ones where single people live—big pool, clubhouse, weight room. He said he was sick of her history . . . history . . ." She stuttered on the word.

"Histrionics?"

"Yeah, that's what he said."

Poor Karla. Even with the grudge Love held against her, she couldn't imagine what she must be going through right now. Love hoped she had friends she could lean on. "Patsy, all I can say is the same thing I told Rett. Things will work out. I know everything seems overwhelming now, but the best thing a person can do when that happens is just take care of each day as it comes. You have another life to think about right now, so make sure every day you do what you can to protect your baby."

Patsy was quiet a moment. "I guess I can't make Dale come back or help my mom's marriage or, you know, change what has happened. But what can I do?"

"You can make sure you eat three good meals a day. You can take a nap whenever you can. Drink a glass of milk. Take vitamins."

"I can do all that," she whispered.

"How far along are you?"

"I don't know. Maybe two months?"

"You should see a doctor. Do you need money? I can send some money."

Then Patsy started to cry.

"Oh, honey," Love said, wishing she could transport herself through the phone wires. "I didn't mean to make you cry."

"It's not that," she said through her sobs. "It's just that's the nicest thing someone's said to me in weeks."

"Do you have someone you can go to besides your mama who can help you find a doctor?"

"Yes. My friend Liz's mom is pretty cool. She said she'd help me. I've known her since I was fourteen. She's a psychologist. She goes to our church."

"Then don't be afraid to accept her help. I'll send you a check today, and we'll keep in touch. This will all work out, even with your mama. She'll come around eventually."

"No," Patsy said, her voice taking on a hard edge. "She won't ever forgive me. I ruined her plans."

Love almost said, yes, she will, but then realized she'd be stating something that she didn't know to be true. Maybe Karla never would forgive Patsy. Love didn't have any idea. But she did know one thing for sure. "She'll always love you, Patsy. She might not be able to show it, and it might not be in the way that you'll always need, but she'll always love you. And she loves that baby inside you. You'll see once she or he is born."

"Maybe," she said, not convinced. Someone in the background spoke to her, though Love couldn't understand the words. "I gotta go, Grandma. Liz has a dentist appointment. Thanks for listening. Can we, like, talk again?"

"Absolutely. I'll tell Rett you called. And take Liz's mom up on her offer. Call me if you need to talk. Do you have my number?"

Patsy took it and promised she'd call. Love took down the friend's address and said she'd mail her a check. "Take care of yourself, Patsy."

"Yes, ma'am. Thank you."

"Well," Love said to Ace after putting Rett's cell phone back on the table. "Maybe I handled that halfway all right. What do you think?" She stood there for a moment, wondering what she should do while she was waiting for Rett to come back.

She remembered the digital camera in her denim jacket. She got it out and downloaded the photos from Big Barn on a disc, then printed out the pictures of the colorful Morse code writing. For not the first time, she thanked the Internet fairies for Google. Within minutes she had a site that gave her more information about Morse code than she'd need in a lifetime. For one thing, she had no idea there were Morse codes for other languages. She printed off the traditional one and took it over to her easy chair along with the photos of what she and Mel assumed was written by August. Even though he didn't remember doing it, it made sense that it was him, since he'd been a signalman in the navy.

Like a preschool child printing her first alphabet, Love slowly interpreted the message.

"Oh, August," she whispered when she was finished, her eyes soft with tears. "Oh, my dear Pops."

WHERE ME GOD LOST WHER ME SOS SOS SOS SOS SOS

TWENTY-FOUR

Rett

While Dale and Rett drove up Pacific Coast Highway, she pretended that they were together, maybe even married. Maybe on their honeymoon. She knew it was a total fantasy, but she couldn't help herself. She stared out the passenger window at the paper-bag-colored hills dotted with patches of bright Kelly green and imagined their perfect life together.

It lasted for about three minutes. Then she remembered that when Dale left, her life would be like the brown parts of those hills. Her grandma said the hills were way greener in the early spring, after the winter and spring rains came. They are so green, Love had said, that it is hard imagining them being any other color. Her grandma said it somehow surprised and amazed her every year. Rett wondered if she'd be here long enough to see what they looked like.

She glanced over at Dale's profile, then past him to the Pacific Ocean, a shiny, glossy blue that made her head hurt, it was so pretty. For this little while, she told herself, she could pretend. This would be all she'd have for the rest of her life, this one moment of pretending that he chose her. She knew she should be mad. He was a jerk and a phony and made her feel totally humiliated. Still, she was glad to be with him. As pathetic as that was, she was glad.

"Where do you want to go?" he asked, glancing at her, giving her that cocky smile that made her stomach lurch like she would throw up if the car turned too fast.

"I don't know. Just drive."

She looked back at the hills. They reminded her of something she'd seen on television once. A songwriter—she couldn't remember who— told the interviewer that there was a story in everything, a reason to write a song, that you just had to discover what it was. It was kind of like what her grandma had said, that Rett should look at this situation as an experience, pain she had to go through to really understand life. That helped a little and also made her see the hills going past her window in a different way. She tried to study them with a more open mind, not try- ing to imagine perfect green hills, but appreciate them for what they were right this moment. As she did, she realized they weren't just a plain brown but a complex palate of browns and golds and tans. If she stared long enough, shapes appeared: lazy-looking lions and the shadowed faces of old men, their crevices deep and mysterious with age, the deep green oak trees looking like eyes and mouths. These were, she realized in that moment, the same hills and oak trees that her father saw grow- ing up. What had he thought as he watched them change with the sea- sons? Did he miss them when he moved to Tennessee? Did they come to him in his dreams like parts of him—his eyes, a word or two, the feel of his hands—sometimes haunted hers? That elusive scent of him, his voice saying her name, like the bridge of a song she barely remembered. She wanted to ask Love more about Tommy. But she was afraid. Maybe her grandma would start crying, and Rett didn't know if she could stand that.

These hills were the same ones the pioneers saw hundreds of years ago and the Indians before them and before the Indians, who knew? They'd been through so much, these hills, these old, gnarled oak trees, these jagged rocks. She tried to imagine that—eternity—time before she existed and time after she was gone. Where did a person go when they died? She knew about heaven and hell, what she was taught, but sometimes it didn't seem real to her. Was her father in heaven? Where was heaven, anyway? Her head was starting to hurt with the complexity of it all.

"Looks like you're trying to solve the problems of the world over there," Dale said, chuckling.

She looked at him, amazed at first by his insight, then a little annoyed. He was joking, of course. She wondered what he'd do if she told him, Why, yes, that's actually what I was trying to do.

She narrowed her eyes. "Why did you tell me you loved me when you were sleeping with my sister?"

Her blunt question caught him by surprise. The car swerved to the middle of the road, hitting the divide bumps, jarring her teeth.

"Man, where did *that* come from?" He pulled the car back to their lane, the road smooth again. "I'm glad no one was coming at us from the other side when you threw that bomb at me."

She studied the side of his face, its unshaven cheeks, his shadowed eyes, full of impossible promises. She knew what those cheeks felt like against her own soft skin, the taste of him, smoky and sweet and full of mysteries she wanted to experience. Then Patsy's face seeped into the picture, a ghost lover, his real lover. As always, Patsy knew so much more than Rett, even in this. Rett wondered for the first time if, maybe, she couldn't have done a lot better choosing her first love. Yeah, right, a little voice inside her cracked. Like a person can choose.

"What in the heck," she said, trying to make her voice hard, "did you think we were going to talk about on this drive? The weather? Your mama's corn bread recipe? Your freakin' upcoming tour of a life-time?"

He frowned and gripped the steering wheel with both hands: ten o'clock and two o'clock, she remembered from her driving lessons in high school. She could see the tension in his flexing fingers. "I assumed we'd talk about how you were going to give me back my banjo. Then, well, say good-bye and stuff. That's what I thought we'd talk about." He glanced over at her, giving her a tentative smile. "Look, we had some nice times. You gotta admit that. We had some laughs."

He abruptly pulled over to the side of the road, coasting to a stop.

He unbuckled his seat belt, turned to her and took her face in his hands. He looked deep into her eyes, that lazy half smile on his face. She tried to pull away, but he held tight, his warm hands enticing her, pulling her back into that place that both intrigued and frightened her.

"Rett," he said, his voice low. "You know I never meant to hurt you. You are so special." He bent his head close, and she knew if she had an ounce of pride, she'd stop him right now. But she couldn't. She had to taste him one more time. His lips grazed hers, a soft kiss full of promise, fake promise she knew, but she could pretend for a few seconds. He pulled her closer and kissed her again, deeply, his thumbs caressing her cheeks, his tongue tasting like butter, his scent enveloping her in a musky, leathery cloud of longing.

"Oh, baby, I've missed this," he said, murmuring against her lips.

Her spine stiffened. He didn't say *her*. *This*. He missed this. Not her. *This*. She shoved him away. "Stop it."

Not appearing surprised or angry, he laughed, rebuckled his seat belt and turned the ignition. They didn't speak for the next few minutes. He whistled softly under his breath while she inwardly screamed at herself: Stupid, stupid, stupid girl.

Up ahead she saw a parking lot filled with cars, a scenic outlook. "Pull over." Better to be where there were other people so she wouldn't be tempted again. Besides, she needed some air.

He flipped his left turn blinker and pulled into the gravel parking lot. There were about twenty or so cars parked facing the ocean. People stood in front of a fence looking out at the deep green and blue Pacific.

"What're they looking at?" he asked.

She jumped out of the car without answering and walked over to the fence. Down below on the wet sand, right on the edge of the ocean, were hundreds of what looked like silvery walruses.

"Our newest pup is over there," an old man in a blue jacket said to her, pointing at what looked like a smaller walrus. He handed her a pink sheet of paper. "Probably weighs sixty pounds or so."

"What are they?" she asked.

"Elephant seals," he said, pointing to his jacket. The patch above his heart read Friends of the Elephant Seal.

"Bizarre," Dale said, walking up to them.

"Not at all, young man," the old man said. "They're really quite amazing. The adult males swim all the way to Alaska and back during the year. Like to see you try that." He winked at Rett, then walked over to another car pulling up filled with young kids. "Follow the walkway to get a better view," he called over his shoulder. "But stay on this side of the fence. Don't throw anything at them. And no feeding them."

"Yes, sir," Dale muttered under his breath. "Hey, this is kinda lame. Plus they smell. Want to go find someplace to eat?"

"No," Rett said. "I want to see the elephant seals." She started walking along the path that ran along the fence. She didn't look back to see if he followed. He ran up beside her, grabbing at her hand. She jerked away. "Let's go all the way to the end of the walkway." He grumbled under his breath but followed her.

The elephant seals' skin looked silvery in the sunlight, though as Rett looked closer, she could make out an amazing number of shades: gray, blue, white and brown. They reminded Rett of the hills she'd just seen. The seals lay next to each other in long lines, like girls sunbathing at a public pool. Other groups appeared to have been tossed there, like bait-fish in a tank. Some lay alone, basking in the weak winter sunlight. The best were the babies, whose eyes looked like shiny black jewels. She wished she could see closer and envied the people carrying cameras with telephoto lenses. One baby was all alone, down near the edge of the water, and she wondered which of the barrel-shaped seals was its mother. She leaned as far as she could over the fence, trying to see better.

"Here," an older woman said next to her. She held out a pair of huge black binoculars. "You can see more detail with these." The woman wore tan cargo pants and a faded navy sweatshirt.

"Thanks," Rett said. She put them up to her eyes. An involuntary "Oh" escaped from her lips. The little seal seemed to be staring straight at Rett, the mysteries of the ocean smoldering in its black eyes.

"Yes, it is quite astounding," the woman said. "Your first time here?"

Rett gripped the binoculars. "They're beautiful."

"Yes, they are. I've come all times of the year, and they are always different. Did you get a brochure?"

Rett nodded, lowering the binoculars to look at the woman.

"They can weigh up to five thousand pounds, and each male has his own territory, where he has thirty to forty females."

"Sounds like a good deal to me," Dale said, grinning.

Rett turned to frown at him. His face flushed. She turned back to the woman, who was brushing back her kinky gray hair. "They seem so peaceful," Rett said.

"Right now they are," the woman said, gesturing over at a bunch lying in a row as neat as canned sardines. "They started arriving in November and, boy, did they put on a rough-and-ready show. They bellowed and fought like a bunch of adolescent boys." She glanced over at Dale and raised her eyebrows. "The females start arriving in December. You're seeing the first of them. The babies are just now starting to be born, and we'll see pups until early February. I've been lucky enough to witness one giving birth."

Rett glanced over at Dale, whose bored expression kind of pissed her off. The lady's remark struck a nerve in Rett, though, a reminder that she and Dale still had Patsy and the baby to discuss.

"Three thousand pups were born last year," the woman said. "There's always something going on: mating, birthing, breeding, pups crying and nursing, females squabbling, males trying to one-up each other. And then they leave. Not all at once, but the females leave their weaned babies to go back out to sea to feed, the babies stay here and learn to swim when the males are out feeding too. Then the juveniles and females come back to molt around March. The grown males come back around July looking like a bunch of homeless wanderers, all scruffy and tattered. Six weeks later after their molting, they are sleek as Vegas con men. The adolescent males are the most fun to watch. They're just big old show-offs." The woman's smile showed beige, even teeth. "I name my favorites, take photos and put them up on my refrigerator. It's exciting if I recognize them the next year. I suppose I should get a life."

Rett listened to the woman, amazed at how she was so excited about these seals, seemed to just love being here. It was cool, really, how people loved things, like she loved making music, like she loved . . . she almost thought, Dale. She turned to look at him. He'd walked away in the middle of the woman's stories. He stood over by the fence, ignoring a duet of squirrels chattering at him, begging for food. He glanced at his watch, then looked over at the car.

"You might want to reconsider that one," the older woman commented. "I've had three husbands. Outlived them all. And trust me, the one I miss the most was my third husband, Mitch. He and I saw life the same way, thought the same things were beautiful. That makes all the difference in the world."

It embarrassed Rett that Dale didn't see how amazing these animals were, how cool this old lady was.

"I'll take that under advisement," she said, not remembering where she'd heard that, but she thought it sounded kinda cool and adult.

The old woman threw back her head and laughed. Her frizzy hair blew around her head like a cotton candy halo. "You do that, young woman. I think you can do better, though I do see the natural attraction. He's a fine-looking one."

Rett laughed with her, although if someone had asked her to put into words what was funny, she doubted that she could have. "Yeah, I guess he is."

"Looks fade," the woman said. "A good heart doesn't."

"Thanks," Rett said, handing back the binoculars. "For letting me use these, and, like, all the information."

"Stay true," the woman said, turning back to the seals.

"Let's go," Rett said, when she walked up to Dale. "I've seen enough."

"Yeah, okay," he said. "I mean, seen one seal, seen them all, right?"

She didn't answer.

In the car, he asked, "Where to now?"

"Back to Morro Bay. Drop me off at the Buttercream Café, and I'll fetch your banjo for you."

He nodded, turning on the ignition. "Are we, like, cool on everything?"

She took a deep breath, wishing she could just let go, scream, hit him, force this car into a ditch. But what would that prove? And who would it help? Be true, the elephant seal woman had said. What did she mean? For Rett to be true to herself, to be a true person, to tell the truth? The truth right now was that she wasn't sure she'd ever forgive Dale. Would she forgive Patsy? If her sister hadn't known Dale was seeing both of them, there wouldn't really be anything to forgive. The fault was all his. Somehow, she didn't believe Patsy knew. For one thing, Patsy was horrible at keeping any kind of secret. And, Rett wanted to believe, she wouldn't do that to her sister.

"No, we're not at *all* cool. What you did was disgusting. I'm giving you your banjo back because it was wrong of me to take it. And me doing something wrong doesn't even out you doing something wrong. I wish I never had to see you again, but because of Patsy being pregnant, we probably will. Are you going to marry her?"

He held up both hands. "Whoa, where'd that come from? Patsy and I aren't anywhere close to that kind of relationship."

At that moment, if Rett had a knife, she swore she'd stick it in his gut. "You make me sick. You're having a baby with her, you freakazoid! You'd better not let her go through this alone."

"I never said that. But, Rett, baby, this gig I was offered is a once-in-a-lifetime opportunity. Patsy wouldn't want me to give it up."

That's where you're wrong, Rett thought.

"Take me back to town," Rett said, buckling her seat belt. "Then you go back to your hotel and wait for my call. I have the banjo in a safe place. You'll have it by tomorrow. My word."

"Why can't I go with you to pick it up?"

She gave him a look—her Killer Karla look, as she and her sisters called it. One of the valuable things their mom inadvertently passed on to them. It never failed. He instantly shut up.

They didn't speak the whole drive back to Morro Bay.

When he dropped her off in front of the Buttercream, he said, "Are you sure I can't—"

"I'll call you," she said, jumping out and slamming the door.

The coffeepot-shaped clock above the cash register read four thirty-two. The café was almost empty, with only two old men in beat-up cowboy hats sitting at the counter eating pie and reading the newspaper. Rett could hear a male voice singing in the kitchen, a Gillian Welch song about a man whose daughter had died and who warned listeners that no one gets everything they want in life and until you die and face Jesus, there's no use wondering why. Rett had always thought it was one of Gillian's best songs.

Magnolia stood in front of the silver and black Bunn coffeemaker singing along with the voice in the kitchen. Rett listened to them, mesmerized by their perfect harmony. Magnolia's voice was as good as any pro that Rett had heard in Nashville. She remembered that Love told her that Magnolia had been a professional singer. Rocky had said she still sang in some bar once a month. Did she ever regret giving up her career in Vegas to be a pastor's wife and a café owner? Magnolia belted out the chorus, still not aware Rett was listening. The words tore at Rett's heart every time she heard them. Magnolia's deep, rich contralto had an aching, mountain vibrato that gave the words an authenticity Rett could feel in her bones.

When the last note reverberated in the room, Rett gave in to her spontaneous urge and clapped.

Magnolia whirled around, surprised. "Oh, my land. I didn't know anyone had come in."

Rett glanced at the cowbell that had clamored when she opened the door.

"That thing," Magnolia said, dismissing it with the wave of a red-nailed hand. "It don't even register in my brainpan anymore." She picked up a white bar towel and folded it in half.

"I love Gillian Welch," Rett said, walking up to the counter and sitting down. "I wish I could write like her."

"She is one talented young woman," Magnolia said. She wiped the counter, despite the fact it was clean as a dentist's tray. "What can I get you?"

"See you later, Magnolia," one old man said, standing up. The other man did the same. "Good butterscotch pie. It's a keeper."

"Thanks, boys. Y'all come back." She turned back to Rett. "So, are you hungry? How about a piece of butterscotch pie? Shug just made it." She nodded her head at the skinny, bald man Rett could see in the kitchen's pass-through. He lifted a flour-dusty hand.

"Sure," Rett said.

Magnolia cut her a piece, poured her a cup of black coffee, then leaned against the back counter. "So, I see that boy dropped you off. Did y'all get your ducks in a row?"

Rett looked down at the meringue-topped pie. Its sweet, buttery scent caused her stomach to rumble. She'd only eaten half her soup for lunch and wondered what Love was going to have for dinner. She took a big bite, then said, "Yeah, I guess so. I suppose my grandma told you the whole pathetic story."

Magnolia nodded. "It's a mess. But not unfixable. I'd say you got the raw end of the deal."

Rett looked up at her in surprise. "I thought everyone would think that Patsy did."

Magnolia contemplated the folded bar towel in her hands. "Oh, I'm not saying your big sister hasn't got herself a hard row to hoe. But at least she'll get people's sympathy when he takes off. And, trust me, he will. Haven't met too many young buck musicians like him who were very dependable. She'll have her some sad, lonely nights. But you have to suffer in silence while you're feeling pretty much the same humiliation. That's hard. I've been there. My younger sister married the man I was in love with, and I had to be one of her bridesmaids. Let me tell you, that was hard. And the worst of it was the dress was ugly as homemade sin. Aqua and gray satin. I looked like a beached whale. Well, I was thinner then. Maybe a beached seal. I always wondered if Rosie picked those ugly dresses out on purpose."

Surprise froze Rett's fork halfway to her mouth.

Magnolia gave a deep laugh. "Girlie, did you think you was the first one that ever happened to? I'm here to tell you, I survived and, frankly, it was darn near the best thing that could have ever happened to me. Hate to imagine where I'd be if I'd've married Varner." She gave a physical shudder. "As it was, their marriage lasted four miserable years. They had three kids, and my sister had to fight tooth and nail for every darn child support penny. Then the flake up and died! Not a speck of life insurance, of course. Whereas I hightailed it out of Chicago to Las Vegas and sang in a variety of nightclubs. I eventually met Rocky, and as they say about history, that's the rest of it." She tossed the damp folded towel into a plastic tub full of dirty dishes. "All I'm saying is it looks like a big old jagged mountain now, but thirty years from now, it'll be a rolling hill."

Rett lowered her fork, thinking about what Magnolia said. "My grandma said I should use the experience, write a song about it."

"Not often Love is wrong about things," Magnolia said. "My advice is you listen to her. She know you were out with that boy?"

Rett nodded. "She was worried, didn't want me to go. But I knew I'd be okay. We drove up the coast and stopped to look at the elephant seals."

Magnolia crossed her arms over her ample chest. "What about the boy's banjo?"

"I told him I'd give it to him tomorrow."

Magnolia raised her eyebrows.

"I wanted to play it one more time. I deserve that much."

"You can't get on with things until you give it back."

"I know." Rett took a last big bite of pie, then pushed the plate back. "I have to go get the banjo. Mel's keeping it for me at the feed store."

Magnolia picked up the plate. "Will you be staying with Love awhile?"

Rett nodded. "At least until I save up some money. I need a job." She glanced around the café. "Is being a waitress . . . uh . . . hard?"

"Can be."

Rett stood up. "Well, thanks for the pie." She reached down into the pockets of her jeans.

"Forget it," Magnolia said. "On the house. From one scorned sister to another."

Rett gave a small smile. "That's a good song hook."

"Go for it," Magnolia said. "Write that man right outta your hair. Want me to call Love and tell her you survived?"

Rett knew there was only one acceptable answer to that question.

"Sure. Tell her I'll be right home."

Rett walked the three blocks to the feed store, watching the sun set on the Pacific Ocean. With the orange-juice-colored sun glowing behind Morro Rock, the beauty of the moment made her wish there was some way she could capture it in a song. But writing about scenery in a way that people could see it was hard. Relationships were always easier.

It was a little before five p.m., the air that unreal purple blue tint that seemed deeper here in the West, when she crossed the feed store threshold. Mel sat behind the counter leafing through a catalog with pictures of flowers and giant pumpkins. She wore a green B & E Feed sweatshirt and brown cords. Behind her a radio was playing softly. Rett couldn't make out the artist.

"Hey," Rett said.

Mel looked up from the catalog. "Hey, yourself. How'd things go with you and the butt wipe?"

Rett grinned. "Is that, like, cop talk or something?"

Mel gave her a half smile and tossed the seed catalog aside. "Nah, that there is scorned woman talk."

Rett laughed. "That's the second time I've heard that word today."

Mel lifted her eyebrows in question.

"Scorned," Rett said. "Magnolia has been scorned too."

"Yeah, well, it's a big club. Lots of members."

"So I hear." Rett leaned against the counter. "I told Dale I'd give him back his banjo."

Mel nodded. "Probably best. Want me to get it?"

"Yeah, but I'm giving it back to him tomorrow. Want him to suffer one more night. And I want to play it one more time."

Mel didn't reply, just stood up and went through the doorway into the small office behind the counter. Rett heard a closet open and close. Mel came back a few seconds later carrying the banjo case.

"This sucker is heavy," she said.

"Tell me about it," Rett said. "I lugged it clear across the country."

"Next time, fall for a harmonica player."

Rett giggled. It felt good to be joking with another woman about Dale. It did almost feel like she'd gained membership into a kind of club. The scorned sisters, Magnolia had called them. Membership requirement: one broken heart. She felt her heart beat faster. That *did* sound like the beginning of a song.

Mel smiled, then like a flash, her expression changed. She stared over Rett's shoulder, a look that Rett could only discern as fury on her face. Rett turned around and saw a heavy-chested man standing in the feed store doorway. He wore a dark trench coat, like those eastern city detectives on *Law and Order*. His hair was short and curly, his complexion shiny red, especially around his nose and cheeks. He reminded her of her second stepfather, Roy, who was a total alcoholic.

"I need your help, Rett," Mel said, her eyes not leaving the man. "Call Brad and tell him I had to leave. Tell him you'll stay here until he can come close up." She grabbed a pen and jotted something down on the wooden counter. "I'll be back soon." Rett could feel some kind of emotion radiating from Mel, like a three-way lamp switched on bright— it seemed like fear or anger or something else? Who was this man? Why could he rattle someone as unshakable as Mel?

Without waiting for Rett's reply, Mel met the man just as he stepped through the doorway.

"Not here," Rett heard Mel mumble. She pushed past him and with a quick glance at Rett, he followed her without uttering a word.

"Okay, sure," Rett called after Mel, nervous about what just happened. She looked down at the countertop where Mel had written Brad's phone number. Under it was written the word *triggers*.

Triggers? What was that? Like on a gun? Was it this guy's name? Was Rett supposed to tell Brad that? She called the number and got Brad's voice mail. She quickly told him what Mel said and hung up, wondering what she should do now. She knew she couldn't leave the store without locking it up, and she didn't have any idea how to do that. Her grandma. That's what she should do, call her grandma.

The answering machine picked up after the fourth ring, and Rett left a quick message for Love to call her back at the feed store. Then she tried Love's cell. Again, voice mail. Why didn't her grandma answer her cell phone?

What now? For some reason, she knew deep inside that she had to tell someone right away about Mel leaving with that scary-looking man. It didn't feel right to her, and the burden of being the only one who knew frightened her more than anything ever had.

Magnolia was the next person who came to her mind. She was looking up the number for the Buttercream in the tattered Morro Bay Yellow Pages when a man walked into the feed store. He was an older guy, not as old as her grandma or Magnolia, but not as young as Mel. Forties, she guessed. He wore a fleece-lined denim jacket, Levi's and muddy roper boots.

"Howdy," he said in an obvious Texas accent. "Mel around?"

She was silent for a moment, not certain what to say. "Uh, she stepped out for a moment, with a . . . She'll be back . . . uh . . . soon?"

He cocked his head while she stammered, his brown eyes serious. "Is everything okay?"

She nodded and swallowed hard, not trusting herself to speak again.

Something in his face shifted. He glanced around, taking in the empty feed store. "Are you here alone?"

She hesitated, not wanting to answer a question that would point out her vulnerability. Should she lie and say Brad or Evan was in the back? Would this guy fall for it? Who was he, anyway? She put the banjo case in front of her thinking that if he tried anything crazy she could throw it at him and run.

He walked up to the counter, pulled out his wallet and flipped it open. "My name is Ford Hudson. I'm with the San Celina County Sheriff's Department. Mel and I are friends. Is there something wrong, young lady?"

She stared down at the badge. It looked real enough, but what if it was a fake? She'd seen on television about how many fake police badges there were out there. She wasn't an idiot.

"Smart girl," the man said. "Yes, it could be fake. What can I do to convince you I'm an actual officer and Mel's friend?"

Before she could answer, the phone rang. It was her grandma.

"Rett, are you okay? What's going on? Is Dale threatening you?" Love's voice sounded out of breath.

"No, I'm fine," she said, keeping her eye on the man. "I'm at the feed store. Did Magnolia call you?"

"Yes, but she said you were on your way home. Then I listened to your message. You sounded scared."

"I'm okay. You know, like, a lot of people here in Morro Bay, right?"

"I suppose you could say I do. Why?"

She gazed up at the man in the denim jacket. "Do you know some-one named Hudson . . . uh . . ."

"Ford Hudson," the man repeated, smiling. "People call me Hud."

"Hud?" Rett said into the phone.

"Of course," Love said. "Hud's a sheriff's deputy. He has a daughter around your age. She was in my 4-H group for years."

"What's he look like?"

"Medium height. Short, brownish hair, gray at the temples. Has a Texas twang. Why?"

"He's here looking for Mel and I wasn't sure—"

"Where did Mel go? Are you at the feed store alone?"

Rett turned her back to Hud, and in a low voice, quickly told her the story. "I left a message for Brad. I can't leave the store unlocked. She left in such a hurry with this creepy guy who showed up and just told me to call Brad."

"Let me talk to Hud."

Rett turned around and handed the phone to Hud. "She wants to talk to you."

He listened, then said, "I don't know what's going on. I just walked in. Maybe Rett can tell me. Okay, sure. Here she is." He handed the phone back to Rett.

"I'll be right down," Love said. "Sit tight. Tell Hud whatever he wants to know. You can trust him."

Rett hung up the phone. "My grandma said you were okay."

"Can you tell me where Mel is now?"

Rett nodded. "She left with a man. It was kinda strange. I mean, she was sort of jumpy. The guy was big, like wrestler big. He wore a trench coat. He had curly short hair. And a red face. Like he was a drinker." She paused. "My stepfather drinks a lot, that's how I know that."

He put both hands on the counter. "Tell me exactly what happened."

She told him everything she could remember. "He didn't say any-thing, but it was like she knew he was coming or something."

"Did she say anything about where they were going?"

Rett shook her head. Then she remembered and pointed at the counter. "She wrote Brad's number for me and something else."

He came around the counter and looked at the message: triggers. "How long ago did they leave?"

She glanced at the black-and-white schoolhouse clock that hung on the wall next to the doorway. "Maybe fifteen minutes? Twenty? Do you know where they went? Does it help at all?"

He reached over and patted her hand. "It helps tremendously, Rett. You did real good. Is your grandma on her way down here?"

Rett nodded, suddenly afraid for Mel, though she didn't exactly know why.

"Then I'm going to take off. Don't worry. I'm pretty sure I know where they went."

"Okay," she said, watching him walk out the door. "Good luck," she called after him. Then added under her breath, "Okay, Mister God, you gotta give Mel a break. She really, really needs your help. Please make everything okay. In Jesus's name, amen."

TWENTY-FIVE

Mel

"We'll take my car," Mel said, walking toward her truck.

"I'd rather drive," Patrick said.

"I drive, or I don't go." She wouldn't give in on this point. She knew that it was crazy even going off alone with him, despite the fact that she'd left a clue on the desk that she hoped Rett would pick up on. It would at least give them a place to start looking if she disappeared.

"Whatever." He grunted and squeezed his hefty bulk into the front seat. "I just want to get this over with."

"No more than I do," Mel said, driving slowly down Main Street.

"Where are we going?" he asked. "Why not just go to your place?"

She stopped at the on-ramp to Pacific Coast Highway and glanced in her rearview mirror. No one behind her. She turned to look at him. "I think that little paint job you did on my garage answers any questions about why you are not welcome at my house."

He had the grace to look embarrassed. His already florid complexion, a rougher, rounder facsimile of Sean's handsome face, turned a deeper red. "I was just trying to get your attention."

"It was juvenile," she said, pressing her foot on the accelerator as they took the curvy on-ramp. "There's a bar in San Celina where we can talk."

"Only thing I want to talk about is you giving back the money."

She didn't answer but pressed down harder on the accelerator. She contemplated more than one of the passing light posts, calculating how fast she'd have to hit one to kill them both. But, somewhere inside her, another voice, one that sounded suspiciously like Cy's, argued against that drastic solution.

"Not many situations on this earth are totally unfixable, Mel," Cy told her once. "With God's help and a little perseverance, most things can be worked out. The secret is not giving up. If something doesn't work, you simply try another path."

They'd been stacking alfalfa bales in the back lot, and she'd not answered. She loved Cy like a father, but when he started talking that God stuff, she just shifted her mind into neutral and let him rattle on. She didn't want to offend him, but it all seemed just too improbable to her. And ironic, she thought now, coming from someone who died from something that couldn't be fixed. But she understood what he was trying to get across to her and what he was trying to do: give her hope.

His words about not giving up made her think of Love. If nothing else, what Love had gone through in the last year was reason enough for Mel not to kill herself. She'd never put her friend through that kind of pain. She'd at least try to heed Cy's advice and try another path with Patrick.

It was dark when they reached Triggers, a bar that Mel had gone to a few times on her lonely night drives when grisly memories kept her from sleep. It was down by the San Celina bus station. The bar was a place that didn't do a thing to attract tourists but prided itself in maintaining its hard-core working-class roots. The flat-roofed, cinder block building had been around for fifty years, had opened and closed at least ten times, and every one of those hard years was apparent in the scarred wooden booths, the chipped dark brown linoleum floor and the rust-stained bathroom sinks. It was past the point of being quaint and was what it was: a place for people down on their luck to sit, drink and brood. The television on the wall was always turned to sports, never CNN. There were only hard-core country songs on the jukebox: Haggard, Jones, Cash, the Williams boys, father, son and grandson. No one knew Mel there—she didn't frequent it often enough—and the bartenders changed as quickly as the tide. It felt like the right place to have it out with Patrick.

She chose a back booth, and once their drinks came, Patrick started in on her. In the background, Dwight Yoakam wailed about being a thousand miles from nowhere.

"Okay, enough of the bullshit," Patrick finally said. "Just give me the money, and I'm on the first plane out of here."

She was ready for him, had been carrying them around since he called, expecting this moment. She pulled her checkbook and savings account statement from her back pocket, slapping them down on the table in front of him. The wooden table jiggled with the force, and his beer sloshed over the rim of the mug, wetting the edge of the blue and white bank statement.

He glanced over them. "What's this supposed to prove?"

"Look at the balances," she said, keeping her voice quiet. She needed all the edge she could get, and she'd learned from years on the force that often speaking low commanded more authority than loud blustering. It forced the other person to lean in to hear you, giving you the psychological advantage. "In case you have trouble with numbers, the checking account has approximately nine hundred bucks in it and the savings a little less than a thousand. What don't you understand? That's all my worldly goods, right there."

He shoved the papers back across the table. "Doesn't prove shit. You could have the money squirreled away in some other account."

She picked up her own drink, a whiskey over ice, and took a sip. She'd make this last, let the ice melt and water it down. She had to keep her wits about her. "Except that I don't."

"Yeah, right." He gave a harsh laugh and rubbed his knuckles across his strong chin. She could hear the rasp of his beard against skin-covered bone.

"Oh, c'mon," she said, frustration rising inside her like a teakettle starting to boil. "You saw where I lived. You've probably been inside my house. I work at a feed store, you stupid ass. Why would I live like this if I had all this money you think I have?"

He shrugged, drained his beer and let out a soft belch. "You're not stupid. For all I know, you're lying low, waiting—"

"Waiting!" she exclaimed, slapping a hand on the table. "For what? It's been three years. What do you think I'd be waiting for? I have a question for you. Why did *you* wait so long to start harassing me? If you thought I had this money, where have you been?"

He looked her straight in the eyes. "You know why. I told you at Sean's funeral that I'd never pursue this until our mother died. God rest her soul." He crossed himself. "I'd've never done nothing to hurt her. Sean hurt her enough."

She wanted to slam her fist on the table. *Not just her.*

"Give me the money, and I'll go away."

"You're hopeless," she said, throwing a ten-dollar bill down on the table. "Find your own way home."

She jumped up and darted for the door, counting on youth and surprise to give her a head start. The unexpected rain hit her hard in the face the minute she ran over the threshold. The semi-full parking lot was slick with wet oil, causing her to slow just enough for Patrick to catch up with her. He grabbed her upper arm, squeezing it hard enough to make her squawk.

Outweighing her by eighty pounds, he easily swung her around to face him. She twisted from his grasp, attempting to knee him in the groin. She slipped on the wet asphalt, missed and slammed her knee into his thigh. His grip tightened; he fumbled, let go, grabbing her other arm.

Rain blinded her, pelting their struggle. She twisted, turned, using speed and her smaller size to make herself an awkward catch. She wished she had her baton or her hefty police flashlight.

"Hold still," he yelled, his hand twisting her arm. "Hold still, you stupid . . ."

She twisted again—a crazy pirouette—pulled a hand free, ramming her palm into his nose. Dead-on hit. Cartilage gave under her hand; warm liquid spewed out.

He bellowed and backed up, cupping his hand to his bleeding nose. In the blink of an eye, his gun was out and pointed at her.

Instinctively, she backed up, hands held up in protest. "Hey, Patrick. Not cool. Not . . ." Where was her gun? Her jacket. The feed store. *Damn.* She was toast.

"Give me the money," he said. Blood flowed freely from his nose, pooling in the flabby corners of his mouth. He twisted his head to the side and spat. His gun didn't move an inch.

At that moment, staring down into the barrel of his 9mm, something in her just surrendered. She closed her eyes, letting her arms drop to her side. Just do it, Patrick, she thought. I'm so sick of all this. *Just do it.*

But seconds later, something—someone—else inside her protested. Don't be a coward. There's always another path. This is not unfixable.

She opened her eyes and started walking toward him. He wouldn't shoot; she knew that now. Not if he really thought she had that money. "Patrick, look . . ."

Before she could go any farther the door of the bar opened, and an old man stumbled over the threshold. He took one look at Patrick's gun, then glanced at Mel and held his hands up.

"Whoa, it's good, people. It's all good." He scuttled back into the bar.

"Put it away, Patrick," Mel said. "That guy's going to tell the bartender, and he's going to call the police. You'll have a lot of explaining to do."

"Tell me where the money is," he said, ignoring her words.

She sighed, too tired to fight, too tired to cry. "I don't have any money."

In seconds, he closed the distance between them, shoving the gun in her side. "We are going to go back to your place, and you will give me the money."

At that moment, though it was totally illogical and probably stupid, she started laughing. He shoved the butt of the gun deeper into her side, causing her to grunt from the pain, but it still didn't stop the laughter.

"What is your problem?" he said, poking her again with the gun.

Before she could answer, a truck pulled into the driveway, a Dodge Ram with enough running lights to double as a small airport runway.

Patrick pulled her closer, whispering into her ear. "One word, and I swear I will pull this trigger."

She felt a giggle start deep inside her again. Didn't he realize what a keystone cop moment this was? As the laughter bubbled inside her, she knew that he was crazy or maybe drunk enough to pull the trigger. And if he did kill her, he'd probably get away with it, seeing as no one knew he was here, no one knew the history between them.

Except Rett. Her laughter died in that split second, sobering her as quickly as if she'd been soaked with a bucket of cold water. Rett had seen his face. And for all she knew, Patrick was crazy enough to make sure that Rett would never identify him. It occurred to Mel in that moment that she no longer lived in a vacuum, that maybe she really never had. What happened to her affected other people. And, though she had the right to play with her own life, she didn't have the right to endanger someone else. Especially an innocent young girl. Especially Cy and Love's granddaughter.

"Patrick," she answered in a calm voice as they watched the man park in the shadows, turn off his lights and step out of the truck. "Let's just go back to my place like you suggested." She could hear his harsh breathing on the back of her neck, smell the stale malty scent of beer, the wet sugary scent of his hair oil.

The man walked past them, his face clear now in the lone parking lot light. He was close enough to them to shake hands. He wore a Levi's jacket with fleece lining. Mel tensed against Patrick, using all her resolve to hold back a gasp of recognition. In that moment, she almost believed in God.

"Evening, folks," Hud said, touching the bill of his dark baseball cap. "Nice night for ducks."

Patrick grunted a reply, lowering his face into the back of Mel's head. She knew what he was attempting, to make sure that Hud didn't see his face. Her heart pounded so hard she could hear it thumping in her ears, blocking out any other sound. Though she knew it had only been a few minutes that she and Patrick scuffled, it felt like an hour. She was glad to see Hud, relief flooding through her veins like good whiskey, but she also knew that Patrick would not give up easily.

She searched Hud's face, looking for a clue about his plans, but he acted like they'd never met. He walked on toward the bar, entering the door and closing it behind him. Had he not recognized her? Was it just a coincidence that he'd shown up? Had Rett called him, told him what Mel had written on the feed store counter? Relief turned into confusion. She felt Patrick's grip on her ease, and she considered pulling away. But no matter how fast she was, she wasn't faster than a bullet. And he was drunk, not thinking clearly. Though she couldn't believe he had any intention of killing her—that would truly only complicate things for him—she also didn't trust his judgment right now.

"Let's go," she said in as normal a voice as she could manage. "It's wet and cold out here. We can talk about this at my place."

"Right," he said. "Like I said to begin with." He loosened his grip on her and pushed her ahead of him. "Let's go."

"Let's not," Hud said behind him.

TWENTY-SIX

Mel

The sound of Hud's voice caused Mel to whip around. It had seemed like only seconds since she'd seen him disappear inside the bar. In the rain, he looked blurry and indistinct, like he'd appeared from the mist. The whole scene was beginning to feel like one long, weird dream.

He held a small revolver inches from Patrick's left ear. "Now, sir," he said softly in his Texas accent. "Why don't you just lay your gun down real nice and easy? I'm sure we all can talk about this in a civilized manner befittin' our esteemed professions as peace officers."

Mel felt a hysterical laugh rise inside her chest, making her feel again like this was some insane dream . . . or an episode of *The Dukes of Hazzard*. Patrick did kind of remind her of Boss Hogg. But would Hud be Bo or Luke Duke? Oh, man, she was losing her mind.

"What the . . . ?" Patrick started to move, then froze when Hud touched the side of his neck once more with the gun barrel.

"Put the gun down *now*." Hud's voice lowered a fraction of a note.

Mel could see Patrick hesitate, and for a split second, she felt sorry for him. He probably thought he was being mugged. As a cop, one of the things you always worried about was some dirtbag getting your gun.

"Patrick," she murmured, shivering slightly. "It's okay. He's a cop."

Patrick coughed, spat blood, his ravaged face confused. "What are you talking about?"

"Just put your gun down. Do what he says."

She could see him hesitate again, weighing the possibilities of whether he could come out on top of this situation. Realizing he wouldn't, he slowly placed his gun on the wet asphalt.

"Back up," Hud said, grabbing Patrick's shoulder and pulling him back. "Mel, pick up the gun."

Mel dashed over and grabbed the gun.

Hud lowered his revolver and stuck it in his shoulder holster. He clapped Patrick on the shoulder. "Now maybe y'all should go back inside and take care of your business with each other without the entirely unnecessary threat of bodily harm."

"Nothing to talk about," Patrick said. "She has my brother's money, and I want it back."

Hud said, "Mr. O'Reilly, if you want my opinion, in this particular situation, I think that you might be huntin' coon with a bear rifle."

Patrick spat again, then gave Hud a disgusted look. "Are you some kinda nut job?" He glanced over at Mel. "Is he some kinda nut job?"

Mel shook her head. "No comment."

"Look," Hud said, throwing an arm around Patrick's shoulder. "Why don't you and Ms. LeBlanc go back inside and deal with this little squabble between you once and for all? I think you losin' your baby brother is sad as all get out, but you both gotta move on. Y'all are alive and, frankly, you don't know for how long. Any one of us could be hit by a Greyhound bus the next time we step off the curb. Would Sean really want you throwin' your own life away looking for money that is probably a figment of your imagination?"

Patrick's face hardened. "It's not. My little brother—"

"Ah, man, your baby brother made some big, big mistakes," Hud said, his voice gentle. "Sounds like he left a whole heap of sadness behind for you, for your mama, for Mel there. I think you know deep in your heart there never was any money left. And I think you and Mel there need to talk about that. But more importantly, I think you need to talk about Sean and how much you miss him, maybe even how he disappointed you. What do you think?"

Mel held her breath, not believing what she was hearing. Was Hud crazy, trying to play amateur therapist? Any minute Patrick was going to blow his top, start throwing punches and shouting obscenities, grabbing for his gun. But she watched in shock as Patrick seemed to deflate. He dropped his head, rain dripping from his black hair. She looked down at herself and realized that she was soaking wet.

"It's wetter than a duck's ass out here," Hud said. "Let's go inside and have some coffee. Mel, you hand me Mr. O'Reilly's gun, and I'll hold it until you two get this thing between you straightened out."

Mel handed Hud the gun without a word and followed him and Patrick into the bar.

"That's them!" the old man at the bar said when they walked into the almost-empty bar. "They's the ones with the guns."

The bartender, a thin, sloe-eyed man with one tattooed sleeve and a shaved head, gave them a hard look. "Do I need to call the cops?"

"No, sir," Hud said, pulling out his deputy's badge and showing it to the man. "Things are under control. If you could just pour my two friends here a couple of big cups of coffee, I think we'll be fine."

The man nodded. "Don't want no trouble."

"Nor do we," Hud said. "I'll have my coffee here at the bar, and my friends are going to take that booth over there." Hud nodded over at the booth where Mel and Patrick had sat only a half hour ago. He faced Mel and Patrick. "We'll stay here as long as it takes for you two to come to some kind of compromise, and then I'll give Mr. O'Reilly a lift back to his car, wherever that is. How's that?"

Mel was again shocked to see Patrick nod, without a peep of protest. They sat in the booth facing each other for a few minutes before he spoke.

"There isn't any money, is there?" he asked.

She looked him straight in the eyes. "No, Patrick. I'm sorry. I think . . . I think he spent most of it. I really do. And I'll be straight with you. If there had been, I would have turned it over to the department. I know there's lots of people there who think I was in on it. No one wanted to believe that Sean would take graft. They would have liked it better if I had been the one on the take, that Sean had been covering for me. But he wasn't. I didn't know a thing. I left the department because I couldn't stand people thinking I was crooked." She swallowed, tasting salt and bile at the back of her throat. Her voice turned into a harsh whisper. "And I couldn't stand being there without Sean."

Patrick hung his head down, and she stared at the part in his thick, dark hair. Even in the dim light of the bar, she could see streaks of silver, and for some reason that caused her eyes to burn. He was ten years older than Sean, and it was like she was seeing a snippet of what might have been.

"Ma was never the same after he died," Patrick said, his face studying the wooden table. He didn't even look up when the bartender slipped two white mugs of coffee in front of them. The man didn't offer milk and sugar, and she didn't ask.

"Were any of us?" she answered softly.

"I'm so tired," Patrick said. "I wish . . ." His voice dropped away.

She had a good idea about what he wished. That Sean was still here. That he'd never taken the money. That he hadn't killed himself. That life was easier. If wishes were horses, her mom used to tell her, we'd all be sitting on a Derby winner every darn day of the year.

"He was mostly a good man, Patrick," she said, resisting the temptation to touch his hand. "He made some mistakes, and the thing was, I guess he just couldn't face up to it. I just wish I could have . . ." She didn't finish the sentence. Loved him better? Helped him? Saved him? Frankly, she didn't even know how to finish that sentence.

She wouldn't tell him the one thing that no one else knew, the one thing she'd never tell anyone. Sean, the day he killed himself, asked her to come to his apartment. He wanted to talk. He wanted to explain one last time. She knew she shouldn't have gone. But she could never say no to him.

They were sitting on his leather sofa when he asked her. He asked her to shoot him and then asked her to come with him.

"We can be together forever," he'd said, his voice so mesmerizing, so convincing. "You and me, baby. Drinking with the angels. Forever and ever, amen."

She'd stared at him in shock. "You're crazy," she'd whispered.

He laughed. "Did you ever doubt that?"

She left a few minutes later, feeling like he'd duped her one more time. She never thought he'd really do it. She thought that, in some insane and miraculous way, he'd beat the rap. He'd somehow walk, not go to prison. Sean was just not the kind of guy you could imagine locked up. Well, he did beat the prison rap. In a way, he did walk away.

The question always haunted her. What if she'd told someone? What if she'd stayed? What if she'd taken his gun? What if, what if, what if?

Patrick looked up, peering at her in the dim light with watery eyes, old man's eyes. "I . . . wanted someone to blame. I'm sorry, you were . . . you were just easy. When I talked to the guys who worked with him, they just said you and him, you were so close. I couldn't believe you'd be so close and . . ."

"And not know about it?" She gave a harsh laugh. "Think of how I felt, Patrick. I thought I knew him. And I was a cop, for Pete's sake. I should have known. I should have . . ." Her voice cracked. She pounded a fist on the table. Her eyes burned again, but she wouldn't give in to tears. "I was an idiot. To be honest, I didn't even know he was using, much less skimming off money. All I could see was I loved him. I did, Patrick. Despite everything, I loved him."

Patrick stared at her a moment, then gave one nod. "I believe you. I'm sorry if I made things harder. His partner said you found him?" His face twisted in agony.

She nodded, feeling a drop of sweat inch down the middle of her breasts. Don't make me tell you, she thought. Please, don't make me. Sean's face stained bright red, tiny bits of his brain sprayed across the hallway wall, stuck to the bucolic scene of sunflowers and wishing wells. When he moved in, they'd laughed until they cried at that wallpaper, both agreeing it was the tackiest they'd ever seen. *The coppery sweet smell of his blood.* She'd gone back to his place a few hours after that last talk. She'd tried his cell phone, and it kept kicking over to voice mail. In her gut, she knew he'd gone without her.

"I'm sorry," he said. "I'm sorry you had to experience that."

She nodded again, unable to talk, knowing if she said one word, she'd start sobbing and maybe never stop.

"I'll go now," Patrick said, reaching over and patting her hand like she was a child.

She slid out of the booth and stood up, not knowing what to say.

He stood up, and they stared at each other for a moment. Finally, she held out a hand. "You take care, Patrick. Stay safe." That customary cop admonition, a prayer of sorts, because they knew that being safe really wasn't in their control.

He shook her hand awkwardly, breaking contact before she did. "You too." He went over to Hud, said a few words, then walked into the men's room without looking back.

Hud walked over to where Mel still stood next to the booth. "I'm going to take him back to his car in Morro Bay, then follow him back to his hotel. Will you be okay driving home?"

She nodded, not trusting herself to speak. It was over. She'd never hear from Patrick again. Though it was a relief, she was also oddly bereft. Because then she'd have no one in her life who knew Sean, who knew how much he loved ranch-flavored Doritos, how he always talked about buying a houseboat, how that little cowlick in the back of his head drove him nuts, how his laugh was so infectious that even most of the people he arrested couldn't resist laughing with him. Patrick would go back to his family and have people to talk to about Sean. She'd only have a small manila envelope of photos and a ruby pendant shaped like a daisy that he bought her the first Valentine's Day they were together.

"Mel?" Hud said.

She jolted back to the present. A deep shudder ran through her, reminding her briefly of Red on cold days. She felt chilled to the bone.

"Here," Hud said, pulling off his denim jacket. Before she could protest, he slipped it around her shoulders.

She could feel the warmth from the fleece lining seep into her wet flannel shirt. "I'm fine. I don't—"

"Ah, pipe down," he said. "It's just an excuse to see you again."

She stared at him a moment, feeling vulnerable. But also, she had to admit, relieved. That it was over. That she'd survived. That she maybe had a shot at having a life.

"Thanks," she said finally.

"Go home, Melina Jane LeBlanc," he replied. "Get in your pj's and make yourself a cup of tea. Sometimes, as my own dear grand-mère used to say, that's just all a body can do."

"Yes," she said.

On the drive back, she tried to put her thoughts on hold. There was just too much to comprehend, too much she'd have to think about later. Right now it seemed imperative that she do exactly as Hud said: go home, get in her pajamas and make a cup of tea. Home. Yes, that's what it was, what this place finally was: home. She knew she'd need to call Love, that Rett would have told her everything and that she was likely worried sick. Mel was already going over the conversation in her head, the explanation, the explanation of the explanation. It was time to tell Love everything. She should have done it long ago.

The house was dark and cold when she walked in. She turned on the hall light and the heater, then walked into the living room. She sat down on the sofa that she'd bought for fifty bucks at the Salvation Army store in San Celina. Moonlight filtered through the blinds, shadowing the room. Her clothes were only damp now; the warmth of the car heater dried them as she drove home.

She pulled the denim jacket closer around her, its warmth coming from her own body heat now. But the scent of Hud was still strong: a sharp, peppery male scent. A sob gripped her throat, trying to escape. It reminded her of all the men she'd ever worked with, the locker rooms where they stored their gear, the scent of their testosterone, their sweat, their fear and their joy. The scent of her old life, the one that would never exist again.

But it had been replaced with the scents of leather and saddle soap, alfalfa and the salty-sweet smell of the sea. Not a bad trade. But she missed her old life. Oh, how she missed it.

"Sean," she whispered, pulling the jacket closer around her, turning her nose into the fleece collar, inhaling the scent of a man she barely knew, remembering another man she thought she'd known, but who had really been a stranger.

"Sean," she cried, louder this time. Her voice sounded harsh in the empty room. The third time she wailed his name. "Seaaan." She sank to the floor where she rocked back and forth, the stranger's jacket pulled tight around her shoulders. She rocked and rocked, not crying, not thinking, just pretending the jacket was her lover's arms. She sat on the cold, cold floor, rocking and pretending, rocking and pretending, until long after the shivering stopped.

TWENTY-SEVEN

Love Mercy

M el, I'm still worried. Call me."

It was the sixth voice message Love had left on her friend's cell phone since she'd picked Rett up at the feed store five hours ago. It was past ten p.m., and the only thing that kept Love from calling the police was that Rett told her that Hud said he knew where Mel was going by the clue she left written on the counter. Besides, what could Love actually report? That a woman, a former cop, no less, had left under her own volition with some man that Love's granddaughter thought looked kind of creepy. Oh, and that Mel seemed a little nervous, even though the man didn't utter one threatening word. Love could almost hear the police dispatcher's annoyed response: And what, ma'am, do you exactly want the police to do?

Mel finally called her at ten thirty.

"I've been worried sick," Love said, trying to keep her voice neutral. She wished Mel was her daughter so she could really let go and give her what for. But that was something a person could only get away with if there was shared blood or, at the very least, a more intimate relationship than what they had.

"I would have called you earlier, but . . ." Mel's voice faded away, sounding as tired as if she'd run a marathon.

"You should have," Love snapped, deciding, what the heck, Mel *was* like her daughter. All this drama was starting to get on her nerves. "You shouldn't do things like that, take off with whoever this flaky guy was, and not let someone know where you're going to be. People care about you. *I* care about you. You could have been hurt . . . or . . ." Her voice faltered.

"I'm sorry," Mel said. "Hud caught up with me. I wasn't alone. Rett did the right thing by showing him what I'd written on the counter. Tell her thanks. Everything's fine."

Love swallowed hard, trying to dislodge an imaginary meat chunk stuck in her throat. "What was this all about? Who was this man? Rett said he looked like a hit man."

Mel's laugh sounded forced. "He's a cop. The older brother of a . . . a friend of mine. I have some stuff to tell you. It's about . . . my life before I came here. Can we talk tomorrow?"

Still irritated, Love almost demanded the whole story right then, but she'd learned from experience that difficult subjects really were best discussed when everyone was rested. It was late. Tomorrow would come soon enough.

"Of course," she said, her voice short. "Call me tomorrow. We can meet at Cy's bench."

Mel's relieved sigh was audible over the phone. "That would be good. I go there sometimes when I need to . . . think and stuff."

Love's anger subsided. "Me too."

"Is Rett okay?"

Love looked over at her granddaughter, who was giving Ace a neck massage. His dark eyes were slits of pleasure. "Yes. She and the boy have come to an agreement. She's giving him his banjo back tomorrow."

"Yeah, she told me. I told her the sooner she did that, the quicker she could get on with her life."

"I agree. Sleep well."

Mel paused, as if she was considering Love's words. "You know, I think I will."

"What's the four-one-one on the mafia hit man?" Rett asked when Love hung up.

"Don't know yet." Love leaned against the refrigerator, her arms crossed over her chest. "Mel will fill me in tomorrow."

Rett stood up and grabbed Ace's leash from the hook. "I'll take the Flying Ace Ball for his last walk."

"Thanks," Love said, her mind trying not to dwell on what Mel would reveal tomorrow. Had she been a drug addict? An alcoholic? Had she killed someone? Was that why she was no longer a police officer? There were so many things it could be. An undercurrent of tragedy had always hovered around Mel. Magnolia and Love had pondered it many times.

"I bet she's got herself some kind of sad story," Magnolia said once.

"Doesn't everyone?" Love had answered, her mind drifting to the question, How would a person reveal someone's life story in a single portrait? The best photographers—like Judith Joy Ross—could reveal a person's backstory and also give a hint about what might come to be in her subject's life. Her portraits of the Hazelton public school kids were breathtaking in their simplicity and vulnerability. Every time Love looked at them, she felt she could see the future of each child. She'd always wondered if she would be able to discern Mel's backstory if she took her portrait. She had not yet had the nerve to ask her to pose.

Love had always suspected that Cy knew much more than she did about Mel's life before Morro Bay, but even he admitted to Love once that Mel had a shell like a Brazil nut: thick, jagged and hard to crack. Even as he neared the end of his life, he never revealed whatever he knew about Mel to Love, something she admired in him even as it frustrated her. Cy's word was something he'd always taken very seriously.

She walked into the living room to wait for Rett so she could lock the door behind her. The battered banjo case sat propped against the sofa. Rett had brought it back with her when Love picked her up at the feed store. Love hesitated, then laid the case flat and undid the clasps. The banjo that had started this whole adventure lay nestled inside its gray fuzzy cocoon, not one bit aware of the trouble it had caused.

She touched the strings gently. When she pulled her hand back, the slight give from her fingers caused a tiny hum. What did Rett sound like playing this instrument? Did she have talent or only wished she did? The occasional episodes of reality talent shows that Love had seen taught her that a person didn't always recognize the difference between wanting a talent and having a talent. The thing that wrenched Love's heart watching those shows was how surprised the untalented people where when they were told by the judges to do the world a favor and find another way to express themselves. It was obvious on the contestants' faces that they truly didn't realize that they didn't have something extraordinary to share. And, she wondered, what if, by pursing a talent they didn't have, they were neglecting one they did possess? How many aspiring singers might actually be extraordinary painters or dog trainers or gardeners or children's game inventors, but they'd never know it, because they continued seeking something they thought they wanted? Honestly, wasn't the invention of Monopoly as important a gift to the world as the songs of Elton John or Willie Nelson? A lot of families would never even talk to each other if it hadn't been for Monopoly.

Love always wondered what happened to those disappointed people who didn't have a chance at making the final fifty or ten or first in those talent shows. What did they go home to? What were their stories? Those were the photos she wanted to take.

She picked up her Nikon. She had ten shots left on this roll of black-and-white film. Holding her breath, she carefully lifted the banjo from the case and set it on the sofa. She took shots of it from all angles, capturing its glossy wood and the shadows the yellow lamplight made on its round body. Banjos were such funny-looking instruments, like a pear-shaped figure gone horribly wrong. She knew enough about music to understand that they were rarely the center of attention in a band, almost always were there to support the other instruments and the main event, the singer. Still, she'd heard some banjo solos in her life that amazed her. She smiled to herself. And they certainly got more respect than a bass fiddle.

There was a full moon tonight, and she would have liked to take it outside and photograph it in that interesting light, but she didn't want to risk harming something so valuable. Maybe before Rett returned it to Dale, she could get a few shots of it outside. For now, these inside shots would have to do.

Love knew Rett would be sad tomorrow. But what her granddaughter didn't know was that it would likely be one of the easier sad moments of her life. It would feel huge while it was happening, she would think her heart was breaking, but time would give her perspective. Maybe Love would give her one of these banjo photos then, and maybe Rett would laugh, recalling how important she thought this shallow young man was.

Love placed the instrument back in the case and sat down on the sofa. She leaned her head back, so weary she felt like she could sleep for days. Sometimes it overwhelmed her, all this sadness, when she studied photos from places around the world where poverty and war and the cruelty that humans manage to perpetrate upon each other is revealed, photos of tornadoes and tsunamis and floods. The wreckage of so many lives. She wondered where the God her mother trusted so faithfully was in all this. At times, Love despised herself for doubting. Other times, she just felt tired and wished God would give the world a break and erase all doubt. Just write across a big chalkboard in the sky who he was and what he wanted everyone to do. She smiled to herself. She should share that with Rocky. He loved stuff like that. He'd get a whole month of Sunday sermons out of that image.

Her mind drifted to the subject of gifts, the subject she'd suggested to Clint for February's issue. Appropriate for Valentine's Day, but her mind wasn't considering sentimental photographs of lacy hearts and chocolate candy or photos of couples walking on the beach. For some reason, her mind floated back to the first days after Tommy was killed, when for the first time since they'd known each other, she and Cy seemed unable to talk. Both of them were adrift in their own personal grief, reliving their moments with Tommy, wondering if there would ever be an end to the long bridge they were being forced to cross.

A sudden memory caused her to sit forward and move the wooden bowl filled with magazines from her coffee table trunk. Down at the bottom of tissue-wrapped family heirlooms of pickle dishes, embroidered pillowcases, her father's folded coffin flag, her great-grandmother's

silver-plated cake server, next to her mother's letters was a large envelope of photos that had rested there for fourteen years. She pulled out
the manila envelope and hesitated. She'd had the photos developed,
then slipped them unseen into this envelope, taping it shut with brown
packing tape.

Why now? Why would it occur to her now to search for the photos
she'd taken while she walked up and down Morro Bay mourning her
lost son? She really should have just thrown them out. Like the fish that
Cy told her he caught when he took the *Love Mercy* out and floated in
the open ocean. He'd fight to bring the fish in, he told her. The harder
the fight, the better he felt. Once he won, he'd toss it back in without a
glance. Over and over, he fought to capture a fish, then throw it back.
At some point, he told Love, he just started feeling better. After that, he
never fished again. Didn't have the heart for it.

While he fished, Love walked. She'd walked and taken roll after roll
of black-and-white photos. Not color, because at the time, color seemed
an emotional extravagance she couldn't bear. Mile after mile she'd walked
on the beach or on the three-mile white sand spit that enclosed Morro
Bay, taking photos of birds. Later, the metaphor seemed painfully clear
to her, but at the time she just felt drawn to photograph birds. She con-
centrated on f-stops and lighting, framing and detail. The mechanics of
photography took over, relieving her from thinking too deeply about the
life that stretched out in front of her and Cy like a long, dark, treeless
highway.

She carefully tore away the tape, curling at the edges after all these
years, and opened the envelope, expecting somehow the brackish, salty
scent of the ocean to rise up to greet her. Instead, there was only the
smell of old paper. The photos fattened the bottom of the envelope, and
she pulled the first one out. She stared at the picture of the one-legged
seagull perched confidently on a rock. A memory hit her like an electric
shock. She dumped the photos out on the floor, sifting through them
until she found what she was seeking. Two other photos. Two other
seagulls. Each of them one-legged. She remembered that day like it was
last week. What were the chances of her photographing three different
seagulls in one day, each with only one leg?

The second gull she'd caught in flight at just the right angle so that its footless stump was outlined against a bright afternoon sky. The other stood next to a discarded McDonald's bag, precariously balanced on one leg, its head half hidden, searching for leftovers. She laid all three photos on the closed trunk lid, staring at them. Two of the seagulls—the one flying and the McDonald's bird—were busy doing what seagulls do: looking for food. The third one, the one posed on the rock, stared directly into the camera's lens, looking—if a seagull could—defiant and strong and, it seemed to her, confident.

She remembered something else. The gulls had caused her to recall a Bible verse that she'd memorized as a child. It was a practice that Mama encouraged, telling her and DJ they'd be grateful someday that she made them do so, that memorizing God's words was like saving quarters for a rainy day.

Love closed her eyes and whispered out loud, "Purify me with hyssop, and I shall be clean: wash me and I shall be whiter than snow. Make me hear joy and gladness; that the bones which Thou hast broken may rejoice."

Psalm 51. Was it verse eight? Nine? She didn't remember exactly. But she did remember that at the time, the verse that the injured gulls flushed from her memory had made her angry. Had God been trying to communicate with her? If so, it was a message she had refused to accept. She didn't want to have broken bones, and she certainly didn't want to rejoice. The whole idea of being happy about affliction seemed sick and horrible and wrong. She just wanted her son back.

Love stared at the photos, wondering what she was supposed to learn from them after all these years. Maybe she'd ask Clint to do something a little different and print three photos. Three one-legged gulls. Gulls that were going on with their gull business despite their broken bones. Because that's what you do. You go on. You put one foot in front of the other. You trust that there's a reason, even if you don't get it. You trust there is someone in control. You go on because the only other choice is to give up, to believe that there was no reason at all that bad things happened. That seemed the most hopeless thing of all to believe. Maybe that was the gift right there.

That would be her caption, her mini essay: "Let the bones which Thou hast broken rejoice." Let people stew on that one. If they asked her what she meant, she could honestly say, I'm not really sure. Could you tell me?

By the time Rett came back from walking Ace, Love had scooped up all the photos and put them back in the envelope. Except the three of the one-legged gulls. She left those on the top of the trunk to take to Clint.

"What're those?" Rett asked. She picked up the one of the flying gull. "Wow, cool."

"Just some photos I took a long time ago," Love said.

The next morning at seven a.m., Love was up before Rett. She heard Ace pawing behind Rett's closed door. He was used to taking his morning constitutional right on time. Love opened her bedroom door, and he bolted out, scampering toward the back door.

Rett lifted her head slightly off the pillow. "Ace?"

"Go back to sleep," Love whispered. "I'll let him out."

"Okay," she said, her head dropping back down on the pillow with a thump. "Thanks."

About an hour later, Rett wandered into the kitchen, her hair pulled back in one long braid. She was dressed in jeans, sneakers and the Morro Bay sweatshirt Love had bought her.

"Yum," she said, sitting down, picking up one of the cinnamon rolls Love baked earlier. "I have a question."

"What?" Love asked, pouring her a cup of coffee.

"I'm supposed to meet Dale at the Buttercream at one to give him back the banjo. But I want to play it a little before I do. And, uh, just kinda be alone, you know? Maybe somewhere outside where, like, no one would be around. In nature or something?"

"Morro Rock," Love said. "It's a weekday and not tourist season. It would probably be you and a bunch of birds. Maybe an old guy or two taking photos, though they usually do that at sunup or sunset. There are always a few folks watching the peregrine falcons. You should be able to find a quiet spot."

"Can I walk there?"

"You could, but it'd be, as we say in Kentucky, a fur piece."

Her lips turned down slightly, a stubborn expression that Love was starting to recognize. "I can make it."

Love pulled a set of keys from the hook next to Ace's leash and tossed them on the table. "You can drive my Honda." She looked Rett in the eyes. "Providing you have a valid driver's license."

"I do," she said, standing up. "I can show—"

Love waved at her. "I believe you. Just turn left out of the driveway, then left again at the next street. That'll take you to the Embarcadero. Turn right on Embarcadero and follow it north. You'll see the road that leads out to the rock. It's a couple of miles."

"Wow, thanks. I'll be real careful. I promise."

Love smiled at her. "I know you will." Then she made a mental note to herself. Call insurance agent and have Rett put on my policy.

When Rett was halfway through the door, she turned around and asked, "You and Grandpa. How'd y'all meet?"

Her question caught Love by surprise. "He was visiting in Redwater with one of his friends from Fort Knox, Jim Shore, a boy who went to my church. They were on leave before going to Vietnam. We saw each other in the Redwater Drugstore. He was drinking a Coke float. I was buying some nail polish."

"So his friend, the guy from your church, he introduced you?"

Love smiled. "No, actually, he wasn't there. Cy just started talking to me. Said he liked the color of red polish I was buying, that it was the color of Pacific sunsets where he grew up."

"Grandma! He so totally picked you up."

Love faked a grimace, then laughed. "Yes, I guess you could say he did. He asked for my phone number, and he called the next day. He wanted to go out that night, but I was already busy with the Vacation Bible School fund-raiser pie social. He came with Jim, whose father was our head deacon. Your crazy grandpa paid seventy-five dollars for my rhubarb pie."

"Wow, he must have really liked you. That's a lot of money for a pie."

"Especially in 1967. After church, he and I and Jim went to a road-house to hear a bluegrass band play. But we told your great-grandma we went to a movie."

Rett leaned against the doorjamb and giggled. "You were a bad girl!"

Love winked at her. "Only semi-bad. I didn't touch a drop of liquor, and he had me home by ten p.m. Then he left, came back here to visit August and Polly, then he was off to Vietnam. I wrote him a letter every day for the whole year he was gone."

"No e-mail? Harsh."

Love started stacking the breakfast dishes. "Yes, hard as it is to imagine, we actually had to wait a little longer than thirty seconds for a reply."

Rett shook her head, the concept beyond her comprehension. "Then what?"

Love turned around and started rinsing plates. "When he returned, we got married. It was small, mostly my family. His parents couldn't leave the ranch to come out, so when we got to Morro Bay, we got married again by a minister here under the lightning tree. We used to celebrate two anniversaries every year."

"That's pretty cool."

Love opened the dishwasher door and started filling it with dishes. The dishwasher had seen more action in the last week than it had in a year. "I loved living here on the Central Coast. I mean, who wouldn't? It's beautiful. And Polly and August were wonderful to me from the start. Then your daddy was born, and everything was perfect." She didn't mention how glad—no, relieved—she was to leave Kentucky. Yes, she'd missed her mother like a physical pain, but she was glad to be thousands of miles from the earth that swallowed her beloved twin brother and rotted her daddy's pink lungs.

"Did you ever go back?"

"Once a year until Mama died when Tommy was five years old. Then, not as much. I have relatives there—Mama's two sisters and a passel of cousins—but by the time Tommy was born, my home was here."

She was silent for a moment. "When my dad died, how did you . . ."

Love turned around to face Rett, waiting for her to finish her question. Rett stared at the tile floor, her expression so stricken that Love wished she had a magic wand to wave over her head and conjure away all the hurt.

Love took a deep breath, not wanting to talk about this, but knowing she had to for Rett's sake. "When Tommy was killed, I thought I didn't want to live myself. I felt like . . ." Love paused a minute, thinking how she could word it. "I felt raw. Like a wound that couldn't scab over. I couldn't read. I couldn't think. I couldn't even pray." Love closed her eyes, thinking, Kind of like now.

"So what . . . how . . . ?" Her voice was hesitant.

She opened her eyes. "It just . . . gets easier. There's no real secret. You've heard that saying, time heals all wounds?"

She nodded. "Yeah, I guess."

"It's not exactly true. It doesn't heal; it just softens. You know it happened, but the details get fuzzier as time goes on."

Rett took Ace's dog leash and started rolling it into a little circle. "Like, you forget the pain?"

Love shook her head. "You never forget that sort of pain. It just . . . at some point it's not the first thing you think about when you wake up. It's a horrible cliché, but life does go on."

Rett pushed herself away from the doorjamb, hung the leash back up and picked up the banjo case. "Do you ever get pissed? I mean, you know, at God?"

Her question startled Love again with its bluntness. Her generation seemed to just cut to the chase, push aside all the flimflam and go for the throat.

"Yes," she said, surprised at her honest answer. "Sometimes I do, I have. But I think he understands. I hope he does."

Rett picked up her banjo case. "So, see you later."

Shortly after Rett left, the phone rang.

"Meet me at Cy's bench in an hour?" Mel asked.

"See you there."

Love left immediately, wanting to sit for a while before Mel arrived. There were rarely any children at the playground that early in the day, probably because it was usually still misty and damp. Once the sun burned away the fog around noon, the bronze whale tail and seals, the wood and concrete ship and the rocking fish would be filled with laughing, screaming children. When the city informed Love where Cy's memorial bench was to be placed, she was overwhelmed with the rightness of it. From his bench you could see the playground, the bay, the boats, Morro Rock and, in the distance, the open ocean. Everything he loved could be seen from this one perch. As she did each time she sat down, she put her fingers to her lips, then touched them to the brass plaque.

"In Memory of Cyrus August Johnson—1950–2007—Beloved Son, Husband, Father and Friend—Born and Raised on the Central Coast—From paradise to Paradise."

"Hey, Cy," she said. "Things sure are looking better. But then, that probably doesn't surprise you at all."

She sat there for a half hour before Mel arrived, enjoying the quiet. Love didn't know what Mel needed to tell her about her past, but before she even started, she was going to make it clear that whatever it was, it would not affect one bit how Love felt about her. Though they'd only known each other a few years and though they didn't bare their souls to each other in the way she and Magnolia did, Love trusted her instincts. She would have bet the ranch on Mel's decency and goodness. She was, Love suspected, someone who cared deeply but who'd seen too much hurt to let anyone get close.

Though Love knew a part of her would always feel missing with Cy gone, she suspected the pain Mel was feeling was very different. Like a motherless gosling, Mel had imprinted on Cy. She was, Love imagined, feeling the pain of almost having something and having it snatched away. Love would always have the assurance that she was loved, and that would carry her through her life. But even through her tears at Cy's funeral, she could see the absolute terror on Mel's face.

"She's carrying a world of hurt inside her," Cy told Love when he first hired her, right after the chicken incident. "I don't know what happened to her, but I feel like the Lord brought her to us, and I want to do whatever I can to make her feel safe."

Mel and Cy became friends immediately—good friends. And Love had become friends with her too. She had never been jealous, secure in Cy's love for her, in her place in his life. She knew his feelings for Mel were special. She'd needed him and, in a way, he had needed her. Not as a replacement for Tommy. More like the daughter he'd never had. Now that Love thought about it, what he and Mel gave to each other had been more like . . . a gift.

Love felt a hand on her shoulder.

"Hey, Mrs. Johnson," Mel said, slipping around and sitting next to her on the bench. "Looks like it's just you and me right now."

Love looked into Mel's tired young face. Pale lavender shadows stained the skin under her dark brown eyes. Her cheeks were flushed crimson from the cold. For a moment, she could imagine the little girl Mel once was, all gangly arms and skinned-up legs, big-eyed and serious. Who had hugged her when she was afraid or lonely? If no one had, would there ever be enough hugs in her life to compensate for that? Love couldn't help herself. She reached over and laid her palm against Mel's cold cheek.

"Melina Jane LeBlanc," she said, feeling Mel's skin start to warm under her hand. "I'm so awfully glad to see you."

Mel's eyes grew moist, though Love would be willing to bet it had been some time since she actually allowed tears to roll down her cheeks, at least in front of anyone. Even at Cy's funeral she'd been stoic as a monk.

"You might not think so after we talk," she said.

Love reached down and took Mel's cold hand in her own. "Sweetie, I truly, truly doubt that."

TWENTY-EIGHT

Rett

Rett drove as far as she could on the road that ended at Morro Rock. Her grandma Love was right: not many people were out here this early in the day. She parked the car facing the ocean and stepped outside. It was cold and wet from sea spray. The foghorn that blew all night was still going, its warning like a slow, mournful heartbeat. Behind her, Morro Rock rose to the sky, looking less spectacular close up than it did from her grandma's back deck, not so shiny. Really, just a big old rock.

Except that close up, she could see the tiny bits of life sustained in the crags and crevices, evidence of birds, wildflowers, insects. She turned away, walked to the edge of the ocean and peered into the churning water. It was so different from the lakes she'd grown up around, whose dangers included poisonous snakes and sometimes quicksand that grabbed your feet and made you feel like you were being pulled into the depths of the earth. This was different even from the ocean she'd seen in Florida. The Pacific Ocean seemed wild and untamable, like the wolves she'd seen on a National Geographic program. The pups were so cute, but then the photographer would zero in on the wolf mama's eyes, and you just knew that she'd rip your throat out without a moment's hesitation. A wave broke against the rocks, spraying her with a fine, cold mist. If she was going to do any writing, she'd definitely have to stay inside the car.

Inside the car it was still cold, but she knew if she turned on the heater, it would make her drowsy, and she'd never get this song written. And it was itching at her, telling her, now, now, get it down *now*. The emotion from it welled up in her—the words, the melody—like one of the waves crashing against the rocky shore. She pulled Dale's banjo out of its case and held it for a moment, letting its heavy fullness rest in her arms. She'd miss it, this hunk of satiny wood and cool metal that accompanied her on what was, for now, the biggest adventure of her life. But it wasn't hers. And it was time, as Mel said, to move on. Dale would always, always have that piece of her heart. It sort of pissed her off, and at the same time she was sort of okay with it. Because it was her experience, her life, and it was hers to use. She wondered what she'd think about all this thirty years from now. Thirty years. It seemed like forever. She'd be forty-eight. Patsy would be forty-nine. This unborn child that was causing everyone so much pain would be twelve years older than Rett was right now. It was hard to imagine that much time passing.

She tuned the banjo quickly by ear, second nature to her since she was ten, then started playing song after song, listening to its full sound once more, feeling the notes ring long after she'd plucked them—"Cripple Creek," "Banjo in the Hollow," "Bury Me Beneath the Willows," "Sally Goodin'," "Blackberry Blossom," "Wayfaring Stranger"—old songs she'd played when she first learned the banjo. She ended with "Amazing Grace," which she sang as she played, in her mind dedicating it to Tommy Johnson, the father she barely remembered. After a half hour or so, she set it upright in the passenger seat, like a fellow traveler, and pulled out her notebook. The words, baking in her subconscious like some kind of slow-cooking cobbler, flowed out of her in a quick, delicious waterfall of detail. For her, there was nothing better than this, not even first love. And, she suspected, there never would be.

* * *

Before Rett realized it, the fog had burned away, and the sun shone through the car windows. She noticed people walking past her car, peering curiously inside as she wrote, played a riff or two, then wrote again. It would have been easier with a guitar, but she liked the idea of composing a song using this banjo. It was something else to remember about this last incredible week. In four hours she'd finished everything except two lines of the bridge. But they'd come to her. Though she probably wasn't the best judge of her own work, she thought this song might be the coolest one she'd ever written. It made her cry, and that was a good sign, wasn't it? She laughed at herself when she put the banjo back into its case. That was so totally self-centered. The song was probably a piece of crap, but, somehow, just writing it all down made her feel better, made her feel like she'd taken some kind of giant step forward in her life.

She glanced at her phone. It was a quarter to one, but the Butter-cream was only a few minutes away. She had plenty of time. It wouldn't hurt Dale to wait a few minutes longer.

She started to call Lissa to tell her everything that had happened. When she got the number half dialed, she disconnected. No, she didn't need to do that. She could deal with this without help from her friend. It was time to take charge of her own life, with no advice from anyone else.

When she walked into the café carrying the banjo, it was a few seconds before she spotted Dale sitting in a corner booth. His face, drawn and shadowed with irritation, softened when he saw her. Her heart skipped, unable to hold back hope, until she realized it was the banjo he was looking at, not her.

"Get a grip," she muttered to herself.

"Coffee?" Magnolia called, as Rett walked toward Dale. An untouched plate of French fries sat in front of him, steam rising from their golden depths.

"Thank you," Rett called back.

Magnolia was at the table two seconds after Rett sat down across from Dale, pouring a white mug full of steaming coffee. "Hungry?"

"Not right now, thanks," Rett replied, looking up at the older woman. Did Magnolia know what a big moment this was in Rett's life?

"You let me know if you need any little thing, darlin'," she said. Then she turned her attention to Dale. Her full lips pursed into a little donut before saying, "Young man, do you require anything more than that lonely plate of fries?"

"No, ma'am," he said. "This is fine."

"Okay, y'all holler if you need something."

Once she'd left, Rett picked up a fry and contemplated it before putting it in her mouth. "How's it going?"

"Fine," he said, drumming his fingers on the red Formica table. "I'm ready to get going. You okay with things?"

She contemplated his words. "Actually, I am. I mean, with things between you and me. I'm so over that, you know." She looked him right in the eyes when she said it, daring him to contradict her.

He looked back at her, his eyes lingering on her lips and throat. She felt herself start to warm, so she decided to squelch whatever physical thing there was between them right now.

"You *are* going to go see Patsy when you get back, aren't you? She needs you right now."

"I guess," he said, his eyes darting sideways, looking in that moment to Rett just exactly what he was: a flaky, shallow guy who didn't think past his next gig, his next bottle of beer or his next hookup. Poor Patsy. In that moment, Rett felt like throwing her cup of coffee in this sorry-ass guy's face for messing up her sister's life.

"You are legally this baby's father, and you should help her," Rett said, coldly. "Step up, Dale. Be a man for once."

"Hey, that's low," he said.

She shrugged. "Low is taking off on your pregnant girlfriend."

"You had my banjo! It was your fault I had to leave Knoxville."

She gave him what she hoped was a withering look. *Withering.* Now there was a good word. Had all kinds of connotations to it. "Just take your precious banjo and go home. Go talk to Patsy and figure stuff out. Grow some balls."

He opened his mouth to say something, then thought better of it.

Though she'd always wonder what his comeback would have been, she knew a good last line when she heard one. She scooted out of the booth.

He slid out and picked up the banjo case. "Guess this is good-bye, then."

She grabbed her mug, turned her back to him and walked over to the counter where Magnolia was cutting a lemon icebox pie. Rett stared at the yellow and white pie, feeling her heart give a little when she heard the cowbell on the door jangle.

"He's gone," Magnolia said, slipping a plate in front of Rett. "Might as well have some pie."

Rett sat down on the stool. "That could be a song."

"You stick around this place long enough, you could write more songs than you could record in a year. Everyone's got a story." She cocked her head. "One of our morning waitresses just quit. It's my job to hire and fire."

Rett picked up her fork and took a bite of the pie. It was sweet and sour and bitter all at the same time. Kind of like the last few days. "I've never been a waitress before."

Magnolia's left eyebrow went up. "Everyone should be a servant at some point in their life. It's good for the character."

Rett took another bite. "I might not be here long. I have plans." They were vague plans—L.A. or Nashville? She couldn't decide.

"Plans need money, and I hope you aren't expecting your grandma to be footing the bill for your music career. We barely make enough to get by with this place. Thing is, I need someone from six to eleven a.m. Tuesday through Saturday. Minimum wage plus tips."

"That's early," Rett said. "I hate getting up early."

Magnolia slipped the pie back into the glass case. "Life's hard, and then you die."

"Will I be working for my grandma? That's kinda weird."

"Like I said, I hire and fire. That was my and Love's deal. She does the books, buys the food and bakes the cakes. I deal with the employees."

Rett thought for a moment. "Okay. When do I start?"

"Tomorrow. Wear comfortable shoes and bring a smile. A lot of screwups can be bought with a sincere smile."

Rett looked up at her and grinned.

"Yeah," Magnolia said, shaking her head, her expression saying she was already regretting her offer. "The old farts will like you just fine."

Before Rett could answer, the phone behind the counter rang. She went back to her pie, wondering how much it would cost to have her old banjo and guitar mailed out here. Or maybe she'd just save up for new ones, to go along with her new life. Living in California, wasn't that something? Lissa was going to be so jealous. Her grandma would be glad. At least, she hoped so. Mom would pitch a fit, but what was new about that? She felt kind of bad that she wasn't back there helping with this crisis with Patsy, but a person had their limits. She could give up Dale, but she wasn't sure if she had it in her to sit there and watch them be all over each other as Patsy grew bigger with his baby. Then again, she had a sneaking suspicion that he wouldn't even be around when this baby was born.

"Rett," Magnolia said behind her. "You need to drive home right now and pick up Love. August is missing."

TWENTY-NINE

Love Mercy

Though Love knew it was only minutes before Rett drove up, it felt like an hour. Rather than chew her nails to the skin while waiting, she tried to keep her wits about her and called Benni Ortiz. Their ranch was the closest to Polly and August. Love knew the best thing was to get someone there as quickly as possible. Though Polly's voice didn't sound hysterical when she called—she'd been a rancher's wife far too long to fall apart when something out of the ordinary happened—Love could tell she was concerned.

"Now, I don't want you to worry," she'd said, her voice holding a hint of a tremor. "But August has been gone for quite a little while, and I'm concerned that he might need some help."

"How long has he been gone?" Love felt her heart rev up like a motorcycle engine.

She paused, thinking. "Oh, a few hours. He left about six this morning. Gone to check some fence up around Siler's Ridge. Said he didn't want to bother Mel with it, what with it being the holidays and all."

Love glanced at the clock on her desk. It was past three p.m. Nine hours. Back when they were all younger, she wouldn't have thought twice about August being gone that long. The Johnson ranch was large, over hundreds of acres, and there were miles of fence, always sections that needed fixing. He'd often left early and come home after dark. Cy and Tommy had done the same. But August was eighty-seven and had been having those memory lapses they'd all been ignoring like they were an irritating cough or a case of hiccups that would eventually clear up on its own. How could she have been so irresponsible? She should have been more assertive about making August go to the doctor. Now, because of it, he might be lying somewhere hurt. Or . . . She didn't want to think any further.

Benni answered on the third ring. She listened to Love's garbled explanation and said in a calm voice, "Gabe and I can be there in a few minutes."

"What's going on?" she could hear Dove call out in the background.

"August went out on a ride and hasn't come back," Benni told her. "We're going to look for him."

"I'm coming too!" Dove said.

"I'm waiting on Rett," Love said. "She has my car, but she's on her way home from the café."

"Meet us at the ranch," Benni said, the calm certainty in her voice a balm to Love's ears. "We'll find him. He's probably just taking his good sweet time like August always has."

"Yes," she agreed. "His own sweet time. August always takes his own sweet time."

While waiting for Rett, she called Mel at the feed store.

"I'll close up now," she said. "Do you need me to pick you up?"

"No, Rett will be here in a minute."

"Meet you at the ranch then."

She poured some dry dog food out for Ace and filled his water dish, in case it turned out to be a late night. What she really hoped was that by the time they arrived at the ranch, August was sitting in his worn leather chair laughing at all of them for being so silly.

Love was at the curb when Rett drove up. When Rett started to get out of the driver's seat, she motioned her back. "No, you drive. I'll tell you how to get there."

Love was glad in that moment that someone else was at the wheel. While she had waited, like an incoming tsunami, all the sorrows of her life seemed to flow over her: losing DJ, then Daddy and Mama, Tommy's too early death and her dear, sweet Cy. All of them gone. Were they all together? Could they see what was going on? Did the saints sit on heaven's sidelines and cheer on the ones left behind as she'd been told by so many ministers? Love wasn't ready to lose one more person she loved.

Benni, Gabe, Dove and Mel all beat Rett and Love to the ranch. They were standing around the round kitchen table looking at an old topographical map chicken-scratched with notations. The sight of Cy's familiar printed letters caused Love to inhale sharply. She longed for his strong arm around her shoulders, assuring her that things would work out fine.

"I called Rocky and Magnolia," Mel said. "They're on their way. Should we call search and rescue?"

"Already did," Gabe said. "They'll be here soon, but I suggested we start looking on our own. We know this ranch better than they do. They agreed." Having Gabe, a former police chief, take control made Love feel less panicked. He spoke directly to Love. "Daisy came back without him."

Everyone was silent a moment. That wasn't a good sign.

"I'll start baking a chicken," Polly said, wiping her hands down her apron. "And I'll make some biscuits. It'll keep while you all fetch August. Heats up easy. He'll likely be hungry."

"That's a good idea," Dove said, heading for the kitchen. "Give me some fruit. I'll make a cobbler."

While Dove and Polly set about doing the thing that they'd grown up doing when disaster struck, the rest of them turned to Gabe, whose high brown cheekbones seemed cut with a diamond knife. Rocky and Magnolia walked into the room just as Gabe started to talk. Zane followed behind them.

"Hey," Rocky said. "Zane was working at the church when you called. Thought we could need another set of eyes and legs."

"Always helpful," Gabe said, nodding at them.

"Okay, let's do this in teams," Gabe said. "Benni and Mel, Love and Rett, Zane and me. Rocky, I need you and Magnolia to stay here to tell the search and rescue when they arrive what we're doing." He pointed at Love. "You take the jeep, since I'm assuming Rett isn't an experienced rider." He looked at Rett, and she nodded, her face solemn. "Take the north side, because it has the most drivable roads."

He pointed to the other sections of the ranch. "Benni and Mel, you two take the south part, starting at the lightning tree and to beyond the old avocado orchard. Zane and I will ride the western and eastern sections over by Smuggler's Cave and Siler's Ridge."

"We only have one horse," Love said. "I'm sure Daisy's in no shape . . ."

"We figured on that," Benni said. "We brought three. Tacked them up while we were waiting for you."

"Okay, everyone coordinate cell phone numbers, and let's get going," Gabe said.

Zane and Rett, quickest at that sort of thing, entered everyone's numbers in their cell phones so that they'd all be in constant communication . . . that is, if the phones worked at all sections of the ranch.

Benni handed each of them a red backpack. "They're actually for earthquakes, but they have everything you need: water, food, basic first aid supplies, flashlights."

"Let's pray before you all go," Rocky said.

They all gathered in a circle and held hands, listening to Rocky's hoarse, sure voice ask God to keep August safe, to keep the searchers safe and, most of all, for them to trust and believe that all things work for the glory of God.

Love felt frozen as Rocky prayed, wanting to join in but feeling like a phony, begging for God's help when she'd ignored him for so long.

She drove the old jeep up the road toward the northern section of the ranch. It was soupy from the recent rain, and a couple of times they had to get out and push the jeep out of a soggy pothole. Love was proud of Rett. She pushed with grit and determination, stronger than her slight frame appeared.

They drove up roads barely wide enough to accommodate the vehicle, and Love scanned the deep crevice on her side, searching for a movement, a glimpse of faded denim. The old engine was loud enough to drown out any cries of help, so she was depending on her eyes to spot any indication of August. But there was no sign of him. Of all times for Ring to go lame and have to stay home. Love was sure if Ring had been with August instead of recuperating in the house, the dog would have led them to him.

They'd driven about a mile following the road that Love knew he customarily rode up to the northern part of the ranch when, like a flash of lightning, it hit Love where August might be.

She turned to Rett. "You know what? I bet he's at Big Barn."

Rett nodded, as if that was the most logical thing in the world that her grandma could have said. "Is it far from here?"

"About another half mile." Love felt her stomach clench.

"Should I call everyone?" Rett asked taking out Love's cell phone.

Love thought for a moment. "Not yet. I could be wrong, and then the search would get all screwed up. It'll only take us a few minutes to get there."

Since the day she and Mel rode up there to check out the strange writing August had complained about, and she told Mel the words he'd put into Morse code, she'd worried about his mind. But she figured they still had a little time. Most of the time, he seemed fine, and there had been so much happening with Rett that she decided she'd talk to Polly about it after Christmas. It was obvious now that had been a mistake. She tried to reel in her imagination, tried not to picture his battered body lying in a deep, brush-covered ravine somewhere, hidden from their view, vulnerable to the elements and wild animals that roamed these hills.

Love glanced up at the sky where the sun had already dipped behind a hill, a tangerine glow making the oak trees like sharp pencil sketches against a lavender blue sky.

Rett followed her gaze. "It'll be dark soon. Do you think the search and rescue can find him if we don't?" Love heard a tremble in her granddaughter's voice.

"I don't know," Love said, both hands death-gripped on the cold steering wheel. But she did know. Once it got dark, they always called off the search until the next morning.

They didn't speak again until they rounded the corner, and Big Barn came into view. Against the plum-colored sky, it loomed like a haunted house, its crooked, sunk-in roof giving it a lopsided, nightmarish quality.

"Spooky," Rett said, her words coming out with a soft breath.

That was the exact word that Love was thinking.

They were about a hundred yards away when something in Love caused her to cut the engine.

"What's wrong?" Rett said.

"It might be better if we walked in," Love said.

"Why?" Rett knitted her pale brown eyebrows together.

Love couldn't explain it. It was something a city person might not understand. Love had not only grown up in the woods, she'd spent much of her life up here with Cy, riding this land, learning its contours and sounds. There was a vibration in the air, something that didn't feel right. She realized now why she'd not really been afraid when she'd come here a few days ago with Mel. She'd not felt anything then. Not like now.

"Stay here in the jeep. Let me check it out first." She climbed out and started slowly walking toward the barn.

"Pops," she called out, her voice clear and strong in the cool, early dusk. "It's Love, Pops. Are you in there?" Suddenly, she wished she'd thought to bring Cy's shotgun. She was too vulnerable out in the open. Anyone could be hiding in Big Barn. She stopped, turned to go back and saw Rett walking toward her.

"Get back!" She waved her granddaughter away.

Rett moved up beside her. "No, I want to come with you. I'm not a kid."

Love was about to snap at her that it had nothing to do with being a kid, when there was a *crack*. A puff of dirt exploded in front of them. *Crack—crack, crack.*

Instinctively, Love tackled Rett, slamming her to the ground.

"What?" Rett warbled as she hit the ground with a thump.

"Don't move!" Love commanded.

THIRTY

Rett

"G unshots," her grandma said in a hoarse voice.

Rett froze where she lay, feeling the damp, cold leaves on her cheek. Though her first instinct was to get up and run, she pushed back her panic. Relax, she told herself. She could barely see her grandma in the darkening twilight. Love had rolled over on her stomach and was watching the barn, where a light flickered somewhere deep in its bowels. She could hear her grandma's harsh, heavy breathing, the sound of wind in the trees, a bird's twitter, a rustling in the bushes to her left. Everything seemed louder, bigger, slower. The last few minutes felt like a movie she was watching in a dark theater.

"Don't move," Love whispered. Rett felt the soaked soil give under her when she shifted.

"Well, dang," her grandma said. "One hit me."

Rett felt her throat constrict. "Are you okay? What should we do?" Are you going to die? she thought.

"Crawl ahead of me. Keep low. We need to get behind the jeep. I'll be fine. It's just a surface wound."

Like some kind of old black-and-white war movie, they crawled toward the jeep, Rett's elbows and knees stained with soil, wet leaves sticking to her chilled skin. Time did that crazy thing it did when she was writing a song: it both stood still and flew by. She crawled and crawled for what seemed forever, waiting to hear another *crack*, another puff of dirt. But the only thing she heard was her own heavy breathing.

Behind the jeep, Love crouched and looked out toward the barn. It was dark and quiet; the source of light had moved deeper into the barn. For a moment, Rett wondered if they'd imagined the gunshots. She shivered and sat back against a front tire, waiting for her grandma to speak.

"Well, that stings a little," Love said, looking down at her shoulder. Blood seeped through her blue cowboy shirt, the stain appearing black in the dusky light. "Stay low, and get the backpack. Find me something to put over this."

Crouching, Rett fumbled with the jeep door, finding the backpack. She sat back down and unzipped it. For the first time in her life, Rett was truly terrified. Mister God, she prayed, help needed here, like, *right now*. Not a muscle moved on Love's face, but Rett knew she had to be in pain. She handed her the biggest gauze pad in the backpack. "Does it hurt?"

Love pressed the pad down on her shoulder, giving Rett a small smile. "Don't worry, Sweet Pea. It looks worse than it is. Try to call someone on my cell while I apply pressure."

Rett nodded, amazed at her grandma's composure. She flipped the cell phone open, the blue light from the screen illuminating her face. "No service." Rett felt like crying. *El Señor*, she prayed, feeling her breathing grow shallow. Stars popped and sizzled in front of her eyes. We really, really need some help.

In seconds, she felt a warm peace wash over her. Her breathing slowed, and the stars started fading away. They'd be okay. Somehow, she knew that.

Love struggled up and peered over the hood of the jeep at the barn. "You know, I wonder . . . Oh, Lord, have mercy. It's August."

Rett crawled over to Love and crouched next to her. She could see a light silhouetting a figure in the window. The figure held some kind of lantern. Even from their distance, maybe the length of a football field, Rett could also see it was August. He cradled a rifle in one hand and held a lantern in the other.

"What's he doing?" Rett asked, confused.

"I don't know," Love said. "But he must not realize it's us."

"August . . . Pops," Love called out. "It's Love. What's going . . . ?"

Before she could finish, he threw open the window and pointed the gun in the direction of her voice.

"Down!" she hissed, jerking Rett's arm.

"You'll not take *me*, you dirty bastards!" he yelled. "Here's one for stinkin' Herr Hitler." The *tat-tat* of his shots echoed through the trees.

Love leaned her head against the jeep's door. "He thinks he's back in the war."

Nervous laughter gurgled in the back of Rett's throat. She knew that was totally not cool, but this was like some kind of insane music video. Did people really do that, go crazy and think they were in some other time? Did her great-grandpa August really believe she and her grandma were German soldiers? That was so messed up.

"Well, okay," she said, not knowing what else to say.

"If we're lucky, Gabe or some of the others heard those gunshots," Love said, glancing up at the early night sky. Stars were starting to show themselves, like tiny white carbonated bubbles. "But we have to find a way to try to warn them. I don't want them riding up without knowing what's happening. Someone could get hurt."

Somebody already has, Rett almost said.

"What should we do?" Rett asked, shivering. A cold breeze shook oak leaves in the trees above them, a soft rattling sound, like an old-time recording of people applauding.

"I'm going to try to move over to that rise over there." Love pointed to a hill behind them. "The phone might pick up a signal there."

"I should go," Rett said. "You're hurt."

"No. I'd never forgive myself if something happened to you."

"But, grandma—"

"No argument!" Love snapped, and Rett could hear the steel in her voice.

Except Rett always argued. Her grandma would learn that. "So, what if you get shot again?"

Love gripped her shoulder. "I won't."

Rett folded her arms across her chest. "But if you *do*."

Love's mouth turned into a slashed line. "Do not mess with me right now, Rett. Just do what I say and wait here."

"Fine, General Johnson," Rett said, holding up her hands. "Just be careful."

"I will." Love's voice softened. She reached over and patted Rett's knee. "I'll be okay. We'll all get out of this alive."

"I know," Rett said, making her voice sound more confident than she felt.

She watched her grandma crawl through the grass until she couldn't see her any longer. Then she turned and stood up slightly, trying to see if August was watching. He'd moved away from the window, but she could see the lantern's light bobbing inside the barn. What was he doing? Was he scared? Did he think that his buddies had deserted him? It made her sad to think he was feeling that way, alone and scared, especially when it wasn't true.

For some reason, she remembered what she'd once read about writing—songs, books, poems, whatever—how it was really just carrying the Golden Rule to its complete meaning, that being a writer meant trying to see things from someone else's point of view, imagining yourself to be them. She tried to imagine August's fear, how alone he felt, what he'd be wishing for, who he'd be hoping to see. It hit her like a slap on the head.

"August!" she called out. "It's Aggie. I want to talk to you."

Behind her, she heard the faint sound of her grandma's voice cry, "No. Lord, me. *Me*—not her. Please. *Please.*"

Rett called out to her great-grandpa again. "It's Aggie. Your baby sister. Can I come see you?"

There was a long silence, and she thought that maybe she'd done something really stupid, when she saw August move back in front of the window and hold up his lantern. His face glowed from the light. "Aggie? Is that you? Are you all right?"

She swallowed hard, then stood up, ignoring the sound of Love's voice behind her telling her to get down.

"Yes, August, it's Aggie. I'm fine. I just want to talk to you. Can I come see you? I have . . ." Her mind went blank for a second. "I . . . uh . . . I have supper. Mama sent it. I have fried chicken."

His laugher rang out, and he opened the old window. "Mama's chicken? That'll sure hit the spot."

Rett moved slowly around the front of the jeep. "Can I come and bring it to you? It's getting cold." She held her breath, watching his figure in the window. He brought the lamp up closer to his face. One hand held the lantern, the other was empty. He'd set his gun down. She exhaled in relief.

"I'm coming to the barn now," she said, walking slowly toward the building. Beneath her feet, the snap of dried grass sounded as loud as gunshots.

Please don't let him shoot me, Mr. God, she silently prayed. I really kind of want to live. She continued walking toward the barn. "I'm almost there, August. Don't forget, it's me, Aggie."

"For heaven's sake, I know who you are," his deep voice said in a slightly peeved tone.

His tall figure in the window bent down to pick up something. She froze. "August?" Her voice wavered.

"Who's that behind you? Stop!" August's voice was harsh. "Who goes there?" He pointed his rifle at something behind her.

Surprised, Rett turned around to see her grandma Love, still clutching the soaked gauze pad to her shoulder. In the moonlight, Rett could see the pain in her shadowed face.

"August," Rett cried in a panic. "Don't shoot. It's . . . it's my friend . . ." Her mind frantically searched for a name that sounded old-fashioned, someone who might be friends with his sister, Aggie. "Lucille. Lucille . . . uh . . ." She almost said Ball. "Jones. Lucille Jones. She's spending the night with me."

"Luci?" he said, lowering his rifle. "Why, I haven't seen her since she was a little girl. How's your mama feeling?"

"She's fine," Love said in the calmest voice Rett had ever heard. "She's gotten over her shingles now. Feeling much better."

"Shingles," August said. "That's a shame. Never had 'em, but I know they can hurt like the dickens. You two come on in and stay for supper. I want to hear more about your mama."

"Okay," Love said, coming up beside Rett and putting her good arm around her shoulder. "We're coming through the door now. Don't you shoot us."

August's deep laugh echoed through the empty barn. "What a crazy thing to say, Luci girl. Why in the world would I shoot you? Aggie, you say you got fried chicken?"

Rett and Love walked inside the barn. He'd set the rifle down on an old wooden box, but it was still within his grasp.

Rett immediately went over to August and slipped her arm through his, pulling him out of reach of the rifle. "The chicken's out in the car, August," she said, glancing over at Love, who had already placed herself between August and the rifle. "Let's take the lantern and go on home."

"Fried chicken," August said, picking up the lantern, not even glancing at Love or at the rifle. "That sure would hit the spot right now. You know, after supper, I think I'd like to take a nap. I'm feeling a little tired."

"That's a good idea," Love said, coming up behind them. "I think maybe we all could use a nap."

Rett hugged August's arm to her side, smelling the sour-sweet old man scent that came from him. He stumbled when they stepped over the barn threshold, and she caught him before he could fall.

"It was a long day in the fields," he said, sighing.

"Yes, I bet it was," Rett agreed, tears suddenly burning her eyes. This man, it just occurred to her, was her blood, her daddy's grandpa. Without him, she would not be here right now. She would not be anywhere. By some mysterious meeting of sperm and egg and sperm and egg and sperm and egg, Loretta Lynn Johnson was on this earth, able to sing and write songs and fall in love and get scorned. And live. Most of all, live. Just like Patsy's baby. Patsy and Dale's baby. For some reason, that baby was now a part of this world, and someday, someday, Aunt Rett would tell him or her this story. The story of the day great-great-grandpa August thought Aunt Rett and Great-grandma Love were German soldiers and how he shot Love without meaning to and how Rett pretended to be his long-dead sister.

She glanced behind her to make sure her grandma was all right. Love walked slowly behind them, carrying the rifle.

"Are you okay?" Rett asked. "Do you need some help?"

"I'm fine," Love said. "Just needs a little antibiotic cream and a Band-Aid."

August stumbled again, and Rett slipped her arm around the old man's waist. "We have some water up in the car. Bet you could use a drink."

He looked down at her, his watery eyes blank. "Who did you say you were?"

She inhaled, no longer needing to lie because they were all safe. "I'm Rett. Your great-granddaughter. Your grandson, Tommy's, daughter."

He cocked his head. "Tommy's daughter? Why, I didn't even know he had a daughter. How is Tommy doing?"

Her heart ached at his question, but she smiled up at him. "He actually has three daughters. I'm number two."

"Tommy's a good boy," August said. "Real smart. Always quick with figuring things out. He can think on his feet, that boy."

"Really?" Rett said, leading him toward the jeep. She turned her head again to check on Love, who was slipping the rifle under some blankets in the back of the jeep. "You still okay back there?"

"Yes, I am. You're going to have to drive, though."

"I can do that," Rett said.

"I know you can," Love replied. "And I can't wait to get back to the ranch and tell everyone how proud I am of you. Sweet Pea, you really saved the day." Rett could tell that her grandma wasn't being sarcastic, that she really was proud of her. It felt good. It had been a long time since someone had said she'd done something right.

"You saved the day?" August asked, cocking his head. "What did you do?"

"Oh, nothing," Rett said, helping him up into the passenger seat. "Just a little quick thinking on my feet."

"Just like Tommy," August said, patting her hand. "He's a good boy. A smart boy. Never had a bit of trouble figuring things out."

"So I've been told," Rett said and laughed.

THIRTY-ONE

Love Mercy

They settled August in the front passenger seat, wrapping an old blanket around his trembling shoulders. Love slipped into the back of the jeep. The bleeding on her shoulder had slowed, so she told Rett not to rush, that these fire roads were tricky at night.

"I'll get us home in one piece," Rett said.

August had grown silent, his head lolling to one side in exhaustion. Oh, Pops, Love thought, tucking the blanket around his exposed neck. I'm so sorry I didn't do something before it came to this. She would never forgive herself for what happened. It would be something that would haunt her for the rest of her life—what *could* have happened. She'd never forget those terrifying seconds when her granddaughter stood up and started walking toward the barn. Love never prayed more desperately or more sincerely: *Lord, please, not Rett. Take me, not Rett. Please.*

He was gracious and spared them all.

Halfway back to the ranch, Love was finally able to reach Gabe on his cell phone. "We found August. He was at Big Barn. We're on our way home."

"I'll let the others know," Gabe said. "Is everything all right?"

Other than her shoulder feeling like someone had burned it with a blow torch? "Yes, we're all fine."

By the time they reached the pasture nearest the ranch house, Zane and Mel were waiting for them on horseback. In the distance, Love could see a trio of police cars and dozens of people milling about the ranch's back patio, lit up like daylight from security lights that August installed years ago.

Zane hopped off his horse and undid the last gate.

"Hey, there, cowboy," Rett called, laughing. "Thanks! I've been having to latch and unlatch every gate myself."

"Why didn't Love—" Mel started, then she spotted Love's bandaged shoulder. A small amount of blood had seeped through. She scrambled off her horse and ran over to Love. "What happened?"

"I'm fine," Love said, nodding over at August. "We need to get Pops home. He's very tired."

Mel glanced over at August, whose chin touched his chest now. "What—"

"Let's get him home," Love said firmly. "We'll tell you everything once we get him settled."

Because Gabe had called search and rescue, and they'd been setting up plans for a search if August didn't show up, paramedics were on the scene. Despite his cranky protests, they gave August a quick exam and said that he seemed okay physically. They suggested it might be good to take him to the hospital for a more thorough exam.

As Love kept trying to tell them as they undid her clumsy bandage, her wound had turned out to be superficial. They cleaned it up, bandaged it much more professionally and also recommended that she stop by emergency. She assured them she would at the same time they took August. When questioned by the sheriff's deputy in charge of search and rescue, Love remained obstinately vague about how she got the wound, insisting that it was accidental; she might have fallen on something in the barn; she really didn't remember.

Rett went along with her story, saying that she hadn't really seen what happened. When the deputy tried to probe a little deeper, suspecting there was more to the tale, her granddaughter looked straight into his disbelieving eyes and said, "Are you saying that my grandma is a *liar?*" When he turned his back in frustration, she shot Love a wide, goofy grin.

Love couldn't help smiling back. Teaching her granddaughter to lie to the police probably wasn't the most moral thing to do, but since they didn't know what would happen to August if the police found out he shot at them, Love decided that this needed to be a family problem. Before she left tonight, she'd make sure that every gun in the house was gone.

Though August was annoyed about Love for calling an ambulance rather than letting Polly or her drive him the twelve miles to General Hospital in San Celina, Love wouldn't back down. He needed to be under observation, and they needed time to search the house for guns.

"I'm tired, and so is Polly," Love said. "We just want to make sure you get there in one piece."

"Waste of money," he grumbled.

"I'll pay for it if that's your worry," Love said.

He sat up straight in his chair. "I pay my own debts."

"Do you want us to come along?" Benni asked. Gabe was outside, tying up things with the police, while Dove helped Polly pack an overnight case for August.

"Thanks, but we can take it from here," Love said. "Y'all have already done so much. Thank you for coming so quickly . . ." The rest of the words choked in her throat.

"That's what neighbors do," Benni said, her wiry arms gently hugging Love. "We were glad to help. Let us know if there's anything else we can do."

"I will." Then Love went over to Magnolia and Mel, who were seated at the kitchen table drinking coffee. Zane and Rett lingered behind them, sipping cans of Coke, their young faces looking a thousand times less tired and worn than the rest of them.

"Mel, Magnolia, I need your help," Love said. Glancing over her

shoulder to make sure that Polly or August wasn't within hearing distance, she gave them a quick rundown of what happened.

"Lord, have mercy," Magnolia whispered. "Y'all could've been
killed!"

"What do you need us to do?" Mel asked.

"Search the house for any firearms and take them out of here," Love
said. "We can't take the chance of this happening again."

"I can help," Zane said.

"Thanks," Love said. "You'll have a pretty long time to look, because I'm going to ask them to keep August overnight. I'll be making an
appointment first thing tomorrow with his doctor to see what we can
do about . . . his memory problem."

She couldn't say the word yet—*Alzheimer's*. If it wasn't that, there
was certainly something firing wrong in his brain. They couldn't ignore
it any longer. And it was up to her to talk to him and Polly about it. She
was all the family they had now.

"We'll let you know tomorrow what we find," Mel said. "I'll keep
any guns at my place."

"Thanks, Mel. I'll see you all tomorrow."

Rett drove Love to the hospital in San Celina. The ambulance allowed Polly to ride with August to keep him from becoming agitated.
Love took the doctor aside and explained how August had temporarily
lost himself, how he thought he was back in the war. He agreed that
having him stay overnight for observation might be wise. He knew August's family doctor and would confer with him in the morning.

So they checked him into a room with a small bed for Polly so she
could stay with him. Once they were settled, Love promised she'd be
back first thing in the morning. She found Rett in the front lobby,
watching a *Leave It to Beaver* rerun on the television. Her face looked
pale and vulnerable in the dim light of the lavender and gray lobby.

"What about your arm?" Rett's forehead wrinkled with worry.

"I'll see a doctor tomorrow," Love said. "I'm tired. I want to go
home. The paramedics bandaged it fine."

Rett sat back on the nubby sofa, her arms crossed over her chest.
"They aren't doctors. What if it gets infected? You probably need anti-

biotics, or you could get really sick. Then who would take care of Polly and August?"

Love stared at her granddaughter, speechless for a moment. Then she laughed. "Well, you certainly know how to make a person feel guilty."

"You have, like, insurance, don't you?"

Love shook her head in disbelief. "Yes, I have insurance."

Rett stood up, resting a hand on her cocked hip. "Then what's the big deal?"

"Okay," Love said, turning around and marching up to the emergency admitting desk. "If it'll make you feel better, I'll have a doctor look at it." After having to lie, yet again, about how she came to have the wound, the emergency room doctor bandaged it again and wrote her prescriptions for antibiotics and pain pills, in case she needed them. They stopped at an all-night drugstore in San Celina and got them filled.

Love took the first one with a bottle of water she also bought. "There," Love said, shaking the half-empty bottle at Rett, who insisted on driving. "Happy now?"

Rett smiled without taking her eyes off the road. "Yes, ma'am, I am."

It was almost one a.m. by the time they got home. Ace greeted them like they'd been away on a ten-day trek through the Congo. Rett sat down on the floor and let him jump all over her, giggling as he licked her face. Then he ran over to Love, poked his nose on her calf, let her scratch his neck, then darted back to Rett.

"Flyboy," Love said, laughing. "I think you might be overacting a little."

"He missed us," Rett said, pushing herself up from the floor. She stretched her long arms and yawned. "Wow, gnarly night."

"The gnarliest," Love agreed. "I think I'm going to have some toast and peanut butter before I go to bed. Would you like some?"

"Sure," Rett said. "I'm going to change clothes." She turned her head and sniffed her shoulder. "I smell like rotten leaves and kind of mediciney."

Love was pouring hot chocolate in two mugs when Rett walked back into the kitchen wearing a plain white T-shirt and Love's striped pajama bottoms. "I have a question," she said, sitting down at the kitchen table.

"Shoot," Love said, then made a face. "Whoa, I'll never say that again without it meaning something entirely different now."

"Does your arm hurt bad?"

"No, thank the Lord for Vicodin." Love put a handful of miniature marshmallows in their cocoa. "Was that your question?"

Rett shook her head. "It's about Grandpa August. What's going to happen to him now?"

Love inhaled deeply while spreading peanut butter over two pieces of toast. "We have to talk to his doctor tomorrow. August is obviously having some serious mental and memory problems, so he and Polly probably shouldn't be out there at the ranch alone." She turned and set the plates down on the table. "I guess we'll just have to wait and see." She sat down across from Rett. "I wish I could see into the future and tell you more, but I just can't."

They were sitting at the kitchen table silently eating and drinking, lost in their individual thoughts, when from her bedroom, Rett's cell phone rang. She ran for it, checking the screen before she answered.

"Man," she said, walking back into the kitchen, staring at the screen, her face a mixture of emotions. The ring tone continued its tinkly song.

"Who is it?" Love asked, suspecting it was Dale.

She grimaced. "Mom." She watched the screen until the music stopped playing.

Love joined her in staring at the cell phone. Why would Karla be calling at one a.m.? Wait, it wasn't one a.m. there. It was four a.m. Or was it only a two-hour difference in Knoxville? She glanced at Rett's face, which only showed annoyance. Her granddaughter hadn't lived long enough to automatically think what Love did: that phone calls coming in at odd hours rarely carried good news. Rett set the phone down on the table.

"Aren't you going to call her back?" Love asked, trying not to show her anxiety. She wasn't sure if she could stand one more piece of bad news.

Rett shrugged and picked at a hangnail.

"You should," Love said firmly, hating how much it sounded like nagging. Though she didn't want to do anything to harm this fragile relationship they'd started, the responsible adult in her knew Rett shouldn't ignore Karla's call. "It might be something important." She rephrased that. "It probably is something important."

Rett sighed and didn't look at Love but continued to pick at her nail. "You forget that it's Karla we're talking about. Me and the sisters call her Mama Diva. She makes everything that happens sound like a Lifetime movie."

"Well, all y'all's lives do sound a lot like a Lifetime movie," Love pointed out.

She raised her head and gave Love a half smile. "All y'all? You're too much, Grandma."

Love laughed, thinking about Cy. "Your grandpa always said my accent got real strong when I was under stress."

"Yeah, this night sure was that." Rett sighed again and picked up the phone. "Okay, I'll call Mom, but I'm telling you, it's probably a big fat nothing."

"I'm finishing my toast. Then I'm going to bed. I feel like a wrung-out old washrag."

"Nice visual," she said, crinkling her nose as she walked into the living room.

Love pushed the swinging kitchen door slightly open and blatantly eavesdropped on Rett and Karla's conversation. She could only hear Rett's side, which consisted of many "uh-huhs" and "yeahs" and "that sucks." Something had happened, but Rett's responses didn't reveal a clue about what it was. Did it have to do with the baby? Or Dale?

"I don't know what to tell you, Mom," Rett said. "I'm sorry." She was quiet a moment, listening. "I don't know! Let me think about it. I'm tired. A lot's happened here with Grandpa August. He's in the hospital. It's a long story, but he's got, like, Alzheimer's or something. They think he'll be okay, but I want to stay here. I *said* I'd think about it. I'll call you tomorrow. Yeah, whatever. Love you too."

From the slit in the door, Love watched Rett punch the cell phone off and toss it on the sofa. Ace stirred at her feet, lifted his head, then laid it back down, unconcerned about the latest human problems. His worry was resolved. His pack—Rett and Love—had been gone but now were back. He could sleep peacefully. Rett bent over and touched her head to her knees. Her soft sobs caused Love to push open the door and approach her.

"Rett," Love said, startling her.

She looked up, her eyes swollen red with tears. "My life sucks."

Love put a hand to her mouth. "Is it the baby? Patsy?"

Rett gave her head a quick shake. "The baby's fine. Patsy's fine. It's Mom. Roy's filing for divorce, and she's all freaked out. He doesn't even want to talk to her. She wants me to come home right now." Rett wiped the back of her hand over her cheek. "Patsy's barfing all the time, and Faith has the flu. Roy wants to marry his big-haired secretary."

"Ouch," Love said. "Not even original."

She rolled her eyes. "He sells office supplies. He's lame."

Though everything selfish in her protested, Love just gave those feelings to God and said, "I'll buy you a plane ticket to Knoxville if you want to go back."

Rett bent over again, touching her head to her knees. "I don't want to go home," she mumbled.

Love didn't want her to either, but the mother part of her empathized with her former daughter-in-law. When things started falling apart, you wanted your family surrounding you. Though Love didn't want to let her granddaughter out of her sight, Rett needed to go home. At least for a little while.

Love sat down next to Rett on the sofa and rested a tentative hand on her back. Her skin was warm; her bones felt as delicate as a cat's. "I know it's hard, but it sounds like Karla depends on you. That's a real compliment, you know. You don't have to stay long, but she could probably use your help right now."

Rett slowly sat up, her eyes damp and red-rimmed. "I'm sorry for what she's going through, but she has tons of friends. She doesn't need me. She just wants me there to run interference between her and Patsy."

Love waited a few seconds before answering. "Well, you understand the situation better than I do. But I'll help you get back there if that's what you want to do." She smiled, trying to relieve some of the tension in Rett's troubled face. "And if you want to come back to Morro Bay, you won't have to hitch rides from truckers. I'll buy your ticket, though you'll have to settle for coach."

Rett couldn't help smiling through her tears. "It was kind of cool, you know. The truckers were totally awesome."

Love gave an exaggerated fake shutter. "Certainly something to write songs about."

"I'll call her back," Rett said, standing up. "It won't take long. Could you put my hot chocolate in the microwave? It's probably cold."

"Sure," Love said, taking the hint that she wanted privacy.

Love didn't eavesdrop this time, though she wanted to. Rett came through the swinging kitchen door five minutes later. Her eyes were dry and her mouth set, though Love couldn't tell if it was from anger or determination. It hit Love with a jolt how much she wanted her grand-daughter to stay. She had this sinking, illogical feeling that if Rett went back to Tennessee, Love would never see her again.

"I put more marshmallows in your cocoa," Love said, turning away so Rett wouldn't see her stricken expression.

"Thanks," she said. Love could hear her pull out the kitchen chair and sit down. "No worries, Grandma. I told Mom I had important fam-ily business to take care of here, but that I'd come home as soon as I could. Definitely after Christmas."

Love's heart tap-danced with joy, despite feeling guilty about Karla missing Christmas with her daughter. She turned back to face Rett. She was using a spoon to scoop up a melted mess of marshmallows.

"If that's what you want to do," Love managed to say with an even voice.

"Like I said, Mama's got a thousand girlfriends to help her." Rett looked up at Love, a bit of sticky white marshmallow stuck to her up-per lip. "What do you think we'll do for Christmas?"

To be honest, Love hadn't thought about it. "I usually go out to the ranch. Polly loves to cook dinner and, well, that's where I've spent Christ-mas since I moved to Morro Bay."

She sipped her cocoa. "Do you think they'll still want to have Christmas this year?"

Love leaned back against the tile counter. "I'm sure they will, but I doubt that Polly will have the energy to make Christmas dinner."

"We should do it then. I mean, it might be their last one at the ranch."

Love stared at Rett, realizing that what she said might very well be true. "You're absolutely right. After we visit them at the hospital tomorrow and see what the tests show, we'll start planning the dinner. We don't have much time."

Rett smiled. "We can do it. I totally work best under pressure. And I bet Mel will want to help."

Love smiled back at her. "Yes, I bet she will." She finally gave in to the yawn that had been dogging her for the last half hour. "But right now, I have to get some sleep. That pain pill is knocking me on my butt."

"I'll clean up," Rett said, pushing back her chair.

Love hesitated, feeling like she was abandoning her.

"Go to bed, Grandma. If I'm going to work at the Buttercream as a waitress, I guess I'd better get some practice. Don't want to look like a slacker."

"What?" Love said. That was news to her.

"Oh, I forgot to tell you. Magnolia offered me a job, and I accepted. I was supposed to start tomorrow, but I'm guessing after last night she'll cut me some slack and let me start the day after."

"I imagine so," Love said, wondering what other surprises waited for her down the road.

THIRTY-TWO

Rett

The next day, Rett's mother called her nine more times. By the ninth call at four p.m., Rett was ready to throw her cell phone in the toilet.

"Mom, I told you, for the kazillionth time, I don't know exactly when I'll be coming home. I told you about Great-grandpa August getting hurt. I want to make sure that everything's okay. Besides, I have a job now." Quit wasting my minutes, she wanted to add.

"A job?" Karla whined. "What about us? We're your real family. Love and them, they're just your extended family. You're barely related."

Rett chewed her bottom lip, glancing over at the kitchen where Love was talking on her landline. She was glad her grandma hadn't heard Mom's words. She wanted to do the right thing for everyone, but right now she felt like a rubber band being pulled ten different ways. Still, her mother's attitude was annoying. "They're my family just as much as you, Patsy and Faith," she said, knowing her words would totally piss her mom off.

"I can't believe you said that!" Karla cried. "It's a knife to my heart, Loretta Lynn Johnson. A big ole carving knife to my heart."

"Oh, get a life," she muttered.

"What did you say?"

Rett felt like stomping her feet like a kid having a temper tantrum. "I said I have my own life. Look, let me get back to you."

"When?" her mother demanded. "We have to make plans."

"Soon. Today. I promise." She crossed her fingers, though it was childish. She knew God totally didn't recognize crossed fingers.

She turned off her cell completely. She was not going to talk to her mom again until she'd decided what to do.

They had spent most of the day at the hospital waiting with Polly while August had tests. Then, after August was checked out, they ate dinner at some steak place called McClintock's in San Celina. Then they took August and Polly home. Jade, one of Magnolia's daughters, was staying with them tonight with the excuse that her kids wanted to feed the chickens and pet the horses. Love and Magnolia were trying to figure out how to help August and Polly stay at the ranch and still be safe. That's who Love was talking to on the phone: Magnolia.

Ace came over and nosed her leg, a blue tennis ball in his mouth. "Okay," she said, picking up the ball. "I can throw this while I think."

She knew that as she threw the ball across the backyard grass, her grandma was watching her from the kitchen window. Rett wanted to do the right thing, make everyone happy, but she also wanted to be happy. "I wish I was an orphan," she muttered, knowing her statement wasn't true even as she said it. She liked having family, and she had to admit that she missed Patsy and Faith. She even kinda missed her mom. She definitely missed the feel of her own bed and the smell of her stuff. A part of her felt sad about her first Christmas away from her family. She kept tossing the ball, and Ace kept bringing it back, though occasionally he'd pause, his huge batlike ears cocked and listening. Then he'd run to the side fence and bark at someone who dared to walk in front of his house. She felt so torn. She'd miss Ace too. And her grandma Love and August and Polly, the Buttercream, this town. Shoot, she'd kinda even miss Mel. They were sorta friends now, she thought. Or something, anyway.

Eventually Love came out holding a cup of cocoa. That made Rett smile. She was already figuring her grandma out. She always brought you something to drink when she wanted to talk serious. It was kind of cool, learning things like that. Grandma Love with her short, reddish hair that always seemed to have a piece sticking up and her long-legged, full-of-purpose stride that made her look like she was hiking in the Alps, kind of like that lady in *The Sound of Music*. Love was already starting to feel familiar to Rett. She wished they could have known each other while Rett was growing up. How cool would that have been, spending her summers in California? Maybe she'd have learned how to ride a horse. Then again, maybe she still could.

"Hey, thought you might be getting chilly out here," Love said, walking over to her. "Made some hot cocoa."

"Awesome," Rett said, taking the mug and sitting down on one of the blue high-backed wooden lawn chairs They looked like the kind she'd seen in a catalog once that advertised stuff for cabins. Adirondack, her grandma had called them.

Love sat down in the chair next to her and tossed a sausage dog treat to Ace. "Well, your friend, Zane, is really doing us a favor. He's agreed to live at the ranch in the attic bedroom for the time being. It works out good for him, because he can live there rent-free, and Polly will adore cooking for him. He wants to work on his songwriting and still work part-time at his mama and great-aunt's vet clinic. I think I'll see if he wants to earn a little extra money by helping August out with ranch chores."

Rett nodded. "He's a nice guy."

Love smiled, raised one eyebrow. "Kind of cute too."

"Chill, Grandma. I'm on the rebound, okay?"

"I'm just saying," Love said, holding up one hand.

"You totally ripped that saying off some lame sitcom, didn't you?" Rett said, laughing.

"Hey, I read," Love said. "We'll all be taking turns going out there every day. Polly called this morning and said that the doctor called in some new kind of medicine for dementia. Starts with an *N*—can't remember it exactly. Says it doesn't cure it, but will possibly keep him stable for a while. It's not for sure, but it's something to try."

"Wow, that's so cool, you know. How everyone pulls together."

"That's what family and friends do," Love said. "So, when do you start at the Buttercream?"

"Tomorrow. I'm kinda nervous. All I've ever done for money is sing."

Love sat down in the chair next to Rett. Ace picked up the ball and dropped it at her feet. "You'll catch on quick. And people will be nice. This is a pretty small town, and you come from one of the old-time families. Don't forget, you're Tommy Johnson's daughter and Cyrus Johnson's granddaughter. Not to mention your great-grandpa August, your great-grandma Polly and your great-great-grandpa and grandma Joseph and Mattie. They were the original owners of the Johnson ranch. You've deep, long roots here, Sweet Pea." She threw the ball, sending Ace bounding.

Rett shook her head. "Wow. That is, like, so . . . wow."

Love smiled and looked out at the ocean, the same ocean Rett's ancestors had watched for the last hundred years. Rett followed her gaze. The water was a deep, dark blue, the color of her favorite pair of blue jeans that she'd forgotten to bring with her.

"I sure wish you'd met your grandpa," her grandma said, her face sad. "I mean, you did meet him, but you were only four. You probably don't remember."

Rett didn't answer, not wanting to tell her grandma that what she remembered about her dad and her grandpa was sort of mingled, almost like they were one person. She was afraid that would make her sad. But they'd disappeared from Rett's life at around the same time. It had always bothered her when she thought about it too much, the fact that she couldn't separate the memories of her dad and her grandpa.

Then, like one of her songs, something came to her. "Juicy Fruit," she said, turning to look at her grandma.

Her grandma's lips turned up in a smile. "That was Cy's favorite gum!"

"He snuck me a piece. Mom caught him. She yelled at him."

"She told him you always swallowed it so she wouldn't let you chew it. She was afraid you'd choke," Love said, nodding, sitting forward in the lawn chair. A slight breeze picked up a piece of her hair, causing a cowlick. "I agreed with her. Cy should have known better."

"He laughed," Rett said excitedly. "I remember bells. And him and I were running."

Love laughed out loud. "We were saved a family argument by the ice cream truck. Cy just wanted to make you happy."

Rett sat back in her chair. "That was awesome, remembering something like that. Do you think I might remember more? Maybe stuff about my dad?"

Love ran her hand through her hair. The cowlick bobbed back up. "Memory's an odd thing. You might. Especially since you're here where he grew up."

Rett almost told Love about the scent, the one she'd been searching for all her life. But, for some reason, she held back. That was still something that was hers, something private she sort of shared with the father she barely remembered. She didn't want to tell anyone about it until she actually found it. That desire was part of why she wanted to stay here for a while. There was so much to discover, a whole part of her life that had always been missing.

Still, she knew her mom was hurting. And that Patsy was probably scared. And Faith. Rett was usually the only one who Faith had to hang with, what with Patsy always at her girlfriends' or obviously sneaking around seeing Dale and their mom with Roy or her friends or trying to score gigs for the Son Sisters. Now that Patsy was pregnant, for sure the Son Sisters were history. Rett knew neither Patsy nor Faith cared much. They'd never really wanted a career in music. Things were changing. But Rett knew she had unfinished business in Knoxville. She had to help her family get it together before she could really start a new life here in California. She turned to her grandma.

"I have to go home," she said. "For a little while. They need me."

Love didn't look at her, but continued to stare at the ocean. "I know you do. I told you I'd pay for your flight."

"I swear I'll pay you back." She stood up, tilting her head back to drink the last of her cocoa. "I'll go call Mom now. Like I said, I won't go until after Christmas. I want to help cook dinner for August and Polly."

When Rett reached the back gate, before she could open it, Love called to her. She turned around to face her grandma, who was standing with her back to that blue, blue ocean.

"I'll go with you, if you like," Love said, using her hand to shade her eyes. "Maybe I can help Karla sort things out. We could drive. With the two of us driving, we could make good time. And we could bring back some of your things. I mean, if you want to come back."

Rett stared at her grandma wondering how she knew that Rett was hoping she'd offer. "You'd do that for my mom? After the way she's treated you?"

A sharp breeze blew Love's hair into a headful of cowlicks. She didn't even try to smooth them down. "Oh, Rett, I'm not that good a Christian. Not yet, anyway. I'd do it for *you*."

Rett felt tears come to her eyes, and she didn't even try to hide them.

"We can leave the day after Christmas," Love said. "We'll stay as long as it takes to help your mom and Patsy figure out what to do."

"What about August and Polly?" Rett asked. "What about my new job?"

"People will cover for us until we get back," Love assured her. "We've got lots of friends here in Morro Bay." She smiled. "And I have some pull with your boss. We have friends who'll fill in for you. Things'll work out."

Rett nodded, feeling happier and less scared than she had in a long time. "I'll go call Mom."

Before she picked up the phone in the kitchen, she paused for a moment and looked out the kitchen window at her grandma, who'd sat back down on the blue lawn chair. Rett could see her from the side because the chair was set at an angle. Even from this distance, Rett could see a cowlick that Love had missed when she'd finally patted down her unruly hair. Whenever Rett saw a crazy cowlick now, she'd always think of her grandma Love.

"Well, Mister God," Rett said. "You really did work things out like Rocky said you always did. I sure appreciate it not taking so long. Thanks."

As she watched her grandma stroke the top of Ace's head, a peace settled around Rett, and for the first time in a long time, she felt like she was traveling in the right direction. She had no idea what lay ahead. Her insides seemed to quiver with excitement. Her life was just beginning, and she couldn't wait.

THIRTY-THREE

Mel

It was noon on Christmas Eve and Mel stood in front of a rack of jewel-colored western shirts at the San Celina Farm Supply. She stared haplessly at the hand-printed sign: Round up a Little Western Fashion for the Holidays! She had only one gift left to buy, something for Rett. She turned away from the rack of shirts. They were too full of rhinestones and fringe. Rett was definitely not a rhinestone kind of girl. What kind of gift did you buy for someone you barely knew?

They were all going to the Johnsons' ranch for Christmas Eve dinner, so Clint, Rocky and Magnolia could join them and not miss Christmas with their own families. No one actually said out loud this might be August and Polly's last Christmas living at the ranch, but the thought hung over everyone like a swollen rain cloud.

August was back home now with absolutely no memory of what happened at Big Barn. Love said he was on some kind of new drug for people in early dementia. The doctor said it could possibly help keep him steady, though he had no idea for how long. That night he was in the hospital, Mel, Magnolia, Rocky and Zane searched every corner of the ranch house. Besides the .22 rifle he'd had at the barn, they'd found two shotguns, a .22 hand pistol and an old beat-up .45 revolver. All the guns were in a closet at Mel's house. So far, August hadn't even noticed they were gone.

Mel, Love and Rett set up a schedule of going out to the ranch every day to help Polly and check on things. Since Love and Rett would be leaving for Knoxville the day after Christmas, Magnolia and Rocky's daughters, Jade and Cheyenne, would fill in until they returned. With Zane living there, and Magnolia and Rocky checking in regularly, August and Polly would be able to stay at the ranch a while longer.

"We have no idea how long this can work," Love had said to Mel Friday night at the Happy Shrimp. Rett skipped this week because she said she was still working on a Christmas present for Love. "But, if there needs to be changes, we'll cross that bridge when we get to it. Christine Nybak at the Alzheimer's Association has been a huge help. There are some options; we just have to figure out what's best for August and Polly. Rett and I will get back as soon as we can, but we have no idea how long we might be. Hopefully, not more than a few weeks."

"How are things back there?" Mel asked.

"Complicated," Love said. "But that's how family is." She smiled at Mel. "I'm thankful we have family here to hold down the fort while we're gone." She reached over and patted Mel's hand.

Mel felt her chest warm with emotion. Never, in a million years, could she express to Love how much she appreciated being included as family.

So, in a way, buying something for Rett was kind of like buying for the little sister she'd never had. Except Mel was a dismal failure at shopping, for herself or anyone else. She never really paid that much attention to what other people wanted or liked. She'd definitely have to work on that. But, in the meantime, there remained the problem of a Christmas gift for Rett. She left the clothing section and went over to peruse the silver Western-style jewelry. Horseshoe earrings? Did Rett have pierced ears? Mel couldn't remember, so she nixed that idea. All she really knew about Rett was she played banjo and liked the

Nashville Sounds baseball team. Wasn't there a new music store downtown? What did you get someone who played the banjo?

She turned to walk toward the exit when she saw Hud come from the back of the building. He carried a jacket-sized box wrapped with red paper decorated with black and green horseshoes.

"Hey, Mel!" he called, seeing her seconds after she spotted him. There was no way she could pretend she hadn't seen him.

She stopped, held up a hand and politely waited for him to walk to her. Why couldn't she have left just one minute earlier? Though she was grateful for his help in resolving things with Patrick and for his call later that night to make sure she was okay, they hadn't talked since. She'd taken to heart his last comment to her on the phone.

"I'm not going to bug you, Melina Jane," he'd said. "I'd like to see you again, but I also know that this is a tough time for you. So I'm lobbing the ball into your court and will just wait to see if it comes flying back."

"Thank you," she'd replied and never called him back. She wasn't ready to deal with even the most basic relationship with a man. Right now, with all that was happening with August, Polly and Love . . . well, her time was pretty much spoken for.

Now here he was walking toward her looking pretty darn attractive in his crisp blue dress shirt, tweed Western-cut jacket, perfectly pressed Wranglers and shiny black boots. He was obviously dressed for some Christmas Eve shindig.

"Hi," she said, when he reached her. "How are you?" Wow, she thought, that's original. Then she chided herself. What did she care about what he thought about her? He'd already seen her at pretty much her worst.

"I'm doing good," he said, touching the rim of his pearl gray Stetson. "Picking up a jacket I ordered for Maisie for Christmas. You doin' some last-minute shopping?"

She nodded, hitching her leather purse over her shoulder. "I'm trying to buy a present for Rett. But, to be honest, I'm at a loss. We're having dinner and exchanging presents at August and Polly's tonight."

Hud cocked his head. "How's he doing?"

"How'd you know about August?"

"Benni told me."

"He's doing okay. Doesn't even remember . . ." She paused, not certain how much Benni had told him.

Hud's dark brown eyes studied her face. "How's Love's shoulder?"

"Fine," she said. Benni obviously told him everything. "I have all August's guns at my place."

"I'm sorry y'all are having to go through this. My gramma Hudson had Alzheimer's. It's a long, hard road . . . for everyone involved."

She nodded, looking down at the floor. Over the store's sound system, Willie Nelson sang "Oh, Come All Ye Faithful." "We're kind of figuring things out as we go along."

"All anyone can do."

She looked up, glanced over his shoulder at the exit. "Well, I didn't find anything here, so . . ."

He glanced at his watch. "Want to have some lunch?"

She looked into his face, trying to decide if she wanted to even start this. There were so many reasons not to: he was too confident, he was fifteen years older than her, he knew too much about her, he was a cop.

"A sandwich, Melina Jane LeBlanc," he said, smiling that cocky smile that both annoyed and intrigued her. "It's just a sandwich. And maybe some soup. A cup of coffee. A pastry if you're feeling particularly adventuresome."

"You are so full of crap."

"Been accused of that a few times. Did you know that there's a procedure called a toe tuck? It's to slim down a person's pinkie toe. They actually remove fat deposits on the tips of the toes. They say it's to fight toe-besity." He shifted the Christmas box from one arm to the other. "I dearly love trivia."

She stared at him, then, unable to help herself, started laughing. "I don't have time for lunch." What she was thinking was, I don't have time for *you*. "I have to buy Rett a Christmas present. I want it to be . . . nice. Or rather, right."

He slipped his arm around her shoulders and started walking out
the Farm Supply's wide front door. She had no choice but to go with
him. At least, that's what she told herself.

"Gift certificate, my little Cajun cutie. When they are that age and
they haven't handed you a detailed list, that's the only gift that is truly
appreciated. We can go by the Chamber of Commerce, and you can buy
one good for any of the downtown merchants. That way she can get
what she wants—clothes, music, food, banjo strings, toothpaste—trust
me, she'll adore you for it."

"Well . . ."

"Have I ever led you wrong?" He walked her out to her truck.

"You've never led me anywhere . . ."

"Not yet. But there's always next year."

She shrugged away from his arm and unlocked her truck's door. "I
don't like being pushed, Hud. You said you'd give me space."

He stepped back one foot and held out one arm, palm up. "Voilà,"
he said. "Magic."

A jolt ran through her. Did he know her father was a magician? Was
he making fun of her? She studied his face, relaxed and smiling. She felt
her spine loosen. He was just kidding around. Maybe she needed to
quit being so uptight. Though she had no desire to even think about
another romantic relationship, lunch was doable. Maybe it would be
good for her. He was easy to talk to, a great . . . what was it called . . .
transition person? Transition to what? Who knew, but like with what
had happened with Love and Rett and August and Polly, Mel had now
realized that there was no peering into the future, no guarantees. Sometimes, like Cy said to her once, you just have to run in the ocean, catch
a wave, see where on the shore you end up.

Here, she thought. I ended up here. Here in this funny little county
in California with a bunch of people who are almost family. She had to
admit, whoever was in control of her particular wave had done right by
her this time. She was here. She was alive, and she was *here*. And here
felt good.

"Okay," she said to Hud. "I'll meet you at Liddie's Café in an hour.

The gift certificate is a great idea. I'll run by the Chamber and buy one."

"You won't be sorry." His smile was nice this time. Not cocky, just nice.

"Well, I guess we'll see," she said and smiled back.

THIRTY-FOUR

Love Mercy

It was four p.m., and the only person who hadn't arrived at August and Polly's house was Clint. Love stood at the sink in Polly's kitchen washing her gold-rimmed Christmas holly glasses. The large window looked out over the front yard and long driveway. This view was one of the things she loved the most about Polly's kitchen. A person could see everything that was going on as they were doing the dishes or peeling potatoes. Polly had always teased August, saying she married him partially because she loved this kitchen and its view.

"I like seeing right away who's here to visit," she'd told him. "I don't like to be kept in the dark about what's coming."

How ironic those words seemed now. There was not any way she'd be able to see what was coming as things started to darken for August. The medical workup couldn't conclusively tell them if it was Alzheimer's, but he definitely was experiencing some sort of dementia. Nothing would be predictable; that was the only certainty.

Love had found someone to stay with Polly and August every minute. It was working, for now. Once Love and Rett returned from Tennessee, they'd have a family meeting and discuss the future. They'd figure something out. Every day they made it through without incident was just another slice of God's good grace. How well Love knew that.

Love dried the holly-printed glass, set it on a tray with the others and looked back out the window. Clint was pulling up in his little green Subaru Forester. They'd have dinner, then open presents right away so that Clint could get on the road before too late. He was driving to San Francisco to spend Christmas with Garth and his family.

"But you probably won't reach Garth's house until midnight," she had said yesterday when he told her his plan to come to the Johnsons' for Christmas Eve dinner. "You'll be exhausted on Christmas Day." They'd met for lunch so they could discuss the best legal strategy for Polly and August. He'd recommended a lawyer he knew in San Celina who specialized in elder law.

"Polly specifically asked me to come," Clint said. "She said it might be their last Christmas at the ranch, and she wanted me there. How could I refuse?"

Love had been surprised that Polly was so open with him. He was an acquaintance, but not family or a longtime friend. She'd not spoken to Love, Magnolia, Rocky or anyone else she'd known for years about her and August possibly moving from the ranch. The worry in Polly's eyes after hearing what the doctor said was obvious, but it was typical of her not to want to burden anyone with her troubles.

Love stared down at her half-eaten Caesar salad. "I wish she'd talked to me about it."

He opened his tri-tip beef sandwich and spooned salsa on the steak. "It's common for parents to want to spare their children the hard details. She trusts me but doesn't have to worry about my emotional state. And she knows that whatever she tells me will eventually get back to you, so it's her way of communicating with you without all the fuss." He gave Love a lopsided smile; his silver-streaked hair fell across his forehead like a teenage boy's. "I think therapists call it *triangulation*. Sounds deadly, doesn't it?"

She looked up into his kind gray eyes. "You're not breaking any legal rules by telling me what she said, are you?"

He shook his head. "No, because I'm technically not her lawyer, just an interested friend. Also because she mentioned that if I felt so inclined, I could talk to you about any of this."

Love had smiled, relieved. "That sounds like Polly." She pushed at the salad with her fork, her appetite diminished. The thought of this being August and Polly's last Christmas at the ranch felt like a knot in her heart. "Well, I'm glad you're coming to Christmas Eve dinner, Judge." She'd bought him a huge handmade coffee mug that read on the side, Trail Boss. He'd get a kick out of it.

She carried the tray of clean glasses into the dining room where Polly was fussing with the red and green plaid napkins.

"Clint's here," Love said, placing a Christmas glass next to each plate.

"Hope everyone's hungry," Polly said, wiping her hands on her crocheted Christmas apron. "We've got enough food for three armies."

"Good," Love said. "You won't have to cook for August and Zane for a week. Maybe you can get some quilting done."

She looked up at her daughter-in-law, her toffee eyes serious. "You and Clint talk lately?"

"Yes, ma'am," Love said. "He says that John Goldstein is the lawyer you need to see to sort things out with the ranch and such. Are you okay with that?"

She held Love's gaze. "Do you think you might have time to come along? I'd sure like to have some company."

"Of course, Mom. You know I'll do whatever I can to make things easier for you and August. Rett and I leave for Knoxville day after tomorrow and will, hopefully, be back in a couple of weeks."

She gave a sharp nod. "Set it up for when you get back."

"I'll call Mr. Goldstein and make an appointment for the middle of January."

While everyone greeted Clint, Love carried the platter of ham and turkey into the dining room and set it in the middle of the table. Polly had agreed to let Rocky carve the turkey in the kitchen, saving August any trouble he might have with the large carving knife. Love gazed over the table filled with the food so lovingly prepared by Polly: baking powder biscuits, sweet corn and green beans frozen from last summer's garden, mashed potatoes, sliced tomatoes, herb and onion dressing, homemade peach preserves, chowchow made from her own secret rec-ipe, her famous dill pickles, which had won first place at the San Celina Mid-State Fair a record ten years in a row. It was a feast.

Love blinked back tears, missing Cy and Tommy at that moment with a pain like the actual wound to her skin made by August's gun. It felt as new as the moment their souls left this earth. Seconds later, her heart soared when she heard the sounds coming from the living room: the deep rumble of August's voice, the high, girlish giggle of her grand-daughter, the animal growl of Zane's young voice, the booming sound of Rocky's teasing baritone and Magnolia's beautiful contralto—like a foreshadowing from the bluesy section of heaven—singing her unique version of "I'll Be Home for Christmas."

She went into the living room and announced that supper was served. It took a few minutes for everyone to find their seat, but once they were all settled down, they instinctively looked over to August, waiting for him to say the blessing like he had at all the dinners they'd had at the ranch over the years. He smiled, looking straight ahead, un-comprehending.

Rocky cleared his throat. "Polly, would you like . . . ?"

"Yes," she said quickly. Next to her, August smiled and picked up a biscuit.

"Let's bless this wonderful meal," Rocky said. "*Gracias, El Señor*, Father God, for this blessed holiday, the celebration of your son's birth, the hope and salvation for man and womankind. Bless this delicious food, bless those who prepared it and we who will partake of it. Bless our men and women in uniform who serve and protect us every day, both here and on foreign soil. Comfort and protect them. Thank you for your continued grace as we attempt to walk your righteous path each and every day. We ask this in Jesus's name. Amen."

The meal was a joyous event with much laughing and joking and reminiscing. More than once Love's throat tightened. This meal was so different from last year when Cy's death was so new, barely a month gone, and Polly, August, Mel and Love forced themselves to gather around this same claw-foot table despite the fact that their hearts were raw and chapped with grief.

Afterward everyone gathered around the Christmas tree to pass around presents and drink Polly's cold, sweet, homemade eggnog dusted with nutmeg. Love had bought a last-minute gift for Zane, a gift card good for twenty-five dollars' worth of downloaded songs for his iPod, a suggestion from Rett.

"You know, Grandma, you should get an iPod," she'd said. "You could put all your CDs on it and listen while you walk along the beach. The Nano weighs, like, nothing. Like carrying a credit card."

"I like listening to the seagulls," Love said, smiling. "But I'll think about it."

Actually, she'd done more than think about it. Yesterday she went to Target in Paso Robles and bought herself a teal-colored one to match the red one she bought for Rett.

As everyone opened presents, Love instinctively took out her camera and started snapping pictures. Her mind already gave the montage a title: "Last Christmas at the Ranch." She quietly moved around, trying to capture the happiness and the sadness: a smile, a faraway look, a moment of peace. One shot of Polly's and August's eyes meeting across the room while everyone tore open presents made Love lower her camera, her eyes too flooded to see through the viewfinder. Like a physical filament of memory, everything of their shared life seemed to pass between them: the joy, the longing, the sadness, the contentment, the whole long map of their joined lives. In that moment, Love sensed that August knew that their life would never be the same.

Love watched while Mel subtly helped August when he had trouble opening a present. There was a peace in her face that Love had not seen before. Was it because the situation with Sean's family was settled? Had her mother finally called her back and wished her a good Christmas? Love hoped so.

Yesterday morning Love had gone to the feed store to get Mel's advice about iPods. The store was empty when Love walked up to the counter. Before she could call out, she heard Mel's voice coming from the back office.

"Hey, Mom," she said. "I've tried calling a couple of times. Guess you've gone somewhere for Christmas. Hope it's someplace fun." Her voice sounded young and uncertain. "Just wanted to say . . . well . . . guess I just want to wish you a merry Christmas. I sent you a card. There's . . . uh . . . a hundred-dollar gift card in there. I didn't really know what you needed. It's one of those Visa ones. You can use it anywhere, I guess. Buy yourself something crazy. Anyway, call me if you have time. I . . . Merry Christmas, Mom."

Love backed quietly out of the store, not wanting Mel to know that she'd overheard her conversation

How proud Cy would have been of her, how grateful for the kindness and patience she was showing with his father. For a moment, Love felt a little of what it must feel like to have a daughter, one whom you trusted and loved and, most wondrous of all, liked.

Love watched Mel open Love's present to her. When she unwrapped the stained glass Christmas tree hanging, her initial expression was as if someone had handed her a suitcase filled with thousand-dollar bills.

Mel glanced up and caught Love's eye. Thank you, she mouthed.

Love grinned at her, delighted. Was there any greater pleasure than giving someone exactly what they wanted? She'd tease Mel later when her friend quizzed Love about how she knew exactly what to buy her.

"You've mooned over that wall hanging for six months," she'd tell her. "Did you really think I wasn't watching?"

When all the presents had been opened, and Polly and Magnolia were serving pie and coffee, Clint stood up and clapped to get everyone's attention.

"There's one more gift," he said, glancing over at Love, then nodded at Rett. She stood up and walked out of the room. When she came back in a few seconds later, she was carrying a beautiful guitar made of some kind of glossy red-tinted wood.

"First, this is my gift to Rett," he said. "It was my mother's guitar. Neither of my boys or their kids have a bit of interest in playing it, so I know my mother would approve of me giving it to someone with so much talent and with such a love for music."

Rett's face turned pink. They'd obviously discussed this already, though Love didn't have a clue when.

"Now we're cooking," Clint said, rubbing his palms together, thoroughly pleased with himself. He looked at that moment like he was Zane's age.

Rett fit the strap around her shoulders and nodded at Zane, who had somehow slipped out of the room and returned with a shiny black mandolin.

She gave Love a shy look and said, "Grandma, I didn't have any money to buy you a present. I'll be able to next year, 'cause now I have a job." She turned and saluted Magnolia. "But I do have something for you. I wrote this a few days ago."

She nodded at Zane and started strumming. The mountain sound of his mandolin notes blended perfectly with her guitar, and for a moment, Love was transported back to Kentucky, to her childhood, when neighbors came to call and you sat on the front porch of an evening and whomever had the talent played for the rest of the folks, singing the words of their lives: the hard, cold mine, how the black got into everything, Daddy could never wash it completely away, days without much to eat but crackers and canned milk, Mama singing a high, thin soprano as she sewed a skirt for Love on her treadle sewing machine, the sound of buzzing insects, the scent of frying oil, the taste of air sweet with spring flowers. How could a few bars of music capture all that?

When Rett started singing, they all hushed, mesmerized by the sound of her voice—an odd mix of soprano and alto—not perfect, but one that held the strains of her heritage, the throat bones of her Appalachian ancestors, a people who'd spent as much of their life starving as filled, but always held hope, always believed that good times were coming. When Zane's raspy young voice swooped in and sang soft harmony, it caused everyone to stare, aware that they were hearing something unusual, two voices that miraculously seemed to be made exactly to do this very thing: sing together.

Love automatically brought the Nikon to her face and started taking snapshots, trying to capture the moment in the best way she knew how. After two or three shots, she slowly let the camera drop, the words that Rett sang causing her to catch her breath.

A California boy on his way to war,
a country kid with chestnut hair,
Cy missed his horse and a lightning-scarred tree
and the town where he lived near the Western sea.

Love sat up front at the country church,
where kudzu grew and coal came first.
She smiled at him in his army greens,
baked a rhubarb pie, and his heart fell free.

He fell in love with Love that day,
with her clear blue eyes and her Southern way.
He brought her home to the Western sea,
and married her 'neath that scarred oak tree.

They settled to the ranching life,
bore a son when the time was right.
Tommy played beneath the scarred oak tree,
galloped his horse 'cross the Western beach.

Cy's flown to Jesus, Tommy too,
still in Love's tales they live anew.
For in her heart she always knew,
love never dies when it feels this true.

He fell in love with Love that day,
with her clear blue eyes and her Southern way.
He brought her home to the Western sea,
and married her 'neath that scarred oak tree.

Yeah, lightning struck
but Love still stands.
Knows they'll meet again
on that golden sand.

Knows they'll meet again
on that golden sand.

The mandolin's final vibrato echoed in the room as Rett and Zane's voices faded. There was a moment of silence, then everyone started clapping. All Love could do was let the tears flow down her cheeks.

Rett came over and sat next to Love, putting her thin arm around her shoulders. "It wasn't supposed to make you cry."

"Thank you, Sweet Pea," Love said, reaching out and cupping Rett's cheek in her hand. "It's beautiful."

"You're welcome," she said. "If you want, Zane and I could record it and put it on your iPod. He's got some awesome music software."

"That would be wonderful."

While everyone was eating dessert, Love managed to slip outside. There'd been so much emotional upheaval in the last few weeks that she needed a moment to be alone. She wanted to go to the place that reminded her the most of Cy. She walked across the dark pasture to the lightning tree.

This ponderous old oak had been here before August was born, and it would probably still be here when all of them were gone. Would Rett's great-grandchildren play underneath this tree? Or Patsy's? Or Faith's? Love hoped the ranch was still in the family then, but you never knew. Things were changing in San Celina County, in the country, in the world. There were no guarantees that the Johnson ranch would survive. That made Rett's song even more precious. It would survive, it would always be there, a testament to the life that Love and Cy had lived. She ran her finger down the jagged scar from the lightning strike. Its edges felt smooth as satin.

"Thank you, Lord," she said out loud to the Creator of this tree, the God she had doubted for so long, but who never gave up on her, never deserted her. She knew that now. "I'm sorry I didn't believe you when you said to trust you, when you said to pray. Say hey to Cy for me. Tell him I hope to see him soon, but there're some things I need to do here first. Tell him . . . I miss him. Tell him . . . I understand why he wanted to go home." She inhaled deeply, the loamy scent of the soil assuring her that for right now, she was here on this solid piece of earth because God had a reason for her to be here.

"Love!" Clint's voice carried like a strong ocean wave. He stood at the gate to the pasture, just barely visible in the purple dark. He pulled out his cell phone and opened it, holding it under his chin so she could see his face—a twenty-first-century flashlight. Her heart warmed at the sight of his smile, thankful for his friendship and his gentle wisdom. She'd need both in the next few months.

"I have to leave now." His voice echoed across the dark pasture. "Wanted to say good-bye and wish you a merry Christmas."

Love traced the tree scar one more time, then called back to him, "Hold on. I'm on my way back."